THREE KINDS OF LUCKY

ALSO BY KIM HARRISON

BOOKS OF THE HOLLOWS

THREE
KINDS OF
LUCKY

KIM HARRISON

ACE
NEW YORK

ACE
Published by Berkley
An imprint of Penguin Random House LLC
penguinrandomhouse.com

Copyright © 2024 by Kim Harrison
Penguin Random House supports copyright. Copyright fuels creativity, encourages diverse
voices, promotes free speech, and creates a vibrant culture. Thank you for buying an authorized
edition of this book and for complying with copyright laws by not reproducing, scanning,
or distributing any part of it in any form without permission. You are supporting writers
and allowing Penguin Random House to continue to publish books for every reader.

ACE is a registered trademark and the A colophon is a trademark of Penguin Random House LLC.

Library of Congress Cataloging-in-Publication Data

Names: Harrison, Kim, author.
Title: Three kinds of lucky / Kim Harrison.
Description: New York: Ace, 2024. | Series: The Shadow Age
Identifiers: LCCN 2023028980 | ISBN 9780593437476 (hardcover) | ISBN 9780593437483 (ebook)
Subjects: LCGFT: Fantasy fiction. | Novels.
Classification: LCC PS3608.A78355 T47 2024 | DDC 813/.6—dc23/eng/20230630
LC record available at https://lccn.loc.gov/2023028980

Printed in the United States of America
1st Printing

Book design by Daniel Brount

This is a work of fiction. Names, characters, places, and incidents either are the product
of the author's imagination or are used fictitiously, and any resemblance to actual persons,
living or dead, business establishments, events, or locales is entirely coincidental.

THREE KINDS OF LUCKY

1

I LEANED INTO THE TURN, BIKE TIRES HUMMING UNTIL THE PAVEMENT ROUGHENED and my smooth ride dissolved into a rumble, unheard but felt as NIN blared in my earbuds. The mirror attached to the handlebar was less than helpful with the vibrations, but traffic had stopped and I slowed, feeling the afternoon heat from the street as I scanned the commuter cars, their windows up and air-conditioning on. My spandex kit emblazoned with a nonexistent bike-messenger service gave me some slack, but I'd had enough near misses with doors to be wary.

That's why the helmet and skidproof gloves. Both had the sweepers' triangle logo on them, as did my backpack and water bottle strapped to the bike frame. So did the blueprint tube over my shoulder, the metal tube heavily stickered with grunge and alternative rock bands.

Reason one for a bike, I thought as I rolled past the cars. Here outside the university campus, the low, squat buildings did little to hide the late sun, and I squinted as I found the intersection. The light changed before I got there, and after making eye contact with the driver on my left, I jammed on the pedals in time with the hard beat in my ears to cross the street.

I kept up with traffic, muscles moving smoothly as I watched the street and sidewalk in a familiar pattern of defense. My gaze, though, kept returning to a glinting shimmer half a block up. It looked like a heat mirage and I stifled a call of warning when a woman stepped right into the hazy glow and picked it up like dog doo. Immediately she tripped on the sidewalk—and the distortion of dross clinging to her heel was gone, used up in a flash of bad luck.

Two doors away, a more certain gleam lurked under a painter's scaffold. The shimmer was unseen by nearly the entire world's population, oblivious as they walked through it to snag wisps of dross and carry them over the entire city. A tiny half percent had some sense that it was there, and an even smaller fraction, like me, could actually do something about it.

The city of St. Unoc just east of Tucson had one of the highest percentages of magic users this side of the Mississippi, bringing the usual ratio of one in a thousand to more like eight out of ten. The ratio at our closed campus, named after the small city, was even higher. But that was what made St. Unoc University special—and my job essential to keeping the silence of our existence.

I signaled a lane shift, checking behind me before sliding over to give the hazy glimmer a wide berth. Dross never broke on me, but it might pop my tire if I drove through it. *No reason to tempt fate,* I thought, knowing someone would be along to sweep it up. It was a rather large chunk of dross, though. A mage was being careless with his or her magic.

Big surprise, I thought as I bunny-hopped up onto the curb, slowing to a crawl as I swung a leg over the saddle and rode on one pedal to the bike rack before a three-story office building. Behind me in the street, a horn blared followed by a crunch of fender. I turned, knowing the accident would be right where that heat-distortion-like haze was.

Or had been, I thought as the drivers in ties and power dresses lurched out of their vehicles, tired and surly from the heat. Maybe I should have tried to gather it up, but I had a pickup, and even the best of us wouldn't sweep dross during rush hour. Besides, the haze of latent energy was gone, used up in the crash. Any left was probably stuck under one of the cars, where it would stay, slowly breaking down as snapped belts and leaking hoses: a long-running total.

The bike rack by the door was a small pocket of stillness between the ornamental cacti and the overgrown lavender, and I jerked one earbud out, letting it hang as I took off my helmet and fluffed my bangs to ease my helmet-head coif. Sometimes it sucked to be able to see the origins of the bad luck that was so common that it was accepted as the natural order of things and not someone else's magical waste.

"Reason two for a bike," I whispered, my blueprint tube and backpack over my shoulder as I timed the revolving door and went inside. "Door-side parking is always available."

I pulled my other earbud out as the cool of the building hit me. There was a definite flow of people leaving, and I got only a cursory check at the front desk as I signed in and opened my bag for inspection. The elevator was empty, and Reznor fought with the Carpenters on the way to the top floor.

The air felt different when I got out. Clearly I was among the point-five percent. Magic. I could smell it more than the unspent jet fuel from the nearby air base: the tang at the back of my throat and a hint of ozone pricking my nose.

Which isn't always a good thing, I thought when the floor receptionist recognized the sweeper insignia on my kit and pointed me down a hall even as she reached for a phone to alert the building manager. Most mages could see the waste they generated when doing magic: a flicker of distortion, a hazy glow near the eye's blind spot. The two required semesters of dross manipulation and capture were usually enough to give magic users the skills to direct dross into traps without touching it, but only Spinners and sweepers had the ability to physically touch dross without it breaking on them in a wash of bad luck.

Which was how I landed my sweeper job eight years ago at the soul-crushing age of eighteen. Eighteen and pigeonholed into a low-status but surprisingly high-demand job, for even though I couldn't do magic, my dross-handling skills made me more than an essential worker but also a frontline defense against deadly shadow.

Most people, though, only saw a trashman, and as I strode down the hall I heard a whispered "That's Petra Grady? She looks like a bum."

My stilted smile faltered. *Bum?* Sure, I looked like a messenger, but they'd called me because they couldn't handle it. Besides, if I had shown up wearing velour robes and carrying three yard-long engraved sticks, I'd end up in an insane asylum.

"Petra Grady? Ms. Grady?"

The man's voice pulled me to a stop and I turned on my heel. A heavy man in a suit a half size too small for him was making his arm-swinging way to me. "Guilty as accused," I said, hating my high voice, but five-foot-four, small, athletic frames seldom make for a low, sexy lilt.

"Thank you for coming on such short notice." The man, clearly the building's manager, strode forward, pulling me into his wake as we continued down the corridor. It went without saying that he was a mage. "Um, I'm Mark," he added. "The psi manager."

Which meant he was the one where the buck stopped when there was a dross issue. He'd whispered the last, but that he said it meant the entire floor was probably mages. Psi manager wouldn't be on his pay stub, but I'd agree he was a manager of some sort as I took in his lunch-spotted tie, ample middle, and scuffed brown shoes. He looked like a mundane, but I was willing to bet that the ornate class ring pinching his plump finger was actually his lodestone.

The piece of glass at the center had been utterly unremarkable until he had bonded to it, allowing him to use and store the light energy that touched it—or at least half of the light energy. Mages used the wave half; Spinners used the particle. What was left after separating light into its two parts was discarded as dross. That was where I came in; for though I couldn't do magic, I could touch the waste they made with impunity.

Still, seeing the stone on his finger, a long-dead envy flickered and went out.

"I, ah, found out about the spill this morning," Mark added, clearly nervous. "But I think it's been free-roaming for two days." He pointed to the left and we went deeper into the building.

"That's two days too long," I said, and he shrugged. You leave dross alone and it gets bigger, attracting other dross until its natural dissociation isn't spilled coffee and crashed computers but six-car pileups and elevators dropping to basement floors.

"And a right here," he said as we turned into a short hall ending in double fire doors. "It's in a back office. Aren't you supposed to have a spotter?" he added as he ran his badge at the reader. The speaker beeped, but the door didn't move. Flushing, Mark tried again.

"My assistant is graduating this week," I said as he tried a third time—and got the same result. St. Unoc's university made a practice of pairing promising new students with experienced sweepers for a yearlong work-study/assessment program. I, though, had been work-ing with the same mage for the last two years as she gathered data for her thesis on dross abnormalities. But Ashley's thesis was written and she'd be gone next week. I was going to miss her. I hadn't thought I'd like a housemate when she first proposed sharing rent, but Ashley had been surprisingly accommodating. For a mage.

"It does this all the time," Mark said, nervous as he ran his card again, and finally the lock disengaged. "It's not the escaped dross."

"Sure," I said, preferring to reserve judgment.

Mark shoved through the doors and held them for me. I fol-lowed, soaking in the feel of the large, close-ceilinged, open-concept room, with its low partitions and full-spectrum lights. It was after hours and the desks were empty. Hazy dross drifts lingered like dust bunnies under chairs and in the corners, evidence of their hidden magic: covert coffee-reheats, avoid-the-boss glamours, forget charms to steal from the fridge and hide illicit computer use. It was small stuff that when left to its own devices did little more than cause a paper cut or spilled coffee . . . a burrito explosion in the microwave at the worst.

As expected, the floor's ambient trap was moderately full, the tripod-like arrangement of sticks conveniently disguised as a water-cooler stand. As I watched, a drift of dross slipped like a living sunbeam under an office door at the back of the room. Goose bumps prickled over me.

Something drew it in there.

"Tyler?" Mark called as I stifled a shudder. "The sweeper is here."

"Oh, thank God." A middle-aged man popped up from behind a distant desk. He ran a hand through his thinning hair before dropping it to fix his rectangle glasses more firmly atop his narrow nose. He, too, had a thick class ring to hold his lodestone. His, though, had been multifaceted to mimic a diamond. "It's in my office," he said as he came forward, black shoes scuffing. A white lab coat added to his professional look, and I wasn't surprised when he angled to the door that the dross had vanished under. Someone had taped a DO NOT EN-TER sign to it, and I rubbed the goose bumps out.

"How confident are you that it's still in there?" I asked as I unslung my backpack and blueprint tube. Despite the low ambient dross levels out here, the security door *had* stuck, and there were signs of accidents: a broken carafe in the trash, a busted chair upside down on a desk. Someone had thrown out a keyboard.

"Pretty sure," Dr. Tyler said, his wince convincing me otherwise. "The only other exit is through the building's servers. I, ah, don't know why I couldn't catch it," he added as he touched the wand in his breast pocket. The stick was disguised as a stylus, unnoticed among the pens, highlighters, and laser pointers. The mild attractant it contained was a convenient way to collect dross in mixed company or if the mage didn't know how to use an attraction spell. I had one myself because even though I could touch dross with no trouble, the initial jolt of connection had always been uncomfortable.

"The longer it's free-roaming, the harder it is," I said, but he knew that. His first mistake was letting it get away. His second was going home over the weekend and leaving it for Monday. *Which would make it three days free-roaming, not two.* I stifled a smirk as I took my phone from my pocket and brought up an e-invoice. *Hazard pay.* "Mark, I'm glad you're here. If you'd authorize this, please?"

Mark took the offered phone, sighing. "I was hoping this might be on our loom contract."

I smiled as my phone dinged. "Picking up a three-day spill is not on your agreement."

"Three days?" Mark looked at Dr. Tyler, who had the decency to flush. "You told me it was two."

"Or I could put you on the schedule," I said lightly. "That would take about thirty percent off. I could probably have someone out here by Wednesday."

"I can't go back in there," Dr. Tyler said, and Mark sourly put his thumb to my phone.

"That bad, eh?" I tucked my phone away and pulled the DO NOT ENTER sign from the door, stifling a shudder at the sensation of pin-pricks tripping down my spine. There was a hell of a lot of dross behind it. I could feel it. "What are you doing to make such a large dross deposit?"

Mark shifted from foot to foot. "Dr. Tyler uses a class-three at-traction spell to clean the building servers of dust and building dan-der to help prevent server crashes. He does the charm in his office. It's quiet, and there are three gated doors between it and any, uh, mundane."

A class-three gravity manipulation to limit dust? Telekinesis at its finest. Most mages who specialized in attraction spells quit at being able to roll a pencil from under their chair or slam a fly against a window. Making a room-wide psi field to hold that much magic meant Dr. Tyler was good. Really good. "And the dross got away . . . how?" I asked.

Tyler sat back against the nearest desk, arms over his chest and clearly not liking that I was insinuating he didn't pick up after himself. "I had it bottled. The seal broke," he said tightly.

Mark's face reddened at the probable lie. Bad seal? How like a mage to blame the loom's seals. Most sweepers were like milkmen in reverse, picking up full bottles of captured dross and leaving behind empties to be filled. Me? I was more of a trashman, taking the stuff that smelled so bad the milkman wouldn't touch it. And like the trashman, you didn't want to get on my bad side or I'd walk away, leaving you *and* your toxic garbage.

"Tyler. Go get a cup of coffee," Mark ground out from between his teeth.

"It's after five," Tyler said shortly.

"Then make it decaf," Mark said, and Tyler pushed off from the desk and stomped away. "Ms. Grady, how can I help?"

Besides sending Tyler to remedial dross bottling? "Make sure no one opens this door until I come out." I put a hand on the door, my expression emptying at the nearly subliminal tingling of heat. "No one," I said. "No reason. Unless the building is on fire."

"Yes, ma'am."

I picked up my backpack and blueprint tube. "This should take about fifteen minutes."

"Fifteen minutes?" Tyler said from across the room, a phone in his hand. "I spent all day trying to catch it."

"Which is why it's costing a week of your salary," Mark said, angry now.

Shrugging in agreement, I opened the door and went in, soaking in the muffled silence as it closed behind me. The dross that I'd seen slip under the door was gone, but a feeling of wrong—of unspent energy—drifted at the edges of my awareness like a warm fog.

Otherwise, it was an office like any other: a little messy and smelling like Tyler's lunch. One wall had an interior window looking into a computer lab with machinery blinking to itself. There was a door to it, but seeing as the servers hadn't crashed, the dross was likely still contained in this room. *Interesting* . . . Dross usually went for technology as if it were candy. Something was keeping it here.

But I was willing to bet it wasn't the standard, medium-grade trap on Dr. Tyler's desk, the three pencil-long, dross-cored sticks bound into a tripod shape with a rubber band instead of the loom-supplied knotted cord—which was probably why he hadn't been able to catch the dross a second time.

Frowning, I poked around until I found the strand of knotted silk that should have been holding the trap together in the trash—frayed in two and useless.

"Stupid-ass mage," I swore, then I shoved his rolling cushy chair to a corner and out of the way. Hand on my hip, I gave the room a once-over before kneeling before the door on the matted blue carpet. I exhaled to settle myself, feeling the familiar, contented haze of a meditative state slip into me as easy as breathing. Holding it, I opened my blueprint tube and tilted it to allow three yard-long notched sticks to come sliding out. They were black, smooth apart from the notches, and their silky coolness pulled my shoulders down as they slipped through my fingers like water.

Unlike most sweepers, I'd made them myself, having spent an entire two years on staff theory and construction before Ryan had lured me away from psi-protection design to become a sweeper like my dad. The sticks in my hand were actually a final exam, and I'd put enough dross into their core to attract and hold most spills, because the only thing dross liked more than technology was more dross. Once collected under the sticks, I could easily put it into a bottle.

One stick, two stick, three, four, five. Stand them straight to stay alive, I thought as I propped my three sticks up like a tripod to make a large cave below the crossed sticks and a small, open vase above, where the containment bottle would rest. *Six sticks, seven, eight, nine, ten. Shadow held, its strength to lend,* I added, fingers tingling as I unwound the strand of knotted silk holding my hair back and used it to tie the three sticks together.

Dross wouldn't break into bad luck once knotted. It was how we'd gotten rid of the stuff before technology gave us the glass-lined vault. But whether knotted or free-roaming, dross always attracted dross. When wrapped around the crossed sticks, the dross knotted into the cord would pull the snared dross up and into the bottle.

The children's rhyme wasn't necessary to make this all work, and no one ever used more than three sticks, but the poem helped me focus, and the hiding dross seemed to settle into my blind spot as I got to my feet and wiped the carpet grime from my hands. Backing up, I tilted my head one way, then the other, as I put my earbuds in and hit play. All I had to do was wait for the dross to show and fill the trap.

But as Reznor crooned, a frown found me. It was as if the room was clean. I could feel the latent energy somewhere, but it wasn't moving to the heavy-duty trap.

"Huh." My hands went to my hips. Clearly the drift was bigger than what my sticks could lure out of hiding. The dross remained unseen, hidden in the desk or a crack in the floor, or possibly it had taken refuge in the wiring, though that was rare. I hadn't brought a long-cord, so I'd have to get creative.

Lattice fair and strong and clear. Keep me safe, both foul and dear, I mused as I took one of Dr. Tyler's trap sticks and used it like a wand, running it across the walls, then the chair, and finally . . . the desk. Sure enough, even with the stick acting as a buffer, a flash of heat shot through my fingertips and I jerked back.

"Found you," I half sang. It was a big drift, too big for a wand, and resigned to a little pain, I tossed the makeshift wand aside. I set my hand atop the desk, grimacing at the pulse of heat as I pulled a hint of haze from the desktop and condensed it into a knot between my moving palms. The agitated dross prickled and stung like a sunburn, threatening to break on me as I rolled it into a ball, coating the latent energy in a psi field until every last hint of heat was gone. Satisfied, I flicked the inky silver sphere of distortion into the waiting trap, where it spun in an ever-smaller circle until the dross slowed and spread out, puddling in the middle.

The test dross showed no signs of trying to escape, and satisfied the sticks would hold, I turned to the desk. I could feel the dross, puddling like a lazy sunbeam, filling the drawers and spilling over to drip onto the floor, soaking the carpet as if it had been there for years, not three days. Dr. Tyler was lucky that he hadn't accidentally rolled on a pencil and cracked his head open to spill those lovely mage brains all over his matted blue carpet tiles.

"The hard way," I whispered as I sank my thoughts deeper into my center. Hands at my middle, I inhaled, drawing my palms apart as I drew a psi field into existence. Exhaling, I brought my hands together to contract it, strengthening it as I inhaled again. Three breaths later, I had a ball of psi energy the size of the desk, diffuse and tingling. The need to breathe seemed to hesitate, and I lazily shifted my hazy distortion-of-self to settle over the desk, in effect making a net to snare whatever might be in it. The technique was not for the faint of heart. It had taken me nearly five years and a migraine prescription I hadn't filled in over two years to perfect a field this large. It was also why I was the one they called when things got sticky.

I purposefully exhaled to contract the field one last time, and a pleasant warmth rippled over me as my will found the dross. A hazy glow began to gleam under the desk, little flickers of distortion showing. Tighter, smaller, I shrank the psi bubble until my very synapses were tingling. Breath by breath, I drew the waste out of hiding, condensing it until it was visible as a hazy sunbeam under the desk.

"Tyler, you are one lucky duck. This thing is huge." Fixated, I pulled my backpack close to get the larger of my two glass bottles. Fingers sure, I set one atop the tripod, open mouth down. "Nice and easy. In you go."

But my confident smile faded when the glow under the desk didn't move toward the trap but continued to shrink on its own, ripples of distortion solidifying into a shadowy form. My skin crawled as a soft sob lifted through the back of my mind. The heartfelt cries came from everywhere and nowhere as if the spaces between mass held voice.

"Ah, shit," I whispered as the dross under Tyler's desk took on a visible form, huddled as if beaten. As if my attention gave it strength, the sobs became louder, slipping from the subreal to the audible. The memory of a woman appeared, her dress torn at the shoulder and silver blood showing where someone had beaten her.

"When did you come from?" I whispered, riveted. The woman wasn't real, but she had been once, beaten to death in the late 1800s by the look of it. Her death had left a mark on reality—a framework that dross could structure itself on in an attempt to scare me into leaving it alone. Some said that when dross gathered into too large a drift, it became pseudo-smart like its big, ugly, deadly brother, shadow. But I was inclined to believe the show was an unconscious reaction. I'd dealt with shadow before, and it was like comparing a hamster to a velociraptor—they could both bite, but one you could walk away from.

Regardless, pretending to be a dead woman wasn't going to put me off, and I set a hand atop the crossed sticks of my trap and used my will to lure the apparition in.

Wailing, the image of the woman began to blur as glittering streamers of dross were drawn from under the desk. Streaks of distortion roiled up behind the sticks, pulled to the cross points until I tightened the knotted silk cord and the trapped haze rose up into the only opening I had left it—the glass bottle.

Slowly a heat shimmer began to fill the bottle, little silver sparkles showing as it condensed. The wailing woman began to fall apart, unable to maintain its form as its mass was halved. Unfortunately the bottle wasn't going to hold what remained. "Ashley?" I called, forgetting she wasn't with me, and grimacing, I fumbled in my backpack for my second bottle.

"And . . . drop," I whispered as I eased the tension of the silken cord around the crossed wood to cut off the flow, simultaneously tipping the full bottle up and capping it. Not a hint of dross escaped either the trap or the bottle, and the new container was in its place in less than a heartbeat. Satisfied, I tightened the silken knotted cord again, and the haze in the trap boiled up. Slowly the second bottle began to brighten. The more waste it contained, the faster the remaining dross rushed to fill it until, with a tiny bump of sensation, the distortion in the trap was gone. Dr. Tyler's desk was clean.

"Fifteen minutes on the tick," I breathed as I capped the second bottle. It was warm in my hand, and I gazed in satisfaction at the glittering haze. Pleased, I tugged my earbuds out and set the bottles on the desk. It was unusual to find an unregistered rez in a building this old, but it would explain why the spill had grown so quickly. Residues, or rezes, were like dross gravity wells, pulling anything within their influence to them and making them larger.

Ashley would have loved this one, I thought. But when I went to take the trap apart, I hesitated. My fingertips were vibrating as if to a distant rumble.

My hand dropped, and I peered into the trap, suspicious. It seemed empty, but my gut said it wasn't, and when I reached again to take down the trap, my hand fell once more. Cold. The sticks were cold. Something was in my trap. And it wasn't dross.

Remember your z-axis, I thought, squinting at where the notched sticks crossed.

Worry flickered through me. "Shadow snot, not again," I swore as I saw the spider. It didn't look like much. The penny-size arachnid had probably been in the carpet when I'd set up the trap. But dross's defining characteristic was that it caused freaky things to happen—and there had been a lot of dross in there with it.

"You just a spider, Fred?" I said hopefully.

And then I backed up when a distortion shimmered over it, gleaming obsidian and silver.

It's gone shadow, I thought, fixated on the suddenly contorting insect. *And it's in my trap! It's in my trap, and I'm out of bottles!*

Worse, it was growing, its edges wispy as the shadow began to mutate the spider. "Oh, hell no," I said, scared as the spider shook the sticks and the knotted silk holding the trap together began to loosen. "Stop!" I stumbled back as my sticks thumped to the carpet and rolled. Furry legs waving, the spider ran to the closest stick and began gnawing on it as if it were candy.

"No, no, no!" Lurching to Tyler's desk, I began searching. I could lure the spider into a bottle with a shadow button, but I needed a friggin' bottle to put it in!

The only thing shadow wanted was inert dross—dross that had lost the ability to break. The stuff was rare and thankfully hard to come by, as it was a veritable shadow magnet. The only natural source of it was the rezes, which was why we worked so hard to get rid of them and probably why the shadow had been in here. But why the shadow was going for the dross core in my sticks was beyond me. The dross in my sticks was not inert.

Maybe it's insane, I thought as I yanked the drawers open to find nothing helpful. Paper clips, stapler, Band-Aids, tube of antibiotic cream, empty ink cartridges, file folders . . .

There! I seized on the nearly empty vodka bottle and unscrewed it, dumping what was left in the trash. Unfortunately the shadow-spider was already too large to fit through the opening. I'd have to lure the shadow out of it.

Without a spotter, I thought as I took the dime-size black coin of inert dross from the top of my stick case and dropped it into the vodka bottle. The button hit the bottom with an insanely cheerful *ting* and I turned, blanching. Chunks of my stick littered the carpet. The shadow-spider had chewed to the core, releasing and consuming the bound dross. Somehow it had not only survived but had used the dross to become as large as a rat. Hissing, it turned to the next stick.

"Hey!" I yelled, and the spider jerked as if surprised. Lurching, I grabbed one of my sticks when the spider started for me, mandibles spread. Wisps of shadow made it hazy and indistinct except for its eyes, and unlike dross, it was black as sin.

"Everything okay, Ms. Grady?" came a voice from just outside the room.

"Keep that door shut!" I shouted, then shrieked, jabbing my stick at the spider. It fell back, mandibles waving, until it pounced on my knotted short-cord and dragged it under the desk.

What the hell! I thought as the spider gnawed through one of the knots to get to the dross. What were the chances that both my sticks and trap tie would go bad at the same time? The anomaly had to be in the shadow, not my tools.

Angry and confused, I jabbed my stick at it. The spider chittered, dropping the cord and latching onto the stick. Panicked, I slammed the stick into the wall, spider and all.

The spider burst with a sickening splat, then hit the floor and stopped, quivering. For one glorious moment, I thought I'd killed it and it was done, but then it gathered itself up—and I realized all I'd done was kill the spider.

"Shadow spit, you leave my sticks alone," I whispered as I shifted back and forth to gauge its ability to see. Yes, the spider was dead, but shadow animated it, and it oriented on me with a hiss, its front legs feeling the air.

The shadow was trapped in a corpse. If I could get it out, it would be free-roaming, and *that* was something I could lure into a bottle, but do it wrong, and there would be two structured rezes in Dr. Tyler's office for dross to pattern itself on.

"Let's see how smart you are, you shadow mother," I whispered as I rolled the vodka bottle at it. If I was lucky, the shadow would abandon the corpse and go into the bottle.

But then the spider corpse did something I never expected.

It ignored the shadow button and jumped at me.

"Hey!" I shouted, terrified as I batted it away. Panicking, I back-pedaled to the desk as its spindly legs wrapped around my hands and wet guts coated my fingers. For an instant, that was all I felt—until the shadow abandoned the broken flesh and touched me.

Oh, God. I was touching shadow.

Living ice flooded my brain. Gasping, I choked back a scream at the sensation of shared space. It was in me, clawing through my thoughts, trying to take me over as it had the spider.

I couldn't breathe. Stunned, I dropped to my knees, the dead spider in my grip as I was suddenly powerless to let it go. Wrongness soaked into me, gritty granules of night sifting into every corner of my soul, searching to find what would turn me to shadow, searching to find what would make me as it was.

I was going to go shadow.

"Get. Out . . ." I rasped, jaw clenched as I forced myself to breathe. My pulse hammered, and my vision swam as if I was seeing the room from two angles. Ice cramped my grip, and I staggered to my feet, knocking into the desk as I fought to reclaim my body. The world shimmered in heat haze. The two capped bottles of dross blazed with an unreal light. A flicker of fear that I might be forced into one to burn flashed through me.

Bleary, I looked down, trying to reconcile the memory of my hands with the violently shaking, burning cups of fire that they had become. Black goo dripped through my fingers, and from the crushed wreckage of the shadow-warped spider, a beady eye focused on me. I saw my face through its eyes, heat lifting from me in waves of smoldering warmth. *I am seeing what the shadow does,* I thought as I felt it struggle to comprehend my cold, bland vision of the world.

Staggering, I shook the crushed spider from my hands. It hit the floor with a dull splat, but it was too late, and I groaned when icy maggots began to eat their way through my sense of self to claim everything I was.

"Oh, God," I whispered as my knees gave way, and I fell face down on the carpet. It was finding out how I worked. It was only a matter of time.

Groaning, I inched to the vodka bottle with a teeth-clenched determination, shaking as I fought with myself, with the shadow. *I am a sweeper,* I thought as the shadow soaked deeper into me, fighting for control. Ice closed my throat as the shadow found a crack in my will. Cold smothered me and my legs went numb. Claws raked me from the inside and I gasped for breath.

I had to get it out.

My fingers touched the cool glass, and success was a bright spark. The shadow freaked, and a violent twitch shook me as foaming oil and water sizzed in my brain. Images of fire and cold rose, blurring my vision as it dug, burrowing to find something with which to stop me.

But as I knelt on the carpet and struggled for control, I realized that though my body was a battleground, my core of thought remained untouched by the cold blackness that was clawing me. The two refused to blend, couldn't mix—oil and sun in the same space. *I am not going to die in Tyler's cruddy little office.*

Panting, I knelt with the empty bottle of vodka and walled off the confusion. It wasn't mine and I wouldn't listen. Exhaling, I sent a bubble of psi energy swirling around the shadow within my mind, coating it as I would a stray drift of dross hiding in a desk.

Like flipping a switch, the confused double images vanished. I had it.

Head lifting, I sucked in air in a gasp. The shadow was still inside me, caught in a psi bubble. I could feel it, the faintest hint of shock marring its hunger to possess. I panted in a hazy relief of nothing, a still point of understanding. I held shadow within me, trapped like a drift of dross knotted within silk. But my prison held both of us. I couldn't untangle it from my mind without freeing it. At least not when we both were in my body.

My hands shook as I pulled the open bottle to my lips . . . and then I exhaled.

Black poured from my lungs as the shadow caught in my psi bubble streamed from my lips—warmth and ice, gold and black, swirling together to fill the bottle until I was empty. There was no will in me, no shadow. I was numb. All I had left was the need to cap the bottle.

Hands shaking, I fumbled for the cap. My psi field holding the shadow rolled within the bottle, spinning like a mad top. And then, only after I got the cap fastened, I let my will go.

Shadow exploded within the bottle, shoving the gold of my thoughts through the spaces between mass. The shadow, though, was denser stuff and was caught. I fell back on my butt, shaking violently until my psi energy eased back into me where it belonged. Within the bottle, the shadow settled over the shadow button I'd put in there earlier as if it were a bird with a mouse. Ideally, it would have gone in there of its own accord, but it was in there, and I had done it.

How the hell had I done that?

Blinking, I looked blearily at the door. The two dross bottles on the desk were no longer a white-hot hell through the shadow's eyes, and I stifled a shudder. I was myself. It was truly gone.

"If I hear one word about this costing too much, I'm going to let this shit go!" I shouted, and from behind the door, the men's intense, hushed conversation went silent.

I felt ill, and I wiped the spider guts off on the carpet . . . the wall . . . Tyler's chair . . . whatever was handy as I used the desk to pull myself up. I was too exhausted to be anything but shaken. Later, maybe, I might congratulate myself for surviving. My skin felt raw, as if I had been burned by ice from the inside, and I lifted my spandex bike shirt to make sure. I was the same blah light-brown tan. There were no gaping holes where my soul could fall out, and I tugged my shirt down. I could have gone shadow as the spider had done. I should have. But I hadn't.

My throat hurt, and I rubbed at the new stiffness in my shoulder. The rat-size spider lay dead against the wall, and the first flicker of anger began to burn through the fear as I scooped up my two gnawed sticks and felt the rough edges. *Great.* Sure, I could polish out the chew marks on one and make an entirely new stick to replace the other, but matching their internal dross levels would be tedious. It would be easier to make an entirely new set. *Or I can buy them. That would be easier yet.*

But what concerned me was why the shadow had gone for the sticks in the first place. Shadow only ate inert dross. What my staff contained should have driven it off, not attracted it. That was kind of the point. And yet I had watched it chew through my stick to get it, then start on my short-cord. *Maybe it can handle normal dross when it is possessing an organism?* I thought, wondering why that little nugget hadn't been in Shadow Containment 101.

Worried, I slid the two chewed sticks in with the last and propped the case by the door.

This was the third time this year that I'd bottled shadow. I'd like to say it was getting easier, but it wasn't, and it was only because the bounty on this little baby would put me solidly in the black that I wasn't in an outright rage. Shadow was as dangerous as all hell when free, but bottled shadow was always in demand to teach rising sweepers how to handle it safely—provided it hadn't gotten too smart. *Nothing like making my weekly quota on a Monday.*

"I can't believe it ate the dross right out of my knots," I whispered as I tied the torn silk around my hair, my fingers feeling for the missing knots like a tongue seeking a missing tooth. I could mend it, but it had been balanced to the sticks. Annoyed, I picked up the vodka bottle.

Black swirled within it, tingly and cold against my hand. "You know what? You suck," I said as I used the wax pencil in my bag to scribe a poison symbol on the vodka bottle in three places plus the cap. *Eyes. There are eyes in there,* I thought, stifling a shudder as I shoved the shadow into my bag along with the two bottles of dross.

"I'm coming out!" I called as I slung my backpack on. Ticked, I grabbed my stick case and opened the door, but my steps slowed as I saw them waiting.

"Is it clean?" Mark asked, his worried gaze on my backpack.

"For now," I said, thinking of my chewed sticks. "But you've got a rez in there. Any more dross spills within two hundred feet and it's going to flare up again."

"A rez?" Mark exchanged a nervous glance with Tyler. "There's no rez in there."

My lip twitched, and I looped my stick case over my back. "I'll send you the charges tomorrow after I know if they are going to want to use or destroy the shadow I pulled off it."

"Shadow!" Mark yelped, ashen as he looked at the open door. "You found shadow?"

I nodded, smug at their sudden fear. *Yep. I'm bad.* "Rezes attract them, so I suggest you keep the area clean so it doesn't flare up again."

"Are you sure you have it?" Tyler said, clearly worried.

Seriously? "You want to see it?" I shifted my pack up higher on my shoulder, satisfied when both men shook their heads vehemently.

"I was in there this morning," Mark whispered as Tyler inched into his office, reassuring me that he at least knew the gravity of the situation.

From Tyler's office came a muffled "Oh, my God!" of disgust.

Yeah, a spider the size of a rat can do that to a person, I thought as Tyler came out of his office, clearly shaken. "If you have any more indication of the rez activity before you get put on the schedule, call it in," I said.

Tyler glanced over his shoulder, clearly nervous. "Uh, the spider . . ."

"Isn't my problem." Feeling good, I took my blueprint tube in hand, my smile faltering as I heard the wood chips rattle.

"And the structured rez?" Tyler added as I walked out.

"It took the form of a woman beaten to death. Right under your desk. Late 1800s by the look of her dress." *How am I going to tell Ashley without freaking?*

"That would explain a few things," Dr. Tyler said, and my anger softened. Apart from his letting the spill sit over the weekend, this might not have been his fault. Both his trap cord and the original seal could have broken from the accumulated dross drawn to the little spot of horror.

Either that, or the shadow broke it. I'd never seen a shadow go for knotted dross, but if it had eaten my short-cord, it might have eaten Dr. Tyler's. I'd ask Darrell.

"Thank you, gentlemen," I said, steps jaunty as I stiff-armed the office door and found the hall. But my mood faltered when I got into the empty elevator and the memory of that shadow-spider clawed its way through me. The ding of the lift shocked through me, and I quickly strode out into the lobby.

The sun had hardly moved, surprising me. It had felt like hours.

Surrounded by thousands and yet alone, I unchained my bike and headed for the university, two bottles of dross and one of shadow heavy on my back. The bounty on the shadow would likely more than pay for a new set of sticks, and life was good.

2

ONE OF THE LARGER LECTURE HALLS HAD JUST RELEASED, AND THE SURRAN building was unusually crowded. I felt out of place in my bike kit, tattered and raw after dealing with that shadow as I wove through the students filling the lobby. It was the end of term, and everyone was clearly reluctant to leave, as they might never see one another again.

"My God," a young woman said as I angled past her, her face scrunching up in distaste. "Look at the dross she's dragging behind her."

"They really should make sweepers use the rear entrance," the second woman said, knowing full well I could hear them. "Dragging dross through the entire hall attracts worse."

"I wouldn't be attracting dross if you weren't making it," I muttered, vowing to remember her. Freshman, blond, dressed nice, pixy haircut: she'd need me someday. True, the three-story stone building belonged to the university, but under it was one of the oldest dross containment facilities in the state. Sweepers had the building first. If anyone should use the back door, it should be the students.

Chin high, I pushed through the outflow, my backpack and stick case over my shoulder as I tried to reach the stairs. But the farther I went, the more I was being noticed, and I finally glanced over my shoulder to see a trail of distortion following me, sparkling like dust in the sun. Wincing, I slowed. Okay. They might have a point. The two bottles of dross in my pack were attracting wisps from the corners and walls, where they might have lain unnoticed for weeks.

Great, I thought sourly. As if I didn't look grungy enough in my bike kit and spider guts under my nails. No, I had to drag dross behind me like a fisherman's net. There were too many people to easily catch it in a psi field, and it was too large for a wand, so I angled to one of the niched permanent traps in the hall. With a little luck, I could lure it into containment.

Sighing, I inched past the students sitting in the chairs arranged beside the nearest trap, making casual eye contact as I took the last open seat. Once the dross got close enough, I could surreptitiously gather it up and dump it into the hall's trap. But even as I sat, the dross behind the three sticks began to filter out, attracted to my haul. *Shadow spit . . .*

There was no help for it. Embarrassed, I took a bottle of dross out of my backpack and set it under the sticks as an extra attractant. Immediately the trapped dross reversed its flow and plastered itself against the bottle. A tendril of heat curled up around my hand as I drew away, the dross tingling as if wanting to break on me in a flash of bad luck.

You wish. Grimacing, I tried to brush it off on one of the trap's sticks, finally having to flick it into the trap like a booger, where it oozed down to rejoin the rest.

"Oh, my God," one of the guys said, having witnessed the entire disgusting show. "Let's breeze," he added as he stood, and the rest gathered their things and followed.

Whatever. I slumped in my chair to wait out the crush, telling myself that I didn't care what they thought.

The hall had two of these five-foot-tall, freestanding ambient traps, strategically placed to give magic-using mages a place to dump their dross, though I thought they were too beautiful to be a mage's trash can. The sticks themselves were too tall for easy use, more ceremonial with the reddish wood beautifully engraved and heeled in silver. We'd once hidden our sweeper abilities behind brooms and woven fabric, but now all that remained was art to remind us.

Tired, I looked over the milling heads to the kimono-like robe behind glass and under a spotlight. Though dusty from the display, it was still stunning, having been woven from knotted strands of rough silk. The shimmery black and green robe was a stupendous example of passive shadow deterrent, its knotted dross allowing the wearer to more safely work with the dangerous stuff.

I'll never be that good, I mused, jerking my foot at the sudden hot-toe touch of dross. The latent energy I'd dragged from the corners had finally gotten close enough, and while the noise continued to grow as more students replaced those leaving, I leaned to scoop up the sparkling heat, feeling it cool in my hand as I wrapped it in a psi field. "Get in there," I whispered as I rolled the little dust bunny of bad luck into a psi field and then into the trap. With a little hiccup of sensation, the nasty stuff abandoned me to merge with the rest.

"Thanks, Dad," I whispered, leaning to touch the plaque set below the oversize tripod. *When three souls fall to one, and one in turn is all. Sweeper, Spinner, weaver. Shadow heeds the call,* I read, my melancholy rising. The art installation was dedicated to my dad, actually, who had died in the shadow break of 2014. I'd been a freshman at the time, and if not for the entire sweepers' guild taking me under their collective wing, I might have quit my studies entirely.

Though no less beautiful, the twin trap at the other end of the hall lacked the commemorative plaque. It was rumored that the identical sticks had once belonged to Herm Ivaros, but I doubted it. The Spinner had gone into hiding after his theories that dross could be used to fuel a new kind of magic had ended with my dad dead.

But it was an old hurt, and I took out my phone, swiping through my music and putting in an earpiece to ignore the world until the hall emptied. I'd forgotten to take my phone off do-not-disturb, and my frown eased when a text came in from Ashley. She'd finished her meeting with her professors and was making dinner tonight to make up for missing our last pickup.

Thanks for handling the spill, came in, posting three seconds after the first, and then, only five minutes ago, **You forgot to turn your phone on again.**

Smiling, I texted back. **Sorry. You would have loved the sweep. Tell you over pasta.** Because it would be pasta. That was all the woman knew how to cook.

But guilt stirred as I scrolled through my news feed to the sound of the Foo Fighters. I wasn't going to tell Ashley about the chewed sticks if I could avoid it. She'd want to know how, blah, blah, blah . . . Telling Darrell would be bad enough. It wasn't as if I could blame it on Pluck, my dog. *Or could I . . .*

Sighing, I gazed out over the students, wishing they would just leave. Surran Hall traditionally housed the university's history program, sandwiching the more popular mage classes between Current Affairs and Middle Eastern History before 3000 BC. St. Unoc was the premier school for higher mage studies, and that the campus was closed went a long way in preserving the silence of our existence. Most mages were happy with the class-one manipulations needed to reheat their coffee or find their misplaced keys—skills gained at home or from a skilled relative. But those who went on to further their studies into the more elaborate magics needed an additional career to point the taxman to in order to evade uncomfortable questions. A double major in history or philosophy wasn't uncommon and often useful in helping to maintain the silence when accidents happened. And they did happen.

St. Unoc had a substantial discipline devoted to political science, allowing graduates to tweak witness testimonies or cloud a mundane's perceptions or memory using a complex class-five ether spell. Many of the graduates in the mage nursing program would go on to become ER doctors and nurses, where their proficiency in air studies allowed them to reach into a body with no incision. 'Course, the same skills could be used to rob a safe blind.

Those with even a class-one rating in water studies could sense when things were wrong, but when developed, finding people and objects that were out of place made for a useful skill in law enforcement. Earth studies was more nebulous, but who wouldn't want to be able to move things with their mind using an attraction/repulsion spell?

By far, the easiest school of magic to master was fire, and just about every mage from the least proficient to the highest professor could warm their coffee by exciting the molecules to move faster. Those who developed the skill generally landed in mage security or demolition. But everyone from a class-one rating to the most proficient professor did what they could to keep the mundane population in the dark.

Part of that was the creation and maintenance of dross traps disguised as artwork. There was an entire program, a double major in art, to satisfy that need. It was one of the few disciplines where sweepers excelled, probably because mages thought it beneath them.

"You are such a slob, Janice," a high-pitched voice said as I scrolled. "Are you really going to leave that?"

I looked over my phone, eyebrows rising. Two young women stood before me, a wisp of dross wafting down from their steaming coffee as they debated whether to sit. "Why not?" she said, her expression mocking as her eyes met mine. "It's not my job." Fingers playing with her lodestone pendant, she walked away, her friend giving me an apologetic smile before following.

Nice, I thought, eyeing the drift of glowing haze rolling along the floor. This was why I hated being paired with new students. Every last one of them, Ashley included, had thought I was the village shit-keeper, following behind their royal asses with a shovel—until I'd taught them otherwise.

True to form, the passing mages ignored the sparking haze of new dross. They all knew it was there, but not one of them would do a damn thing to pick it up. It irritated me, though, so when the hall began to empty, I gathered myself to go get it—only to hesitate at a familiar voice.

Benny? Pulse fast, I sank back into the cushions, flustered. It *was* Benedict, his pressed shirt tucked into his jeans and his hard-soled shoes reminding me that he had recently begun to teach intro-level mage studies. His tall frame put him a head over most everyone else, making him easy to find among a group of fawning students. He had dark curly hair like mine, a scrumptious olive skin tone, and a lanky build. In short, he was beautiful, and I shrank down, hoping he didn't see me in my spandex messenger kit as he made his way to the main door.

Unlike most everyone here, I'd known Benny since grade school. Our two families had been the only magic users in a five-mile radius, but because he was a mage and I was clearly not, we'd all but ignored each other until I broke my ankle in seventh grade and had to sit out gym. As luck would have it, Benny had busted his leg at the same time after traipsing through a dross drift in his backyard like an idiot. Long story short, we'd spent three months in an unsupervised art room playing paper-triangle football and blowing up balloons.

We were supposed to be doing art, but the only art we ever did was making full-size fans for our football stadium. It was Benny who had taught me how to put a balloon in a balloon without even using magic, and we spent an entire three days blowing them up before cramming them into the music room as a prank.

I'd thought we were friends and had told him stuff I'd never told anyone—only to find out later that I'd been nothing but a pleasant distraction, that our "friendship" had been contingent on the art room we were trapped within. *Not one smile, not one acknowledgment that I even existed,* I thought, warming at the old hurt as I remembered his utter disregard when I'd tried to talk to him in the hallway and his cutting comments to his friends when he'd walked away.

I forced my jaw to unclench, telling myself that I didn't care. It was more bad luck that Benny hadn't left St. Unoc after graduation. Like most of the university's best, he had remained, and he was now working on a project that, if successful, would revolutionize how we dealt with dross. The process was being hailed as a godsend, but in my mind, it only meant there'd be less impetus to dispose of dross properly—resulting in more of it lying around. If it ever reverted, we'd be in trouble.

It went without saying that Benedict was smart—wickedly so—but if you asked me, he looked a little frazzled as he spun as if to return to the lecture hall, only to be called back by his assistant, who then handed him first his phone and then his lecture notes. I knew Benny wasn't good at explaining complex things simply, and why he had taken on a class was beyond me.

"All that, and so . . . charmingly oblivious," I muttered, as he headed right for that wisp of dross that Ms. Coffee had left behind. I knew he couldn't see it. It had been one of his art room confessions. The more powerful a mage you were, the less attuned you were to dross, and as much as he irked me, Benedict was *very* good, excelling in not one discipline but two: fire and earth.

Not knowing why, I moved my backpack from beside the trap and closer to the aisle in the hope that the waste in it might pull the dross out of his way. Yes, he was a wanker, but that didn't change that I had liked him . . . even if it had only gone one way.

It sort of worked, and I winced when someone else stepped into the haze. There was a twinkle of light as the dross broke on him . . . and the guy promptly dropped his phone. It hit the floor with a crack, and I surreptitiously shifted my backpack to where it had been tucked out of sight. *No good deed goes unpunished.*

"Who left that?" the student said, swearing when he saw the spiderweb cracks in his screen. "Someone left a dross wisp in the hall. My screen is busted!"

I buried my attention in my phone, scrolling, scrolling, scrolling.

In my ears, Slipknot screamed about people being shit. It was hard to find fault with the thought.

"Damn sweepers, dragging in dross," the guy accused, and I slowly lifted my head.

He was staring at me, and my eyes narrowed. "Are you referring to me?" I said sweetly as my feet came down to land solidly on the scratched tile floor.

"Who else would I be talking to?" he said, ignoring his friends urging him to let it go. "How much dross you got there, princess? Two bottles? In a high-psi zone?"

Princess? I turned my music off and stood, pulling myself up to my distressingly average height, and shifted to stand right in front of him. The hall had gotten progressively quiet, and I leaned forward, deeper into his space. "I'm thinking you need to take your lumps and leave," I said, my high voice carrying well. "This is the sweeper hall. You simply decorate it. What's your name?"

Someone snickered, and the guy backed up, clearly startled. A whispering was rising, and my jaw clenched at a hushed "That's Petra Grady? She's not very big."

Damn it all to hell. I wasn't short! Just because I didn't wear heels . . .

"Hey, hold up there," a pleasant, low voice intruded, and I jerked. *Benny?* "That drift couldn't have come from her."

I froze, startled. *Benny is sticking up for me?*

The guy with the broken phone spun. "Yeah?"

"She was sitting next to a dross sink," Benedict said, gesturing at the decorative trap. "If she had accidentally released anything, it would have gone there, not rolled halfway across the room. I think it's more of a 'he who felt it, dealt it' situation."

Someone laughed, and the guy flushed as his friends tugged him into their circle. "Come on," one of them complained. "The big tables go fast. I don't want to string out along the bar."

Phone Boy gave me a dirty look and walked away. Smirking, I

turned to pick up my pack—only to lurch to a halt. Benedict was there—right in front of me. I flushed as I remembered finding a note in my locker after he had dissed me in the hall, saying that he wanted to be "secret friends." Bullshit. Yes, it had been over a decade, but it still hurt.

"Hey," I said, and he smiled. Something in me dropped to the pit of my gut, pulling my ability to speak with it. *Crap on a cracker, Petra. Get a grip.* "Ah, thanks for that."

"No problem." He half turned, gesturing to his assistant that he needed a moment. "You're going to think this is weird, but I was just thinking about you. You work for the loom, right?"

No, I simply like wandering around in spandex with bottles of dross. "Yep." I put a hand on my hip to hide a spider-gut stain. "I've been a loomer for the last eight years."

A flicker of what might be guilt crossed his face. "Word is you took on an unregistered rez today by yourself. Three bottles. Is that it?"

His attention had gone to my backpack, and I slowly exhaled, glad he wasn't looking at me. "It was only two." *Why are you talking to me? We aren't stuck in an art room.*

His attention went over my shoulder to the dross-covered bottle in the ambient trap. "You, ah, were using it to pull that free-range drift from across the room, weren't you."

I shrugged. "I was waiting for the hall to clear before I took my haul down, and it bugged me."

He nodded, thoughts distant. A big chunk of glass winked from his class ring. His lodestone, obviously. He hadn't been allowed to have one when we were in school. No lodestone, no magic. But that hadn't stopped him from having a secret one he kept in his pocket. Even so, one good pop and he was helpless unless the sun was up to recharge it.

Which might be why Ashley always seemed to have a spare, now that I think about it.

"Hey, ah, you want to go get some coffee or something?" he said, and I felt myself burn when he eyed me up and down as if in evaluation. "I could use some help with—"

"No," I said flatly, and his brow furrowed. "Goodbye, Dr. Strom."

"I suppose I deserve that," he said. "See you around, Ms. Grady."

Black curls falling into his eyes, he walked away, head down, pace slow as his assistant hustled to join him, glancing at me as if I had insulted the king.

"Whatever," I whispered. Annoyed, I turned to the trap and did what no right-minded mage would do and stuck my arm right into it. Fire enveloped my hand, quickly muted as I sent a psi field around the trapped dross, jolts of tingles protesting at my intrusion. Even with the psi field, sensation prickled over my hands as I brushed the dross off and took a moment to examine the bottle on all sides. Satisfied there were no hangers-on, I stuffed the bottle away.

"What was that all about?" I heard Benedict's assistant ask when they left the building, and I felt myself warm as I paced through the emptying hall to the sweeper lounge. I was wondering what that had been all about as well. Faculty and sweepers got together all the time, but Benedict was a known quantity, and I wasn't going to be his trophy sweeper / adoring girlfriend who picked up his dross along with his socks.

Not even if the world were ending.

3

TAKING THE ELEVATOR WITH TWO BOTTLES OF DROSS WASN'T PRUDENT, AND I opted for the stairs. It was only two flights down, and I was already through the fire door and halfway to the loom before the heavy a door to the stairs slammed behind me. My stick case bumped against my back, and my soft shoes scuffed. But my pace slowed when I realized someone else was coming up.

"Hey, Marge," I called, recognizing the woman at the twin double doors. Marge wasn't a sweeper but a Spinner, the designation putting her one step above and sideways, neither an all-powerful mage nor a dross-toting sweeper but a little of both. "Shoot, is it that late? I meant to get here before the loom closed."

Marge waited for me by the doors, a pleasant expression on her broad brown face. "You're good. I saw your invoice pop up, so Darrell kept the vault open when she clocked in."

But it was still after hours, meaning the sweeper lounge would be empty. The fewer who knew about my chewed sticks, the better. "Thanks. I didn't want to take this home."

"Exactly." She shifted her books to the other arm. "So . . . how many bottles?"

"Two," I said, telling myself it wasn't a lie. "There was an unregistered rez."

A frown pinched her brow to make her look old. "At the Lance building?"

"Third floor." I shifted the bag higher up my shoulder. "Dr. Tyler doesn't strike me as being especially careful with dross, but that might change."

"No doubt." She flashed me a smile and coded in the door for me. "Hey, if you want to do anything this week, let me know. Darrell has the night shift all this month, and I don't know what to do with myself."

The thump of the magnetic lock was loud, and I nodded. Everyone knew Ashley was leaving. Maybe sharing rent hadn't been the best idea. "Will do," I said, and then I gave her a wave as the door shut behind me, sealing with an ear-pressure shift.

The short passage went right under a huge, unseen tripod, the dross-cored beams hidden behind the walls ensuring I wouldn't drag anything in on the soles of my feet. The floors were white, the walls were white, and the dross trench under the walkway was white. A slight shiver rose from me as I passed under the huge trap and tiny, unseen drifts of dross clinging to my sticks or containment bottles peeled away like smoke from a long-dead fire to settle in the trench. The loom was a mage's version of a clean room, and this was the first and only needed defense.

I coded in my individual passcode on the keypad by the door, and with another hissing click, it opened. "Darrell?" I questioned as the loom's computer, affectionately named Henry, dramatically announced me as "Petra Grady. Sweeper first-class."

"Give me a sec!" Professor Yanna called back, and I unslung my backpack and stick case. The air smelled faintly of citrus and cloves, and it was quiet but for Darrell's ambient music. The sweeper lounge was decorated in soft tones of gray and blue, comfortable with companionable couches and low tables. Its tall ceiling made it feel less basement despite the no-window theme. One wall had a galley kitchen stretching along it, the dishwasher quietly slushing. Three desks sat almost behind the entry door: two pristinely clean, the third cluttered with papers and knickknacks that overflowed onto two file cabinets. An older, petite Black woman sat at the messy desk, and Darrell waved me in as she tried to wrap up her phone conversation.

Yes, it was the sweeper lounge, but it was manned twenty-four/ seven by at least one Spinner. The Spinners' guild was a step up, the small group consisting of sweepers who, over time, had learned how to bond to a lodestone. Short story shorter, they could do magic as did the mages. They could also touch dross with impunity, and the mix of sweeper and mage abilities was paramount in maintaining security if the vault should ever break and the accumulated dross threaten to escape. If there were more of them, mages might not be so smug, but as it was, Spinners were treated almost as badly as sweepers.

Relaxing, I dropped my backpack at the end of a couch and sat down. It was one of several, all curving around a yin-yang coffee table. The informal meeting area made for a pleasant place to decompress after a hard sweep, but it was empty now, as were the racks of hooks beside the door. A second door led to the actual lockers and showers.

Both sweepers and Spinners could knot dross without harm, but Darrell was an expert, and an antique loom for weaving cloth sat under a dimmed spotlight in one corner, the knotted warp making it look impossible to work. It was Darrell's latest piece, each silken knot holding a captured drift of dross to repel shadow. It was how dross had been stored before the technology for the vault had been invented, but this was pure art, the silken strands having a beautifully shaded, muted color. All animal-born fibers, from wool to angora to horsehair, could hold dross when knotted properly, but silk was the best and Darrell would use nothing else.

St. Unoc's university had only a handful of Spinners, four of whom were devoted to the loom. Darrell had seniority, and she invariably took the late shift. She kept the lights dim once the door was locked, but seeing as sweepers and Spinners both had an unusually high number of rods in their eyes, it only made things seem sharper . . . if a little on the bland side.

The wall behind the desks held formal university-taken pictures of past sweepers and Spinners. They had once graced the upper floors, but time and a slow decline of importance had shoved them down here to be forgotten by everyone but us.

Though the entire room was called the loom, the loom itself was somewhat anticlimactic, being little more than a chemical exhaust hood with sterile, poke-through gloves and three small doors or gates: one to get the dross in there; a second leading to the vault behind the wall; and a third, a trapdoor affair, to funnel used bottles back to the stockroom.

True, the industrial hood was nothing like the loom that Darrell sat at to weave knotted dross. The terminology of sweepers and Spinners harkened back to our beginnings. Sweepers had once collected dross with dross-cored brooms. Spinners had spun it into something safe to handle by knotting dross into tiny strands where it couldn't break into bad luck. Mythical weavers were said to have taken it a step further and woven the snared bad luck into good—sort of a cradle-to-grave SOP for magical waste.

Now dross-cored sticks were used to collect dross, which we put into glass bottles, and the only spinning Spinners ever did was a good story. There were no weavers, and there likely had never been. But the terminology had stuck—an indelible link to our ancestors.

"Right, right," Darrell said into her phone, clearly impatient as she stood, the beads in her hair clinking faintly. No one dared ask, but rumor said the woman knotted dross into her hair, too. A misshapen chunk of glass hung from her neck like a pendant. It was her lodestone, front and center as a source of pride and sign of her station. Unlike mages, Spinners had lost the art of making lodestones, and the lumpy, greenish glass was older than the university itself.

"Hey, I gotta go," Darrell said. "My last spin of the day is here. As a matter of fact, it is. Talk to you later." The beep of her cell was loud, and I turned. "Hi, Grady. I saw the pending invoice. An exceptional sweep."

I drew my backpack across the sleek black-and-white table, remembering the conversations I'd had around it, the camaraderie, the way I'd been helped through a rough spot, the way I'd helped someone else. "Kind of like my luck—both good and bad," I said, reluctant to tell her how my sticks got mangled and why I had a vodka bottle full of shadow.

"Yes?" She came out from behind the desk, her woven skirt a swaying mass of color as she dragged a tablet off her desk in passing. "You were working alone. How'd that go?"

"Okay," I lied. "I used to work alone all the time." *And I will again if I get my way,* I thought, smiling at the charismatic woman in her ratty slippers, long skirt, and knotted shawl over a colorful blouse. There was a fray in her shawl, and my curiosity pinged. The loom was a low-dross zone despite the vault's entrance being sixty feet from her desk. Everything here was focused on containment and detection. That fray meant that something had gotten loose.

"Well, let's have it," she said as she closed the distance between us.

Usually I'd simply drop the bottles off and leave, but the shadow made things different, and I followed her to the table beside the loom hood. Guilt for my ruined sticks and short-cord rose up, was quickly squelched. "Two bottles, plus."

"Plus?" She glanced over her shoulder, her thin eyebrows high. "From a spill? Wow. Someone will be eating steak tonight."

I lagged behind, hiking my stick case higher up my shoulder. "Two dross bottles from the spill . . ." I hesitated, not wanting to bring up the spider. How I'd handled it was not standard practice. "There was an unregistered rez," I said truthfully. "It went active and drew in everything within two hundred feet of it. The Lance building."

"Lance, huh? Ashley will be sorry she missed it." Darrell settled herself on the wide stool with a sigh, waiting as I put my bag on the table and unzipped it. I took the dross bottles out one by one . . .

wincing as my fingers tingled, cramping with cold when I brought out the shadow. A shudder threatened to ripple over me—and I stifled it. The shadow had ripped my stick apart to get to the dross inside—dross that should have killed it.

Worried, I set the bottle down and wiped the chill from my hand.

"Oh." Darrell stared at the vodka bottle. "New vice?"

I quashed my embarrassment only to have fear flicker up in its place. "I ran out of bottles. It would have been nice if they had told me it was in there, but I don't think they knew." I hesitated, afraid that my sticks and tie had gone bad. I'd made them, and the thought that I had been using substandard tools was scary. "It didn't behave right. The shadow, I mean."

"Shadow's nature is to be unpredictable." Darrell took up the vodka bottle. The shadow pressed against the glass as if trying to get away from her, but that was how knotted dross worked—usually—and she was wearing a lot of it. Frowning, Darrell set the bottle down. "What happened?"

"It, ah, might have eaten the dross out of his trap cord," I said, voice rising, and her eyes slid to my backpack. "I found it broken in his trash can."

"Shadow can't eat active dross, only inert."

"Yeah, I know," I said, still not wanting to show her my sticks. Instead, I reached for the bottle, reconsidering when the shadow flung out a wisp of black as if to strike me.

"We'll vault your haul, then look at it." Her thoughts clearly somewhere else, Darrell checked a monitor under the glass wall before opening a small door on the front and putting all three bottles into the loom. "This is the third time you've brought in shadow this year, isn't it?"

Her voice was casual, but I felt a twinge of worry as the memory of that spider crawled up from where I'd shoved it. "Yeah. Does it ever get any easier?"

"Three seconds before it turns you shadow," she said, the beads in her hair clinking as she stuffed her hands into the poke-through gloves. "Or so they say. What happened to your short-cord?"

I flushed, wishing I had stowed the trap tie instead of using it to hold my hair back as I usually did. *She sees everything,* I thought, but before I could come up with an answer, she opened the bottles of dross. Immediately two waves of distortion billowed out, shifting to cling together with random sparkles until a haze of wispy glory slowly plastered itself against the wall where the vault lay. Ten years of magical waste lay beyond, an irresistible, magnet-like lure.

"Let's see what you got," she said, peering at her tablet as a wave graph rose and fell, the level landing somewhere between nice and very nice. "Not bad," she murmured, gloves making a popping sound as she pulled her hands out to make a notation. "Sixty-seven macro-pules."

"Sounds good," I muttered, knowing that as much as that was, I'd get five times that for the shadow—if they could use it.

"Invoice?" she prompted.

I scrolled through my phone until I found it and touched it to her tablet. My eyes strayed to the unusual pull on her shawl. "How did you snag your throw?" I asked as she played trombone with her tablet to get the print visible.

"I've got a leak." Darrell tapped at the pop-up keyboard. "How did you tear your short-cord?"

I stifled my reach for my tie, useless now except for holding back my hair. Either the shadow was different or my dross knots were subpar. Either did not bode well. "A leak? Seriously?" I scanned the quiet, dimly lit space. "Down here?"

"I can't find it, and it's driving me nuts." Darrell paused while she brought up a new window and resumed typing, one finger at a time. "A regular trap won't work this close to the vault. I'm going to have to find the leak by hand." Darrell half turned, her gaze going to my stick case on the table, then to my frayed cord. "Talk to me about this shadow."

"Yeah, about that." I took my stick case in hand and let the sticks slide out, chips and all.

Silent, Darrell fingered the chewed lengths. "A shadow-imbued organism did this?"

"Maybe it could handle the dross because it was in a spider?" I offered, watching in worry as her slim fingers delicately traced the damage.

"No," she said, voice preoccupied. "It doesn't work like that. You made these sticks yourself, yes? I'm guessing the dross you used had been made inert to make shadow buttons and you got it by mistake."

Relief that it wasn't my skills was quickly followed by horror. "I've been using shadow-attracting sticks?" I said, and Darrell smiled.

"Inert dross attracts dross just as well as active, but it might explain why you keep running into shadow. How long have you been using these?"

"Eight years," I said, appalled. It was like learning that your spare parachute had a rip. *Shadow spit* . . . "They were my final exam. I got the dross from Professor Brown. You think someone tried to prank me?" I hadn't been in the sweeper program at the time, but someone would have used the sticks if not me.

"Mmmm. I wouldn't worry about it," she said as she eyed my sticks as if they were a personal affront. "It was lucky that you busted them before you got yourself in trouble. You need a new set."

I stared, startled when she threw all three across the wide room to clatter against the wall by her desk as if they were nothing. "I think fighting off a shadow-imbued spider the size of a rat is the definition of trouble," I muttered, appalled at her casual disregard of something my life had depended on.

"Let me vault this," she said as she stuffed her hands back into the gloves. "And we'll see if your shadow is too smart to use."

Oddly, it was Darrell's very disregard that I found most comforting, and my shoulders eased as she prepared to "spin the dross" from the loom into the vault. "Hey, I'd appreciate it if you didn't mention my new sticks to anyone," I said, as she hit a button to open the vault and allow the dross to flow into it, drawn like a magnet to the huge, glass-walled containment facility under the building.

"Petra Grady, you know discretion is my middle name." Eyebrows at a saucy slant, she closed the vault and opened the vodka bottle. A black, sparkling haze boiled up and out, swirling in the open space until it puddled in a corner of the hood as far from the vault entrance as it could get. The amount of dross behind the door would kill it a thousand times over, and if it could sense that, it was too sentient to use. It would be forced into the vault and destroyed.

"We can't use this," Darrell said as she studied it. "You say it took over a spider?"

"Yeah." Arms over my chest, I remembered its malevolence, then frowned when the dross began to drift, a thin stream rising like a cobra to orient on me. "Jeez, Darrell. I swear, the more there is of this stuff, the smarter it gets. I think it remembers me. Look at that."

"I'm looking," she said, low voice worried.

"Hey, don't open the vault yet," I added, an idea drawing me straight.

"Grady," she growled in warning, but I'd already pulled my ravaged short-cord from my hair. If the knots held inert dross, it should follow it. Maybe I could find Darrell's leak.

Pulse fast, I held a knot close to the glass, shuddering as the shadow oriented on it.

"That is definitely too smart to use. What are you doing?" Darrell said, wary as I held the knot out and ran it across the loom's glass-welded seams.

"Finding your leak." But I was far more interested in the shadow, black and shiny as it followed the knotted dross in my hand like a living oil slick. *Shadow spit, she's right,* I thought.

Until the black haze sharpened into a sudden point beside a seam and began to burrow.

I jerked my hand away, breath held and hiding the knot as the shadow continued to dig . . . until it abruptly lost interest and began to haze.

"There it is," I said in relief, wondering if I'd been stupid to show her. "You got a pen?"

"Yep."

I couldn't tell anything from her flat tone, and I stared at the shadow until she fitted a pen in my hand and I drew a squeaking arrow pointing to the crack. "What?" I complained when I gave her pen back.

Her expression thoughtful, she tucked the pen into a pocket beside her wand. "When was your last Spinner skills test?" she said, and I choked out a nervous laugh.

"Are you serious? No, thanks," I said, though being able to do magic would be a definite boost to my ego—if I could make the jump.

"Think about it," Darrell said. "You clearly have skill handling shadow."

But when I shook my head, she put her hands in the gloves and opened the vault. The shadow fled, darting over the small airlock until it retreated into the bottle, where it huddled in an evil-looking puddle. It was clearly afraid, which meant the abnormality was in my sticks and short-cord, not the shadow.

"Way too smart," Darrell said, her expression grim. But instead of using a psi field to force it into the vault, she fumbled for the cap and put it back on.

"Ah . . ." I started, watching as a thin wisp rose up from the puddle of black, touched the cap, and sank back down. "You're not going to dump it?"

Darrell's thick lips crooked in a wry smile as she tightened the cap and left it where it sat in the loom. "I want to show Ryan how you found the leak or he'll never believe me."

And with that, Darrell locked the vault for the day. The substantial, wall-thumping *clunk* stirred the inky black puddle, and then it sank down as she leaned to check the monitor before opening a second chute and chucking the empty dross bottles. "I take it you need some empties?" she said brightly.

"No." I felt myself warm. "I'm good. I just underestimated. I could use a few more shadow buttons, though."

She stood, her good mood obvious. "Right this way, ma'am. Buttons and sticks."

I fell into place beside her, relief and guilt twining around themselves. "I really appreciate you not telling anyone about this," I said as she stopped at a series of long, low cabinets built into the wall.

"If anyone finds out, it won't be from me." Beads clinking, she pulled open a drawer.

My breath escaped me in a sigh as I saw the carefully racked stick sets. They glistened black and gray in the electric light, and I smiled in anticipation. "I wish I had time to make a new set. I'm going to have to deduct the cost from my hauls. It's, um, what? Ten percent every week until it's covered?"

But Darrell pushed past them as if they were store-bought dowels, rummaging until she came out with four three-foot-long sticks, her smile sad as she handed me one.

My lips parted as I took it. The wood was a deep red, beautiful and engraved with esoteric loops and swirls. Silver capped the ends like on the ones upstairs, giving it a nice weight, and I marveled as I ran my hand across its length and sensed the dross trapped inside. "Darrell, I can't afford these," I said as I recognized their strength.

Darrell's smile was fond as she drew a strand of red knotted silk from the cabinet and shut it. Still smiling, she handed me the remaining three sticks along with the knotted cord balanced to them. "They were your dad's."

My head snapped up. "My dad's?"

Darrell nodded. "Part of his old set," she said, eyes lingering on the reddish wood. "You've seen the monster sticks upstairs in the hall? They are too long to do anything with, but he made those as well. At the time, I thought it best I keep these for you, seeing as you were only eighteen. I was waiting until you broke a couple. That, and for Ryan to lure you from Professor Brown."

"Uh, thank you," I said, stepping away to spin one to better sense the balance of dross it held. God help me, they were magnificent, all the way to the silver-heeled ends. *My dad's?*

And then I slumped when I realized what she'd meant by her comment that *she* wouldn't be the one to give away my secret. I couldn't refuse them. Everyone would know the first time I brought them out. Sweepers lived in a small world, and word traveled fast by magic.

"My dad," I said again, softer this time. "How come there are four?"

"He used to go through them fast. Let's hope it's not a 'like father, like daughter' thing." Chuckling, Darrell went to another cabinet for a soft velour casing to put them in. My blueprint stick case was a few inches too short. "The cost of the buttons will come out of your pay-check," she said, and I stifled a shiver when she dropped three black shadow buttons into my palm. "I'll ask Dr. Brown if he knows of anyone who might have switched out your dross. Even as a prank, it is inexcusable."

"It doesn't matter." I shoved the buttons into my pocket. I was far more interested in my new sticks, and I let her walk me to the door, oblivious to everything else.

"Big day tomorrow," Darrell said, snagging my empty backpack as we walked and handing it to me. "Incoming-freshman tours."

My mood dimmed. Ashley was leaving. "Tell me about it," I said glumly, wondering if I should volunteer as a tour guide so as to check out the freshmen, but I was tired of educating wanna-be-a-mage newbies on how the world really worked.

I slung the velour case over my shoulder as Darrell followed me to the door so she could lock it. I'd stop on the way home and get a longer blueprint tube. Maybe Ashley wouldn't notice.

"So . . . what do you think about that new dross-modification process the university is working on?" Darrell asked, surprising me with the shift in conversation.

"I think it's a mistake." My focus blurred as I remembered Benedict standing up for me, casual and confident in his tight jeans and crisp shirt, his softly curling black hair falling into his eyes . . . And then how he lingered, asking me out for coffee as he sized me up. *As if,* I thought sourly. Yes, I had tried to lure the dross away from his idiotic feet, but that was as far as it went. "If it's inert, no one is going to bother bottling it. What if it reverts?"

Darrell halted at the door, her eyes pinched in worry as she opened it. The hall to the stairs was glaringly bright after the cool dimness of the loom. "That's my concern, too. I'm glad you're thinking the same way."

"Thanks for the sticks," I said, and she made that doesn't-matter gesture that she was famous for, a waving, frivolous motion, as if she were swatting at flies.

"Don't thank me, thank your dad," she said, and I smiled, wishing I could. But feeling the heavy weight of his sticks on my shoulder made him feel close. "Petra, give the Spinner skills test some thought," Darrell said, and I shook my head even as I walked toe-heel backward into the hall. "You clearly have the chops to handle shadow. If you don't want to man the loom, you could always teach. I know for a fact that Dr. Brown would take you on as an apprentice. You could even go into the arts if you want."

She looked pained saying the last, and I smiled. "Thanks, but no," I said. "You aren't tricking me into being stuck down here all day."

Darrell took a protesting breath, then let it go. Beads clinking, she shut the door. The thump of the lock sliding into place was comforting somehow. Halfway up the stairs, my phone dinged, and I smiled at my new balance.

Me? A Spinner? I thought, wondering what it would feel like to have a lodestone and be able to harness the light as the mages did. There wasn't a sweeper alive who didn't know the theory, who hadn't practiced it at night, desperate to break through and become more. We all started with the same primer books, the same potential. It was only when proving we couldn't break light that we were quietly shifted to another course of study.

True, it would be wonderful to be able to do magic and leave the slights and whispered comments from stuck-up mages behind. But as I remembered the feel of the shadow fizzing against my thoughts, I stifled a shudder. Deal with that on a regular basis?

Never.

4

MY STREET BIKE WAS SURPRISINGLY LIGHT, MAKING IT EASY TO CARRY UP THE single flight of stairs and angle it around the corners without marring the walls. The wide communal hallway was quiet, and the sound of my wheel ticking was loud compared to the muted TV and conversations from my neighbors as I rolled my bike down the color-fully tiled floor.

Scuffed ride-on toys were parked against the wall under messy, hand-painted signs designating parking spots, and I smiled at the garbled sound of kids arguing as I passed. Someday I wanted a fam-ily, but right now, the idea of kids was more terrifying than facing a dozen shadows with only my sticks to fend them off.

My apartment was at the end, the spacious flat totally out of my pay grade if not for it having belonged to my dad. I had inherited the mortgage, which was why I had jumped at the chance when Ashley suggested she move in. The money had been nice, but the friendship better.

The soft click of a door opening behind me pulled my attention up, and I turned at a pleasantly masculine "Hey, Petra."

It was Lev, and I smiled as I scuffed to a halt, eyeing the some-what short, narrow man in his running shorts and tee as he came into the hall. "Hey. You got tonight off?" I asked.

He bobbed his head. "Yeah. Sorry to bother you, but I got your mail again."

"Seriously?" I held out my hand as he extended it. Lev was in his early thirties, and his blue eyes, dark hair, tight abs, and sensuous lips made him a poster boy for either cheap cologne or the military. The man had rented the apartment across the hall a few weeks after Ashley had moved in, and his immediate interest in her would have been annoying except that for all the time Lev spent at my apartment, it had become obvious that no matter how much he made Ashley laugh or how many times he offered to take her out for a movie or dinner, she was always going to put him on the friend couch.

For all his gregarious nature, Lev didn't talk about himself much, and it was only last week that I'd found out he'd gone right from high school into the mundanes' military to get the training needed to become a marshal for the mage court system. Four years and an overseas tour of duty later, he had decided law enforcement wasn't for him and he left with little more than a car and lots of stories.

The four years spent hiding his skills from the government was probably the source of his confidence and toned body, at odds with his too-long hair and the day-old stubble on his somewhat narrow chin. Though having been discharged from the nearby air base over two years ago, he clearly appreciated the Arizona climate and had yet to leave, content with his after-hours hotel job.

Today he had traded out his usual flip-flops for a pair of running shoes, and his jeans and lightweight top for a light-reflecting spandex "yummy suit," as Ashley would have called it. The sun was almost down, and my guess was he was going out for a run. A diamond earring glittered from one of his earlobes, his lodestone, obviously. He'd given Ashley the matching stud sometime last year. I'd never seen her wear it, and I felt bad for the guy. Always trying.

A cowlick of hair had spiked in the back, and the faint hint of obsidian haze on his shoulder told me a drift of dross had broken on him. The guy invariably had a drift or two on him. Messy hair was the least of it, and my shoulders slumped as he handed me the letter, not just open but clearly full of crisp hundred-dollar bills. *Great. Now I have to explain that.*

"I would have shoved it in your box, but I accidentally opened it," he said, ears red. "I didn't want you to think the postman did it. Um, sorry." He hesitated. "You win the lottery?"

"No." Annoyed, I shoved the letter into my pocket to deal with later. "It's my uncle," I lied, feeling myself warm. "He still thinks I'm a starving student. I told him I'm okay, but he keeps sending me money."

All of which was untrue. Herm Ivaros wasn't my uncle. The man was slime, and the money was the latest in his ongoing guilt payments for having been responsible for my dad's death. I'd told Ashley the money was from my "Uncle John" when she'd accidentally opened up one of his letters shortly after having moved in, and the lie had taken root, as most lies did. I had no idea where the man lived, but it had to be close, seeing as the canceled stamp was from the local post office.

"Nice." Lev lingered, clearly wanting to talk. "I'm really sorry. I didn't know it wasn't mine until I opened it up. No one ever sends me money." His lips quirked. "Except my grandma, and that was a five-dollar bill for my thirteenth birthday."

"You, um, want to come in?" I took a rocking step to my door. Herm had been adding handwritten notes to the mix lately, and the need to find out what he had said was a growing itch, even if I hated the man. "Ashley is making pasta. There's always room for one more." Grimacing, I took my wand from a back pocket and spun the dross up from his shoulder, gathering it before it reached the cell phone strapped to his arm. "Honestly, Lev. Don't you have a trap in your apartment?" I muttered.

"What, and have to pay you vampires to take it away?" he said with a grin. "It breaks and I move on with my life. Thanks for the dinner invite, but I want to hit the trail before the sun sets and I have to worry about coyotes."

Vampires. As in the loom sucking him dry . . . I managed a thin smile, adroitly holding the dross-coated wand between two fingers as I steadied my bike against a leg. Coyotes wouldn't harass a full-grown man, but they'd been known to lure off-leash dogs from the bike path into the many washes and, um, yeah. "Maybe next time," I said as I began to roll my bike down the hall, and his attention flicked past me to my door.

"Next time," he agreed. He turned, one hand fiddling with his phone until his music started. "Tell Ashley I'll be by later tonight."

"You got it," I said, and he took the stairs and was gone. "Watch out for dross bunnies," I whispered as my thoughts drifted back to my new sticks. Pride for their existence mixed with the desire to keep them hidden. Ashley would want to know what happened to my old ones, and telling her that a shadow-imbued spider ate them would be a mistake.

I hiked my backpack and sticks higher up my shoulder and reached for the knob without bothering to find my keys. Ashley never locked the door. It drove me crazy. As expected, it was open, but my irritation evaporated at the anxious whine of eighty pounds of happy dog.

"Hey, Pluck," I said as the black Lab nosed the door open and pushed himself into the hall. The scent of cooking pasta rolled out with him, and for a moment, I was preoccupied with placating the wiggling animal, wand held high and bike leaning against me as his heavy tail thwacked the walls, me, everything.

"How you doing, boy? Did Ashley take you out already?" I asked, not seeing any indication that he wanted to go for a walk as he snuffed my new stick case. "If she hasn't, we'll go after dinner, okay?" I added then, "Hey, hi! It's me!" as I struggled to get in.

"I figured!" Ashley called from the kitchen, her voice even higher than mine. "Pluck has been stuck to the door for the last five minutes. I swear, he must hear your bike clicking."

"I ran into Lev," I said, still trying to get past the dog. "He'll be over later tonight. Come on, Pluck, move!"

Curiosity satisfied, Pluck trotted to the kitchen in search of a handout. There was a small table trap by the door, and I cleaned the dross from my wand before tucking it into my pocket with my phone. Tired, I dropped my backpack on the red-and-orange-tiled floor, then hung my bike on the wall before propping my sticks in the corner to hope for the best.

The glow of sunset lit the building across the street, bouncing in through the balcony sliders to mimic the sunrise in a weird display, but I flicked the lights on anyway as I made my way to the kitchen. The kitchen was open to the rest of the apartment, and though there was a breakfast bar, we usually ate in front of the TV. The living room was comfortable if small, most of the natural light coming from the sliding glass door out to a narrow balcony. Two doors led to our separate rooms and shared bath.

Ashley had the nicer room, with sun in the morning and a view of the street. It had been mine as a child, but putting her in my dad's hadn't been an option. It now gave off a frilly, feminine vibe, with bright colors and pillows. It was nothing like my dark, spartan room, which stayed cool even on the hottest days. *Maybe that's why I gave it to her.*

Ashley and I had redecorated shortly after she had moved in, leaving only my autographed record album from Tool and the small house trap on the table beside the couch. I would have felt slighted, but the room was beautiful now, with a mix of Mexican art and Midwest overindulgence, and I didn't have either the eye or the stamina to decorate. Besides, it wasn't as if I hadn't helped pick everything out.

"Smells good," I said as I shut the blinds, and she flashed me an honest smile. Though we were nearly the same age, that was where the similarity ended. Ashley was blond, blue-eyed, and willowy. She was also tons more gregarious than I, having friends all over campus. Though not athletic in the traditional sense, she could shop me into the ground, as her designer shoes and trendy clothes could attest. She changed her lodestone with her mood, and it stung every time I found her discards in the trash. The smart woman was always doing something, and that balanced my cursory interest in most everything not revolving around my job remarkably well.

A Band-Aid decorated her pinky, the box on the counter telling me that she'd just put it on. Her brand-new sandals were scraped, and there was a little arc of sunburned skin on her neck where either she'd forgotten to put the sunscreen . . . or more likely, breaking dross had caused it to fail prematurely. The woman lived in a world of bad luck, but my sympathy was tempered with the knowledge that it was likely her own fault. Like Lev, she knew how to pick up dross and simply chose to take her lumps. Not me. I liked a clean space.

"Have you showered yet?" Ashley asked as she dropped a square of chocolate into the sauce. Pluck was beside her, his nose in easy reach of the counter.

Duh? I plucked at my sweaty bike kit, but she was probably making conversation. "I got to the sweeper lounge late. Darrell wanted to lock up, so I came right home."

"I can put this on hold if you want." She still hadn't turned. "The pasta is almost done, though."

"I can wait. Ah, I'll be with you in a sec. My uncle sent me another wad of cash."

"Shopping spree!" Ashley sang out, stirring the melted chocolate into the sauce as I took the note from my pocket and unfolded it, curiosity getting the better of me. With his typical conspiracy paranoia, Herm had written it on hotel stationery, and my brow furrowed.

Dear Petra. I hope this finds you in good health. I trust your work is going well at the university. Let me know if anything strikes you as odd as your skills progress. You can reach me at your dad's old phone number. Your dad was special, and you are, too.

I am special? I thought bitterly as worry and anger pinched my brow. How about odd, as in shadow deciding to make my sticks into lollypops, maybe? And how the hell did he have my dad's old phone? It had been ten years. I wasn't sure I had my dad's old number anymore.

But I knew I did. I even had his last voice mail.

"He wants me to call him," I said, struggling to keep my expression pleasant as I crumpled the letter and tossed it into the trash. Like that was ever going to happen. The man was a pariah, not just for being responsible for the last shadow break, in 2014, but for his foul theories that dross could be used to fuel magic—which was probably what had caused the incident in the first place.

"What, like on the phone?" Ashley's motion to stir the sauce hesitated. "Dude, you never told me you had his number. You have to do it. Or better yet, maybe you could meet him. I'd go with you if you're scared."

"God no," I said, scrambling for a reason. "What if he wants to give me a car?"

"Then you learn how to *drive*," Ashley said brightly. "You should do it. Family is family."

"I suppose." But there was no way I was going to tell her my pretend uncle was Herm Ivaros and the money was to soothe his guilt. Not many had seen the firsthand accounts, as well-meaning sweepers and Spinners glossed over the atrocities of one of their own. But I knew. Darrell had made sure of it. My dad had trusted Herm, and my dad had died for it. Accident or not, using dross to do magic was deadly, and my dad had paid the price.

Frustrated, I came into the kitchen and grabbed two oranges from the hanging basket to cut into half-moons. Beside me, Ashley's brow slowly furrowed as she looked into the living room and at the cash on the coffee table. It would be going to the ASPCA tomorrow. "Uncle John" had funded St. Unoc's entire spay and neuter program last year. *Hurray, Uncle John . . .*

The sound of my knife through the oranges mixed with the soft pops from the sauce, and she turned down the heat. *Maybe I should say something,* I mused. My sweep was probably all over campus by now. "I, ah, found a new rez at the Lance building," I said hesitantly. "I pulled two bottles off it."

"Damn," Ashley breathed, her disappointment obvious. "Figures you'd find one the first time in two years that I wasn't with you. What was it?"

I stretched to reach a bowl for the oranges. "A woman beaten to death in the late 1800s. She didn't give me any trouble." Which was the truth. It was the shadow-animated spider that had been the problem. "So." I put the oranges in the bowl. "How was rehearsal, Miss Valedictorian?"

She smirked as she forked a strand of spaghetti out. "Boring." She ate it, silent as she considered its state of doneness. A new pendant swung from her necklace, but I wasn't willing to bet that the bauble was her lodestone—yet. She might still be storing light energy for use after dark in the dangling earrings that she used last month or the pinky ring she'd been wearing the last two weeks. They were all glass.

"I gave them a copy of my speech and they asked me to tone down the rebellious content," she added as she turned the burner off. "No way. It's my fifteen minutes."

"Damn straight."

"Mmmm."

It was pensive, and I silently watched her carry the pot to the sink and pour the pasta through a colander. If I didn't know her better, I'd say she was avoiding something.

I took two strands and gave one to Pluck. "What do you want to drink?"

Ashley ladled the spaghetti onto the waiting plates. "Hard cider."

"Ooh! We're celebrating!" I pushed off the counter and got two bottles. "Your exit interview went well, then?"

"The Spinners' guild took my sticks," she muttered, clearly upset as she ladled the sauce. "Thanks for the stellar review, by the way. Callahan five-starred my application for the two university positions I put in for, and I was invited to apply to a third. That's the one I want."

"Cool. Who with?" I asked, the bottles hissing in turn as I opened them. If she landed a job on campus, she wouldn't have to move until she wanted to. "Rowen?"

"No . . ." Ashley put a slice of bread on her plate. Grabbing a bottle, she went to the seldom-used table and sat down. Pluck's nails clicked as he followed her, the dog happy as he sat at her side. He was my dog, but she was by far the softer heart of the two of us.

She's at the table? Worry was a quick flash as I wrangled my plate, my drink, and the oranges. "Who?" I asked again as I set everything down and moved a stack of mail off my chair.

Ashley's chin lifted. "Dr. Benedict Strom. He wants a dedicated sweeper for his team."

My motion to sit jerked to a halt. That was why he wanted to go for coffee. He had been fishing for information on Ashley. *Nice . . .*

Her blue eyes narrowed as I settled into my chair. Silent, I sucked on my teeth, trying to plan my attack. Arguing with Ashley never ended well and I tended to pick my battles. This one was a hill I'd die on. It wasn't that I cared if she went to work with a man I thought was a dweeb. Ashley wasn't a sweeper; she was a mage.

"They're in the final stages before release, and he needs someone to prep their study dross and monitor it for changes. The Spinners' guild agreed he needs a dedicated sweeper."

Want to be sure he isn't lying. Check. "You're a mage, not a sweeper."

Her cheeks reddened. "I can see dross pretty well. My psi fields are rated at a solid four for breadth and density, and my attraction and repulsion spells are even better. Add a wand to that, and I can handle dross as well as any sweeper can touch it. Me being a mage makes me perfect for the job," she said, head down as she aggressively buttered her bread. "I won't be going in with any preconceived notions that it won't work."

I took a swig of my hard cider, feeling the earthy burn. "Setting aside that it's a sweeper position, Benedict's entire theory is flawed," I said flatly. "If you're smart, you'd stay the blue blazes away from it. It's a career ender."

"It *will* work, and I want to be a part of it." Ashley dabbed a napkin to her lips. "If that means I have to clean a few traps, it's no skin off my nose. Jeez, Petra. You use a wand to empty the house trap yourself half the time."

I used a wand because the dross burned my fingertips until it cooled. No one else seemed to have a problem with it but me, and I set my bottle down hard, embarrassed.

Tail down, Pluck slunk into the living room and hid behind the sofa.

Appetite gone, I frowned. Ashley wouldn't be able to stomach the second-class vibe she'd have to endure if she took a sweeper position, and though Benedict had couched the job as something more, they'd put in for a janitor to clean up after snotty professionals who thought they were above shoving their own dross into a trap.

"Ashley," I said flatly, and she flushed. "Using psi fields and attraction spells to gather dross for your thesis is one thing. But you can't touch dross without it breaking on you. Besides, you can't change dross—"

"They *are*," she interjected hotly.

"And even if you did, dross's nature is to cause the unlikely to happen. Which would be to change back."

We'd had this argument before, but not when a potential job was in the mix, and fork in hand, Ashley squinted at me. "I think you're worried about losing your job if this works."

"That's not it at all," I said, though the thought had occurred to me. "He's making dross inert, right? Inert dross attracts shadow. What if it works like a shadow button and it pulls in every stinking shadow in a hundred-mile radius?"

Ashley spun spaghetti onto her fork. "I saw the proposal. They have a way around that."

Frustrated, I took a swig of my drink. "Okay. Let's say it *all works* and the treated dross stays both inert and invisible to shadow. People will do more magic than they should. Dross is going to pile up even worse."

"Who cares, if it's inert?" Her mood had softened, and I picked up my fork. I could at least pretend to eat as she aimed her promising career squarely at destruction.

"The only reason anyone collects dross is to avoid the bad luck when it breaks." I spun my fork, spindling up a wad. "What if it doesn't break at all? Ever?"

"Isn't that the point?" Annoyed, she focused on her food. "No dissociation, no bad luck."

"Everything breaks eventually," I said patiently. "I wish you hadn't put your app in."

"Well, thanks a hell of a lot," Ashley said loudly, and Pluck slunk into my room. "You'd rather I work at some dead-end job making complexion charms and selling them under the counter in a mall in Tucson? This could be the biggest innovation in dross handling since we quit using brooms to sweep it up and wheels to spin it into knots and looms to store it. *I* want to be in on it," she said forcefully. "*I* want to make a difference in the world. Dr. Strom is going to change everything."

"Ashley, I've known this guy since I was twelve. Don't do this."

"Yeah? Well, you're just afraid of change." Angry, she twirled her fork, but her wad was too big, and she let it drop, frustrated.

"I'm not afraid of change," I said. "I'm afraid that Benny doesn't understand or respect the fundamental properties of dross. I'm afraid that his arrogance is going to bite him, and everyone else who uses his new charm, on the ass. Making dross smell pretty will mean more magic being cast. Best case is we're going to be knee-deep in dross by the end of winter. Worst case is it will draw in enough shadow to cause another shadow break and maybe force us out into the open."

"A shadow break isn't going to force us into the open," Ashley grumbled, and I exhaled my tension, agreeing with her. But the risk of ending up as a government lab rat haunted everyone. The mundanes outnumbered us a thousand to one, and if they knew about us, it wouldn't be hard to suss us out. A simple eye test would do it, seeing as the more light-sensitive rods you had in your eyes, the better you could see dross. The most skilled sweepers had so many rods they could see in the dark like a dog.

"I don't want to argue," I said as I stabbed my fork into a pile of pasta and twirled it. "Benny's procedure is flawed, and frankly, I don't think you could handle the slights a sweeper has to endure."

"His name is Dr. Strom," she said tightly. "And I've never slighted you."

"You used to," I said, warming. "'Petra?'" I added in a mocking falsetto. "'The bathroom is full of dross again! When are you going to clean it up?'" My voice dropped. "I can't make dross, and I'm still finding dross bunnies under the sink."

"Sometimes it gets away." Ashley put her fork down, cheeks reddening. "You know what? I think you want this to fail because you're worried once the mages don't need you to store dross, you won't have a place in mage society at all. Unless you learn how to use dross to do magic, and we *know* how that ends."

My mouth dropped open and I stared at her. Lips pressed, I stood. Okay, I might have brought up a past argument or five, but comparing me to a dross-eater was way over the line.

"Petra, I'm sorry," she said as I took my plate to the kitchen and oh-so-carefully set it on the counter. "I shouldn't have said that. Please, I'm sorry. It was cruel."

But my appetite was gone, and I looked at her, more than the kitchen counter between us. Her brow was creased in worry and she seemed sincere. She knew that if not for sweepers, mages would be up a creek without a paddle. Actually, I'd always thought that was half the problem. They knew it and were mean because of it. They needed us. At least they would until Benny got his new process online. She was right about that.

"I'm probably not even going to get the job," she said, melancholy. "There's like a hundred people who put in."

And she wants it, I thought, realizing this was where her anger was coming from. She wanted it bad and felt helpless. "But *you* were invited," I said, the knot in my gut tightening. They had offered it to her, and she was going to take it. And I was going to be caught in the middle for the next half decade as they tweaked and prodded and forced it onto the market.

Ashley smiled, thinking I'd forgiven her for that stunted comment. "I was, wasn't I." Her smile faded. "Please be happy for me. You're the only person whose opinion I care about."

My shoulders slumped and I sighed. "I am," I finally said, and with a clear heart, I lifted my cider. "I am happy for you. To new beginnings."

Her smile returned, and for the moment, the world was okay. "And happy endings," she said as she stood so our bottles could reach.

Nodding, I clinked my bottle to hers, and we drank to whatever came next.

5

~

THE WARMTH OF THE SWEEPERS' BULLPEN ON THE TOP FLOOR OF THE SURRAN building was somewhat oppressive with fifty or so people, but the cheerful chatter and obvious camaraderie more than made up for it. As a sweeper assigned to the loom, I wasn't required to attend the daily bullpen sessions unless I had something to report. Finding a new rez was right up there, but the reason I'd risen early and dragged myself in was because if I was going to get a new tagalong when Ashley left, I wanted to be on the team who would be evaluating the incoming students—hence the casual jeans and heavy metal band T-shirt instead of my usual cyclist kit.

"Coffee," I whispered, acknowledging a few familiar faces before going to the table set against the wall and the tall urn beside a half-empty box of doughnuts. The long room wasn't so much the top floor of the old building as a converted attic, the air conditioners already going full tilt against the expected heat. And whereas a mage might find fault with the peak-ceilinged, dormer-window-lit room, being this high up meant the entire floor was naturally clear of dross—partly because there was no reason for a mage to be up here, but also because dross tended to move downhill.

The noise was considerable as everyone waited for Ryan. A few were dressed as bike messengers, some in suits, but most looked like students. A few, the older and most skilled, were dressed as if homeless, their worn clothing smelling of detergent. My back was to everyone, and I turned as the first welcoming sip of coffee slipped down—nearly running into Kyle.

"Hey, Grady," the man said, his sly smirk telling me something was up. "Can I get you anything with that? A vodka, maybe?"

I smiled, one finger on his chest as I pushed the tall guy—he was in his early twenties—out of my way. "You are so funny, Kyle. How *do* you make it through your day without someone breaking your nose?" Hips swaying, I headed for a chair in the back.

Behind me, someone made a whistle/explosion, but my smile faded as I realized every seat had been taken except for one. It was in the first row—and there was a liter of vodka on it.

"Grady!" a heavy man in rags sitting beside it shouted. "I got your seat. Right up front."

It was Terry. To his left in a suit was his best friend, Webber. Jessica waited on the right side of the empty seat, smiling as if she were going to burst.

"Right here, honey," she coaxed, patting the chair. "We know you're busy, so we all chipped in and got you a new bottle to save you a trip to the storeroom."

Shoulders back, I swayed to the front of the room as if I were a queen. "You are all so kind to think of me," I said loudly amid the shouted pointed questions I had no intention of answering as I put the bottle under the chair and sat, more than a little disconcerted when the three of them clustered close.

"Well, let's see them," Terry said, and I stared blankly at him. "Them what?"

Jessica inched closer. "Your new sticks."

"Oh!" I unslung my new blueprint tube and twisted the top. A black shadow button again decorated the center like an enormous rivet. A second was stuck to the inside of the lid right under it. The third was tucked behind the laces of my shoe like a penny. One might think it was risky, keeping inert-dross buttons in the open like that, but shadow was rare, and if I found one, I wanted something to lure it into a bottle with. Besides, the dross bound in my new sticks would repel any shadow that noticed the inert dross.

Or at least that's the theory, I thought as I remembered the shadow-animated spider. I didn't like that I had been using sticks with inert dross at their core. That someone had tried to prank me didn't sit well. True, I hadn't intended to use them at the time I'd made them—they'd been a grade, nothing more—but someone might have.

"Wow, word gets around fast," I said as I shook a stick out.

"See, I told you." Terry held out his hand, and Webber smacked a twenty into it. "She wouldn't get a new case unless she got new sticks to put in it."

The tightness in my chest eased. It had been the stickerless tube that had given me away, not gossip. But my anxiety came back two-fold when more people clustered around at Jessica's admiring "Ooooh."

"Those are amazing," Kyle said, his earlier smart-assery gone. "Can I?"

Against my better judgment, I gave him one. A feeling of protection stirred as he backed to the podium and swung the unusual red stick dramatically to find its balance.

"Fantabulous," Jessica said, her eyes fixed on them.

"They have silver caps? Like the ones in the hall?" Terry said, and I shook out a second one to show him. "Darrell sold you these?" he added, a thick finger running down the runes. "Damn. Maybe I should bring shadow back in vodka bottles, too."

"Those were her dad's, if I'm not mistaken," came a slow drawl, and I looked up at Nog. The old man was in street rags, clearly on free-range duty. It took a deft touch and a class-four rating on your psi fields to collect dross from a public place and not get noticed, and Nog was one of the best. St. Unoc was a closed campus, but mundanes still walked the streets.

"May I?" he asked, and I gave him one, thinking he was an odd mix of confidence and power dressed in rags smelling of fabric softener.

Again came that twinge of reluctance as it left my grip, but I appreciated the respect Nog held it with compared to Kyle's wild swinging. "Darrell was holding them for me," I said, adding a quick "Kyle?" with my hand extended.

"Figures your dad was a university sweeper," Jessica said.

"Spinner." Nog's focus was distant as he ran a thumb across a rune. "And a good man. I miss him."

My expression was empty and my mind was full when he handed the stick back. "Thank you," I said as I slid it away. "Kyle, if you dent that, I will seriously kill you."

Kyle finally quit swinging the stick and handed it to me. "Have you used them?" he asked.

"Not yet."

"Are you selling Ashley your old ones?" he added.

But Ryan came in, saving me from answering. Tight-lipped, I recapped my tube, my heavy thoughts on my dad as the man made his way to the front. Kyle had commandeered the seat of the person behind me, and I stifled a jump when he leaned forward, whispering, "Can I buy your old ones? I'll give you more than Ashley," before settling back.

"Okay, we got a busy day, boys and girls!" Ryan shouted, shunning the podium to sit on the nearby table instead. "Let's get to it."

Slowly the room settled. Ryan, in his early sixties, was one of the university's best Spinners working, not only taking a shift at the loom but also in charge of us: giving out assignments and handling the rare promotion and even rarer disagreement. I'd always thought that his limp would have made him an excellent free-ranger, but Spinners never went back to dross duty.

His eyes widened when they found me front and center with my vodka bottle and three of my friends, all grinning ear to ear, and I shrugged, feeling my face warm. Darrell had probably talked to him.

"First order," he said once the rustling abated. "A note of acknowledgment to Grady for finding a dormant rez at the Lance building yesterday."

"Thank you, Ms. Grady," Kyle mocked in a sugar-sweet voice, and Jessica turned to give his shoulder a little smack.

Ryan glanced up at Kyle's startled yelp, then shuffled his papers. "Olive, make sure it gets on the list for quarterly checks until we know its cycle. We don't want this one getting active again. They're doing class-three and -four manipulations in that building. Grady, anything you want to add?"

"Uh, no," I said, not having expected this. "Except the guy whose office it's in is a ten on the PITA meter." My eye twitched at the memory of the shadow. "Actually, I'd suggest monthly checks until we know how clean they will keep that floor." Ryan seemed to hesitate at the odd request, and I added, "There was evidence of long-term dross issues."

The older man swallowed back his next words, his sudden unease telling me he knew about the shadow. *Thanks, Darrell.* "Sounds prudent," he agreed as he nodded at Olive.

"Got it." Olive shot me a smile and tucked her phone away.

"Great." Ryan tapped his papers even to gather the room's attention. "Reevaluate in six months. Which brings me to graduation week."

There was a collective groan, and I sipped my coffee, glad to be out of the spotlight.

"Since I'm not going to get any volunteers for the graduation party at the arboretum, Daniel, Naide, Len, Kyle—thank you for stepping up."

"I did it last year," Kyle complained.

"Then you should still be able to fit in your tux," Naide said loudly, and I smiled, noting that Kyle was decidedly younger than the rest. Either Kyle was really screwing up or he had shown some hidden promise that Ryan wanted cultivated. I was betting he'd screwed up.

"I'm expecting more free-range dross than usual this year, so go prepared," Ryan added.

"I had plans." Kyle pouted, and Naide put her arm over his shoulder.

"Suck it up," she said cheerfully. "You should hang around until the end this time. We have our own party afterward."

Daniel pretended to drink something and Kyle's irate expression smoothed.

My eyebrows rose. *Not screwup. Hidden promise. Will miracles never cease?* But though graduation celebrations traditionally had a lot of unclaimed dross generated by too much magic and copious amounts of alcohol, it was considered easy work and hazard pay. No one ever complained about the free food, either. *Thank God St. Unoc is a closed campus.*

"Pace, Archie, Sara, Harry, Saul," Ryan continued, and I turned to the front. "Freshmen are touring the university today. You're on evaluation. Admissions is expecting you ten minutes ago. Sorry. My fault. We have a lot of graduates this year, so I'm going to need at least eight potential ins."

Five sweepers rose, one of them getting a last coffee before filing out of the room to take the freshmen on a tour of the university while surreptitiously evaluating their sensitivity to dross to help cull out the best. I leaned into my chair, arms over my chest, surprised he hadn't called me. He knew I was up for a new tagalong. As ranking sweeper, I'd get my pick of the litter.

"Nothing of note for our bike messengers on regular pickups," Ryan said, head down over his paperwork, showing his thinning hair. "Be aware that the new invoicing is now fully in use, so please check that you have signatures *before* you leave. If you make Marge track you down, don't complain to me if you don't get paid on a timely basis.

"Don, you pulled quad duty," Ryan added, and I smiled when the man swore under his breath. "We have alumni on the grounds this week, so as a personal favor to me, could the free-rangers stow the rags and put on a letter jacket or something? You don't have to be bums to collect dross. Get a blanket, sit under a tree with a guitar, and be a beatnik."

"No one looks at beggars," Nog complained as Ryan tapped his papers on end to order them. It was his signal that the meeting was over, and chairs began to scrape. "I don't have a letter jacket," he added, his low, rumbly voice pathetic, but no one was listening.

"Hey, one more thing," Ryan said loudly over the new noise, and I slumped back into my chair. "We're ditching the school's logo pin to mark alumni this year. It didn't work as well as hoped, and we got too many complaints of memories being erroneously erased because someone forgot to put their pin on or it couldn't be seen. We're back to the old passcode to get into the closed events. It should make a more mundane-free environment, but if you see something, do something. Memory-altering stations will be at every venue."

There was a heartbeat of silence, and then the noise redoubled as Ryan waved everyone off. "I guess I'm on messenger," I said to Terry, disappointed. I could have used a day off showing freshmen the campus. "See you around," I added as I stood and finished my coffee in a last gulp. I'd have to change into my kit and bother Marge for a list of pickups. They hadn't popped into my inbox as usual that morning.

"Grady, if you have a moment?" Ryan said loudly over the leaving sweepers.

"Or maybe not," I said, startled when Webber put a hand on my shoulder, giving it a squeeze before turning to walk out with Terry and Jessica.

"Suck it up, Kyle," Daniel was saying as he and Kyle left. "Every-one else has family."

"Grady doesn't," Kyle said, and then they were gone and it was only Ryan and me in a breath-hot room at the top of Surran Hall.

The older man's balance bobbled as he came down off the low stage, his usual pleasant expression twisted into a frown. "Sorry about that. Kyle has the tact of a bull in lust."

"Well, he's right." I leaned on the back of a chair. "How come I'm not on evals?"

Ryan's expression widened, but his smile didn't reach his eyes, making me uneasy. "You have been assigned permanent placement," he said as he extended a nine-by-three envelope.

"Really?" And now it made sense. I wouldn't be coaching fresh-men on how to corral free dross if I had a regular situation.

"Long-term," Ryan was saying as I opened the envelope. "Nine-to-five. Easy work."

I eagerly pulled out the slip, my expression immediately falling. Dedicated Dross Collector with Strong Manipulation Skills and Data Interpretation. My gaze darted to the letterhead, and my lips parted. *Dr. Benedict Strom?*

My thoughts flicked to the way Benedict had looked me up and down yesterday, and I felt myself warm. His project was hot right now, which gave him the clout to request a private janitor for his labs, but not just no but hell no. This was the job that Ashley wanted.

I shoved the paper into the envelope and handed it back. "Ah, thanks, but no."

Ryan eyed me, refusing to take it. "This is a direct request from a senior team leader," he said, and I set the envelope on the podium behind him with a sharp tap.

"Don't care," I said sourly. "Ashley was invited to put in for this, but more importantly, I don't think it should be done. Dross isn't static. It attracts more dross. It moves like a slime mold to shadows and under angles. Trying to make it inert won't last. I want nothing to do with it."

"Good." Ryan took the envelope from the podium. "That's why I *strongly* suggest you accept this position. In addition to keeping their building dross-free and prepping their samples, I expect you to evaluate their results and keep me informed in a separate, confidential report."

My brow furrowed, and I took the envelope. *A spy?*

"Ashley Smyth is a horrible fit," he said, his gaze going to the open door behind me. "She's not a sweeper. I need my best, and you're it."

"Ryan," I protested, suddenly feeling like Kyle. "They don't want me there. Trust me. I'm surly and sour. And I'm *not* a janitor." I couldn't bring myself to work for Benedict. The hurt was old, but it was as sharp as if he had dissed me in the hall last week.

"You are not a janitor," Ryan agreed. "I've already talked to Dr. Strom, and he assures me that they will pare that part of the job down to a minimum. They want you. Benedict asked for you specifically. Apparently you impressed the hell out of him yesterday when you tried to lure a wisp of dross across the hall with your afternoon's haul."

This is not happening. "It wasn't me. I was standing beside a full trap," I said, but Ryan wasn't listening.

"And seeing as he requested you, I think we should take the opportunity to get in there and see what they're doing."

A sigh pulled my shoulders down. "No good deed goes unpunished, eh?" I said. "Ashley put in for it," I said, trying again. "They asked her to apply and she's expecting to get it. If I tell her I got it, she's going to be as mad as hell on a Monday. I told her not to take it. We argued."

Ryan was clearly unmoved. "That's unfortunate. But how long do you expect your relationship with Ashley to last? Her thesis is done." He hesitated, a new thought visibly crossing his features. "You aren't a couple, are you?"

"If I say yes, will you take this envelope back?"

"No."

I winced. "She's my friend and I can't do this to her."

Ryan's expression creased, wrinkles falling into each other as he refused to take the extended envelope. "You've taught Ashley everything she can learn from you. Don't hold her back by letting her take this job. It's a sweeper position and it will ruin her entire career."

"That's what I told her," I muttered. "She thinks it will make it."

"Look, I know it's a shit job, but I need *your* opinion, not Ashley's. Will you set aside your wants and do this for me?"

I rubbed my forehead, feeling a headache coming on. He wanted me to spy on Benedict. *That,* I could stomach, and Ryan smiled in relief when I nodded.

"Thank you," he said, voice subdued, but I still felt uneasy. Ashley was going to be pissed. "Dr. Strom asked if you would meet him this morning and he'll take you out to their new lab space himself. Introduce you around. Meet everyone. He's talking to the incoming freshmen right now before they divide up into their tour groups."

My eyebrows rose. "He's giving the orientation speech? Seriously?"

Ryan nodded, his grin wide. "I think he's doing some headhunting of his own. His new space needs a crapload of enclosure cleaners, and freshmen work cheap. Big auditorium across the street."

"Got it," I said glumly, all the while wondering how I was going to tell Ashley. Maybe Hallmark had a card for it: SORRY I STOLE YOUR JOB, BUT YOU KNOW I'LL ALWAYS BE YOUR FRIEND. This *sucked.* "Do me a favor, will you?" I added as I stuffed the envelope into my jeans pocket. "See if you can get in front of any thanks-but-no emails to Ashley. I want to tell her."

"Of course. Grady? Thank you."

Thank you? He'd practically forced me to do this. "You owe me,"

I said, and he nodded, showing his slightly overlapped teeth as he smiled.

"Big-time," he agreed, and I turned away, steps slow as I found my way into the hall and the narrow stairs.

But my mood only grew worse as I worked my way out of the building, unlocked my bike, and coasted across the street to the big auditorium. This cake was not going to go down well no matter how much bullshit icing I put on it. Ashley had wanted the position— wanted it bad—and now I had the job.

6

A DULL ACHE SETTLED BEHIND MY EYES AS I LOCKED MY BIKE TO THE RACK outside the university's largest auditorium and stomped up the wide stairs. My stick case thumped against my back, and I gave my shoulder a little hitch when I reached the double glass doors to hike the unfamiliar weight higher. Pulling the doors open, I hesitated, enjoying the flow of cooler dry air rushing out before I consigned myself to the high-ceilinged lobby, echoing with whispers.

The two-story space with its closed bar and huge restrooms had the air of a theater lobby—which in all honesty the place served as from time to time. A large decorative trap pretending to be a teepee sat between the two main doors to the auditorium itself, the stanchions engraved and sporting metal inlays in a beautiful expression of Native American art. There was no dross within it despite its obvious function. The dross it attracted dropped through a grate to a holding tank, safely out of sight. My first year as a sweeper had been spent emptying a handful of such tanks across campus.

The squeak of a door pulled my attention across the lobby. It was a woman in her midforties, her fixed-gaze beeline to the coffee and doughnut table almost comical. Benedict's low, expressive voice slipped out behind her, faint until the door swung shut . . . and then it was gone.

"Ryan, you owe me so big . . ." I whispered as I padded across the lobby, feeling underdressed in my jeans and band tee as I eased the heavy door open and slipped inside.

"I guess what I'm trying to say"—Benedict's voice pulled my gaze to the distant stage—"and, parents, don't come down hard on me for this . . . is that if you don't know what you want to specialize in or what course of direction your studies should be, that's okay."

There was a nervous titter. My eyes were still adjusting to the dim interior, but Benedict was in a spotlight, sitting casually on the edge of the stage, feet dangling, instead of standing behind the podium. He looked scrumptiously casual in his jeans and pressed shirt, and my eyes narrowed at the rapt, almost adoring attention the female student body was giving him.

Why do you care, Petra? I asked myself, hand trailing across the back of the chairs as I came down a few rows and sat, so far into the shadows that Benedict wouldn't be able to see me. The auditorium was large, holding about fifteen hundred people. It wasn't used much apart from guest lectures, graduation, and theatrical presentations where magical special effects were hidden behind mundane science. Occasionally a lower-level class would be taught in it, one that every freshman needed.

There was a raised central stage where Benedict now sat, his feet hanging into what would be the orchestra pit if it wasn't currently holding five rows of widely spaced students and their parents. Behind him was a podium with a single-use coffee cup, and behind that the large backstage area with dressing rooms and set storage. The sound system was good enough for the film festival at the end of summer, and the chairs were comfortable. The space itself was probably four stories tall and the acoustics good.

"If you do know what you want to do, great," Benedict said, his voice reaching all the way to me. "Talk to your counselors and they will show you the most efficient path that will allow you the freedom

71

to do some self-exploring. Your magical skills can dovetail beautifully into any mundane career."

Blah, blah, blah, I thought, turning my attention to the group listening attentively to his expressive voice. It was obvious who were the mages and who were the sweepers. That they had unconsciously segregated themselves made it easy. It wasn't a small group, but the space of the place gave them room to spread out.

"You are here to develop those skills," Benedict was saying, and I tilted my head, studying him, seeing him as he was now in casual jeans and a button-down shirt—and remembering him as he was, in jeans and a band tee, his hair down to his shoulders, his brow smooth, and his confidence paper-thin. Though who in their right mind had real confidence in high school?

"And I'm not simply talking about working with lodestones but dross as well."

Wait. What? My wandering attention snapped back to Benedict. The parents, too, stirred as he touched on a dangerous topic.

"Dr. Strom," a man in a suit and sporting a huge twinkling lodestone ring interrupted. "Are you suggesting that there is a way to use dross to power magic?"

Benedict stiffened. "No, no, no. Good God, no," he said, and a nervous chuckle rose. "I'd be out on my ear, and for good reason. You can't power magic with dross."

Because doing so creates shadow, I thought, lips twitching. Duh.

"No, what I'm saying is that those who can manipulate dross without it breaking have a unique ability that mages can't hope to duplicate with psi fields or wands."

My breath sort of caught. Lips parted, I strained to hear. *Is he serious, or is he fishing to find a couple of starry-eyed sweeper freshmen to clean his rat enclosures?*

But the sweeper kids at the outskirts were listening, no longer fidgeting as if none of this was for them.

"At St. Unoc, those dross-handling skills can be honed to as sharp of a point as any mage skill," Benedict said, speaking to them and them alone.

"Yeah, 'cause picking up trash is so hard," someone said, and my eyes narrowed, spotting the blond, wide-shouldered kid sitting between his clearly affluent parents, lodestones front and center like a badge that gave them the right to be cruel and dismissive.

Benedict sat there, silent, until the elbow nudges and titters silenced.

And then he sat there a few seconds more.

"Earth, air, fire, water, and ether," he began again, his words clear and sharp as he fell into his lecture tone. "They are age-old mage-originated designations that still have weight, but in essence, they are manipulating gravity, mass, and molecular vibrations, and in the case of water studies, tapping into intuition and an as-yet unstudied hive awareness, and in ether, the ability to manipulate a single mind, the skill critical to maintain the silence of our existence. All of which I think we can agree are important, but not as much as the basic need to clean up after ourselves."

It was the mages, now, who were fidgeting, and Benedict held up a hand for patience. "Sweepers," he continued, "have a skill that no mage can duplicate, that of being able to safely handle the imbalance of energy we create with even our smallest magic. I truly believe that there is an entire field of study and magic waiting to be developed based on sweepers' abilities. Maybe one of you will be the one to crack into it."

He smiled, but the grateful expressions of the sweepers were somewhat stilted. It was too close to what had gotten Herm Ivaros exiled.

"Dr. Strom, you aren't advocating teaching our kids how to use dross," one brave soul piped up. "That creates shadow."

I shifted, crossing my other knee over my leg. To be honest, no one knew for sure whether the waste from dross created shadow or simply attracted it, mostly because the result was the same: whoever tried it, died.

"Good Lord, no," Benedict said, grinning to cover the misunderstanding. "Never."

My attention lifted from the stage, tracking to one of the exit doors as it opened and Pace, Archie, Sara, Harry, and Saul all came in, doughnuts in hand and slurping coffee. The tour guides for the incoming mages were already here, messing around with their phones in the corner. *Separate, and definitely not equal,* I mused. Benedict's stirring words aside.

"I'm not advocating using dross to power magic, and neither is the university," Benedict said, decidedly relieved when he noticed the tour guides. "I'm saying that sweepers have a unique skill set and there is room for that to be developed within current parameters."

A kissing sound came from the tour guides, and Benedict's posture stiffened—even as one of the seated parents cleared his throat.

"Dr. Strom." The man's voice rang out, the tone antagonistic. "Are you implying that a sweeper, who can't manipulate light, is stronger than the lowest-order mage?"

Benedict stared at the parent. "Potentially, yes. And before you seek out the dean and demand that he fire me, answer me this. Even if you disregard a sweeper's uncanny ability to safely manipulate energy existing in a state of imbalance, can you handle shadow?"

The seated parent huffed. "That's not my responsibility."

I shot a glance at the waiting tour guides. All of them were listening. Even the mages.

"That's what I'm saying," Benedict said. "It is, and may I say so, correctly, the realm of the sweeper to use that potential energy, dross, to safely effect change. Not using it to power magic, no. But to apply it for a certain outcome. To allow the universe to balance its books in a controlled manner, not in spilled coffee or a lasagna explosion in the microwave, but perhaps to crack shale for oil, or break bonds in a chemical soup to create fertilizer. To direct the dross's natural expression in a known and predictable way."

I stared at Benedict, sighing at his total misunderstanding of what you could do with dross. *Even if it did make the sweeper students sit a little straighter.*

"There is more for a sweeper here than learning how to clean a trap or develop your psi skills to get a job or supplement your mundane career. St. Unoc is a chance to open your eyes, see possibilities that you won't see anywhere else."

No one said anything, but even from my distant perch, I could tell that most of the mages were peeved. The sweepers, though, looked interested. "Damn it, Benny," I whispered. "If this is to find someone to clean your cages, I'm going to fill your toilet with dross."

"Okay!" Benedict said loudly, clapping once. "Your tour guides are here. Let me close by saying I hope you enter this phase of your life with an open mind. Have some fun as you investigate to find out what you're both good at and interested in. If you're lucky, they will be the same thing. If not, remember that though hard, it's always easier to find a way to make a successful career out of what you love than it is to learn how to love what you can make money at."

There was a small smattering of applause, and I stood when the rest of them did. Some were smiling; others not so much. *Maybe he is trying to get out of doing this again,* I thought. It was a rather unorthodox welcome speech, and I was sure he was going to hear about it.

"Sweeper studies to the right," Benedict said loudly as he awkwardly got to his feet. "Mage studies to the left. Be sure to grab some coffee and doughnuts in the lobby on the way out, and thank you. I hope this is the beginning of a stunning opportunity for all of you."

I gathered my things and started down the aisle as the rest began to make their way to the doors, water bottles and coffee cups in hand. Benedict had gone back to the podium, his head tilted as he took a long gulp of water.

"That was an interesting welcome speech," I said when I got close enough, and he spun.

"Oh. Hey. Hi." Benedict looked at the top of the auditorium as the last of them left. "I, ah, thought I'd try something new."

I scuffed to a halt about five rows back. "So . . . do you believe it? Or is it all feel-good noise to convince a couple of freshmen to muck out your rat cages?"

Hurt flashed over him, making me feel bad. "That's not fair," he said stiffly, and I raised a hand, agreeing that that had been a douchebag comment. "I'm simply trying to encourage sweepers into pure research. I'd love to know if there is a method to direct dross into breaking a specific way."

"There isn't." I went silent, watching his anger filter away as he packed his notes into his satchel, the way his muscles moved, how tight his butt was. All these years, and nothing had changed but for the better. *Stop it, Petra.* "Dross is too unpredictable," I added as I forced my eyes to the tall ceiling. "You want to crack shale, and you end up starting an earthquake or accidentally flooding an aquifer with toxins from the seventies."

I came closer until I put an arm on the floor of the stage and leaned in. "Find new ways to bottle and store it, sure. Slathering it on a building slated for deconstruction?" My lips quirked in an almost smile. "You're riding the Nuh-uh train to Noperville, Benny. Can't be done."

He turned, his satchel over his shoulder and a large, crinkly grocery bag in hand. "Maybe someday." Benedict started for the stairs. "Thanks for agreeing to join my project."

My eyebrows rose. "Agreeing. Sure."

"I, ah, had this made up for you." He closed the gap and handed me the bag. "Everyone has them, sort of a team thing."

I set the bag on the stage and shuffled about, not knowing what I was looking at until I pulled the length of white fabric out. "It's a lab coat," I said, adding, "It's got my name on it."

Benedict bobbed his head, clearly pleased. "I had them made up for everyone," he said again. "I think they help foster a team environment."

"Ah. Thanks. I've never had a piece of clothing with my name on it before." My eyes flicked to his, reading his genuine pleasure. "Not counting my backpack from kindergarten," I added, and he chuckled. "Thanks." I folded it up and put it back into the bag.

He hadn't stopped smiling, and I followed his gesture to start for the exits. "Code," he said as he dug out a slip of paper and handed it to me. "The place is wired, but seeing as we're doing a lot of high-impact manipulations, it's necessary."

I read the code and stuffed it into a pocket, my steps in time with his until I hitched my stick case higher. The plastic bag in my hand rattled, and the silence grew.

"I really appreciate you coming out today to give me a dross baseline before we get settled in. I know it's short notice, but we just got the keys to the place and we want to get moving."

Benedict sounded a little breathy. But that could be from the steep incline. "No problem."

"The place needs a good sweep to ensure that the ambient dross levels don't interfere with the study," he added, his smile worried.

"Sure. Unused buildings tend to get drossy." I thought of the excitement he had instilled in the kids coming in for their sweeper studies. That had been real, even if it got him in trouble. *In trouble because it might be real?*

"It's a nice setup compared to the basement we had been in," he continued. "We have the entire building, since the theory has proven out. There are a couple of built-in traps the place came with, but I'd really like your opinion on where we could do better with keeping a clean environment. We were constantly fighting settling dross in the basement."

"Absolutely." Maybe this wouldn't be so bad. "How many on the team?" It sounded like a simple question, but the more there were, the more stuffed shirts I'd be picking up after.

"Four at the moment. Three mages, plus you." A soft smile found him as we paced uphill, our steps hitting together. "I've got a posting to find a couple of sophomores to clean cages. Everyone has at least two jobs, but you are *not* cleaning cages or supervising the people who do."

"I appreciate that." Either he didn't recognize my sarcasm or he was ignoring it.

"Anton is our ether specialist, but he also keeps track of the money," Benedict said, taking an extra-long step to get to the door before me. "Laura is good with earth magic. She's hands-on in helping me run the tests."

"Sounds great. And you need me for . . ." The light brightened when he opened the door, and I balked until my eyes adjusted.

"Prepping samples, mostly."

I couldn't look at him as I strode out into the large, two-story lobby. "And building maintenance." Which was a nice way to say dross janitor.

"Everyone has two jobs, Petra," he said with a soft sigh, and I turned to look at him as we walked.

Two jobs. Right. "So if I'm prepping samples and doing building maintenance, I won't be emptying the desk traps?"

He had the decency to wince. "That's lumped in with building maintenance. So, you ready? I can drive you out there. I can't wait for you to see the place. It's so much better than the basement."

I scuffed to a halt before the big glass doors, reluctant to leave the cool and comfortable auditorium for the bright light and slowly increasing temps of the campus. *And it isn't even noon yet.* "I don't think my bike will fit in the back of your car."

Benedict stopped short and blinked, clearly realigning his thoughts. "Oh! Right!" He sent his gaze down the steps to find it. "Ah, you want to leave it here? I can bring you back when we're done. It's only a walk-through and then lunch."

It might be all that was there for him, but if there was dross, I'd be picking it up, which meant I'd be there all afternoon. "That's nice of you, but I have to stop at home first." I plucked at my T-shirt. "Change my clothes to something more suitable."

"You look fine." Benedict looped his arm in mine and shoved the door open. Heat rolled in, and I let him draw me out into it, sure that I wasn't getting in his car. No way would I be stranded and at Uber's mercy.

Not to mention I still had to tell Ashley before this all blew up in her face.

"Benny, I was expecting to be taking incoming freshmen around campus. Not meeting a bunch of professors."

"They're just people," he said as he drew me down the stairs. "Like me."

Like him. And therein was the problem. "People who will be in slacks and jackets with power ties and high heels," I said. "If I walk in there dressed like this, comfortable and casual, they will see me as the trashman, embroidered lab coat or not. Don't set me up to fail."

Benedict took a breath, his steps slowing as he thought about that. "I can pick you up from home and go from there."

He was really trying, and I felt a smile find me, real and unstoppable. "Why don't you give me the address. I will bike on out after I talk to Ashley." I hesitated. "Unless you want to tell her why I got the job and she didn't?"

At that, he winced. "Ah, I might have sent you something," he said, shifting his weight from foot to foot. "Kind of a welcome-to-the-team thing," he added, and my shoulders slumped. "Sorry."

Maybe she was still in bed. "I should go."

"Right." He glanced at my pocket. "The address is on the card I gave you," he said flatly. "It's just outside campus. Are you sure you don't want me to—"

"I'll see you there," I said, hoping it wasn't far. *Good God, I'm actually doing this.* "Give me an hour."

"An hour," he said, head still bowed as he turned and walked away.

7

THE HEAT OF THE SUN WAS GROWING DESPITE THE EARLY HOUR, AND I WON-
dered how I was going to get out to the research facility without
becoming a sweaty mess. Taking the bike path that looped around
and through St. Unoc would get me off the street, but much of the
paved path wound through what was basically desert: no shade but
always wind.

The ticking of my bike's wheel slowed as I rolled up to the landing of my apartment building. Swinging a leg over, I balanced with
one foot on a pedal, one hovering behind me inches above the ground.
The lab coat Benny had given me was carefully stowed in my backpack. I was pretty sure I had a stash of desk traps in the front closet.
Next to my steel-toed shoes from my woodworking labs, maybe? None of
which I'd actually wear on the trip out there. Not in this heat.

But my slow pace faltered when I noticed Ashley's tiny car in the
covered pick-up/drop-off zone, the hatch of the two-door open to
show her matched luggage and clothes hamper.

Weight shifting, I slipped from the pedal, the thump jarring all
the way up my spine. *Benny's welcome-to-the-team gift?* I thought,
then, *She's leaving?*

Guilt pinched my gut as I left my bike against the long letterbox
stand. The common front door was unlocked as I pushed through it,

but it would be this time of day. "Ashley?" I called up as the air-conditioning shifted my sweat-damp hair. I practically bolted up the stairs, pulse fast as I shoved open the door to our apartment to nearly hit Pluck.

"Hi, jellybean," I said, absently fondling the big dog's ears. He was distressed, thick tail waving as he huffed, clearly glad to see me. His collar was twisted, and I took a breath to call for Ashley again, my eyes fixing on a small balloon arrangement on the eat-at counter. The dozen or so palm-size balloons looked cheerful at the end of their little sticks, all arranged like flowers around a pink balloon bunny, complete with a drawn-on smile and little whiskers. The bunny tickled a memory as I snatched up the card.

Glad to have you on the team, Petra. Can't wait to spend time with you again.

It was signed *Benny*, and I set the card down with a snap. Nice thought. Bad timing. No wonder she was upset. But she didn't have to leave because of this. We could work it out.

"Let me finish this," Ashley said from her room, voice resentful. "I'm so close. And I don't have to actually be on the team to be effective."

I took a breath, but my urge to call out faltered, not at the softly masculine voice twining with hers but because the entire living room was full of dross.

What the hell . . . "Pluck, wait. Sit," I said, holding his collar as I studied the glittery stuff strewn from the kitchen to the balcony, energy shimmering like a heat haze. I could almost smell it, it was so thick. The apartment's trap, though, was predictably empty.

"Chaperoning Strom's process was your idea, not mine," the raspy, unfamiliar voice said, and Pluck wagged his tail, completely okay with whoever it was. "It's a waste of time, and you are better than that."

This has to go, I thought, cringing at the idea of Pluck walking through the dross-strewn room. Still holding his collar, I inhaled slow and deep to make a thin psi field, eyes closing as I sent it to the outskirts of the room.

A burning tingling skated across my skin as it went out, goose bumps rising as it passed over the multitude of dross drifts, shifting them as if in a breeze. Breath held, I tweaked my field to a denser, class-five state, and then inhaled to collapse it to the size of an apple, in essence, gathering the multitude of hazy dross distortions into a now-cool lump of potential energy in my palm.

It was an admittedly high-level procedure, one that wasn't foolproof but close. I'd probably gotten ninety percent of it with my first sweep. Most mages only used psi fields to give their spells a place to act, but Ashley had become nearly as proficient as I in handling large gathering fields to collect her data. Why she had made such a mess was beyond me. It felt petty, even for her.

Pluck whined as the field passed over him, a faint glimmer pulling from his foot before the dross could break on him to make him splinter a nail or worse. I gave him a smile and a pat, knowing he could feel the energy. It was the reason he had come home with me from the shelter. "Better, eh?" I said as I looked at Ashley's open door and toward the faint conversation, the condensed, hazy dross ball in hand.

"We're done talking about this. Your skills are better used elsewhere," the voice said.

"This is my job," she said loudly. "And I'm close. Sikes, I'm so close."

"No, you're done," the man said. "You gave us all we need to know. The rest can be handled from distant surveillance."

Distant surveillance?

"Yeah?" Ashley said, clearly annoyed. "You don't know her like I do. She's going to blow it all to hell. I can promise you that. And you will have nothing."

"Ashley?" I called, my frown deepening when her voice cut off into silence.

"In here," she finally said, her tone high in welcome, but I could hear her anger and was glad it wasn't directed at me. *Yet,* I thought as I glanced at the balloon bouquet. Someone had made a mess in the living room, leaving it as if my sole reason for existing was to pick it up. It could have been Ashley, but I doubted it.

I gave Pluck a pat and crossed the now-clean living room, dumping the dross ball into the trap in passing. A much happier Pluck trotted at my side, and I scuffed to a halt at Ashley's open door, gaze flicking from her next to the clothes-covered bed to the unfamiliar man in a casual suit beside her dresser.

"Hey," I said, and the man set Ashley's perfume bottle back on the dresser. "What's up?"

Ashley's expression twitched. "I'm leaving for a few days," she said, then turned her back on me to rummage in her closet.

The man beside the dresser cleared his throat. Early forties, shock of dark hair, leathery skin that had seen too much sun: he belonged to the desert. *And tall* . . . "I'm Samuel Sikes," he said, a faint accent showing as he tucked his hands behind his back, clearly not wanting to shake hands. The dark glass bauble decorating his bolo necktie had to be his lodestone, and it went with his suit remarkably well, like a tie.

Yeah, this is why my living room was filthy.

"Petra Grady," I said stiffly. "Nice to meet you." But they were just words. I didn't like him. His attitude reminded me of every stuck-up mage I'd run into. Worse, Pluck clearly knew him, knew him well enough to flop at the man's feet and beg for a warming hint of magic. This guy had been here before.

"I thought you were at work." Lips pressed into a thin line, Ashley tossed her best sandals into a roller bag.

"I was. Am. I came home to talk to you." I hesitated, feeling the tension. "Looks like I'm too late."

Ashley exhaled, jaw clenched as she turned to the man. "Professor Sikes is my career counselor," she said sourly, and the man smiled as if amused.

My eyebrows rose as it began to make sense. "He told you not to take the job," I said, and the man put a hand to his mouth to hide a small chuckle. It would explain why she was ticked, but not why she was leaving.

Ashley's gaze flicked to Professor Sikes's. "Ah . . ."

"That is exactly what I told her, yes," the man said, his voice holding a hard, directive tone. "Ashley is a mage. A damn good one. She learned a lot from you, but a sweeper position is beneath her."

"Mmmm." My arms went over my chest as I leaned against the doorframe. It hadn't sounded so ugly when I had said it over pasta. "That's what I told her."

Silent, Ashley dragged a pair of jeans off a hanger, groaning when the pocket caught and ripped. "I have a couple of out-of-state interviews that Sikes set up." Motions abrupt, she dropped the torn jeans on the floor of her closet and took a second pair. "I'll be back in a few days."

"We will find you something suitable to your talent," Sikes said, and my eye twitched.

I took a breath to tell him Ashley could find a job here, only to let it slip from me in surprise. Herm's letter was on her dresser. The wrinkles from where I had crumpled it had been carefully smoothed out, and I snatched it up. "I threw this away. Why do you have it?"

Ashley's gaze flicked to mine. "I was trying to figure out where he is," she said, her eyes fixed on mine. "I wanted to do something nice for you," she added, her expression twisting as she glanced at Sikes. "Maybe get you two to actually, I don't know, talk? He's all the family you have."

Sikes pushed up from the dresser, and both Ashley and I sort of jerked. Clearly she didn't like him any more than I did. *So why is she listening to him?*

"Ashley, I will be waiting for you down in the car," he said as he walked to the door. I was still in the threshold, and he actually stopped and waited for me to shift, as if I had cooties that could jump three feet.

Pluck, though, had scrambled to his feet the instant the man moved, the dog's tail waving as he escorted him to the door. Peeved, I watched them both until I was sure Sikes wouldn't "accidentally" let the dog out.

"Like you would ever reach out to your uncle," Ashley muttered as I stuffed Herm's letter into my back pocket. "Not Petra Grady," she mocked, angry as she flipped her bag closed. "How long have you had his phone number? Years, I bet."

"Hey, not all families like each other," I said, peeved. "It's not a prerequisite."

"Yeah. I get that." Lips pressed together, Ashley zipped her bag closed with a quick fierceness. "Everything would have been fine if I had gotten the job."

"You do not have to leave because I got the job," I said, and she went still, her eyes meeting mine. "This is not my doing. I told Ryan no three times."

"You really expect me to believe that?" she said. Clearly frustrated, she gathered up the clothes she'd left on the bed and dumped them on the floor of the closet. "He sent you a friggin' balloon bouquet! I *needed* that post," she added, her high voice angry. "Damn it, Petra, they asked me to put in for it. I told everyone it was a sure thing, and I never had a chance. What am I supposed to do now?"

It was almost as if she'd already spent the higher paycheck that came with the job, and I stared at her, not knowing where this frustration was coming from. *Pride, maybe?* "I don't know, but you don't have to leave. You will find another position. I can handle the mortgage until then."

Her eyes narrowed, and her held breath slipped from her. "You are so oblivious," she muttered as she yanked her large bag and it thumped to the floor. "I'll be back for graduation. Can you hold on to my stuff until then?"

"Ashley . . ." I followed her out as she pushed past me to the door. "Look. I'm sorry. I wanted to be the one to tell you. The balloons don't mean anything. He's probably trying to be funny." *Though an apology would be better.* "He used to make them for me when we were kids." *When he said he was my friend,* I thought bitterly. "Sikes is right. This is a sweeper position. You wouldn't believe the crap you'd have to swallow. I know you don't believe me, but you not getting this job is a good thing."

"Not for me." She walked to the door, her roller bag bumping behind her until the wheels jammed from a wisp of dross I'd missed, hidden in the rug. "I hate living here!" she shouted as she jerked her resisting bag forward. "I thought it would be easier living with a sweeper, but all my stuff breaks and nothing ever happens to you!"

I said nothing, seeing as the reason was obvious. Her jaw set, she awkwardly pulled her resisting bag to the door before kneeling to give Pluck's ears a rub. A hint of softness came back to her as she whispered to him, and I inched closer.

It's only a job, I thought, wondering why she was taking this so hard. "You don't have to go," I said, and her eyes narrowed. Mood again bad, she grabbed her bag and kicked it into motion. "Ryan is making me do this!" I added as I followed her. "If I don't take the job, I'm fired! Is that what you want?"

I jerked to a halt as she turned. Face red, she worked the key off her ring and dropped it tinkling in the bowl by the door. "I had this one shot, and I blew it," she said coldly. "My chance to have more than a bit part in something that changed the world forever."

"As a sweeper?" I said, not believing this. "You think sweepers get their names in the history books? It was going to ruin your career, not make it. God, Ashley, you're too good for a sweeper job!"

"And yet you got the job, not me, and you're going to screw it all up. Tell the world it's not safe when it is," she said. Hesitating, she looked at Pluck. "Bye, bean." Her eyes came to mine. "Take good care of him."

"Ashley. Wait." She was walking out the door, and I grabbed Pluck's collar, holding him back. We'd both known that we wouldn't be able to work together after she finished her thesis, but this was totally unexpected. "Keep your key," I said, as I slid it from the bowl and held it out. "After your interviews, we'll go out somewhere. Fix this. I'm not trashing two years because of some stupid job."

"It's not a stupid job!" she shouted as she started down the stairs. "It's everything!"

The thump of the busted roller bag on the stairs hit me hard. "Stay," I said to Pluck, then slipped into the hall. "Ashley!"

The door down the way clicked open, and Lev ambled out, one towel loose about his hips and another working over his long hair. "Whoa," he said, eyes going wide. "What did I miss?"

Ashley peered up at him in what might be anger but looked like more. She stared for a moment in silence, then her gaze returned to me. "Sorry about the mess. That was Sikes, not me. I was going to clean it up. Can you keep my stuff until I find a place?"

That last had been caustically bitter, and my own anger flared anew. "She's being a purple snowflake," I said to Lev, then louder, "You don't have to leave. I can manage rent until you find something."

But Ashley didn't answer, tripping on a drift of dross as she stiff-armed the main door open and dragged her busted roller bag into the sun.

I took a steadying breath as Lev inched closer, the small man damp from his shower and smelling of soap as we stared down the stairs at the tiny lobby and empty slice of sidewalk beyond. "What happened?"

Good God, he has nice abs. "She told everyone she was going to get the job I was assigned to." It sounded stupid when you said it aloud, but it felt like more than that, lots more, and my brow furrowed as Lev made a surprised noise.

"I, ah, gotta go," I said as I started a toe-heel amble backward, the key she had left behind hard in my hand. Pluck was whining from the other side of my door, and he needed some reassuring. So did I.

"Sure." Lev stood before his door, his bare feet on the cool tile. "You want to get together later?"

"Lev, I can't think right now," I said quickly, and he quirked his lips, smiling.

"I only thought you might want to vent at someone," he said. "I'm not asking you out on a date. Let me know if you change your mind. I'm a knock away. Dinner is at seven." His eyebrows rose high. "Mac and cheese. Bring a six-pack. I'm into hostess gifts."

Hostess gifts? Somehow I found I could still smile. "Thanks. Let me think about it."

Lev gave me a sloppy salute and went into his apartment, leaving nothing but damp footprints on the tile and a faint scent of soap in the air.

I don't give him enough credit, I thought as his door clicked shut and I shuffled to my door. Pluck was right there, the dog pressing into my leg as we went to the front window. He whined at Ashley as she slammed her hatchback shut and got inside.

I watched her drive away, my arms over my middle in worry. She was coming back for graduation, obviously, but she wouldn't be staying here. We'd known that eventually one of us was going to want their own space again, but to end it like this? Over a cruddy job?

She was overreacting, and a confused anger found me as I turned to see that stupid balloon arrangement. Things might have been different if I'd been able to break it to her myself instead of her jumping to all kinds of conclusions over Benedict's attempt to smooth over a childhood tiff.

But it had been more than that, and my chest tightened as I remembered the horrible feeling when he had ignored me, the laughter of his friends when he made some excuse for pretending to like me. And then him turning his back on me and walking away.

In a sudden anger, I focused on that stupid pink rabbit, imagining a heavy psi field around it and expanding it, taking the balloon with it until it popped.

The harsh sound shocked through me, and I didn't even see the card he'd hidden inside it until Pluck went to nose it.

Annoyed, I scooped it up from the floor. *What do you get when you pour hot water down a rabbit hole?* I read. Frowning, I flipped the card over. *Hot cross bunnies!*

My eyes narrowed, and I threw the card away. I wasn't going to be his starry-eyed foil to show how clever he was. Not this time.

8

⌒

"IRCLE WITHIN CIRCLE. STAR WITHIN A STAR. BOUND BY ONE OR OTHER. INWARD *sight sees far.*"

Knotted Cord's latest hammered in my ears, my legs pushing on the pedals in time with the beat as I rode across campus to the industrial side of town. It went without saying that either Jimmy Tross or the woman he wrote his lyrics with were mages or sweepers, which might account for their popularity on campus. Who wouldn't enjoy hearing about their culture in such a public way, even if it was hidden in the music? Or maybe especially because it was.

It was only ten, and already the heat was beginning to build and pull the desert air into motion. Ashley had left me feeling frustrated and raw. I didn't want this job. I hadn't put in for it. Worse, I didn't understand why she still wanted it after her career adviser told her the same thing I had. It sucked three times over, but I wouldn't call her until she'd had time to process.

It felt good to be moving, burning off my frustration on the bike. My sticks were a comfortable bump against my shoulder, and the lab coat Benedict had given me was carefully tucked into my messenger bag next to a pack of desk traps. The bag shifted as I took a corner fast, and I slowed, not wanting to take myself out on a wisp of free-ranging dross and gravel.

The traffic was light, and I kept a close eye on the Toyota coming up behind me as I stood to stomp on the pedals to go up a steep rise and not lose speed. Wheels humming, I leaned into a sharp turn to enter the industrial park set at the outskirts of university property. Easing into a coast, I took in the desert-landscaped buildings, marveling at the size of the occasional saguaro cactus. Clearly the industrial park had its origins long before it had become illegal to go out and dig up one of the now government-protected cacti.

Traffic here was nil, and the cactus wrens warbled as I spun past long, low buildings set back from the street. The parking lots were small, hot, and cracked. Swaths of scattered sage and paloverde trees spread between them. Lizards basked on the road, and I wasn't surprised when a roadrunner sped from the shade of a cactus to snag one that I'd scared up. The area seemed deserted, abandoned almost. A frown took me, and with one hand on the bars, one on my phone, I checked the street address Benedict had given me.

I hadn't known the university had property out here, but it quickly became obvious where I was headed, and I angled to the stone and metal two-story set to the side. Unlike most of the industrial buildings, this one was relatively small, with minimal landscaping and a lot of in-and-out activity. Benedict's gray sports car was under a large solar panel set over the parking lot, right between the dented contractor trucks and a university vehicle.

"Laboratory Animal Breeding Facility," I whispered as I read the sign. It was as good a front as any. There'd have to be live-animal testing on any dross-related technique. The university probably made some money, too. Genetically known animals were always in demand.

The heat billowed up from the pavement as I came to a halt at the front door, and I jerked my earbuds out. There was no bike rack, and because my bike was my life, I hoisted it up and carried it in through the twin glass doors. Knotted Cord was faint through my dangling buds, but I didn't turn my music off, feeling as if Jimmy Tross gave me a needed sense of identity.

The scent of animal bedding and cut two-by-fours was an odd mix. Loud calls and the sporadic pop of a nail gun drew my attention to the contractors hanging a sign in the dusty lobby. I flashed the contractors a neutral smile as I wheeled my bike behind the unused front desk, only to get suspicious looks in return.

There was no computer, not even a chair, and I propped my bike behind the counter as I took off my helmet and fluffed my sweat-damp hair. I was the sweeper, damn it. I would not take their elitist crap.

Head high, I strode to the double doors at the back of the room. There was a dross trap worked into the artwork in the corner, but that didn't mean there weren't any mundanes around. The sticks were dusty and the trap needed to be cleaned; a ribbon of dross hazed the edges underneath. A hand-lettered sign on the door said animals and offices were to the right, and that was where I'd find Benedict.

"Ma'am! Can I help you?" came a low, loud call, and I spun, stick case thumping. I probably wouldn't need my sticks, but I wasn't about to leave them with my bike.

Foreman? I guessed as I studied his work-stained jeans and flannel shirt. The circled Y emblem on his dusty hat made him more than the boss. He was a mage.

"Petra Grady," I said. "I've been assigned to Dr. Strom's team."

The man nodded, his suspicion easing. "He said you were coming. Can I see some ID?"

"Sure," I said, surprised as I reached for my wallet, currently shoved in my back pocket. My sticks were usually enough to grant me access anywhere in the city, but I'd never worked on a university project before.

He waited, his gaze neutral as I shuffled through my cards and finally handed him the laminated photo ID with my picture, rank, and emergency contact information all highlighted by a holographic sweeper symbol.

"Thank you, Ms. Grady," the man said as he squinted at it, then me. "Sorry about the inconvenience. I'm Wallace. Physical security. I'm glad to have you on board." He handed me my ID, and I stuffed it away. "Word is you're the best when it comes to the odd and unusual."

He was smiling now, and I returned it, sure he wouldn't take me for granted as most mages did. "Depends on who you ask," I said, then jumped when a light fell, the shattered glass invoking catcalls.

Wallace was still wearing his grimace when he turned back to me. "Strom is on-site. He said he gave you the door code?" I nodded, and he began to drift away. "Good. Can you excuse me?"

I took a breath to say it was nice to have met him, but he was already yelling at his crew.

"I told you. Iron, insulator, iron! You can't let them touch! Where are the spacers? They aren't doing any good in the box. Use them!" he bellowed, and I flushed at his loud voice.

My gaze went to the dusty trap in the corner. "Wallace?" I called, and he turned from the man he was yelling at. "You mind if I clean that trap and put up a second?"

Wallace's expression brightened, his hand moving in a flamboyant gesture. "I'd be grateful, madam sweeper," he said as the man he was reaming out beat a hasty retreat. "It's a low-dross zone, and my crew is not careful. There are bottles in the lab. Help yourself."

It felt more than good to be appreciated, and I opened my messenger bag on the dusty lobby desk to set up a small trap, making a mental note to check out the "art installation" in the corner before I left to make sure there were no nicks or dents that would impair its function. Someone probably knew where the trap's short-cord was— I hoped. Otherwise, I'd be manhandling the stuff into a bottle.

Confidence restored, I made my way through the double doors and into a narrow hall. I stifled a shiver as the door closed behind me and the comfortable chatter of the work crew cut out. It wasn't the separation; I was walking under a trap. It was smaller than the one leading to the loom, but the higher security was unexpected, and concern pinched my brow as I punched in the code and entered the facility. I'd have to do some digging to find access to the dross ditch under the floor. I was sure no one had cleaned it in years.

"At least it's cooler," I said as I walked past a smaller, but still deserted, lobby desk. I could hear voices, and I followed them to animal containment, feeling the humidity shift and the scent of bedding grow strong.

"Wow," I whispered as I pushed through a glass door at the end of the hall and entered a two-story-tall room bright with sunlight from the room-wide skylight. The rustling of rats was creepy, and I studied the large, toy-enriched common area full of animals in a decidedly zoo-enclosure-like setting. The white-furred, red-eyed lab animals were huge, seemingly happy as they ate, slept, and made more rats in their twenty-by-twenty play yard. I didn't see any dross, though there were several traps that the rats couldn't reach. I guessed it was to duplicate a free-range dross zone, like a street, a subdivision, or perhaps a mixed-population building.

There is dross here, I mused at the soft prickling against me, and my gaze turned to the second-story overhang. Under it were rows of stacked caged animals in more traditional enclosures. It was a prison compared to the enriched area at the center of the room. The cages were free of any haze of dross, but the lids incorporated chew-proof slats, making it obvious that dross would eventually be introduced.

"Sorry, guys," I whispered, knowing they would bear the brunt of the dross tests.

Between the two extremes was a U-shaped lab bench and a time-battered rolling chair. Voices echoed from the balcony, and I headed for the industrial-heavy metal stairs leading up.

Benedict's easygoing voice was obvious, but I didn't recognize the higher, supercilious voice twining with his as I rose. The clean tingle of a low-dross zone prickled over me, and the light brightened as I emerged into the upscale, glass-and-wood office area encircling and looking down onto the rat play yard. It was an odd mix of new corporate and old-school desert sensibility, with small tinted windows looking out and glass walls within. Benedict's tall silhouette was obvious in one of the corner offices. A woman was with him, both hazy through multiple panes of green glass. Laura, presumably. Not wanting to interrupt, I went to check out the break room.

Jimmy Tross was a whisper as I set my messenger bag on the circular table in the middle of the small room. There was a row of gray lockers, and I mentally claimed the one on the end. Other than the faint sound of rats, it was a typical break room, with a counter, sink, and coffeemaker. As usual, a toaster oven took the place of a microwave, seeing as the latter was notorious for gathering dross, dissipating the bad luck in boiled-over soup and exploding pasta. Dross distortions hazed the corners and the toe kicks, and I grimaced. *Oh, goodie . . .*

I grabbed a sticky note, scrawled my name on it, and stuck it on the last locker before shaking out the lab coat Benedict had given me and putting it in there with my sticks. I'd set two traps here: one on the counter and another in the empty fridge. There was a reason kitchens were a high-accident area, and it wasn't because of the knives. Lots of magic equals lots of dross.

"For the sweeper?" came the woman's voice, clearer now as she moved into the hall. Her tone was heavy with scorn, and my face warmed. "Why? If she needs a desk, give her the one downstairs with the rats. That's where she's going to be most of the time, isn't it?"

"Her name is Petra Grady, not 'the sweeper.'" Benedict's voice was soft, and I sighed.

"Mother of cats, couldn't I be wrong just once?" I said, gathering my cool as I prepared to meet my coworker. Benedict's protesting murmur had gone soft, and I forced a smile as I saw him and a stylish brunette coming my way down the wide balcony overlook. Benedict had a wad of tissue around one finger, a flash of blood showing. *God grant me the strength to not throttle the stuck-up mage,* I thought. "And the wisdom to know the difference," I whispered as the woman spotted me and the furrow in her brow smoothed to a condescending, benevolent smile. Sometimes it was easy to tell. It was the ones who sucker punched you that hurt the most.

"I don't know why you even requested a sweeper," she said, her eyes fixed on mine. "Everyone on task knows how to bottle their own dross."

"And yet most of them don't," I said.

Benedict's head jerked up, his surprise making it obvious that he hadn't known I was on-site yet, much less within hearing distance. His lips parted, but whatever his next words were, they remained unsaid. I felt short again, underdressed in my black slacks and collared shirt, the hint of sweat showing. I hated it, hated it all.

"Petra." Benedict lurched into the break room, his tissue-wrapped hand held close. "You found the place. Good. Good. This is great."

Jimmy Tross was still singing, and with thoughts of balloon animals drifting through my mind, I tapped the buds to turn them off. "You were right," I said. "This place needs a good sweep. How long has it been empty?"

"I'm not sure. Three years?" Benedict glanced at the woman as she pushed her way in, heels clicking and smile firmly in place. The two of them seemed more than just associates by how close she was sticking to him. A flicker of jealousy burned, and I quashed it.

"This is a nice setup," I said, leaning back against the table. "It sucks if you're in the caged group, though."

Bloody hand held high, Benedict glanced over his shoulder as if he could see the rat room. "Mmmm," he said, voice breathy, and my eyebrows rose. *He's nervous?* "I suppose."

The woman beside him pointedly cleared her throat. Her makeup had been painstakingly applied, but I thought her lips were gaudy, not the sophisticated she was probably going for.

"Oh. Sorry." Benedict shifted to include her. "Petra, this is Candice. Candice, this is Petra Grady, the university's best sweeper, though you can't really call her a sweeper. She's more of a fixer of large dross issues." His words tumbled out fast, and my gaze flicked to Candice's thinly veiled disregard. "We were lucky to get her."

Good luck or bad? I mused as I extended my hand. *Time will tell.* "Nice to meet you," I said, glad my guess that she was Laura was wrong, especially after her telling hesitation before taking my hand. She hardly met my fingers before letting go. Every single one of her manicured nails had a chip, and the chain her lodestone pendant was on had several obvious repair links. And the elaborately set glass pendant *had* to be her lodestone, the silver wrapped about the red glass orb so ornate that it was probably a family heirloom passed down through the generations.

Candice smirked when she saw me looking at it, and my faint sympathy that it must be hard having dross break on you all the time vanished as Benedict's almost frantic desperation became clear. Candice was sweeper-phobic, and he was afraid she might do something rude and insensitive.

"What a remarkable . . . hair tie," she finally said, her eyes on my sweat-damp hair, having found the fray in the cord like a magnet. "Is it knotted dross?" she asked as Benedict edged to the sink, and I nodded, bristling at the hidden slight. "How interesting," she added. "Knotted dross attracts more dross. I suppose that would be an asset in your line of work."

Only because you make it, sweetheart, I thought silently. "It is, but I also wear it to repel shadow, a definite possibility, as you say, in my line of work." No need to tell her I had accidentally used inert dross to knot it and it would do the exact opposite. Maybe I shouldn't be wearing it, but I carried shadow buttons and that was the same thing. Eyebrows high, I stared her down. Benedict hadn't said anything about Candice when he briefed me on the team, but I might have conveniently forgotten her, too; her attitude was appalling.

"What office have you picked out, Candice?" I added as Benedict fumbled for the first-aid kit bolted to the cabinet. Like everything else in here, there was dross on it, and the lock broke with a startling ping. Rolls of tape and gauze fell out, thumping and bumping as they hit the counter. One bounced twice before landing squarely in the garbage disposal with a tiny *thurmp* of plastic.

Six points! I mused darkly, reminded of our paper-triangle-football games. "I'll set up double traps for you," I added as Benedict stoically tried to dig the tape out, his cut finger making a bloody mess of it. "You look like a hot-coffee kind of a girl. One on the desk, one by the door should do it."

The implied insult that she didn't pick up her own dross hit home. Eyebrows high, she wiped her fingers off on her jacket. "I'm not part of Ben's team," she admitted, and I felt a knot of anxiety ease. *Thank God.*

"Oh," I said lightly. "That's too bad." *Ben? She calls him Ben? He hates that.*

The sound of a Band-Aid tearing open was loud in the obvious tension. "Candice is one of our most passionate donors. She's here checking out the new digs," Benedict said as he wrapped his finger with a quickness born of experience.

As Benedict turned to replace the rolls of tape and gauze, I leaned to make a show of looking at her non-lab-regulation heels and nodded. There was a wisp of dross eddying closer to her, pulled into the room in her wake. *To pick it up, or not pick it up—that is the question.* "Okay. Good to know. Will you be coming in often?"

Candice looped her arm in Benedict's as if he were a prize at the fair. "Ben clearly thinks you're an asset, but there's only one reason you are here. The Spinners' guild wants to shut us down, find a way to keep the process from passing Spell Approval. Good luck with that. Ben's procedure is perfect."

My smile widened to meet hers with a honey-drenched sweetness. Sure, bantering with a muckety-muck donor on the first day wasn't a career-boosting move, but what were they going to do? Fire me? *Please . . .*

"Candice." Benedict pulled his arm away in a mild rebuke. "I asked for Grady because she's the best. She knows how dross behaves under stress, not in theory but practice, *and* she knows how to deal with it in such a way as to minimize its destruction. Her insights and skills could be the difference between a rollout plagued by setbacks or one that is smooth and incident-free."

My next ugly words died unspoken, and as the silence stretched, I watched Candice file that away to bring out when they were alone with her checkbook. A twinge of guilt took me when she gave Benedict's face a fond pat.

"I don't know how you got this far being so trusting," she said, the red of anger breaking through her perfect makeup. "She's here to sabotage the rollout so she doesn't lose her job."

"Hey!" I said, and Candice beamed her ugly smile as Benedict withered where he stood.

"Every mage-based company pays hundreds of thousands a year to get rid of dross," Candice said as if it were a new concept she'd unearthed yesterday. "Ben is going to put an end to the gouging. The Spinners know it, and this is their only chance to stop it." Eyebrows high, she gazed mockingly at me. "Your luck has turned bad, Ms. Grady. This is happening."

I bobbed my head, motions slow as I took a desk trap from my bag. "I'm glad you brought that up," I said as I adroitly set it up, looping and tying the knotted cord without looking. "We wouldn't have to pick up dross if you would all collectively bottle it properly instead of letting it drift about to coalesce into ugly piles." Smug, I simultaneously pulled my wand from a back pocket and swooped down to snag the dross she'd brought in with her. Candice stepped back, clearly surprised.

"Dross exists because every mage and mage-based company blissfully makes it," I said as I spun the dross on the wand like cotton candy, deftly handling the tingling energy that would break on her faster than a bug hits a newly washed window. "If you don't like the fees, don't engage us. We are a service, like everything else, doing what you could do yourself if you cared to—but don't."

I flicked the wand, sending the dross to the tabletop trap. It passed under the set of sticks and was caught, rolling in a narrowing spiral until finding the center and settling into a hazy sulk.

"Ex-act-ly." Candice bit the word off sharp, her jaw tight as she gave Benedict a professional peck on the cheek. "I'll see you next week," she said, spinning to walk out, her heels clicking as she took the staircase down.

"Um, looking forward to it. Bye, Candice," Benedict said belatedly, his worried expression becoming apologetic when he faced me again. "Good God, Petra, I'm sorry about that," he said, but I couldn't help but notice he was keeping his voice low so she wouldn't hear. "Candice has some strong ideas, most of which I don't agree with. But she's our biggest donor, and I have to put up with it."

"Oh, I don't know." I adjusted the trap on the table, feeling the dross behind the thin sticks prickling against my fingers. "I appreciate knowing where I stand with people," I said, and he cringed. "She's right about one thing. I'm taking the desk downstairs with the rats."

His lips parted, his obvious dismay pulling a twinge of guilt from me. Maybe that had been a little catty. "No. I want you to have the office next to mine," he said.

I chuckled, but it wasn't a happy sound. "And deal with *that* twice a day? No, thanks."

Benedict's eye twitched as a distant door banged shut. "She probably won't come back."

Eyebrows high, I stared at him. Did he really think we could pick up where we'd left off without even an acknowledgment of what he'd done? "I was talking about the rest of the team."

Benedict's brow furrowed. Candice's opinions, though not usually so up-front and biting, were common. "Giving you a nice office will help elevate your sweeper standing," he said, and I shook my head, mildly insulted that he'd made it into a gift, something not earned but given.

"It will cause resentment that I can avoid by taking the desk downstairs. Thanks anyway." I drew my bag from the table, but he was in my way and I couldn't leave. "I'll set up a few more traps," I said, motioning him to shift, and he jumped to the side. "No real work until tomorrow, right?" We didn't have to be friends to work together. I could do this.

Benedict fidgeted, his wide shoulders hunched. "Well, apart from an informal lunch meeting. The rest of the team won't be here until noon. I've got some work-study kids to clean the cages, too, that I want you to meet."

I cringed at the thought of lunch with a bunch of mages, and he rushed to fill the silence. "Petra, you're a valued member. I asked for you, and I'm glad you're here. I want this to be a safe product. I feel that it is, but I want to know for sure, and if you see anything that strikes you as potentially dangerous, I want to hear about it."

"Okay." Peeved, I set the messenger bag on the table again. "Since you ask, I find the entire idea of changing dross's fundamental properties of spontaneous dissociation fraught with inherent problems. The nature of dross is change. It will find a way to revert. My advice is to slow this down until you find out what it does long-term."

Benedict's eyes showed no hurt, no anger. He was that confident. "It won't revert," he said. "We've seen nothing to indicate it's dangerous. Actually, that's one of the reasons I wanted you to have the office next to mine. So we can more easily talk about the data concerning our progress so far. I'm confident once you see everything that you will agree."

Why didn't you say that in the first place instead of making it sound as if you were doing me a favor? I thought sourly. "You asked my opinion," I said, disappointed. "There it is."

He was silent, face empty as he leaned back against the counter, arms over his chest. "Huh," he said, voice flat. "I'm sorry about my behavior in school. It was wrong of me, and if I could, I'd take it back. But I was twelve and stupid, and I regret it. You think you could look past that and be an adult?"

Whoa, what? Shock flickered over me, settling into a hard burn. *What kind of half-assed apology is that?* Ticked, I forced my hands to unfist. "You think sending me a balloon animal makes up for humiliating me in front of your friends? That I'm going to ignore that you treated me like a *thing* put there to ease your boredom? It doesn't come close, Benny. But yeah, I can look past you pretending to be my friend and then dissing me in front of your boys' club so you could play the cool card, because it happens all the time."

I took a step forward into his space, and a flash of worry crossed him. "This has nothing to do with you other than the fact that you are trying to make something that isn't possible," I said softly. "And if I find it isn't safe, if I see a *hint* of your modified dross reverting back to its natural state, I'm going to shut you down faster than new corn goes through an old goose. And trust me. I can do it."

His eyes narrowed. It was the first hint of anger I'd seen in him. *Hazel,* I mused, only now remembering. "I doubt that," he said, voice devoid of its usual pleasant lilt. "The university wants this, and the process works."

Chin high, I pulled my messenger bag off the table and pushed past him and into the hall. "I hope you're right that it works. Because contrary to Candice's belief, I don't like dealing with dross and shadow. They both have the potential to be deadly, and I would much rather do something else with my life. Anything else."

Benedict's expression froze as if he'd never thought of that before. He pushed from the counter, his foot hitting the table leg to make it jump. The small shift was enough to knock over the trap I'd set up, and the sticks clattered into an unusable pile.

"There's nothing wrong with my process," he said, his neck red as he reached for the wand tucked into his shirt pocket like a pen and wanded the fallen trap to collect the dross as if it were still there, not already oozing down the table leg like a glittering slime mold. "I've given you access to our preliminary data. I expect you to go over it."

He still can't see dross? I thought as he dexterously held the unencumbered wand between his fingers and righted the trap—only to have it fall apart as soon as he let go.

Grimacing, I came forward. "Just . . . stop. I've got it," I added, pushing his hands aside. "Your wand is clean. The dross is already under the fridge."

Our fingers touched, and he retreated a step, silent as I retied the sticks, my motions fast from long practice. They shouldn't have fallen to begin with, but causing unexpected things to happen was what dross did.

I stiffened when I realized he was still standing there, watching me. "I'm going to finish my walk-through of the building," I said, suddenly feeling awkward. "I'll set up personal traps in each office and the common areas, but I'd appreciate it if everyone would do a better job of cleaning up after their own spells. I am a sweeper, but I'm not your maid. I'll see you tomorrow."

"Lunch. Noon today. You need to meet the rest of the team. I'll be in the lobby waiting," he said as he tucked his wand away. "I'm driving. You can't ride your bike out there. You'd be a sweaty mess and it's a nice place."

"Fine. Lunch," I agreed as I walked out, not looking forward to it.

9

MEETING THE REST OF BENEDICT'S TEAM HAD TAKEN AN ENTIRE TWO AGONIZING hours over salad and pasta, all of it wasted as they talked shop, predictably ignoring me once I admitted I'd been a sweeper straight out of the university. My walk-through afterward had been from ceiling to basement. I'd saved the offices for last, when everyone had gone home, and if there was dross there now, they'd made it themselves. Tired and cranky, I coasted through campus in the cool dusk to the sound of low-flying jets from the nearby air base. I was hungry, too, since I'd tried to be professional at lunch and had ordered a salad. I had no idea what I was going to have for dinner, and Pluck needed a walk first. Lev had let him out around two, but that was hours ago.

Or maybe not, I thought as I slowed before Surran Hall. A big black Lab surrounded by helpful people sat on the steps. Hearing my bike, the dog stood, head down and his heavy tail wagging as he came to greet me, clearly knowing he was in trouble.

"Pluck?" I swung a leg over and propped my bike against the low wall. Stray drifts of dross littered the front steps, looking like trash, and I wove around them, not caring if the students thought I was overly cautious. Sure, dross didn't break on me, but that flash of connection was uncomfortable without insulating myself with a wand. "How did you get out?"

The big dog shoved into me and I fondled his ears, reassuring him I was okay and wasn't he a clever boy to find me?

"Is he yours?" one of the students said, and I nodded, my day somehow both better and worse. I mean, he was here and safe, but how had he gotten out?

"He's mine," I said as I gave his neck a good rub, my smile faltering. *Ashley* . . . She'd probably come back for her things and left the door open, giving the dog a chance to escape.

I stood, one hand on Pluck. "But he's supposed to be at home," I said as the students closed in. "Thanks for watching him. I think he slipped his walker." Ticked, I reached for my back pocket and my phone. "I'd better call her," I said, tone tight. "She's probably worried sick."

"He's such a sweetie," one of the women said, misreading my anger. "What's his name?"

"Pluck." I scrolled, grimacing when I found Ashley's icon. "Because he's got a lot of it." They hadn't recognized me as a sweeper without my sticks, which I was already beginning to regret having left in my locker.

"He's just a big lover!" the woman said, voice high as she baby-talked him, and Pluck's thick tail wagged. "Bye, Pluck!"

"Thanks again," I said as the threesome walked away, my head down as I texted to Ashley, **I've got Pluck. We need to talk.** I hesitated, then added a **Please.**

Pluck nosed me as I put my phone away, and I scanned the dusky campus. I had a couple bottles of dross to dump, but more telling was that I didn't want to take Pluck home yet. Ashley would probably be there in the hopes that he'd come back, and despite my text, I wasn't ready to talk to her. *Out-of-state interviews, my ass.*

Frowning, I sent my gaze up the Surran building's wide stairs to the impressive oak doors. The hall was likely empty, and I pushed my bike to the rack and chained it to the stylized cactus and roadrunner done in twisted metal. "You want to come with me to the loom, bean?"

Pluck wagged his tail as I shouldered my messenger bag. Helmet tucked under an arm, I led him up the stairs. The SERVICE ANIMALS ONLY notice gave me pause, but then I shoved open the door and Pluck happily followed me in. He wasn't on a lead, and I didn't have my sticks with me to give me any clout—such as it was.

But my good luck held and I saw no one. I breathed easier once past the fire door and Pluck took point, tail waving as he went down before me, not a clue in his furry head where we were going, just happy one of his people was with him. He waited at the landing, tongue lolling as I punched in my code, and I held the door for him.

"Feel that, eh?" I said when he sneezed, his entire body shaking as we passed under the trap. "Wait until we get to the loom."

I entered my code again at the second panel, and the pleasant automated voice announced my arrival as Pluck nosed the door open and pushed through.

"Pluck!" I heard Jessica call, her high voice eager, and I slumped at the two masculine voices twining through hers. I'd been hoping to dump the dross and go home to sulk, but no. Jessica wanted the gossip and had lingered—with Kyle and Nog, by the sound of it.

"Good boy!" the woman called in delight as I went in. "What are you doing here?"

Sure enough, Jessica, Nog, and Kyle were at the round table, Kyle standing over the dross-go board and Nog watching him push a dross drift through the maze with a specially made shadow-cored wand. If I knew Kyle, there'd be money on the outcome, hence Nog's interest. The older man was still in his beggar uniform, sipping on a beer from the fridge.

Jessica, who was giving Pluck a good ear rub, had a glass of wine, and my eyebrows rose. Darrell kept the sweeper fridge well stocked, but wine was reserved for special occasions. This wasn't one of them. They'd been waiting for me—for a while if the second, empty bottle beside the box of replacement dross-go buttons was any indication.

Really? I thought, tired as I met Darrell's gaze from across the large room, and the woman chuckled, beads clinking as she studied her paperwork.

"Hi, Grady," Jessica drawled, giving Pluck a last pat as the dog trotted to Nog.

I didn't like the knowing lilt in Jessica's voice, and I set my messenger bag on the table with an obvious clunk, heavy with bottles and about half a ream of paper detailing Benedict's process. "Wow. Wine? Busy day on the streets?"

Kyle was riveted to the four-by-four maze, the young man standing over it to better direct the drift of dross. Sure, he could touch dross with no ill effects, but gaining dexterity with a wand was the point of the game. "No, no, no! Got it!" he said, wand spinning as he made it through the first loop without his dross hitting any of the lit buttons and shorting them out. Dross-go was first and foremost a mages' game designed to increase their skills at collecting and moving dross to traps, but sweepers played it as well. *And played it better,* I thought smugly.

There were any number of ways of getting from the outside in, ranging from long and winding to a short, direct route called the alley. Lighted buttons called dross-gos were set in the walls and floor. The shorter the path, the more were in your way. And that was the trick, because if your dross hit a button, the light went out and points were added to your time. The buttons themselves had been originally developed as a way to dissociate dross before it reached sensitive electronics, but as the story went, bored sweepers in Detroit had turned it into a game.

Nog gave Pluck a thump, clearly fond of the dog. "I told you she'd come in with dross," he said as he poured a glass of wine and handed it to me. "Grady doesn't know how not to clean."

Glass in hand, I gingerly sat on the edge of the couch. Wine on an empty stomach? Not a good idea. "The place was filthy," I said in my own defense.

"Forty seconds," Jessica said, and my gaze went to the board. The rules were simple: using a dross-repelling wand, push your drift to the center without busting any buttons. It was a loud game, especially when alcohol was involved. Anywhere from one to six people could play at once, and the more there were, the more strategy came into play. Score was based on time and mistakes, each busted dross-go button adding five seconds to your time. I wasn't allowed to play anymore. At least not when money was on the line.

Wand waving wildly, Kyle swore as his dross hit a button and the light went out.

"Forty-five," Jessica added, grinning as she met my eyes. "Hey, we heard you were assigned to Benedict's group. How's that working?"

Nog glanced up from the board as Kyle continued to contort and swear. "It's not," I said shortly, not sure if I was glad to see them, even if they were my friends. I was still raw, and when I was raw, I lost my filter and said things I regretted. Every. Single. Time.

Yeah, let's add some wine to this, I thought as I held my full glass, wincing when Kyle's dross got too close to a button and the light went out.

"Darrell? Something is wrong with this wand!" Kyle said, beginning to look frantic.

"The wand is fine!" Darrell shouted from her desk, and Nog chuckled.

"Boom!" the older man said. "That's your third one. No way can you beat my time now."

"No fair," the kid protested, his gaze alternating between the board and Nog slumped contentedly on the couch with Pluck. "I was distracted by Grady's dog."

Nog took another swig of his beer. "Distractions are a part of the game, grasshopper," he said, and from the far side of the room, Darrell snorted.

I set my untasted glass down and leaned over the board to study his strategy. He was going the long way, hoping for fewer buttons and therefore a faster pace. I preferred the alley, the straight shot having buttons every four inches.

I took a breath to give Kyle a word of advice, startled when I realized Darrell was standing right next to me. She'd seen the bag and probably wanted to dump it so she could kick us all out. "I'll take that. Sit," she said as she dragged the messenger bag from the low table. "Talk to your friends. I'll get you some replacement bottles."

"No need." I winced as Kyle hit a fourth button. "They have tons."

Darrell peeked into the bag, her eyebrows rising in appreciation. "Lab grade," she said in approval. "Nice. I'll be sure you get credited for these."

Jessica stood, her focus going from the stopwatch to the board. "One more hit, Kyle, and Nog's won. You can't go fast enough to rub out the points."

"Go, you little dross shit!" Kyle shouted, wand extended as he danced around the table, manipulating the drift. I winced, knowing he was getting too close. My breath hissed in as his dross touched the button—and the light went out.

"Shadow tits!" Kyle swore, and Nog chuckled when Jessica told him to watch his mouth.

"No, don't stop," I said as Kyle slumped. "You got this. Go left."

"Into the alley?" Kyle said, and I inched to the edge of the couch so I could see better.

"You've taken five hits, right?" I said, and he nodded. "Then you've lost enough dross to thread the alley." I hesitated. "Maybe . . ."

Nog sat up with a grunt. "Hey. No fair coaching the kid."

Kyle's face lit up, and with a renewed interest, he twirled the wand and pushed the dross into the first opening. Jessica's eyes went round as he passed one, two, then three dross buttons, their lights never dimming. "My God, she's right!" Jessica said, gripping Kyle's shoulder and bouncing up and down. "Go! Kyle, you got this!"

Kyle's face was creased in concentration, wand twirling and arm moving in grand gestures as he pushed the wisp faster. Nog inched forward to the edge of the couch, brow furrowed until—right at the very end—Kyle's dross hit the last dross-go and triggered it. With a soft pop, the energy dissociated completely. Not even a faint sparkle danced across the finish line. He'd lost even if he had beaten Nog's time.

"Oh no!" Jessica cried, disappointed. "You were so close!"

Smug, Nog settled back into the couch with his beer. "Nice run."

It *was* a nice run, and I wasn't going to feel bad for not telling Kyle that those last buttons were three times more sensitive than anything else in the alley. You had to go high over them. Almost out of the maze.

Kyle slumped into a discouraged lump on the couch, Jessica beside him. "I'll never break three minutes," he said, dropping the wand into the maze in disgust.

"Don't take it so hard." Nog leaned to top off Kyle's He-Man tumbler with wine. "I've been playing dross-go since before you saw your first rainbow."

Kyle's gaze lifted to find mine. "You want a run, Grady?"

"No!" Jessica shouted, startling me, then softer, "No one plays against Grady. She can do the alley in twenty seconds and only one hit."

Nog clinked his bottle against Jessica's wineglass. "And that's only because she wants to thin out her dross," he said, gaze coming to me. "Don't think I didn't notice you hitting the same buttons every time."

I grinned as I lifted my glass and took a sip. The astringent wine bit at the sides of my mouth and I began to relax. They were good people.

"The alley?" Kyle said, still interested. "I'd pay to see that."

Jessica tugged him into a sideways hug. "Not if you want enough of your paycheck left to take me out to dinner tonight."

"Yeah, there is that," Kyle said, his expression shifting.

I pushed deeper into the cushions, legs rising to put my arches on the edge of the table. "Thanks, Jessica. I could have used the rent money," I said, immediately wishing I could take it back as Darrell perked up, beaded hair clinking.

"Your uncle finally quit sending you money, then?" she asked sourly as she vaulted the dross, and I sighed. That shadow I'd brought in yesterday was still in the loom, safe in its capped vodka bottle, and I wondered why she hadn't dumped it yet.

"Yeah," I lied, remembering her agitation the last time I brought him up. Darrell didn't like it that *her sweepers,* as she called us, struggled to make it on one paycheck. But that was par for the course. Either that, or she knew "Uncle John" was really Herm Ivaros. Yeah. Probably not. No one liked him or his theories about using dross to do magic.

I bet she knew him firsthand, I mused, seeing as she had helped end the last shadow eclipse, the one that my dad had died quelling. The one that Herm started.

Jessica leaned over the game, her fingers pulling spent buttons. "I've never seen anyone move dross with a wand like Grady," she said as Kyle filled the empty spots with new ones.

A faint glimmer of dross hazed the table, a remnant of a previous run probably, and I took my wand from my back pocket. "If I can't decant it into a bottle, I use a wand," I said as I spun the haze up like candy. "I don't like getting burned."

"Burned?" Nog looked up from fondling Pluck's ears. "Dross burns you?"

Embarrassment was a quick flash. Damn it, even Darrell was listening. "No," I said as I eyed the tiny spot of hazy nothing perched on the end of the stick. "It's more like a flash of connection?" My gaze flicked to Darrell, not liking her suddenly tense shoulders. I'd never told anyone apart from Benedict, and that was when we were kids. *Like he'd ever remember that?*

"It goes away as soon as I coat it in a psi field," I said as I studied the tiny drift of glittering dross. "But if I use a wand, I don't even have to do that. It acts as an insulator, maybe." I sighed as I remembered Wallace shouting at his crew, *Iron, insulator, iron!*

Their silence grew, and I looked up, wincing. They were all staring at me. Even Darrell.

"All I feel is a warning tingle it wants to break," Kyle said, his expression unsure. "And that's kind of nice. Is that what you're talking about?"

Jessica snapped the last new button in place. "It's not breaking on you, is it?"

"No. Not ever," I said, and Darrell seemed to relax. Still, I was uncomfortable for having admitted it, and I flicked the dross off, wincing when it hit a button and burst it in a flash of light.

The thump of the vault closing echoed, and Nog's gaze went from me to Darrell, then back to me. "Strom has you working already?"

"Bastard," Jessica said, and Darrell grumbled at her to be nice as she shuffled to her desk.

I didn't want to talk about it. Silent, I tucked my wand away. "I should get Pluck home. I'll see you all later." Tired, I set my hardly tasted wine on the table and gathered myself to stand. "Thanks, Darrell," I called, but my motion to rise faltered when Jessica put a hand on my shoulder and practically shoved me down.

"Whoa, whoa, whoa, little sister." Kyle's lips curved into a smile. "Not so fast. You had a bad day. I lost ten bucks to Nog. We both need libations to ease the pain in our souls, and Darrell let us open a bottle."

Nog's low laugh rumbled about his wide frame as he pushed my full glass closer to me. "Not to mention loosen your tongue. Let's hear it."

I hesitated. A part of me needed this, wanted the camaraderie. "I have to take Pluck home."

Lips wry, Nog patted the couch, and Pluck jumped up to put his heavy head on the man's thigh. "What's the poop?" Nog said with a sigh, his hand fondling the dog's ears.

Darrell had settled at her desk, four bright red strands of silk weaving through her fingers as she knotted it. If she really wanted us out, she'd say so. Settling back with my glass, I upended it and I took a large gulp.

"Damn, it's bad," Kyle said, and I almost choked, grimacing as it went down.

"That was for Benedict's *charming* benefactor," I said, then took another gulp, shuddering until the bitter taste shifted to a heady numbness. "That was for Benedict," I said, hardly lowering the glass as I took a third, draining it. "And that was for Ashley," I said, blinking as I set the glass down. *Probably shouldn't have done that.*

"Ashley?" Kyle asked, and Nog's dark eyes pinched in sympathy.

Jessica reached for the bottle to refill my glass. "Ashley put in for the job, too."

I nodded, the quick motion making my vision swim. "Put in for the job, and left when I was forced to take it," I said, hearing my voice as if outside of my head. *Let me finish this. I'm so close,* lifted through my memory, and Sikes's haughty attitude.

Kyle sipped his wine from his He-Man tumbler. "It's a sweeper position. What did she expect?"

Nog's fingers against Pluck never slowed. "Kyle, you're not helping."

"I'm only saying. If it's a sweeper position, why does she even want it?"

Nodding, I slumped back into the cushions, my refilled wineglass held to my chest as the weight of the day crashed down on me. *Nope. Shouldn't have done that.*

"Petra, honey, it's going to be okay," Jessica soothed, and I blinked, trying to focus, when she patted my shoulder. "Ashley will get over it or she won't. You knew that it was only until she got her thesis done."

I pushed myself up and set the glass aside, remembering her saying she hated living with me. Though, to be honest, she'd just busted her roller bag.

Slumping forward, I put my arms between me and the cool glass top of the table. "She's my friend," I said, my words muffled and warm as they bounced back to me. "And she's so full of anger that she won't listen." I exhaled, dizzy and wanting no more wine. "Right now there's no room in her for anything but her own disappointment. I didn't have a choice. And the job is going to *suck*."

I pushed up to see Nog grinning, his wrinkles folded into a beautiful smile. "Mages are stuck-up pigs," he agreed. "I have yet to meet one who didn't believe their shit didn't stink."

"Benedict isn't that bad," I protested, not sure why I was defending him. *Damn it, I do not still like him!* But seeing him silent when that high-maintenance mage with her dross-chipped nails had slighted me had hurt. Again. "Candice, though . . ." I added, "I'd like to drop a ball of dross down her toilet." Sullen, I swirled my full glass of wine. That apology of his hadn't been very good, either—even if it was likely sincere. Benny had never been good at the talking thing.

Darrell laughed from across the room, her fingers moving dexterously as she worked beads and rings into the four-ply silk strand.

"Not that bad?" Jessica pulled her feet up onto the couch to look pensive. "You came back with old dross. Something set you off, or you wouldn't have cleaned."

"The building was a dross pit," I said, a smile threatening as I remembered Benny's cut finger. He had come to class with a new bandage so often that I'd made a game of trying to guess what he'd done. He was always breaking dross on himself. *Kind of like Ashley,* I thought, and my smile faltered.

"My guess is you gave him your opinion and he didn't like it," Nog said, his stubbly chin high as he finished his beer.

"Oh, he asked," I said, and Kyle snorted. My eyes, though, were drawn to the hint of dross oozing to the dross-go table, the little spot of sunshine slinking about in search of something to break on. Clearly Darrell hadn't patched that hole yet, and I idly marked it to pick up before it found my dog and gave him tooth tartar. *So I clean when I'm upset. So what?*

"Well?" Jessie prompted.

"Let's say we agree to disagree," I said as the distortion drifted closer. "But if I see *one hint* that that stuff wants to revert . . ." My words faltered and my shoulders slumped. I wasn't sure what a difference my words would make. Benedict was right. The university wanted this, and for all of Benedict's flattery about *choosing me* and *respecting my opinion* and wanting a *safe product*, if my words and opinions were not acted on, much less recognized, I was nothing more than a trashman sitting at a desk with the rats. *Crap, I should have eaten first.*

"Damn bureaucracy," Nog muttered as I settled into the sofa with my glass of wine to have myself a big old pity party. This was not where I had expected I'd be in my life right now. I'd gotten used to having the spendable income, but I could find another roommate. Lev, maybe. He didn't seem to mind letting Pluck out.

His wrinkled face scrunched, Nog slid out from under Pluck and stood. "Let's go."

Jessica's hand-patting sympathy flashed to anger. "Nog . . ." she protested, and the big man gestured at Darrell calmly weaving knotted strands of silk at her desk.

"We aren't helping," Nog said, his low voice rumbling. "You got the gossip—"

"That's not why I'm here," Jessica said as she gave me a sideways hug.

"I'm good. I'm okay," I said, but my nose was threatening to run, and I sniffed everything back. "I should have eaten first is all."

Jessica's hug became tighter. "Come on, Petra. You're with me tonight," she said, shooting Kyle a sharp look when he took a breath to protest. I appreciated it, but I wasn't sure I could stand up at the moment. "Your bike will fit in the back of my car," she added. "My landlord won't say anything about Pluck for one night."

"What about sushi and a movie?" Kyle said, and Jessica nearly bared her teeth at him.

"No," I said, more grateful of the gesture than she'd ever know. "I'm fine. Pluck and I will be fine." I blinked at the dross maze, focus blurring. "I'm going to sit here for a little is all." My head lifted. "Is that okay, Darrell?" I said, getting a distant "Yes, ma'am!" in return.

Still Jessica hesitated, concern pinching her eyes as she stood. "You and I will have dinner this week, okay?" she said, giving my shoulder another squeeze. "My treat."

I nodded, and she reluctantly headed for the door, pushing Kyle before her. Nog was there and waiting, having already keyed it open. "That Ashley is an entitled bitch," I heard Jessica say as they went out. "I never liked her."

Sighing, I took a sip of wine. "I did," I whispered. *I do,* I reiterated silently.

Pluck was stretched out on the couch, and he did a doggy shuffle-lurch across the cushions until his head touched my thigh. I dropped my hand to touch him. "Darrell, why do I let them get to me like that?"

"It's your nature." Her voice was clear in the silence, even from across the room. "Your dad was the same."

I missed my sticks, stuck in one of those gray lockers halfway across St. Unoc's campus. "I should get going," I said, but after setting the glass on the table, I couldn't find it in me to get up, and I put my elbows on my knees.

And there I sat, unmoving.

"No rush." Beads clinking, Darrell came forward and put my empty bag on the floor, sighing as she settled onto the couch. That red strand of knotted silk was still in her hands, and as I watched her loop it about a metal ring she'd put in the end, I realized it was a dog lead.

"Oh, thank you," I said as she extended it to me. "This will make getting him home a lot easier. It's beautiful," I added, feeling no tingle of dross. The knots were decoration only.

"You're welcome. It's dross-free. I didn't want to risk him attracting anything." Hesitating, she took a swig right from the bottle. "I shouldn't be drinking. I have stuff to do. Put the dross-go board away. Patch that hole, maybe," she finished sourly.

But she didn't move to get up, either. Sitting more or less upright, I took what I told myself was a last sip. That free dross had reached my feet, and I extended my foot to step on it, feeling a flash of connection right through my shoe until I coated it in a psi field. *Bad dross,* I thought as I rolled the drift into a ball between my foot and the floor, squishing it. *What will you dissipate your bad luck on if I let you go? A busted chair leg? A run in Darrell's sweater? A broken nail?* Tired, I squished it again, feeling it tingle a warning. Kyle was right. The warning was almost pleasant, nothing like the brief, painful flash of connection.

"I don't know why I'm even there," I said as Darrell began to put the game away, carefully checking each dross-repelling wand before settling them in a velvet case. "They don't want my opinion regardless of what Benedict says. Why did he ask for me?"

Darrell snapped the case shut and rose to take it to the game cabinet. "He probably sees the light in you."

"Light?" My foot stopped moving and I stared at her in surprise. "What light?"

The older woman's gaze meeting mine held a smidgen of surprise. "The light," she said, as if she shouldn't have to be explaining this. "The stuff that mages and Spinners use to do magic." Her expression emptied as a thought struck her. "You can't see it, can you. At all."

My shoulders slumped, and I fiddled with my wineglass. "Darrell, all I see is dross. Everywhere." Frustrated, I kicked the psi-coated drift across the floor. It rolled until it hit the wall, where it stayed, shimmering like a little heat mirage. "From little dust bunnies to women who were beaten and killed in the late 1800s," I finished sourly. "I'll get that as soon as I can stand up."

But Darrell went to retrieve it, fumbling in a pocket for a little vial. Maybe she was going to keep it to knot. "Not at all?" she asked, groaning as she bent to catch the dross with a wand. "Most sweepers can see a hint of it, a glow."

I shook my head. The disappointment of not being able to do the magic was an old one. "Nope," I said with a forced cheerfulness. "No magic for me."

"Well, that might explain why you can see dross so well," Darrell said. "Most sweepers can see a smidgen of light. Just as most mages can sense dross to varying degrees."

"Not me," I said again, voice thready. "Never even once."

"Grady, don't be so hard on yourself," she said as she set the vial on her desk and shuffled back to the table, slippers scuffing. "Your psi fields are class five. And then some."

Class-five psi field. That sounded glamorous, and it was if you could do magic with it, but I couldn't do anything but catch dross. "Damn it, Darrell, I don't want to go back to my apartment," I said as she returned. "It's either going to be empty or Ashley is going to be there."

Darrell smirked. "Sit. Stay," she said, and Pluck thumped his tail. "I'll get Pluck some water. You can hide here for one night. And then you talk to Ashley, yes? Work this out."

I nodded, thankful as I swung my feet up and stretched out on the half-circle sofa, my arm draped over Pluck. "Thank you," I whispered, eyes already shut when I felt the warmth of a knotted blanket falling over me.

Tomorrow was going to be hell.

10

L AURA AND BENEDICT'S CONVERSATION FROM THE NEARBY LAB COUNTER MIXED pleasantly with the classical guitar being piped in to enrich the rats' environment. My lab station was far enough away to make it difficult to follow their words, but I was pretty sure their talk revolved around tomorrow's graduation and the chance to secure more funding. The space between us had felt accidental when I'd begun to weigh dross into small ampoules that morning, but now I was beginning to wonder: I was too distant to easily join the conversation but close enough that Anton had been able to bark orders at me without moving his ass from his lab stool.

I'd come in early to check the ambient traps as much as to avoid the morning heat, but no one else had shown until almost nine. Shortly after Anton had trained me on the dross scale, Benedict had asked him to take care of some paperwork. I'd like to think that it was because of Anton's repeated jabs about my lack of speed, but really, changing dross into inert lumps was hardly a two-person job, much less three.

Bored, I twisted a new, glittering bottle of dross onto the separator. The apparatus looked nothing like the one Darrell used to dispense dross to knot into her scarves and shawls, the valve opening not to my hand but to a small tube, where it was "weighed" to the smallest pule.

My head hurt from the stress, not last night's wine. It could have also been the dross magnet that Benedict had given me to make the job go faster. The attractant ring held more dross than a sorority party, and I swear I was getting little pinpricks of sensation from it.

The theory was that I could use the magnet to pull the dross through the tube and past a sensor. I'd used something similar when making my three sticks, and there, like here, I'd found it was easier to manhandle the dross through the sensor with a psi field.

Ampoule in place, I opened the valve to weigh out the next sample. As expected, the sparkling waver of potential bad luck lingered at the tip of the dispenser, refusing to move. "Come on, you little dirt wisp," I whispered, ignoring the jolt of heat as I wrapped a chunk of it in my thoughts and drew it over the sensor. The machine clicked, and I closed the valve, cutting the dross field in two. Satisfied, I drew the measured dross into the ampoule and sealed it, leaving what was left in the tube to slowly drift back to the mouth of the dispensing bottle.

Sweepers generally stuck to terms like a "drift" or "clump" or the occasional "blowout" to describe dross. After a morning of this, my best guess put an average drift at about a macropule, meaning the hundred pules I was measuring were tiny, hardly enough to make you sneeze—certainly not enough to make you spill your coffee.

It was the last ampoule in the box of forty, and I stretched, cracking my back as I opened the dispenser valve to allow the leftover to return to the holding jar. Glassware clattering, I took the pinky-size ampoule and snuggled it into the last open spot in the foam tray: forty measured wisps of dross safe for their transport of all of twenty steps. I thought it overkill, but Benedict was a stickler about adhering to safety protocols. After seeing him try to wand a nonexistent drift of dross yesterday, I could see why. It must be hard working with something you couldn't see, relying on repetition to keep yourself safe.

My lab stool scraped the linoleum as I got to my feet, and Laura turned as I came closer.

I'd found Laura to be pleasant enough, the dark-haired woman in her lab coat and plastic-frame glasses second in the pecking order after Benedict. Even so, I still didn't feel as if I fit in, even with my lab coat embroidered with my name.

"Forty vials," I said, wondering whose job had been decanting the dross before me. The foam rack I'd taken over there earlier was empty, and I set the tray beside it. "One hundred pules each."

"Thanks, Grady." Laura reached for the first, her purple silk gloves giving me pause. *As if that will prevent escaped dross from breaking on you?* "We're on D-1," she said as she used a wax pencil to scrawl the number on the ampoule before setting it into a reader. The machine ran a faint current through it to measure the potential activity the dross contained. She'd measure it again after Benedict turned it inert. Apparently after lunch, they'd switch jobs.

His brow furrowed in concentration, Benedict gave me a quick smile, his gaze lingering on the torn short-cord holding my hair back. "We will need four more sets after lunch, but your target will be two hundred pules."

"Sure." I glanced at the wall clock, stifling a groan. This was going to drive me nuts. Ashley owed me big. But Ashley would have thought the mind-numbing, repetitive task cooler than candy as long as Benedict was involved.

"Holy cats, Grady," Laura said as she noted the number of pules in the ampoule. "You are spot-on down to three decimals. How do you do it?"

I lingered, not eager to go back to my side of the lab. "The magnet moves it over the sensor too fast, so I ditched it for psi fields," I said, wondering why the rims of Benedict's ears had gone red. Maybe he'd been the one filling the vials.

"Petra has always been good with psi fields," Benedict said ruefully. "Even when we were kids. I swear, I think she used them to win at paper-triangle football."

"Me use fields in a mixed setting? Never," I said, smirking. I had. Every time.

"The art room wasn't a mixed setting," he grumbled, watching as Laura set the measured ampoule back in its foam-fitted slot, number side up.

"Well, whatever you are doing, keep it up. You're raising our accuracy five percent."

I pulled the empty tray to me. "Glad to help," I said, fatigued at the easy work.

"Hey, um, this is the last tray before lunch," Benedict said. "You want to see how it works? Seeing as that's why you're here."

I stopped short, empty tray in hand. "I don't know. If I find a flaw, will you listen?"

Laura's laugh was nervous. "Probably not. It's his baby."

"It is not flawed," Benedict said tightly as his blush crept down his neck. "Can you look at it with an open mind? No preconceived opinions. That's all I'm asking."

Laura cleared her throat, her focus tight on measuring the next ampoule. Exhaling, I tossed the empty tray onto the counter. I'd read the highlights of the specs that morning after taking Pluck home. I read the rest while waiting for everyone to show up. Benedict's process was basically heat-treating dross, and its very simplicity made me nervous. "Sure. Shoot."

"Oh, if only I could," Benedict whispered as he set the first ampoule in a stabby device to break the seal. He was wearing gloves, too, and my bare hands made me feel like a Neanderthal.

"It's too easy a process to be flawed," Benedict said. "Anyone can do it." His gaze flicked to me. "Um. Sorry. I mean, if you can manage a class-one heat shift, you can make dross inert. It's similar to how shadow buttons are made but eliminates the expanded structure that attracts shadow. That was where I got the idea, actually," he added. "Anton was a lot of help in the initial stages. He came to us from the shadow-button industry. But we didn't figure out how to make it unpalatable to shadow until we turned our attention to the rezes."

Now I was interested, and I came closer. "But rezes attract shadow."

"Yep." Benedict focused on his work. "Because they turn dross inert."

I knew this, and I leaned against the counter, wondering where he was heading. "Go on."

Laura wedged a second, twice-measured ampoule back into the foam tray. "What we discovered was that inert dross has an expanded molecular structure compared to active dross."

And with that, they lost me.

"Shadow attraction hinges on the density of the dross," Laura added as she saw my confusion. "Okay. Water expands when it gets cold, like pipes bursting in the winter."

I didn't know winter from space aliens, but I nodded. Ice cubes take up more space in the ice tray than water. *Check*.

"Dross does the same thing," Benedict continued. "Rezes cool and expand dross until it goes inert. Shadow can identify this naturally expanded state. We found that if we can cool dross without it changing its density, shadow doesn't touch it. It can't tell that it's inert."

My eyebrows rose as it began to make sense. "Heating it to an extreme temperature before cooling it keeps the density the same?" I said. His explanation was far easier to understand than the gobbledygook notes he'd given me. Clearly he'd practiced for his donors.

"Exactly," Benedict said, clearly confident in his science. But I wasn't so sure.

"How do you know it doesn't attract shadow?" I asked.

Laura's wax pencil squeaked as she wrote on an ampoule. "I run it through a pule meter to check its potential activity, but Anton passes random samples over a shadow to be sure."

"You have shadow? On-site?" I asked, suddenly worried.

"Anton is certified to handle it," Benedict said. "He works with shadow all the time."

No one worked with shadow *all the time.* "Okay." I glanced up at the silent balcony. *Please tell me Anton isn't keeping it in his office.*

Laura pushed her safety glasses back up her nose as she set D-2 back in its spongy slot and took up D-3. "We're making inert dross for group four now."

Benedict's gaze was on the ampoule inside his psi field. "The process starts by releasing the measured dross, simulating its creation at the end of a spell."

"Ta-da," Laura said at the soft *pudunk* as Benedict broke the ampoule's seal with a spike.

The dross spilled out, a glittering distortion curling up to show the shape of Benedict's field. "Following you so far," I said, and Benedict's brow furrowed at my sarcasm.

"A quick heat treatment," he said as he concentrated on his field and the dross began to glow, clearly wanting to break. "Followed by an immediate cooling to freeze it in place."

The glitter vanished. A tiny ping like cooling glass sounded, and I leaned closer.

I'd always envied a mage's ability to heat the air to make a light, but my lips curled in disgust at the black, thimble-size, spiky ball with its curving, frozen tendrils now resting on the bench. It felt, in a word, wrong. I'd seen pictures in the report, but the reality, though smaller than I had expected, was far more disturbing.

"That is so creepy," I said, and Benedict blinked. Laura looked up from her work as well, and I pointed to the solid dross on the counter. "That. It's spiky," I said, and Benedict stiffened as if I had told him his dog was ugly. "How do you get it into storage if it can't move?"

Clearly annoyed, Benedict reached out and actually *picked it up*, settling the solidified dross into the partitioned tray where the ampoule had been. "You pick it up and put it in," he said, clearly offended at my horrified expression. I mean, he touched it. Gloves or no, he touched it! Only sweepers and Spinners could touch dross

without it breaking, and yet, that was exactly what he had done—
was doing—did.

"It will make your job easier." Benedict tossed the used ampoule
into the trash. "Fewer spills and no free-ranging dross because it will
stay on a shelf until it can be disposed of. In an industrial setting such
as the loom, you could simulate the heat and cold treatment with
external heat and liquid nitrogen. Do the entire vault at once or in
parcels. You won't have to set up a new long-term dross field every
few decades. Simply clear it out and reuse it."

"Just bury the waste in a great big hole," I said, and Laura winced.
"What about the dross you made heating and cooling the stuff?
Where is it?"

"It merges with the initial dross and is made inert." Laura measured an ampoule and jotted down the energy. "We got it down to
ten percent."

Benedict focused on the next ampoule. "It was thirty when we
started."

*It makes more dross? Shadow spit . . . How did I miss this little nug-
get in the spec sheets?*

"Like anything, it is skill," Benedict added, clearly not appreciating my concern. "But once you know how high to heat and cool it,
you cut back on the waste."

"A skill no one will bother mastering," I said. "Okay, you froze a
hundred pules of dross. But now you have a hundred and ten to get
rid of."

Laura set another measured ampoule back in the rack. "True,
but none of it is dangerous."

My eyebrows rose. "If it doesn't revert."

"It's not going to revert!" Benedict caught his temper, the glass in
his ring shining right through his gloves as he exhaled his frustration.
Yep. It's his lodestone. "It hasn't in the eight months we've been working on it."

"Has anyone intentionally *tried* to get it to revert?" I asked, not caring if I came off as bitchy. Having an opinion might get me fired, but I hadn't wanted the job. Someone needed to bring up the hard questions, seeing as everyone else seemed to be too enamored of the university's wonder boy to do so. "If only to find out what its triggers might be?" I added.

"It won't revert," he practically growled as he set an ampoule in the stabby thing.

Arms over my chest, I put my weight on one foot. "Seems to me all you've done is make a trash compactor," I said, and the ampoule broke to spill the dross into Benedict's waiting psi field. "It's taking up less space, but it's still the same trash. Actually, it's more, and I'm not sure how that spiky dross will get into the vault. You can't spin that."

The dross in Benedict's field flared brilliantly, and then it was gone. "You don't have to," he said as he picked up the spiky, ugly thing. "It will be stored in a separate underground silo."

My eyes narrowed as I imagined that. If a hundred pules made a thimble-size nugget of frozen dross, then the amount in the vault would make . . . one the size of the auditorium? *Good God!*

"Grady, we've been monitoring the lab's waste morgue for months," Laura coaxed. "Anton hasn't seen any indication that it attracts shadow. There's no activity. None."

Until the day there is. It sounded too good to be true and I didn't trust it.

Benedict's jaw tightened at my disbelief. "There's no difference between storing it inert and storing it when it's malleable other than one causes trouble and the other doesn't."

He had a point, but what happened when it was stored wasn't my biggest worry. No, my biggest worry was that if there was a way to make dross inert, magic use would rise dramatically, with very little reason to take care of the resultant dross.

"Benedict? Benedict!" came Anton's shout from the balcony, and I looked up.

"Good God," Benedict muttered as Laura wanded the area clean. "Now what?"

Anton stomped past the offices and break room, a sparkling drift of dross trailing him. "You did this, didn't you!" the angry man said as he started down the stairs.

I took a breath to warn him as, with a little ping of distant sensation, the dross following him broke. Anton's anger shifted to panic as his foot slipped right off a step and he went down.

"Anton!" Laura exclaimed as the disoriented man reached to stop his fall. His hand smacked into a railing post, and with a little crack, the metal rivet popped free.

I gasped as Anton caught himself, his butt finding the stair as the broken post flipped end over end through the air to land straight up in the free-rat enclosure like a flagpole.

"Shadow spit, are you okay?" Benedict stood, lab stool scraping, as the dazed man sat on the step, pale from the narrow miss. It was a good twenty feet down.

My gaze, though, was on the rats. One had already gone to investigate, climbing up the post until its weight shifted it and it tipped majestically over to land on the railing.

"Ah, the rats?" I warned as the animal leapt for freedom, scuttling across to the wide retaining wall and from there to the floor.

"Catch it!" Laura called as two more rats scurried up the post.

"He's headed for the cages," Anton blurted, red and sweating as he pointed from his high perch.

Laura and Benedict went for the rats. I went for the enclosure, grabbing the post before any more animals could escape. Post in hand, I turned to one of the runaways, inhaling to set up a psi field right over it. Exhaling, I made it as thick as I could. It wouldn't stop a determined effort, but it was enough, and the confused rat slid to a halt at the sensation.

"Got one!" Laura sang out, and I looked to see that she'd done nearly the same thing with a spell, and with a little thump, the rat fell over, stunned by the suggestion that it was tired and needed to sleep.

"Nice work, ladies." Benedict smiled, lodestone in his ring glowing as a third psi field settled over the last rat, carrying an attraction spell. He might be good with manipulating heat, but he had clearly developed his earth magic as well, and the rat squeaked, fixed to the cool tile until Benedict grabbed him by the tail and picked him up. "Wow, Petra," he said as the rat hung helplessly. "I didn't know you could make a psi field strong enough to hold something. That's on par with anything a mage can do."

I smiled, feeling the compliment. "Yeah? I'm beginning to see how you kept all those balloons on the ceiling with no helium." I scooped up my rat and let it settle on my arm. They were wickedly smart but docile. I wasn't worried about getting bitten.

"Laura, quick thinking," Benedict added as she brought her rat back to the enclosure, a distasteful grimace on her face. "This could have been a lot worse."

"It is," Anton said from above as I dropped my rat over the side of the enclosure. His skinned hand was fisted about something, and I felt a sliver of warning at his hateful expression aimed at me. I didn't like Anton, and the feeling seemed to be mutual.

Laura wiped her hands on her lab coat, clearly not liking having touched the rat. "Good God, Anton. You're covered in dross. No wonder you fell. What happened?"

"She happened," he said as he stomped down the last of the stairs, the sparkling haze in tow. "Almost every one of today's samples is attracting shadow. She did something to them."

I jumped, startled when he threw an object at my feet. It hit with a little ping, and Laura lurched to get the inert dross before it was lost.

"Petra didn't do anything. It's got to be a mistake," Benedict said, his expression a mix of worry and disbelief.

Anton's chin lifted as he settled in before me. "The only mistake was letting you bring your high school crush onto this project. I told you she would sabotage it."

My lips parted in outrage. "Excuse me? I did *not* sabotage your ugly dross spikes. If they went bad, they did it all on their own."

"Yeah?" Anton's hands fisted and relaxed. "I have run thousands of spikes past that shadow with nary a quiver. You tell me why today it tried to eat them and then me."

"How should I know?" I said, my anger growing as Laura fingered the spike he'd thrown at me. "I didn't even know you had shadow on-site until a few moments ago."

"It reacted?" Brow furrowed, Benedict took the spike from Laura. "Are you sure?"

"Yes, I'm sure." Anton glowered at me. "It got through the first wall before I stopped it."

"Shadow gets smarter the longer it exists," I said. "It probably figured out that your cooled dross is palatable. You need a new shadow." But just the fact that the shadow *had* figured it out was a problem all in itself. Benny's process wouldn't be viable without a ton of safeguards.

"Oh, yeah. You'd like that, wouldn't you," Anton said as Laura settled into her workstation with the spiky dross. "She did something to that shadow." He turned to Benedict, eyes narrowed. "She was here by herself yesterday. And then this morning. She could have done it then."

"I was making sure you had a clean work environment," I said, but no one was listening.

"Okay. Calm down," Benedict soothed. "We can figure this out. We need to know what changed, the shadow or the dross. Do we have any samples from the old lab to run past it?"

Anton shifted uneasily. "Ah . . ."

Laura peered over her glasses. "The shadow is fine," she said, tapping the screen. "It's the dross. It's still inert, but somewhere we lost the tight molecular structure. It's basically a shadow button."

"See? She did something to the samples." Expression ugly, Anton squinted at me. "The shadow busted right out of containment to get to them. I'm lucky I'm not dead!"

Work with shadow long enough, and it happens, I thought, but I wasn't about to say it. The dross he was trailing made sense now. He'd have to do some high-level magic to contain it.

"Good God, Anton. Are you okay?" Laura asked, and the man seemed to find a new confidence.

"I don't care how long you've known her," Anton intoned, a stiff finger jabbing at me. "She's here to shut us down because our process will put an end to the loom and the sweepers, make her no better than a mundane because *none* of them can do any magic."

"Anton!" Laura said, eyes wide at the insult.

I stayed where I was, my chin lifting. "I want to see the shadow react," I said, and Benedict nodded.

"Me too," he said, and a feeling of gratitude rose up. He believed me.

At that, Anton seemed to deflate. "I, ah . . . I destroyed it."

"It's gone?" Benedict's expression was pained. "That shadow was a fifth of our budget!"

"You'd rather I let it kill me?" Anton said, but a hint that he might have made a mistake pinched his brow.

"So all we have is your word that it reacted?" I said. "Sounds as if you're the saboteur, not me."

"You little—"

"Anton," Benedict interrupted, and I pushed off from the low retaining wall.

"Is that why I'm here?" I said, ticked. "To be your scapegoat? Get off my case, Anton. If your spikes are attracting shadow, it's not my fault."

Anton took a step, hands fisted.

"Whoa, whoa, whoa!" Benedict drew Anton back, his nervous laugh fooling no one. "Everyone, relax. This is the first time we've seen a reaction from shadow in over six months. It's not Petra's doing. We moved buildings and changed something is all. How long will it take to get a new shadow? We need to run some of the old samples past it along with the new to verify what you saw."

Anton had begun to calm, but I didn't think it was because he agreed. "I, ah, a week or two?" he said reluctantly.

Benedict winced. "Petra, you brought one in a few days ago. Is it still available?"

Last I knew, it was still sitting in Darrell's loom waiting to be spun into the vault, but I wasn't going to tell them that.

"You brought in shadow?" Laura said, her voice high. "Like, caught it? Alive?"

"In a vodka bottle," Benedict said, and Laura's lips parted.

Yeah, I'm bad, I thought even as I appreciated her surprise. "It's my job, and before you ask, the shadow is gone. It was too smart to use and was destroyed." Okay, that last had been a lie, but they couldn't have it. It had been sucking on a rez for who knew how long. Which was probably why the rez had been dormant, now that I thought about it.

"Mmmm." Benedict leaned against the counter, his mood lifting as the tension eased. "It will pinch the budget, but I'll ask if we can work the cost into the building move."

"Take it out of her pay," Anton said belligerently. "She's the one who tampered with the process and set it off."

"Yeah, well, I'm not the one who panicked and killed it," I snapped.

Anton's face went purple. "You shut up, you little dross-eater!"

I recoiled as if slapped, and Laura gasped. "Anton!" she said, face red.

My eyes narrowed. "You want to say that again? I don't think the rats heard you."

"Anton," Benedict said, his expression horrified. "That language is totally inappropriate in a work setting. Grady, I am so sorry."

"Don't apologize for me," Anton said hotly. "If anyone needs to apologize, it's her. She's making things up to cover for her mistake." But a slight wrinkle in his brow said he thought he might have gone too far.

"Okay." Benedict glanced at his watch, his embarrassment obvious. "It's early, but I'm calling lunch. Everyone back here in an hour. Without their attitudes, please."

I tensed as Anton spun on his heel and stormed up the stairs, his feet finally going silent on the carpet.

"Ah . . . right." Laura looked between Benedict and me, then slid off her stool. "Anton?" she called, low heels clicking as she followed him. "Anton! Let me run a psi field over you before you hurt yourself. You're covered in dross. How did you kill that shadow?"

Just fire me now, I thought as I returned to the bench and grabbed the empty foam rack.

"Grady, I'm sorry about Anton," Benedict said as I tried to smack the rack on the counter, but it was foam, and yeah . . . "He knows better than that. I think he's scared from that shadow and lashing out."

I didn't turn around, settling my ass on the stool before the machine. *Rationalize it. Sure. It doesn't mean anything then, does it.*

Benedict turned off Laura's equipment with a click. The almost subliminal whine vanished, and my slight headache eased. "Um, the dross is still inert, even if it is expanded. There are lots of reasons we might have lost shadow immunity. We need to identify what it is and account for it. It's a setback, but I'm more worried about getting another shadow. Problems are part of the science. We'll figure it out." He hesitated. "Do you want to go to lunch? You and me. My treat." He winced. "Unless you'd rather not. I know how you are about paying your own way."

A tiny wedge of anger melted, and I eyed his pinched expression. He looked kind of forlorn there, a little lost. "Thanks, but I'm going to fill a rack and then grab a quick bite."

Benedict leaned against the counter, a piece of that frozen dross in his hand—probably to convince me it was harmless. It wasn't working. I could smell his aftershave, and the clean scent went right to my core. *Go away, Benny.*

"Um, about Anton," he finally said. "I'll talk to him." He hesitated, watching as I fixed an ampoule in place. "What he called you is not on the red-flag list, but do you want to file a complaint?"

"No." Uncomfortable, I opened the gate and focused on the drifting haze, collecting a wad of it in a psi field and dragging it into the calibration tube and past the sensor. He looked too good there to ignore, standing beside the counter in his lab coat, his worry pinching his brow—and yet ignore him I did as he eased himself down on the nearby stool.

"Still, he had no right to call you a, ah, what he did. If you don't file harassment charges, I will. He called you that to shut down communication. He needs a formal reprimand or he'll think what he did was acceptable."

I glanced up, surprised. Another knot of anger eased, and I snapped the gate shut when the machine dinged. "No. It's only a word. And as you say, it's not on the red-flag list."

"It's up to you, but I still want to take you to lunch."

The measured dross went into the ampoule and I sealed it. *Dang, he smells good.* "Benedict, I appreciate what you're trying to do, but you just had shadow identify your frozen dross as yummy goodness, and you'll forgive me if I'm not convinced that eight months of watching stored dross is long enough to know if that spiky mess is going to stay that way."

I thought he'd be mad, but Benedict brightened, his expression making him more attractive yet. "Hence the live-animal trials," he said as he rolled the inert dross in his hands. "And I haven't been working on this for eight months. I've been working on it since I was ten."

"Ten?" I echoed, and he nodded, a rueful smile softening his eyes. That was about the time he moved to my school. I remembered the day. I had been so excited. *Silly girl.*

"That was when I managed my first mage event. I didn't know about the dross, couldn't see it. My dog picked it up. Three seconds later, he snapped his lead and ran out into traffic." Benedict's focus blurred as he looked at the dross in his hand. "I swore I'd find a way to make it safe. That something I made hurt something I loved was intolerable."

"Mackerel, right?" I said, remembering Benedict talking about him as we made "cheer" posters for the hallway. I'd known he had a dog, but the story was new. "Like the fish."

Benedict grinned. "Because that's what he smelled like. Anyway, he scared the crap out of me. And my mom."

"You ran out after him," I said as I lured two hundred pules out of the dispenser.

"Yep." Benedict studied the dross in his hand, shifting it back and forth. "That's why we had to move. My mom blew up the road between me and the oncoming car. Saved me a lot of pain, but memories had to be shifted, and adjusted thoughts stick better when the person who caused them isn't there to remind you."

He smiled ruefully, and I swear something in my gut flip-flopped.

"They blamed it on a freak gas line explosion." Head down, Benedict rolled the spiky dross across the lab bench, his curls falling into his eyes, making him look endearingly vulnerable. "I've spent my entire adult life building on the existing technology of dross buttons and rez research, and I've seen a lot of freaky things. We'll figure out what parameter we changed, and then we will know that much more about it. It happens when you're working with applied science. But for now, we have a working product."

He wasn't worried, but I was. "Can I see it?" I said, my chest hurting as I held out my hand and he put the solidified dross in it.

I silently studied the sensation of spiky velvet against me. It didn't feel like normal dross. The outer layer was solid, but I could sense a malleable core, trapped behind the cold-treated skin. *Oh, that can't be good.*

"Okay," I all but whispered as I extended it to him, stifling a shudder when Benedict's hand touched mine and the stuff seemed to quiver at its center. "But you need to slow it down. The process might be safe in an industrial setting where you have protocols, but I saw how hot you needed to get it. I can tell you right now that not everyone can heat it that high or freeze it that fast or deep enough. You're working from a scientific principle of precision and dedication, but what about the office assistant who is juggling three bosses and a deadline that was twenty minutes ago? What if the process isn't performed properly?"

Benedict's relief that I was talking was kind of embarrassing. "Good question," he said, voice bright. "If the process isn't performed properly, either on the heating end or in the cooling period, the dross won't turn solid. You know right away if it doesn't work."

I couldn't match his enthusiasm. The thought of even one person trying and failing and trying again, each time making more dross until their traps were full and overflowing in the unfulfilled promise of cutting their sweeper fees, made me ill.

"Grady, the university wants this," Benedict said, clearly seeing my reluctance.

"And what the university wants, the university gets."

"Generally speaking," he said, his sudden, boys-club confidence scratching through his previous allure like nails on a chalkboard. *This is who he is, Petra. Stop thinking with your lady parts.* "Which is why the process is being tested by our beta users even as we speak. What we're doing here is for long-term studies."

My expression blanked. *Beta users?* "Who? When?"

"Since yesterday," he said, his obvious pride marred by my unease. "Phase two was enlarged from live-animal studies to include a study group to collect and analyze frozen dross created in a real-world setting."

"Who?" I said again, alarmed. "Who is using it?"

He shrugged. "Students?" Benedict studied the spiky dross in his hand, then flicked it into the trash with the used ampoules. "The official release will be on graduation."

Tomorrow? I slid from the stool, pulse fast as I went to fish the spike out. "It's in use," I whispered as I cradled the inert dross as if it were a grenade, not sure what to do with it but damn sure it didn't belong in the mundane trash stream. I felt sick as I imagined his careless attitude all over campus. The theory behind the process wasn't hard. Those in the study would tell their friends, and by week's end, everyone would be trying to do it—all of them tossing their waste in the trash, partly because they didn't care but mostly to stick it to the sweepers.

My grip tightened on the spiky nugget of bad luck. It wasn't inert; it was waiting.

Worried, I started for the stairs.

"Great!" Benedict called, the geniusly stupid lout misunderstanding. Smiling, he looked at his phone. The screen was cracked, but then again, his always was. "You ready for lunch? I've got a standing reservation at Chomps."

Of course you do. "I'm getting my sticks," I said, breathless. "And then I'm going home to write up my findings, which I will then file with the sweepers' guild. Then I'm probably going to have to move because I'm going to get fired and won't be able to afford my mortgage. And you know what? I don't care. This is a time bomb," I said, holding the spiky thing up between two fingers. "Even if it never attracts shadow again, the dross this campus alone will make trying to duplicate your process is going to flood the streets. The world isn't like you, Benedict. It doesn't share your passion for positive change that requires dedication and commitment. People will always take the cheaper, faster way. If they didn't, we wouldn't have to pick up their trash."

"You can't quit," Benedict said, red in anger. "I *gave* you this job!"

"You didn't *give* me anything," I said, hating that he assumed working for him was a coveted position—hating myself for thinking he was anything more than he was in high school. "My boss forced me to take it, and I'm done. You guys are on your own."

11

⁓

'M ONLY HAPPY WHEN IT RAINS," SHIRLEY MANSON CROONED, MY EARBUDS MAIN-
lining attitude straight into my brain. Garbage fit my mood perfectly, and it seemed only fitting when my phone gave a warning
beep and threw itself into power-saving mode. "Shadow snots," I
whispered sourly as the music died.

Annoyed, I jerked the earbuds out and scooted my chair deeper
into the shade of the coffeehouse's umbrella. Between the glare and
the afternoon wind pushing my curls into my eyes, it was hard to see
my laptop's screen as I sat outside and worked up my resignation letter. It wasn't for Benedict—he'd gotten the message loud and clear.
No, this was for Ryan and the university's sweepers' guild—and my
chest hurt.

I could've gone inside where it was cool except that Pluck was
with me. I could have done this at home if I wasn't avoiding any
chance of running into Ashley. The ice in my coffee had melted, and
the table jerked every time that damned roadrunner across the parking lot dared Pluck to chase him. In short, I was having a bang-up
afternoon—and now I had to find an outlet.

I looked up from the faded screen, hot and envious of the couple
across the patio as they chilled their coffees with a flash of magic. One

waved the dross from the table to the tiled patio, and I thought about memorizing their faces; they'd need me someday.

And then I slumped, tired and jaded. "Give it up, Petra," I said as I tucked my feet deeper under Pluck's middle. It wasn't worth it.

The wind had pulled my hair from my short-cord, and I retied it as I read over the letter already digitally signed and dated. *Unable to perform the requested duties . . . Hereby tender my resignation . . . Thank you for the opportunity . . . Blah, blah, blah . . .* But still I hesitated, my finger curled under my palm, reluctant to hit send.

Can I work with Benedict and his team? I thought, wanting to be sure. Was it pride making me walk away? Or anger that Anton was right in that I counted myself less because I couldn't do magic? Did I have a responsibility to stick it out in the hopes of making something wrong less bad? Was I overreacting?

The hot, dusty wind was no relief, pushing through my hair as I touched my pocket and the spiky dross I'd taken, but my gaze was on my dad's sticks, safe in the blueprint tube beside me, a touchstone of guidance. *What would you do, Dad?*

A sour huff escaped me. My dad would have pinned Benedict to his chair and barked at him until Benedict listened. But my dad never would have been asked to be part of the team to begin with. They needed someone they could cow, someone with that perfect blend of accountability but no voice to stop the madness. Quitting might be the only way to bring to light what they were doing.

Am I rationalizing? I thought, wincing when a mundane walked right into that wisp of dross the couple had discarded. Two more steps and it broke, causing the man to trip on a raised patio block. His coffee spilled as he lurched, but he caught himself, red-faced as the two women giggled. He was just some guy paying the cost for their magic. No big deal.

I averted my gaze in embarrassment, my attention drawn to a glint under the scarred aloe between the patio and the parking lot.

Someone had left a broken bottle, and a chunk of it was catching the light to look like a tiny slice of the sun itself. I slumped as I imagined Benedict's process filtering through the campus by way of parties and best friends, and with a new resolution, I hit send.

Done. My heavy sigh drew Pluck's attention, and the big dog panted happily up at me. All too soon, though, my flush of relief ebbed, pushed out by the memory of Anton's accusation. I was not trying to shut them down because Benedict's process would drastically reduce the need for sweepers, turning an entire demographic into little more than mundanes unable to do magic and no longer having anything of value to add to mage society. But as I studied the couple with their chilled coffee and smug attitudes, an old hurt that I couldn't bind to a lodestone rose anew. And I let it.

I had tried—tried and failed, both in public and in private, again and again, until I had to admit that the sunlight that the mages used so glibly would not stoop to speak to me, that I would never be able to link my mind to it through a lodestone.

My attempts had not been entirely tilting at windmills. Every so often a sweeper was able to bind to a lodestone and acquire the ability to manipulate the energy the stone collected. The unique combination of mage and sweeper skills was necessary to fix the loom if the vault broke. It hadn't failed to impress me that Spinners usually found their ability later in life. *I am not doing this,* I thought as my gaze returned to the broken glass amid the stones.

And yet I leaned toward it, almost falling out of my chair as I worked the small shard of glass free and brushed the dirt away. *Don't,* I thought, but Darrell's advice to take the Spinner skills test pulled at me. She thought I might be a Spinner, that my skills handling shadow might mean something. I had tried and failed so many times. What was one more?

My thumb rubbed the last of the dirt off, and I held the shard to catch the light. It was said that the first lodestones were tubes of glass created when lightning hit sand, and whereas many stones were handed down through the generations, they were no more powerful than the ones you made yourself. Most mages, like Ashley, had several, using and discarding them like jewelry or when fashion shifted.

Just give me one, I thought as I exhaled, focusing my awareness about the broken glass, feeling its warmth grow in my palm as the sun hit it. I eased my posture, exhaling as I emptied my mind of everything. With a soft *om* of breath, I felt myself center, a psi field easily slipping around the glass as if it were an errant drift of dross.

A smile found me as the collected warmth of the sun in the glass pushed into the corners of my mind, spreading from there to my body. This I could do. Every sweeper could. It was getting the glass to cool—slowing the heated molecules that made it up so you could bind it to your thoughts—that was the jump I could not make.

Slow, I thought, feeling the energy the sun poured into it humming through the glass, warming my hand. *Cool,* I whispered in my mind, even as a quiver of restlessness began to grow. Like an itch, it gnawed, and I forced more psi energy into the glass, trying to quiet it. *Be still* . . .

For one glorious moment, I felt a lessening of wrongness . . . and then the energy the glass was absorbing billowed up in a flame of heat, burning me from the inside out.

My fingers sprang open and the glass fell. It hit the pavers with a ping and shattered in a tinkling of glass. It wasn't the fall that had broken it but the quick influx of energy.

"Shadow snot," I whispered, my thumb pressed to the slight burn as the glass dissolved right before my eyes, fracturing into sand. Embarrassed, I rubbed the hot sand into a flat nothing with the toe of my shoe. Pluck whined, and I gave him a pat to tell him it was okay. I'd cracked glass before, but nothing like this. It wasn't magic. I'd failed to cool the glass enough to form a connection, and it had shattered. Big whoop.

"Cheap glass," I said to Pluck, slumping as I drew my psi energy back and let my will settle into well-worn patterns of thought. I was what I was, and resigned, I nervously checked my email to see if

Ryan had gotten back to me. My heart gave a thump at the little envelope in my inbox, and then I frowned. It wasn't from Ryan.

"Herm?" I whispered, feeling a little ill. What the hell did he want? And how had he gotten my email? But then I figured it out. If he had my dad's old phone, then he had everything: number, email, old texts, pictures. *Yuck . . .*

Uncomfortable, I opened it up. Petra, it's imperative I see you. Please call me at your dad's number. H.

I closed my laptop. *Yeah, like that's going to happen.* I didn't have time for this. And why would I want to talk to him? My dad would be alive if not for Herm trying to use dross to power magic. Self-imposed exile should be the least of it.

Shoulders slumped, I stared across the cracked parking lot and watched the roadrunner stalking lizards in the sun as the two women got up and left. It had been ten years, and it still hurt. Herm had killed him as sure as if he had held his head under water. The vault had cracked, and instead of working with the rest of the Spinners to contain it, Herm had tried to seal the vault alone using the power of dross, calling up the shadow that had killed my dad.

My dad had paid the price for Herm's theories that Spinners could handle dross-based magic, finding an age-old balance that we had forgotten so long ago that it had fallen into myth. The man had been shunned without trial for fear of him using it as a soapbox to push his foul theories. But my dad was still dead, and it still hurt. Herm Ivaros was a dross-eater if anyone was, filthy and uncouth, and that my dad had paid for his mistakes still burned.

"What is it, Pluck?" I said listlessly as the dog began to wiggle and whine, making the table jump when he pulled to the end of his lead. Clearly he saw someone he knew, but my smile faded as I followed his attention to Ashley coming across the lot, a big dog toy in her hands.

I thought you were away on interviews, I mused as I leaned back, acknowledging her.

"I am so sorry he got out," she said loudly as she halted with those ugly, broken aloe plants between us. "I told Sikes to shove the interviews, and when I came back to talk, I forgot to shut the door. Thanks for telling me he was okay. I totally freaked when I realized he was gone." She hesitated. "You got a minute?"

"Sure," I said flatly, fighting Pluck. "It's a good time, actually." But it wasn't, and I closed my laptop as she pushed sideways through a gap in the plants, her skirt snagging on an errant spine as a hint of dross broke on her.

"Hey, Pluck. How's my big boy?" she cooed, oblivious to the tiny rip as she gave him the toy and sat across from me. "There you go. Chew it up. Make that rat squeak. Get 'em!"

Pluck pulverized the new toy, the harsh squeaks drawing amused smiles from the foot traffic in and out of the coffee shop. Ashley looked more professional than usual in a pair of dressy shoes and nice skirt and top, hot even in the shade of the umbrella. Her best purse sat on the table, making me wonder if she'd told Sikes to stick it because she'd found something better. I wasn't a slob beside her in my jeans, lightweight shirt, and frayed cord holding my hair back, but it was obvious that we belonged in different worlds. "How did you find me?" I asked when her loving on Pluck slowed.

"Drove around until I saw your bike." She gave Pluck a last ear rub, a flash of bad mood crossing her when she noticed the rip in her skirt. "I, ah, wanted to talk to you."

I glanced at my red bike in the rack, obvious among the silver and blues. "You coming back?" I said, hiding the words behind a sip of my blah, diluted coffee.

"No. Petra, I'm sorry I got so mad," she suddenly gushed. "I know you didn't have any choice. I really wanted the position, and you *always* get what you want," she practically whined. "So good at your job. Nothing is hard for you."

I lowered my cup, not believing this. "Seriously?" I said. "Have you seen the crap—" I swallowed my complaint. Her mage status would make her forever blind, and I opened my laptop and glanced over my report. *Poses an unknown security risk compounded by a lack of understanding basic dross properties* . . .

"I'm still looking for a place, but I found a job," she said as she petted Pluck. "And with the increased paycheck, I can afford something on my own."

She wasn't here to get her key, and I eyed her over my screen. "You working in Tucson?"

"No. Right on campus. Um, about Dr. Strom's position. I heard you quit—"

"You heard right," I said flatly. Great. If Ashley had found out, it was all over campus.

"Then it's true?" she said, voice high. "Why? Was it Benedict? What did he do?"

"Benedict didn't *do* anything." *Which is kind of the problem.* "You should call them. They need someone and the job isn't that onerous. You'll fit right in." It sounded bitter even to me, and I hid behind another blah sip of coffee. *Why do I buy this stuff if I can't keep it cold?*

And then my gaze rose from Pluck's squeaky toy to Ashley's pinched brow, my expression blanking as I took in her casual best. There was no way she could have known I'd quit unless she'd already talked to them—talked to them and taken the job.

A surge of anger flashed through me, dying almost as fast. Tired, I saluted her with my melted iced coffee. "Congratulations. Did you buy Pluck's toy before or after you took the job?"

"They called me," Ashley said, her color high. "What did you expect me to do? Say no?" Her expression shifted. "Petra, why did you quit? It's the perfect position."

I reached for the spiked dross in my pocket to show her, then stopped. She'd see it soon enough, and anything I said would fall on deaf ears. I could blame it on Anton, but to claim I was leaving because of something that idiot might have said stuck in my craw. "Ashley, if you ever trusted me, call them up," I said. "Tell them that you won the lottery, anything. Don't take the job. It's a career ender for a mage."

"Are you serious?" Anger colored her cheeks again. "You found fault with it, didn't you. *That's* why you quit? It's going to revolutionize everything! What are you telling everyone?"

I hunched over the table, wishing she'd lower her voice. "The process is flawed," I said, knowing I was talking to a brick wall, even if she had asked. "They're using lab-grade techniques that no one on the street will be able to reproduce. There are ongoing issues with maintaining its shadow-resistance, and they practically lied to me about the release date. This was supposed to be a long-term study, not a last-minute CYA assignment."

"You made up your mind in a day? You didn't even give it a chance!"

She was clearly angry, almost as if she had a vested interest in it, and I stared at her. "I agreed to take the job with the understanding they wanted my opinion," I said, my rising voice making Pluck whine. "They were not listening. They didn't want to listen."

"Were you?" Ashley said tightly, and I pushed back, deeper into the hot shade. "You have to call Ryan. Tell him it's not as bad as you originally thought."

"*I* have to *what?*" I said caustically, and she caught her breath, knowing she'd gone too far. "Ashley, I know you think this is a godsend and that I'm doing this out of spite or to save my job, but all Benedict wants is someone from the sweepers' guild to give their stamp of approval to cover their asses if something goes wrong. I am not changing my report, and I can't believe you asked me to. Listen to your adviser and walk away. They're looking for a scapegoat."

"Petra . . ." Ashley coaxed, looking almost desperate. "It can't be that bad."

"It is!" Frustrated, I put a hand to my forehead, then looked up.

"My God, this is a sucky week. If it's not Benny trying to throw us into a new shadow eclipse, it's my Uncle John wanting to get together. I can't decide which is worse."

"You called him? He's coming?" Ashley's anger vanished in a stark surprise. "When?"

I hesitated at her suddenly stiff posture and wild expression. Alarm? Excitement? *Why does she even care?* "He, um, emailed me. Sometime after graduation, probably," I said, not wanting to talk about it now and knowing if I didn't set it way off in the future she'd worry it to death.

"Um, that's great." Fidgeting, her gaze went across the parking lot to her car parked in a distant spot of shade. My eyes narrowed as I recognized the dark shape in the passenger seat sipping on a cold drink, the car's air-conditioning going. *Sikes?*

"Can I meet him?" she added. My attention jerked back to her and she smiled, thin and anxious. "I've been trying to get you two together for years. I want to be there when he sees you is all."

"Maybe. I don't know if I even want to." Right. Like I was going to introduce Herm Ivaros to her as my uncle? *What a tangled web we weave . . .*

Ashley stood, her chair scraping on the patio. "Um, I gotta go. I have stuff to do."

Graduation, I thought. Between us, Pluck held his new toy, a worried slant to his doggy brow. "Ashley, don't take this job," I said again, but she was backing away, her thoughts on something else.

"Ah, let me know when your uncle comes in. I'll take you both out to dinner. Bye, bean," she said, giving the dog a solid ear rub.

"Ashley?" I called as she pushed through the aloe again. "You're not going to take that job. Tell me you're not taking it!"

"I'll call to get my things when I find a place!" she shouted over her shoulder.

I didn't move, sitting in a narrowing scrap of shade as she walked away. Exhaling, I grabbed my laptop and bent to unhook Pluck to run her down—only to hesitate when someone called my name. It was Ryan, lurching out of his car with his dress shirt half untucked and his tie loose about his neck.

I flashed warm. Apparently he'd gotten my resignation letter.

Torn, I watched Ashley slam her car door shut. On my other side, Ryan frantically waved, clearly wanting to talk. Exhaling, I slumped back into my chair and scrubbed a hand over my eyes. *Shadow spit . . .*

"Late lunch?" I said sourly as he halted before me, his long face flushed from the heat.

"I got your letter. Right in the middle of Benedict's call," he said, breathless. "My God, it's hot out here."

I gestured at the chair in the shade. "I'm not going back. They can't pay me enough."

Ryan sat with a groan and ran a hand over his thinning hair to put it in some sort of semblance of order. "God help me, you made me run. It's got to be a hundred out here. How can you stand it?"

"No dogs inside," I said, glancing down at Pluck panting in the shade.

Ryan dabbed at his neck with a napkin. "I'm not letting you quit the university."

"You made it clear it was work the job or else," I said as I pretended to sip my coffee.

"That was only to get you to do it," he said, wincing. "I'm not accepting your resignation. You're on administrative leave pending a possible return to the lab."

"Then you should fire me now because I'm not going to." I reached to soothe Pluck, and the big dog settled at my feet, panting happily. "How did you find me?"

His attention flicked to the bike rack, and I sighed.

"You drove around until you saw my bike, huh?" A faint smile quirked my lips. Somehow it was okay when a friend did it.

Ryan eased deeper into the hard chair. "I called, actually. You're not exactly unknown on campus. Grady, please reconsider. We need you there. Anton—"

"Isn't the problem," I interrupted, and Ryan blinked, clearly surprised.

"Benedict said he called you a, ah, dross-eater," Ryan said, almost whispering it. "He feels really bad. Said he talked to Anton about his attitude. Language like that in a professional setting is intended to shut down communication and bully—"

"Anton isn't the problem," I said again. "I can handle some ignorant mage calling me names. *This* is the problem." Twisting, I took the spiked dross from my pocket and set it on the table. Ryan stared at it, the pointed obsidian bur looking even more ugly outside.

"Ah, yeah," he said, his attitude telling me he'd seen it before. "I, ah, have to take that."

I snatched it up before his reaching hand could get close. "You know about this?" I accused even as I stifled a shudder at its dead, prickling feel. "You could have warned me."

"I wanted your unvarnished thoughts." His thin eyebrows were high in apology. "It belongs to the lab. Benedict wants it back."

My grip on it tightened as I shook my head, feeling like a fifth grader with a stolen cookie. "Then he shouldn't have thrown it away in the mundane waste stream."

Ryan stiffened. "He . . . damn," he whispered. "He knows better than that."

I held the dross up, perching it between my thumb and finger. "I think he was trying to prove it wasn't dangerous," I admitted. "Has Darrell seen this? It doesn't feel right."

Ryan leaned closer, studying it in my fingertips. "How so?"

A cold feeling slithered up and over me as I angled it into the sun and back to shade, watching the black sheen shift with the temperature. "A hundred pules shouldn't feel active, and it does, even if it is frozen in that tight molecular state." My gaze flicked to him. "There was an issue today. The shadow they've been passing samples past triggered on it."

"It saw it?" Ryan went still, his gaze searching mine.

"And went for it. That idiot, Anton, destroyed the shadow before anyone else could see how it reacted. Laura says the dross still retains its inert condition so it's not going to break, but if shadow is attracted to it, it's not safe."

"Mmmm."

His voice was both doubtful and worried, and I stifled the urge to tighten the cord around my hair when I realized he was looking at it. "All he's done is create a new way to make cheap shadow buttons. Benedict says it's the process of science, but if this stuff attracts shadow, it's too dangerous no matter how cheap it is." My fingers closed around the spiked dross when someone walked past, three overpriced, high-caloric drinks in a one-use tray.

Ryan frowned. I could almost see the thoughts plinking through his mind. "You think it's going to revert?"

"That was my first worry, but not my last, and certainly not my greatest concern," I admitted. "It's still inert, whether shadow is attracted to it or not, and that's where the problem is." Ryan's eyes flicked up from the spiky dross, and I added, "They're ignoring that people are going to misuse the process, either by trying to reduce their trap intake and causing even more dross when they fail to perform it properly and it never solidifies, or if they do manage the process, they will begin to do more magic than is prudent. We have to store it, solid or not. I suppose we could put it in a silo, but it's going to pull dross in from everywhere. Make a mess, best case; make a high-dross zone, worst case. What if it reverts in a high-dross environment? They haven't tested for that."

"I want Darrell to see it," he said, and my shoulders eased as I handed it over.

"Me too," I said, relieved. "It's dross; causing the unlikely to happen is its nature. Are you sure you can't feel it?"

Again he was silent, focus going distant as he stared at it. "No," he finally said. "But I respect your perceptions. The last time we ignored a Grady's advice, we got the shadow eclipse of 2014."

I didn't have to look at my sticks. I could feel them hanging from the back of my chair, and I shifted my foot to touch them, finding reassurance.

"I still regret losing your dad," Ryan said, clearly following my thoughts. "He was an extremely talented Spinner, and I know he loved you. I'm glad you have his sticks. He had a great feel for dross." A wistful fondness found him. "He could see it like I'm seeing you. Play with it." Ryan shifted as he pocketed the dross. "I once saw him use a wand to sculpt a dross drift into the shape of a rabbit. He was amazing with a wand. Are you sure you won't reconsider?" he asked, and my focus sharpened on him.

"To be your spy?" I said. "No. So maybe you should accept my resignation."

"Oh, just shoot me now!" he complained, head lolling to the umbrella over us. "I'm sorry I ever said that. Look, you don't have to go back, but it would have been helpful to have a pair of eyes on the inside." Hesitating, he scanned the parking lot. "Ashley took the job. Her opinions will be less than useful even if she would tell us. But I guess you heard that."

I grimaced. He'd seen her walking away, heard what she said. "Yep," I said. "But you don't need me in there now. They moved phase three up. Big reveal is tomorrow at graduation."

"Benedict doesn't have permission . . ." Ryan's eyes narrowed, making me think I should have opened with this. "This is Ulrich's doing, the money-grubbing idiot. He has the right to grant permission for early releases, but the entire council was supposed to be in unanimous agreement before phase two was implemented, much less a campus-wide release. Are you sure?"

"That's what Benedict said," I said, and his focus blurred. "That's why I quit, not because Anton is a prejudiced butt-wipe. Benedict released the process to the study groups yesterday, and after he announces it at graduation, there is no putting it back in the bottle."

"Ulrich has overstepped himself." Ryan's brow furrowed, and his gaze went to my laptop. "Could you do me a favor? Can you write something up and get it in my inbox before six tonight? I can't have been the only council member unaware of the soft release, much less of their graduation plans. Anything you say will help me prove my point, but I need it in writing. Can you make that deadline?" he asked, and I nodded, a sliver of hope finding me.

"Great." Ryan stood and absently tucked his shirttail in. "In the meantime, I'm going to show your little nugget to Darrell. Get her take on it. She should have been allowed to study it in the first place." He turned to his car, clearly eager to be gone. "Write your report and relax. I've got more pull with the university than Benedict thinks. If it wasn't for us, they wouldn't be here."

My pocket felt light without the dross in it, and I managed a smile. "Thanks, Ryan."

He nodded, his gaze touching on my blah-warm coffee. "Six at the latest. And try to keep your personal feelings out of it. Meet me at the loom tomorrow before sweeper shift change and I'll tell you how it went. Darrell will have some feel for this stuff by then, too."

"Will do," I said, and Ryan began walking to his car. He got all of two steps before spinning back.

"Oh, yeah," he said, his gaze on my hair. "Is that the old cord from your chewed sticks?"

I touched the frayed silk. There was still some knotted dross in it, but it was useless for anything now but holding my hair back. "Yeah . . ." I said hesitantly.

"Darrell would like to see it," he said, and I began to unwind it. "She and Dr. Brown are trying to track down how you got ahold of inert dross."

"It was a prank," I said as I handed it over.

"Even so." He looked at it in his hand. "Ah, tonight. Six."

I nodded, and he spun away, his jog back to his car a listless slog in the heat.

Laptop open, I reached for my coffee, surprised at the layer of ice on it. The Spinner had cooled it for me. "We might not have to move after all, Pluck," I said, and the happy dog huffed and settled down to wait.

12

⁓

BIKE HELMET TUCKED UNDER MY ARM, I SCHLUMPED DOWN THE STAIRS TO THE loom, my shoes scraping loudly on the concrete steps. It was early, making the usual ten-minute ride into five despite the campus filling up with alumni wandering about with their cups of coffee and over-priced croissants. The four-acre commons under the paloverde trees had been busy, the echo of the sound check reflecting off the nearby buildings as racks of chairs for tonight were rolled onto the temporary stage to be set up by grumpy students before it got hot.

I was doubly glad I'd dodged cleanup duty and the inevitable result of alcohol and magic mixing freely. It would be worse this year with everyone trying to master Benedict's new process if Ryan hadn't stopped it. I was hoping he had—even if it meant Ashley would never speak to me again. If they hadn't identified why it was attract-ing shadow, it wasn't safe.

Impatient for news, I hit the entry pad hard when I reached the bottom of the stairs. "Petra Grady. Sweeper first-class," Henry the computer announced as if I were the queen, and I went in, the cool of the loom a welcome relief from the stairway's dead air.

"Grady! Perfect timing," Ryan called, and my eager steps faltered as I saw him and Darrell seated at the big yin and yang table with their oversize mugs of coffee.

The loom was otherwise empty. It wasn't unusual this early on a Friday, but they looked suspicious, and the light strains of Darrell's ambient guitar music made a pleasant background as I hung my helmet and stick case on a hook by the door. That bottle of shadow I'd brought in was still in the loom, and I swear, a snakelike head lifted as if to find me.

"I'm in trouble, aren't I," I said flatly, and Ryan chuckled.

"That's your first thought?" he said, but his cheerful mood had an undertone of unease. Clearly the meeting with the university's board hadn't gone well.

"Good morning, Grady." Darrell resettled herself on the half-circle couch across from Ryan. My frayed short-cord was in her hand, and she set it on the table. "Coffee is in the pot."

"Smells great," I said as I went to the spotless counter. I seldom saw the kitchen clean. But I usually didn't show up at the loom until nearly closing and the sink was full of mugs. The coffee, too, was decidedly fresher. I could actually see through the carafe steaming on the plate. But my reach for it hesitated when I noticed the pristine white mug waiting beside it, my name embossed on it in a beautiful silver foil.

Okay . . . I thought as I sent the coffee chattering into it. I turned to the two Spinners, wondering if I was seeing their daily shift-change tradition or if this was just for me.

"So . . . you weren't able to stop the campus-wide release?" I said as I sat between them.

Darrell's brow rose, her wrinkles making her appear old. "What makes you say that?"

"You don't seem happy," I said, and Ryan hunched deeper over his knees, his own chipped, personalized mug before him on the table.

"It's still a go," he said, clearly annoyed. "Fools out for fame and notoriety. We are a university, not a money-making machine."

The coffee was hot, and I blew across it. "You should start a gossip thread telling everyone that the sweepers were against this. The mages already think we're money-grabbing asses, but at least this way when it hits the fan we aren't the scapegoats."

Ryan slumped deep into the couch, his sour expression almost hidden behind his mug. "The board thinks we're against it because it ends our cradle-to-grave dross involvement."

"Oh, I don't see that happening. Unless they plan on shooting it to the sun." I hesitated, eyebrows high in question. "So . . . did you feel its core?" I asked Darrell.

"No. But that doesn't mean you didn't."

"It's a shame Anton destroyed their shadow," I added as Ryan and Darrell exchanged an odd look. "If he had more guile, I'd say this was his warped plan to get me kicked off the team. Blaming me for the dross regaining its shadow attraction." I huffed. "Like I can change the molecular structure of dross."

"Mmmm." Focus distant, Darrell sipped her coffee. "Ryan, remind me to run some additional tests before we okay putting Dr. Strom's waste in the vault. Collect a few more of those spiny dross balls and see what happens when they're exposed to high levels of dross."

"You want to put it in the vault?" I said, thinking that was a bad idea.

"It's that or a hole in the ground." Darrell's beaded hair clinked as she leaned forward to set her coffee down. "Grady, do you always wear your trap's short-cord around your hair?"

Startled at the topic shift, I nodded, my gaze going to it as she pushed it closer for me to take. "Yes, but I usually don't have two of them," I said dryly, fingers bumping over the familiar knots as I tied it around my hair. I hadn't worn my new red one today, the one she'd given me with my dad's old sticks. "Did you and Dr. Brown find anything out about the dross I used?"

"Yeah . . ." Ryan drawled, glancing at the loom and that bottle of shadow. "He doesn't keep records that long, but he did verify the dross within the knots is inert."

Great. I was wearing a shadow button. No wonder I kept running into the stuff. "Well, what's the plan?"

Darrell's eyes widened. "What makes you think we have a plan?"

I set my mug down, the porcelain grating as I turned it a hundred and eighty degrees to make my name obvious. "Why am I here? I'm not going back to Benedict's team. Don't ask."

Ryan took a breath, but Darrell interrupted him with a terse "How long has it been since you tried to bind to a lodestone?"

I flushed, wondering if Ryan had seen me yesterday. "Why?" I asked, evading her.

Ryan smirked, his mug almost lost in his clasped hands. "You quitting Benedict's group has left you in a precarious position."

"Yeah?" I barked. "I'm not worried about my paycheck." But I was.

Ryan chuckled. "We're not asking you to go back."

"Good, because Ashley already has the job."

Darrell waved a graceful hand in the air, clearly trying to defuse my anger. "Good Lord, Ryan. Leave it to you to mess up good news. Grady, as of this morning, you're my apprentice."

My next words choked to nothing. "What?" I said blankly, my attention flicking to the mug and back to her. "I'm not a Spinner. I can't bind to a lodestone."

Darrell beamed. "Not yet you can't."

"But I'm not a Spinner." Panic wound about my heart. I liked who I was, what I did.

"Neither was I," Darrell said in a quiet confidence. "Until I bound to a Spinner's lodestone."

A Spinner's lodestone? I thought, confused, as I shifted my gaze between Darrell's satisfaction and Ryan's eagerness. *There's a difference?*

"Grady," Darrell said, and I started, scrambling to catch up. "Despite the university's love affair with Benedict's research, the sweepers' guild agrees that widespread use of his process will be problematic, their conclusion in no little account due to your foresight at how the general public will abuse it. In light of that, your name shot to the top of a very short list. We need another loom-dedicated Spinner. Someone who can handle dross and do magic both."

They want me to man the loom? Alarmed, I stood to leave. "Then hire a mage and teach him or her how to collect dross. Done."

Ryan put a foot up on the table to block my easy way out. "To do their job, a Spinner must be able to touch dross. Not just roll it in a psi field. Mages can't without disastrous results. You *can*, however, teach a sweeper to do magic—with the right lodestone."

Good God, they were serious. "I can't bind to a lodestone," I said, angry that they would play with my emotions like this. "I've tried."

"Sit," Darrell insisted, pointing until I plunked down on the couch. "We need a dedicated fifth. Someone who can touch dross as easily as you see and touch that mug of coffee."

I squinted at them, peeved. Fine. I could play their game. It wasn't as if I had a job to get to. "I tried to make a lodestone yesterday. I broke it."

I thought they'd be disappointed, but Ryan grinned. "Told you she was the right choice."

"She's our only choice, and a good one." Darrell's faint wrinkles melted into a fond expression. "Don't fixate on failure," she added. "Trying and failing isn't bad. I'm more pleased that you tried than upset that you failed."

It sounded like wise-old-woman crap to me, and I made a sour face. To be able to do magic would be fantastic. But mages were mages, and sweepers were sweepers. Sure, most Spinners didn't find their ability until their forties, but to dangle a long-abandoned hope before me like this was cruel. *Not to mention I am nowhere near that old.*

"You don't want to man the loom, fine," Darrell said, her lips quirked in amusement. "How about this. Ryan and I teach you how to bind to a lodestone. If Benedict's new process doesn't cause problems, you can watch over the loom a few days out of the week and I can plant a lemon tree in my garden. If nothing else, you can ice your own coffee."

I stared at my new mug and sighed. *Stuck in a sunless room all day?* But to do magic . . . "This is not me," I said, head shaking. Sure, I complained a lot, but really?

Darrell leaned forward across the table, her dark eyes alight. "It could be."

"Grady, can I talk to you for a moment?" Ryan said, and I groaned as I remembered he was my boss.

Smirking, Darrell levered herself to her feet. "I'll get the stone."

"Why are my choices never my own?" I said, and Ryan inched down the couch.

"I thought you'd jump at this," Ryan said. "It comes with better insurance," he coaxed. "Invites to all the campus functions, from football games to council meetings. A campus parking space under the solar panels. You could get a car."

"I like my bike," I said flatly. I couldn't care less about the football games, but having my opinion heard at a council meeting had a lot of appeal. My aptitude to see and manipulate dross, however, had already gotten me a dead-end job. I didn't want to land in a better-paying but even more mindless career, especially if it put me in the basement watching sweepers come back with stories. "Darrell doesn't even like gardening," I grumped.

"Stop trying to convince her this is for her benefit," Darrell said as she came back. "Grady, we need five Spinners if things go bad."

"Bad, as in how?" I asked, still not believing this was happening.

Darrell's knotted skirt shushed as she swayed closer and sat with a sigh. "We need three to stop a shadow eclipse, but five is safer. Me, Ryan, Akeem, and Marge can't do it alone."

"You think Benedict's new process—" I started.

"Merely a precaution," Ryan said, but I believed his worry line, not his coaxing voice. "The most likely scenario is that when Benedict's process is released, people will find themselves chin deep in dross until they learn how to do it or decide it was a bad idea and stop trying. Sweepers sweep up, things go back to normal. But the signs . . ."

"There are signs?" I pushed to the front of the couch, my elbows on my knees as a headache threatened.

"Shadow turned to promise. Darkness born in light," Ryan said, his voice sing-song. "Black grows, oath fails. Death begets sight. When three souls fall to one. And one in turn is all. Sweeper, Spinner, weaver. Shadow heeds the call."

I stared at them. "The lyrics to 'Light Side of the Dark'?"

"Your dad's favorite song, if I recall." Darrell's wrinkles folded into each other as she patted my knee.

But Ryan's eyes held regret. "Music is an efficient way to make a public-wide statement in a world we are not supposed to exist in."

I slouched, eyeing them in mistrust. "Yeah? According to the song, we all die."

"Jimmy made that part up." Darrell set a tarnished class ring on the table before me. It was a man's ring, too big for anything other than my thumb. The university's logo was on one side, and the sweeper emblem on the other. But it was the stone that held my attention. A dusky green and roughly textured, it was nothing like the transparent glass that most lodestones were. It did, however, look a lot like Darrell's.

"The reality is," Darrell added as I pretended to ignore it, "it took five Spinners to eliminate the shadow the last time it rose, and because of that, we lost your dad. I'm not doing that again. We need to be better prepared."

"For another shadow eclipse? The loom has plenty of dross to handle anything," I said.

Ryan shrugged. "Shadow grows. Light fails. Three become one. One becomes all. Sweeper, Spinner, weaver."

Shadow heeds the call, I finished silently. There was no such thing as a weaver, but it was said a weaver had been able to blend shadow and light, in essence weave good luck and bad luck together to make a new kind of neutral or delphic . . . luck. "You think Benedict's procedure will shift the balance of dross and shadow?" I asked, concerned.

Ryan huffed. "We don't think anything of the kind."

"We're merely thinking of the future," Darrell added. "Regardless, we need to swell our ranks, and we can't pull on a Spinner already working as a teacher or borrow anyone from another loom. Not when we are the premier para university on the continent. And why would we? There should always be five Spinners to every loom who can effectively manipulate dross. We want to give you the tools."

I said nothing. The stone set in the ring didn't appear to be anything special. Actually, it was kind of grungy, with dust filling the rills and bumps that covered the rough, matte greenish-black stone.

"Unless of course you can't bind to a lodestone," Darrell said, and my attention rose to her. "Before I enslave you in the basement, let's see if you can."

I licked my lips, suddenly feeling small between the two of them. "I tried yesterday," I admitted, embarrassed. "I fractured it into sand."

"Really?" Ryan said, but he was impressed, not appalled, and my worry tightened.

Clearly tired of my reticence, Darrell picked up the ring. "Try this. It's sterner stuff."

"Darrell," I protested as it hit my palm—and then my words died. It felt different. It felt . . . alive. "This isn't glass," I said flatly, and Ryan grinned.

"See?" he said triumphantly. "Didn't I tell you?"

Immediately I extended the age-grimed ring to Darrell. "I don't want to break it," I said, feeling its loss even as Darrell reached to take it. "And—"

But Darrell folded her hands around mine, imprisoning it in my palm. Both rough and smooth, the stone seemed to send little pinpricks of sensation into me, but unlike dross, it was cold, not warm. "This can handle anything you can muster," she said, her expression soft in memory. "Even if it *is* glass, naturally formed in the heat of a meteor hit, then cooled when the molten rock and sand were flung into the upper reaches of the atmosphere."

Her hands dropped from around mine and I gazed at the dull stone set in the ring, then at her pendant. Her stone was twice as big and decidedly more green than black.

Ryan inched closer, his eyes on the ring. "It was made not of earth or space but of both."

His ring looks more like hers than mine. I hesitated. *Mine?* Reality slammed into me and I took a shaky breath. The ring was not mine. It wasn't. "I can't bind to a lodestone. I've tried."

"There's a reason you keep failing," Ryan said, encouragingly.

"*And* why you keep trying," Darrell added, and I warmed, embarrassed to have been caught still entertaining adolescent dreams. "Surround it in a psi field and let your energy bring the stone's lattice awake. You already know how. You just need a primed moldavite stone."

I couldn't put the ring down, and as the cold tingles turned warm from my body heat, I ran my thumb across the stone's bumpy ridges and stared into the small flecks of trapped air glinting like whispered promises. Hints of green slumbered at its depth. "I can't do magic."

Darrell's beads clinked as she shook her head. "You can. You're not a sweeper, Grady. You have too much skill with dross. You're a Spinner like your dad. You've been trying to bind the wrong stone in the wrong way."

Could it be that simple? I thought as I studied the heat-warped glass in my hand.

"*That's* a Spinner's lodestone," Ryan said. "Not a mage's. We lost the skill to make them, but we can still bind to one that has been passed down."

Hence it already being set in a ring. My jaw was clenched, and I forced it to relax. "It's been bound before?"

Darrell bobbed her head, shooting Ryan a look when he took a breath to say something. "You only need to quicken it," she said. "Return it to its heat of origin to shake the dust from the latticework, and it will adhere to your psyche. Once you do that, it can hold energy for you until you need it. Day or night."

My pulse quickened. *Heat it up?* I'd have no problem with that. "Why am I only now hearing about this?"

Darrell's hand went protectively to her pendant. "We only have a few left."

"Perhaps a few thousand in the entire world," Ryan added.

"So they don't get handed out to just anyone."

"And we keep their existence a secret." Ryan's brow furrowed in worry. "Otherwise, the university would give them to whoever had the deepest pocket, not the most promising. The most adept."

I blinked fast at his last words. I knew I was good, but to hear it verified . . . My gaze flicked to my sticks by the door. "Was this my dad's?" I asked, my grip tightening on it.

Darrell and Ryan exchanged a nervous glance. "Ah, no," Darrell said, decidedly uncomfortable.

"Go on. Quicken it," Ryan encouraged, and yet I hesitated. What if I melted it to slag—a priceless stone—right in front of them.

"There's no sun down here," I said in relief.

Darrell pushed my cupped hand to my middle, her smirk heavy with satisfaction. "Exactly. Put a psi field around it. In it. Heat it with your energy, not the sun's. That's why you keep overcooking your would-be lodestones. Spinners pack more punch than mages, and mundane glass can't take you and the sun both. Heat it up with your will alone. It will adhere."

Heat it? I thought, and Darrell nodded, beads clinking.

Damn. I was really going to do this. I felt ill, and I stared at the ring in my hand, centering my will and sending a field lightly around the ring with a practiced inhale, as if it were an errant drift of dross needing to be caught. The uneven rills of the stone seemed to rub against the folds of my brain, and I slumped, my eyes closing as a cool chill whispered through me. It was the stone's essence. Long cold. Ancient.

You've been trying to bind the wrong stone in the wrong way. Darrell's words echoed in my memory—and I began to believe.

The ache to be something more was almost a pain, familiar even as I pushed it aside and gripped the stone more firmly. I closed my eyes to focus on the feel of the glass in my thoughts. Inhaling, I sent my awareness down into the dark depths, drawing my will and the heat of my soul after me like a willing puppy as my strength pooled in the glass with a subliminal hum, spreading out to muddle its structure like a hazy fog.

Little trills were trying to escape the stone, and I tightened my field about it, compressing the ring. Within the glass, a faint flicker of heat began to grow, pushing the stone's disorganized latent energy into an increasingly complex latticelike structure. An almost subliminal chime rocked me as the glass began to vibrate.

Eyes closed, I felt a smile find me. It was nothing like I'd ever done before, and I poured more of myself into it, delighting when a tinkling crackle seemed to echo through the stone, and the remaining free energy was drawn into rills and threads.

"Wonderful," Darrell said, her voice warm with pride. "You've found its molecular structure. A little more heat, it should adhere to your thoughts, linking you to the stone."

My God. I really am a Spinner, I thought as I felt the stone's structure begin to vibrate. Elated, I sent a gentle wave of raw energy into the stone.

"That's it," Ryan enthused, and a feeling of satisfaction found me.

Until a soul-thumping crack rocked my mind.

It was like missing a step in the dark, and my thoughts hiccuped, my awareness flickering for a moment as I scrambled to figure out what had happened. Energy was spilling from the stone, leaking out in an uncontrolled flood, and in a wash of panic, I dropped my thoughts deeper into the glass, searching for the break.

"Ah, Grady?"

Darrell's voice sounded hollow, as if an eternity away. My grip on the stone faltered, snaps and crackles pulling through me like a sparkler. *No!* I thought, flooding the glass with a wash of heat, illuminating every crevice of its perfect crystalline form as I searched for the break. Holes were forming, and I scrambled to plug them even as I felt something shift.

With a soundless thud, the glass's structure imploded in a backwash of energy, burning.

I yelped, jerking my thoughts out of the stone as my eyes opened.

"Petra!" Ryan exclaimed, and I jumped, my hands springing open an instant before I heard the ring hit the floor with a dull splat.

My pulse pounded, and I knew before I asked that I'd done it wrong. My head throbbed from the released energy, and guilt hit me when I looked down.

I'd melted it. I'd melted the entire ring.

"Oh, shit," I whispered as I reached for it—gasping when Ryan yanked me back.

"Don't touch it. It's hot!" Ryan said as he pulled me to my feet and farther away. I couldn't take my eyes from it, though, and I told myself it was the rank scent of hot metal that was making my eyes burn, not that I had failed. Again.

"I am so sorry," I whispered as I turned to Darrell. "I ruined it. I'm sorry."

Ryan licked his lips, his grip on my biceps never easing. "You did," he said, gaze fixed to the molten mess slowly adhering itself to the tile floor, and I jumped when the glass snapped, cooling faster than the metal. I had broken it. This couldn't be fixed.

"Petra, this wasn't you." Ryan's hold on me eased and fell away. "It was an old stone, probably damaged before you got it. Listen. It wasn't you."

His smile faltered, but the honesty in his eyes stayed true and a lump found my throat.

"You had it," he said in what had to be pride. "I saw it. If it broke, it wasn't you."

"Are you sure?" My voice was high, and I hated the hint of pleading in it.

"Absolutely. We can try another stone tomorrow. I think Dr. Brown has one."

"Ryan." Darrell's voice cut through my relief, her warning lilt crushing my fragile hope.

My next words caught. Her expression wasn't one of recrimination or annoyance for destroying a priceless sweeper stone. Or even understanding. She was scared.

"Tell you what." Ryan tugged my gaze back to him. "Go home," he said as he began to lead me stumbling to the door. "Chill out. Take Pluck to the park. I need to think about this." He hesitated, lips quirking. "And get a new stone. One that isn't already cracked. I'm really sorry about this. Petra, it wasn't you. The last thing I want is for you to blame yourself for this."

But my gaze lingered on Darrell as he led me away. The fear was gone, but I'd seen it. "I, um. I'm really sorry," I said, and her attention shot to me, her expression empty.

"Stop apologizing." Ryan's gaze went over my shoulder. "You know how sure I am that you're a Spinner?" he said, but his words were too fast, and I couldn't meet his smile. "Hey, Henry!" he shouted to the loom's computer, and I jumped, startled, as he halted by the hooks to hand me my helmet and stick case. "Open file. Change of status. Petra Grady. Remove status sweeper. Instate status Spinner third-class."

That brought Darrell back, and she seemed to choke. "Ryan, she's not a Spinner."

"Well, not yet. Not technically," Ryan said, his voice a shade too jovial. "We have to get her a new stone."

But I'd broken the one they'd given me, and I wasn't sure I could bring myself to try again.

"Petra Grady," the loom's computer echoed. "Spinner third-class. Voice recognition?"

Ryan nudged me, and I jumped. "Ah, Petra Grady," I said loudly, and there was a cheerful chime.

"Verified," Henry said, and Ryan put a hand on my shoulder.

"There," he said, smiling, still smiling. "Now you can come down here anytime you need to. And you need to! We will make a Spinner out of you yet."

"Ryan, she melted the stone," Darrell said, then went still in thought as Ryan stared at her helplessly. "You need to think about this," she said, suddenly angry at Ryan, and the man's smile went even more stilted.

"Darrell, I'm sorry," I said, wondering how I was going to pay for it. They wouldn't make me pay for this, would they?

"It's going to be fine." Ryan hustled me to the door with my stuff in my arms. Behind him, Darrell lifted a hand to her forehead as if tired.

Damn, I'd really put a dent in their budget this time. Ten percent out of my loom paycheck every week wasn't going to handle it.

"I think we have poked and prodded you enough for a morning," Ryan said with a forced cheerfulness. "Besides, I'm going to have sweepers strolling in with early dumps in about fifteen minutes. Go home," he said as we halted by the door. "Come back tonight after closing. Um, don't tell anyone. Especially Kyle. He will tell Jessica, and then everyone will know."

Because if I really wasn't a Spinner, it would be mortifying.

Stuff in hand, I hesitated. Darrell stood behind Ryan, slumped as she leaned against the back of the couch. "I overdid it," I said, fishing, and Ryan made a dismissive huff.

"Everyone overdoes it the first time. Come back tonight. We'll get you a new stone. I'm going to be busy all day with incoming dross, and when I'm not, I'll be working with that spiky stuff of Benedict's. It was a hundred pules, right?" Again he flashed me that worried smile. "But I want to see you tonight during Darrell's shift."

"You want to look over Benedict's dross *now*?" Darrell said, and Ryan's eye twitched.

"Tonight," Ryan said again as he opened the door. "Bring Pluck with you. I like Pluck."

"Okay, but—" My words cut off as he shoved me out and slammed the door shut.

I stared at it, my gut tightening. I'd completely destroyed a price-less Spinner stone, but Ryan seemed . . . excited? Eager? Darrell, though, was scared.

Hesitating, I put an ear to the door.

"Everyone overdoes it the first time?" Darrell said mockingly. "She melted the ring, Ryan. I don't know how, but she did. She's not a Spinner."

"Yes, well, the only way she could have melted that ring was with magic." Ryan's voice was soft, hardly there, and I held my breath, listening. "It will be safer if everyone thinks she's a Spinner until we figure this out."

"Figure what out?" Darrell blurted, her confusion obvious even though muffled.

"Did you see the shadow?" Ryan said, voice intent. "When she melted the ring?"

"What about the shadow?" Darrell hesitated, then, "No, no, no, no, no, no," she said, the single word tripping from her in a fast sound. "She's not what you want her to be. Ryan . . ."

"Yeah? Then you tell me why that shadow totally freaked when she melted it."

"Leave it alone," Darrell said, voice thick with warning. "It's too smart to play with."

"I'm not playing with it. You still have that dross drift, right? That little dust bunny she wrapped in a psi field and kicked at the wall last night?"

"Yes," Darrell said, sounding affronted. "I was going to vault it with this morning's haul. Why?"

"She wrapped it in a psi field. You're sure of it. I want to see what the shadow does . . ."

I pressed my ear tighter as their voices became softer.

"Oh, my God . . ." Darrell said. "It went for it."

"Because it's inert, just like the dross in her sticks and short-cord," Ryan said.

"She said . . ." Darrell murmured. "She said she uses a wand because dross burns until she wraps it in a field. Ryan, what if she is? Were we blind?"

"Damn you, Herm," Ryan said, sounding angry now. "It wasn't Herm; it was her dad."

My dad? Their voices went indistinct, and I pulled back, my good mood tarnished as I gripped my stick case tighter. *What does Herm have to do with anything?* Ryan had said I'd melted the ring with magic, but I clearly wasn't a Spinner.

What the hell was I?

13

M Y SHOULDERS SWAYED TO MARILYN MANSON'S "PERSONAL JESUS," THE MU-sic's aggressive thump and sultry croon doing nothing to rid me of my disjointed mood as I prepped an early dinner just to have something to do. Frustrated, I went still as I stood at the counter and stared out over the living room. The reflected orange of the sun showed strong against the first of the black desert shadows, but it would be hours until the sun set.

It had been a mentally exhausting day as "I'm a Spinner—no, I'm not" tugged me from elated to depressed and back again until the emotional slurry had dissolved into a bland numbness right around three. Tired, I licked the waffle batter from my finger, gauging it perfect before pouring a cup of it on the hot iron. Waffles for dinner had never sat well with Ashley, but they were one of my comfort foods, and I needed comfort.

"Syrup . . ." I whispered as I left the batter to cook and went to the fridge. The memory of Ashley pulled my gaze to her door, and I slumped as I took out the syrup and butter. It would have been nice to run my confusion past her, even if we were still arguing.

"Go home. Don't tell anyone," I muttered, thinking that had been easy for Ryan to say. Grimacing, I tapped my music off, and the speaker across the room went silent. The glass doors to the balcony were open despite the heat, and the faint sound of a marching band drifted in with the first breath of the evening's cooler air spilling down the mountain.

"Tell you what, Pluck," I said as I gave him a piece of bacon. "We'll walk to the loom tonight. Give you a chance to stretch your legs."

Pluck gulped it down and wagged his tail for more, his chin almost even with the counter. I ruffled his ears, smiling as the distant band played the procession march. Walking would double my time, but the campus would be busy and I didn't want to risk me on a bike and Pluck on a lead when there were so many distractions.

A black van rumbled past in the quiet street, the sweepers' triangle and dot logo a silent nod to the coming festivities. It was likely empty at the moment, but come sunrise, it would be full of glittering bottles. Everyone on campus seemed to be at the auditorium, applauding the students moving up and on, and I wasn't sure how I felt about that anymore. I might be moving up and on, too. Maybe. Maybe not.

It wasn't Herm; it was her dad, echoed in my thoughts, and I picked up my phone. I had his number. I hated the man, but I needed answers.

Back against the counter, I pushed Pluck's feet off the counter and opened my text messages. Herm's original email had been cryptic at best, and my pulse quickened as I scrolled until I found my dad's picture. My shoulders slumped, and I hesitated. I didn't like that Herm had my dad's phone. I wasn't going to call him, but shifting this to texting would make things easier, safer maybe?

"Sorry, Dad," I whispered as I started a new thread, ticked that the memory of my dad had to host the slime.

Stop sending me money. I'd rather have my dad's phone. Speaking of which, Ryan says it was my dad, not you, I wrote, having no intention of sending the word vomit. **What gives? Bunches of love, Petra.**

I stared at the message, trying to figure out what I should say, not what I wanted to. Maybe: *You suck. Keep your guilt money.*

"Pluck, down," I whispered as I pushed his foot off my gut as he begged for more bacon. "No!" I exclaimed as a big black paw smacked the phone, and I scrambled to keep it in my hand. "Pluck, sit!" I demanded, and then I stiffened at the feel of dross breaking—not on me but my phone.

"No, no, no, no, no!" My words were a quick staccato as the whoosh of an outgoing text sounded. It had been Ashley's career adviser's dross. I'd missed a drift, but that wasn't surprising. There'd been a lot of it.

"Shadow snot, Pluck!" It had been sent. "Shit, shit, shit," I muttered, pushing Pluck down as I tried to remember how to recall a message.

But I froze at the cheerful ding, slumping where I stood. Wincing, I read, **Have you touched shadow recently?**

His word choice seemed fraught with peril. Touched, he said, not caught, and I frowned when another message came in. "Hey, look at that, jellybean," I said, frowning as a street address popped up on the screen. "He wants me to meet him at his studio now. Alone." *Yeah. Right.* His letters had always come through the St. Unoc post office, but I had always assumed that he lived in Tucson. That he had a residence here gave me a squeamy feeling. How he had remained unrecognized?

The scent of hot dough pulled me from my brooding, and I jammed my phone into my back pocket, ignoring the incoming message as the light on the waffle maker went out. I lifted the lid, carefully pulling the baked dough free before adding more batter and setting it to cook. Standing at the counter, I opened the tub of butter and slathered too much of it on my waffle, my mood turning introspective as I swung from "I'm not a Spinner" back to "I am."

I didn't know if I could be like Darrell, Marge, and Akeem, working all day in a basement with bottles of dross other sweepers had gathered, my only contact being the stories they brought with them. Ryan had it better, but even so, he didn't catch dross, only assigned others to do so. I liked what I did, and I was nowhere near jaded enough to want to quit.

And then there was the lodestone. I had melted that ring with magic. But you couldn't do magic unless you had a lodestone. Maybe I had bound to it, then broke it. Which didn't mesh with Ryan saying that it would be safer if everyone thought I was a Spinner until I figured this out. *No, until they figured this out.*

The university's fight song was rising high, and as I finished my first waffle, my thoughts turned to Benedict, probably at a party being heralded as the great emancipator from sweepers' punishing waste fees by faculty and fawning students alike. *Am I jealous?* I wondered as I stood in my kitchen and ate waffles while he was entertaining multiple dinner invites, basking in the accolades of his new process as everyone down to my roommate tried to claim a piece of it.

People, though, were people, and I knew that the mages would take to Benedict's new charm like ducks to water. Why should they pay a sweeper when they could make it inert?

Pluck was at the balcony, his tail waving slowly as he watched something in the street. "Who is it, Pluck? Is it Ashley?" I asked as I forked the last waffle out. But in all truth, Miss Valedictorian was probably at the auditorium.

My phone dinged again, and this time I checked it. *Great. Two more messages,* I thought sarcastically. *Henry will let me in? WTF?*

"This was such a bad idea, Pluck," I said, fingers shifting fast as I shot off a text for Herm to stop talking to me or I was going to tell the police he was a stalker and give them his address. *Henry . . . Like the loom's computer, Henry?*

"Petra Grady!" came a shout from the street, and I jumped, almost dropping my phone. Pluck was still staring over the balcony, his tail waving. *Benny?*

"Petra Grady!" he shouted again. "I would like a word with you if you can find it in your cold, miserable, unsympathetic heart!"

That was just rude, and I frowned as I shoved my phone away

and went to the balcony, spotting him in the street, his convertible parked askew to take up two spots. He was facing the building across from mine, clearly upset. Maybe they'd gotten smart and canceled his release.

"Hey!" I shouted, and he spun comically fast, almost losing his balance. "This is a nice neighborhood. People don't yell up at each other. What is your problem?"

Benedict tugged his black suit straight and oriented himself. Clearly he'd been on a stage somewhere, as there was a flower in his lapel and his shoes were obnoxiously shiny. "I . . ." he said breathily, "want to know where you have been this afternoon."

I leaned on the railing, ankles crossed. *Brooding,* I thought. "I don't work for you. Even if I did, it's none of your business." My phone dinged as a text came in, and I ignored it. *Go away, Herm.*

Benedict let go of the tree he'd caught his balance on and crossed the street, his hair perfect and his steps holding the barest hint of hesitation. "I never accepted your resignation."

"That's the thing about quitting, *Dr. Strom,*" I said, hitting his name hard. "You don't get a say."

"I was onstage," he said as he took the curb, needing to grab onto another tree to keep his balance. "Not two hours ago. You weren't there. Anton was there, and Anton is an idiot."

Good Lord. Has he been drinking? "You need to leave," I said, and he stared up at me.

"I need to talk to you," he said. "Come down so I can talk to you. Something is wrong."

No duh, I thought, then slumped in defeat. "Fine. Come on up. I'll buzz you in. Two-D."

"Two-D," he echoed, his long legs beating out a stiff pace as he headed for the stoop.

"Pluck, be nice. Don't knock him down," I said as I went to the door and unlocked it. Frowning, I unplugged the waffle iron, hesitating before shifting the uneaten waffle into the toaster oven. *Coffee,* I thought as I ran the cold tap. I was going to need coffee if for nothing more than to give me something to do.

Something is wrong? I mused as my intercom beeped, and I buzzed the downstairs door open. Maybe Ashley asked him out and he wanted some advice.

"Stay," I said when Pluck tried to nose the door wider. "Pluck, stay!" I said again, but Benedict was clomping up the stairs, and I had to yank the dog back. "Come on in!" I called as my short-cord gave way and my hair swung into my eyes. "Stay down. Down!"

Finally the dog sat. Blowing the hair from my eyes, I found Benedict waiting in the hall.

"Are you sure?" he asked, and I nodded, my grip tight on Pluck's collar.

"Shouldn't you be at a party somewhere?" I said sourly. Damn . . . If Benedict had looked good in a lab coat, he was fabulous in a pressed shirt and suit, his tall height lanky and that flower in his lapel. Somehow, even the Band-Aid still on his finger added to his charm.

"Yes," he said flatly as he hesitantly inched in. "I should, and it's your fault that I'm not."

"Mine?" I squinted at him. But he had said something was wrong, and I buried my urge to kick him out. "You want some coffee?"

"No." Eyeing Pluck, he shut the door, his hand extended for the dog. "And don't try to be nice to me," he said as Pluck trotted over to sniff his fingers. "It's too late for that."

I took a slow breath to center myself. Lips pressed, I scooped up my fallen short-cord and tossed it to the counter. "I'm having coffee," I said with a forced lightness as I went into the kitchen. "Let me know if you change your mind. What do you want?"

Benedict's steps were slow as they followed me. "Your lack of professionalism is appalling. No one has *ever* walked out on me."

"Uh-huh." Back to him, I put grounds in the filter and hit the brew button.

"I could have had anyone with me on that stage," he said, eyes roving my apartment. "I wanted you there to help explain the sweeper stuff. Laura and Anton don't have a clue. Ashley was AWOL. I looked like a fool." He stiffened at a thought. "She isn't here, is she?"

I turned, leaning against the counter with my hands braced to either side. A sparkling drift of dross clung to his shoulder, and I stifled the urge to pluck it from him. Serve him right if it broke and he lost a button. "See, I find that funny," I said as the coffeemaker began to *ch-r-rrump-thump* to itself. Sure, I could have a more sophisticated coffeemaker, but the simplicity of a percolator was harder to short out from dross. "You wanted me there to handle the hard questions because I know what's going on, sweeper-wise, right?"

He nodded, his eyebrows high as his wandering gaze continued to take in my apartment, replete with Ashley's flair for decorating. "I would have thought that obvious," he said.

Pluck lay down between us with a huff, and I tried to find a less antagonistic stance. "And yet you refuse to consider that my insight might be accurate when it means your process might need more study," I said, and his attention flicked to me. "God help you, Benny. You don't even know why those samples lost their tight structure, and you released it anyway?"

"It's only the samples that you handled that showed the problem," he said, patting his knee for Pluck. "You have a nice apartment. I like your dog. What's his name?" he asked, long fingers searching for a tag. "Pluck?" he read. "Seriously? I thought Ashley was kidding."

A flash of memory rose and fell, of me finding paper-triangle-football notes shoved into my locker. They had made me feel special until he suddenly refused to acknowledge me in the hall. I wasn't his *secret friend*, as he put it. I was the one he was ashamed of. Because I was a magic user who couldn't do magic.

But kids were clueless, and I shoved the old hurt down, poured him a cup of coffee, and slid it across the breakfast bar. "Drink it. Sober up. Get out."

"I am not drunk," he said, but his shoulders slumped as he

reached for the mug. "'S good," he added after a cautious sip. "Thank you."

His compliment bothered me for some reason, and my frown deepened as I realized there was dross all over my floor. It hadn't been there until he'd come in. "You've been doing your spiky dross charm, haven't you," I said, but it really wasn't a question.

His eyes met mine from over the rim of his mug. "Of course."

I gestured at the floor, disgusted. "You missed some."

Benedict eased himself onto the barstool, the mug in his hands and his eyes closed as he breathed the steam. "Sorry." He took a slow breath. "I'll get it in a moment."

But he wasn't moving, and I finally used my wand to spin his dross up and flick it at the empty trap. *Great. Now I'm paying to dispose of his dross.* "You still can't sense dross?" I asked as I shoved my wand into a back pocket, and his eyes opened, an old anger in them.

"What of it?"

I shrugged, my expression carefully bland. "My guess is that's why you really wanted me on that stage. You couldn't care less about what I think, the dangers I see that you refuse to acknowledge. You simply wanted someone there to clean up your mess so no one could tell that you can't see it."

"That's not it at all." Benedict pulled himself straight, his long face tight.

"I am *not* your mother," I said, not caring if I was really talking to all my old boyfriends. "You know what? Keep the mug. You need to leave. Now."

Benedict set the mug down with a dull thump. "I didn't want any coffee to begin with."

"Then there is nothing stopping you from walking out my door."

He stood, and Pluck slunk to me. "Okay," Benedict said, his eyes somewhat unfocused. "But I'm going to say something first. I invited you to take part in the biggest innovation our generation is going to see, and you made me the laughingstock of campus."

"Yeah? Well, I am not your arm candy, either. Get over yourself."

"You don't get it, do you!" he shouted. "My theories are being questioned because Petra Grady says they are flawed!"

My pulse quickened in a sudden flush. *Someone cares what I think?*

"You should have talked to me," Benedict said. "Not gone to your . . . Spinner guys and complained like a little girl. And where is my inert dross? You took it. I want it back."

Pluck whined as I stomped across the room to get in Benedict's face. "First, they are my mentors, not my *guys*," I said, and he took a step away, startled. "Second, I did talk to you. You chose to not listen. Third, I didn't *take* your dross. You threw it away. In the mundane waste stream. And lastly, I gave it to Darrell to look at, something I shouldn't have had to do. She should have been involved from day one so your procedure would be safe and effective!"

"Darrell?" Benedict blinked, the coffee starting to hit him. "It's at the loom?"

"I advised you to slow down," I said. "I told you more time needed to be spent on seeing what happened during storage, or if you got too much of it together, or in a high-dross zone like the vault. Don't get me started on why some of it lost its tight molecular structure and began attracting shadow. If nothing else, we needed more time to organize more sweeper runs for when your lab-grade processes can't be duplicated and we find ourselves up to our armpits in dross."

Benedict dropped back another step, finally listening. Or maybe not.

"I had at least half a dozen ideas to make your release go more smoothly," I said, tone easing. "But you weren't listening because it might mean that your grand and glorious initiative to save the world had a few issues you would rather ignore."

He opened his mouth, and I pushed up into his space again.

"That stuff of yours might be inert," I said, a fisted hand at my side. "But what happens in a high-dross zone like the vault or a trap? Have you done any studies on that?"

"No." Benedict seemed to rally. "It's dross."

"And that," I said triumphantly, "is where you keep making the same mistake. Dross is not garbage. It's potential energy. And because of that, it will not stay that way!"

Pluck huffed, tail waving as he went to the door at a sudden knock.

"Grady?" Lev's muffled voice came from the hall. "Hey, you got any sugar?"

Benedict froze, his next words unsaid as we stared at each other. "Spider snot," I muttered, and Benedict's expression went sour.

"I didn't come here to argue with you," he said, but it was too late for that.

"Grady!" Lev called, the light lilt to his voice gone. "You okay?"

"Be right there!" I said loudly, then frowned. "It's my neighbor," I muttered as I went to the door. "He probably heard us, though I would have thought the walls were too thick for that."

"Mundane?" Benedict tugged his suit straight.

"Mage," I said, annoyed as I pushed Pluck aside and opened the door. "Hey, hi," I said, embarrassed as Lev stood there, a chipped Pyrex cup held in his hand like a weapon.

I'd never seen him without a smile on his face, and I cringed when he looked past me at Benedict, a wary squint to his blue eyes. Yep. He'd heard us yelling. "I ran out of sugar," he said flatly, his gaze coming to me for a searching instant. "You want to come with me to the store?"

Immediately I slumped my shoulders in a wash of gratitude, thankful that I had people who cared about me. *Don't trust anyone, eh?* I mused, remembering Herm's text. "Sorry," I said softly. "I didn't realize we were that loud. Come on in." *Needed sugar. Right.* He knocked on my door to make sure I was okay.

Pluck wagged his tail, snuffing as he went from man to man, anxious as they silently evaluated each other. Lev moved with an odd readiness I hadn't seen before, his lodestone earring glinting and his military experience showing strong. Benedict just seemed annoyed. "Hey," the smaller, sinewy man said as he halted beside me, that glass cup at the ready.

I felt awkward, and I gave Pluck a pat. "Lev, this is Benedict Strom. Benedict, this is Lev Evander. My neighbor." I wasn't sure what to call Benedict. He wasn't my boss anymore, and high school crush was pathetic.

Lev seemed to start, his hand almost springing from Benedict's grip. "Benedict?" he said, then seemed to catch himself. "My, ah, sister married a guy named Benedict. I should be able to remember that. I'm terrible with names." A smile quirked his thin lips. "Nice to meet you, Ben," Lev said as he shook his hand.

"Likewise." Benedict smiled, but it was obvious he'd been drinking.

"We were discussing me quitting his project yesterday," I said.

A quick flash of emotion crossed Benedict's face. "I should go," the well-dressed man said, and Lev shifted to get away from the door, closer to me.

"Yeah, enjoy your party," Lev said, and a thread of guilt found me.

"Benny, wait . . ." I started.

Pluck yipped, and my voice cut off as the dog bolted to my bedroom as if stung.

And then I cried out as I was shoved to the floor.

What the hell, I thought, pissed as a flash of pain went from my elbow to my skull. Benedict's yelp of surprise was louder than mine, and I looked to see him on the floor, too, eyes wide in wonder. With a soft thump, Lev rolled to the door, a hand to his hip as he crouched there as if expecting someone to crash through the wall.

"What the . . ." I said, and then a boom of thunder rolled over us, drawing our attention to the balcony as the dishes in the cupboard rattled.

Lev's expression was empty. "That was an explosion," he said as he got to his feet.

I stood, brushing a wisp of dross off me as I followed Benedict and Lev to the balcony. My lips parted at the weirdly tinted sky. Up and down the street, people were leaning out their windows or coming out onto the sidewalk. Alarms were going off, and my worried expression blanked when I followed the pointing fingers to the billowing haze rising up over the trees like an invisible flame.

It was dross, more dross than I had ever seen before, moving like a wave hitting rocks as the freed energy slammed into the university buildings and flooded the campus.

"Was it the base?" Benedict said, squinting into the middle distance.

"No, the base is south of here." Lev searched the skies. "That came from the campus." Dropping back, he reached for his phone.

They can't see it, I thought, my hand on Pluck pressed up against my leg, terrified.

"It took out the towers," Lev said, brow furrowed. "Phones are down."

"Um, I have to go." My pulse quickened as the distortion washed over the library, burying it in a haze before it moved on like a slow-motion avalanche. "Benny, I'm taking your car. You coming?"

It hadn't really been a request, and Benedict frowned.

A horn blared, and I winced at the obvious crunch of a fender. There'd been a release. Dross had flooded the university campus. There was only one source for this much dross. The vault. *Oh, God. What if they had put some of that spiky dross in the vault and it had blown?*

"Go where?" Benedict huffed, his gaze flicking to the window at a siren.

In my lifetime, dross had vastly outnumbered shadow all but once. Maintaining high levels of contained dross ensured that we had a place to dump the free-roaming shadow we didn't need to teach shadow containment. Only by forcing shadow into a closed dross system like the vault could we take it down.

But if the vault had blown, shadow again had a chance to bolster its numbers in a way that hadn't happened in nearly two hundred years. *Not a shadow eclipse, a shadow age.*

I dashed into the kitchen, unplugging everything I could get to as the two men stood at the balcony and tried to make sense of it. That much dross flowed like lava. You couldn't stop it. Couldn't catch it. You simply had to get out of its way. Most of the buildings in St. Unoc were retrofitted for dross, but until it was contained or flowed into the desert, it would be a nightmare.

Breath fast, I grabbed my phone to call the loom. But something told me it wasn't there anymore, and panic wound tighter about my heart as I couldn't even find a tower.

This is useless, I thought as I jammed the phone into my back pocket. "Um, Lev, could you watch Pluck for me?" I said breathlessly. "I have to go. Benny, you're coming with me." I hesitated, staring at his blank expression. "To the loom!" I shouted, and Benedict's face went ashen.

"That was the loom?" he whispered, and then he bolted for the door.

"Benny!" I grabbed Pluck's collar before he could follow him out. "Wait for me! Damn it, Benny! You're going to run right into it!"

But he was gone, his shoes thumping on the stairs until the front door slammed.

"Let him go," Lev said, attention fixed to his phone. "You'll only get in the way of the emergency people."

"I *am* the emergency people," I said, and he looked up, jaw clenched.

"Ashley is at graduation," he said. "I'm coming with you."

I turned to the window when Benedict laid on the horn. "Lev." I took a breath. "Please. Stay here. I need to know Pluck is safe. If I see Ashley, I'll send her home."

Again he squinted at me, his gaze flicking to my sticks by the door as he patted Pluck and drew the dog closer. "We're going to talk when you get back. I'm not the babysitter."

I nodded, thinking, *If I get back.*

"Thanks, Lev. I owe you." I gave Pluck one last ear rub and ran down the stairs before Benedict got tired of waiting and drove right through a dross-filled gully and killed himself.

14

~~~~~~

THE SOUND OF DISTANT DISTRESS WAS AN EERIE BACKDROP AS I JOGGED BESIDE and a little ahead of Benedict. His car had gotten us to within three blocks of the Surran building before the accumulated emergency vehicles and the dross-filled rills blocked our way. That dross didn't break on me didn't mean squat when I was in a car, and unlike a Jeep with a snorkel, driving Benedict's convertible through a desert wash full of sparkly dross would stall it.

People stood in the street in clumps, mages, sweepers, and the occasional mundane mixing in confused knots. No one seemed to know what to do. It was as if the campus had been hit by an unfelt earthquake, and in all likelihood, that was how it would be explained.

"That sidewalk is okay," I said as I pointed to it. "Walk straight to the bus stop. Do *not* get close to the bench. There is a wad of dross under it."

Grim-faced, Benedict stomped along beside me. Everyone but a mundane should have known better than to drive a car through a dross flow, but logic didn't seem to matter, and fender benders and stalled cars were becoming the norm. The initial wave of dross had passed, but it lingered under benches and cars, trapped in tree branches, and, lower down, filling the empty watercourses—anything that made an angle or shadow seemed to hold it.

No one thought about their dross after we took it. Before the sixties it would dissipate about as fast as we made it. Now we created it far faster than was prudent or safe. What had been released from the vault wouldn't naturally disintegrate for another fifty years. An instant of self-gratification—followed by a fifty-year life span. *Something has to change.*

Sirens wailed as fire and ambulance services converged on Surran Hall. "This can't be from the vault," Benedict said as he strode beside me. "The vault is unbreakable."

"All glass breaks," I said, mesmerized at the weird mix of water and dross as a broken water main spouted twenty feet into the air. "A seal break ten years ago caused the shadow eclipse of 2014. This is a hundred times worse. It has to be a containment system failure." And my friends were down there dealing with it.

"There is no way . . ." Benedict said, then hesitated at the pop of a transformer. It was only a few streets off, and we moved faster, trying to work our way through the increasingly agitated crowd. The phones were still down, and everyone was trying to get to those they loved.

"Power is out," Benedict said, voice tight, as we paused at a corner.

No kidding. I squinted into the rank smoke as I sussed out the best way forward. "We're good to that blue Volvo," I said, pointing. "Don't get close. There's probably dross under it."

Benedict nodded, his expression blank as he stepped off the curb.

"And don't walk under that lamppost," I added as I hustled to catch up.

Wonder of wonders, he not only shifted his path but slowed to wait for me, actually stopping in the dead center of the street. And when I followed his mouth-agape gaze to the university's largest auditorium, I realized why.

The building was still there, but the roof was crumpled inward to open it to the sky. The Surran building was still standing across the street, but the corner that had housed the loom, the one nearest the auditorium, was completely gone. The nearby cars were all the same color under a heavy layer of brick dust. A steady stream of dusty people in their best were being helped from the auditorium to the nearby park, some frantic as they called out for their loved ones, others clinging to each other as if their world had ended.

"My God," I whispered as I halted beside him.

"It took out the roof," Benedict whispered, his face riven. "Anton and Laura were in there."

"Benedict, wait," I said, hand outstretched when he lurched into a staggering run.

I let him go. The dross was minimal here, having either moved on or dissipated in the damage to the auditorium's roof. Guilt pricked as I picked my way through the rubble to the Surran building. He had his people. I had mine.

Marge had been manning the loom today. *She might be okay,* I thought, hoping it wasn't a lie. The bulk of the vault was under the auditorium, and most everyone there seemed to be all right.

A wooden rasp stopped me short, and I stared down at a familiar length of wood, blinking at the silver caps and engravings. My breath came in and I bent double as if I'd been struck. It was a stick, and my hands shook as I drew the reddish length from the rubble, recognizing the silver ends and unusual length. It was from one of the commemorative traps in the great hall, and I wiped it free of dust, blinking back the tears as I compared it to the sticks at home and counted it perfect.

Until my attention jerked up at the clink of a stone. Adrenaline was a quick flush as I saw a curl of smoke eddying toward me. *Shadow . . .*

"Get away," I all but hissed, jabbing the long stick at it, and it drew back as if afraid. The core of dross in the stick was clearly too large for it. That was kind of the point.

Emboldened, I looked up, my gaze following a line of clean steel into the sky. It was one of the legs from the trap over the loom, the thirty-foot length exposed now that the building was broken. My pulse quickened, and I moved faster, having oriented myself. *Marge could have survived this,* I thought. She was a Spinner, a master of dross.

So intent was I on finding Marge that I almost stumbled off the edge of the rubble and into a large pit. For a moment, I stood and stared, trying to figure out what I was seeing until I realized I was looking two stories down into the loom.

Or what is left of it, I thought, aghast as sirens wailed behind me. Most of the large space was open to the sky, the ceiling and floors above it having been blown clear. It was hard to find the original walls, and I struggled to make sense of it, unable until I saw the broken weft and weave of Darrell's loom. From there, I found the rubble-covered yin-yang table. My grip on the stick tightened as a gust of wind fluttered a scrap of beaded orange and brown. *Darrell.*

Staff held clear from the rebar and cement, I half slid down the steep embankment. "Darrell? Darrell!" I shouted, breathless, my pulse catching when she lifted her gaze to find me. Oh, God. She was alive.

I lurched to the bottom. The beautifully inlaid floor with the gold and black sweeper emblem was lost under the broken rock. *The force of the blast must have blown the corner of the building above clean away.* "Darrell . . ."

She was sitting propped against her desk as if she'd dragged herself there. The gash above her eye was slowly bleeding. Her brown skin was gray with rock dust, and she blinked, crying out when she lifted her arm to wipe her eyes.

"Hold still. I've got it," I said, almost whispering as I slid to kneel beside her. The stick clattered onto the rubble, and she smiled thinly at it as I used the inside of my sleeve to wipe her eyes. "You're going to be okay."

"No . . . I'm not," she rasped, her hands shaking.

"What happened?" I said, and a flash of pain furrowed her brow. "Where's Marge? I'll get you out of here."

"No," she said, then she held up a hand for me to wait as she coughed, pain bringing her to a hunched, clenched stillness. "Is that from the hall? Do you have the others?"

She was looking at the stick I'd found, and I shook my head. *She's worried about sticks?*

"Marge . . ." she said between her coughs, and I followed her tear-wet gaze to a slumped form beside the broken glass walls of the loom. "No," she added, pulling me down when I tried to stand. "She's gone. She took the full brunt of it and had a stroke, I think. I'm sorry. I don't have a lot of time."

Fear snapped through me. "You've got years," I said as I touched her shoulder, and she grimaced, a pained slant to her lips. "Benedict is up there. We'll get you out of here."

"Grady."

"I can get you out of here." I squinted up at the top of the pit. "Benedict!" Why the hell was no one here? But it was obvious why. Surran Hall had been empty, the auditorium full.

Darrell was tugging at me and I arranged her beaded hair as she began to falter. My chest hurt. I couldn't stop this. There just wasn't enough of anything.

"Listen," she said, her bird-bright eyes fixing on mine. "You have to find him."

Him? Him who? "You're going to be okay," I said, stiffening when a ribbon of shadow eddied out from the rubble. It was heading right for her. Infuriated, I grabbed that stick from the hall and stabbed at it. The clang of the metal-shod staff rang out, and the shadow hesitated. "Get back. Go away, you filthy thing!" I shouted, and it retreated into the jumbled brick like an ill serpent.

Darrell's pained expression held wonder when I turned to her. "My God. Ryan was right. How long have you been directing shadow?" she said, and I stared, lips parting.

"I don't."

Eyes closing, she rubbed her brow, making a clean spot in the dust and blood. "You were right about Strom's inert dross," she whispered, and I leaned to hear. "Ryan raided Strom's basement lab this afternoon. Got samples from the last six months. Three boxes of them. Marge and I were running them past your shadow to get unvarnished findings of if it attracts shadow or not. Maybe it was a mistake using one that smart, but it was the only shadow we had."

Eyes tearing, she looked toward the empty shell of the loom. "It only recognized one. The one from yesterday. The one Ryan first gave me. Your shadow went right for it," she said, her hands gripping mine, slick with her own blood. "It got bigger, Petra. Angry. When it tried to burrow out through that crack, we decided to dump it. It wasn't as if we were going to drop Strom's samples into the vault, just the shadow. I went to get my tablet while Marge opened the vault . . ."

Darrell's face scrunched in an ugly, heartrending pain. I held her hands, and her tearing eyes flicked from Marge to me. "I don't know what happened," she said. "The loom was empty when I turned around. All the spike samples, the shadow: everything was gone. Marge was staring at the loom as if she'd seen a ghost, but before she could say anything, it filled with dross and broke. Blew out the ceiling, everything. Grady, the dross was so thick I couldn't see, couldn't breathe. I don't know why I'm still alive. I think . . . I think that Strom's spiky dross lost its tight molecular structure when exposed to the dross in the vault. They reverted. All of them."

Explosively, I thought, thinking of water pipes breaking when the water in them froze.

"It was only three sample boxes," she said, eyes tearing.

Her voice had gone raspy, and I inched closer, trying to get my arms around her. "I'm getting you out of here," I said, but she waved at me to stop, groaning when I tried to pull her up. Terrified, I let her slip down again.

"I turned the vault into a pipe bomb," she whispered, tears of guilt tracking her face. "Marge—" Her voice broke. "Marge, oh, Marge . . . I'm so sorry."

She sobbed as she reached across the distance for her friend, and I drew Darrell close when she began to shake. I didn't think she knew it damaged the auditorium's roof, too. I wasn't going to tell her.

"It was only three boxes of samples," she said, voice breaking. "I don't know what else it could be. Oh, Marge . . ."

"This wasn't your fault," I whispered, holding her as she cried.

"Grady!" A harsh shout came from the top of the pit, and I looked up to see Benedict silhouetted at the top. "There's one hell of a dross pool between us and a bunch of people. We could use your help to see a way past it."

Darrell's breath caught in a harsh sound. "The auditorium," she whispered, horror etching her creased face. "Oh, no. No!"

"Help me get Darrell out of here!" I called up, and then Benedict yelped as the floor under him gave way.

"Graduation," Darrell whispered, her hand fumbling for her lodestone as the tall man slid to the bottom, swearing all the way.

"We're getting you out of here," I said, blinking back the tears as I got to my feet. Benedict could help me. *Had his inert dross really exploded?*

Clearly stunned, Benedict sat for a moment at the bottom, trying to get the world to make sense. "What the hell happened?" he said, and Darrell began to laugh—until it turned into a cough and she began spitting up blood.

Frantic, I tried to help her as she wiped it away, all the while eyeing Benedict from under a low brow. "You happened," Darrell said. "Your inert dross regained its natural expanded state when exposed to high levels of dross. Congratulations, Dr. Strom. You made a bomb."

His expression blanked. "It can't. It goes against all physical laws," he said, aghast.

"You did!" Darrell shouted, then she gasped, her fingers falling from where she had been trying to work the knot of her necklace. I reached to help her, and she fell back, her lodestone held to her chest.

"We all did," she said, fevered gaze fixed on the tall man. "We all did, Dr. Strom, with our collective arrogance and belief that we could twist the laws of nature to serve our needs. Our best are dead, soaking in dross, buried in it. They died in pain . . . and confusion . . . and their souls have been chained here. They will never find peace. They will become rezes, feeding shadow until it grows. We have lost it, lost it all. We never should have put our waste together like that. We never should have made it at all—"

"Darrell?" I interrupted, and her gaze jerked to mine. "There has to be a way to fix this. Remake the vault. Gather the dross. Contain it."

"And start it all over again?" she said, clenching in on herself as she began to cough again. "No." Her eyes went wild. "We need a weaver. Only a weaver can fix this. Grady, you have to find Herm. He knows everything."

Weaver? She was becoming delirious. "Darrell?" I knelt close, holding her shoulders to keep her from shaking, and she made one of her half waves of dismissal before fumbling for her lodestone.

"Take my lodestone. Leave. Now. I can't hold it back anymore," she said, breath raspy.

"Hold what?" I said, motioning for Benedict to get his ass over here and help me, but he was arranging Marge's limbs, standing up to drape his suit jacket over her sightless eyes.

"My lodestone," she said again, her bleeding hand fumbling to press it into my grip. Take it to Herm. Tell him I'm sorry, that I was afraid. Ask him to help you."

Benedict rose from Marge's side. "Herm Ivaros?" he said, horrified. "He's a dross-eater."

It wasn't Herm; it was her dad, echoed in my thoughts, terrifying me. *My dad?*

"You shut up!" Darrell said, then hunched into a spasm of coughing. "You know nothing! You didn't listen, and everyone who died in there is our fault," she choked out.

"Darrell . . ." Her hand covering mine was cold, but she gripped it with a shocking strength, forcing me to hold her lodestone.

"Find Herm," she said, her eyes bright with pain as she pressed her bumpy lodestone into my grip. "This was his stone before it was mine. Give it back to him. He was right. We never should have put dross together like this."

"We're getting you out of here," I said, but the lump in my throat had thickened until I could hardly breathe as I looked at our joined hands, the greenish-black lodestone between them. Her gaze flicked to Benedict as the man scuffed to a halt beside us.

"Find Herm," she said. "Tell him I'm sorry. That we all are. That he is right. Listen to him. You can fix this."

Shadow spit, she wants me to find the man who killed my dad? He did kill him, didn't he? I wasn't so sure anymore. Oh, God. What if my dad had been the one who drew the shadow in?

Her eyes closed, and panic took me. "Darrell? Darrell!" I pulled her hand to my chest.

"Three souls fall to one," the woman whispered as I gripped her fingers. "And one in turn is all. Sweeper, Spinner, weaver. Shadow heeds the call."

"It's going to be okay. You're going to be okay," I begged, and she opened her eyes.

"Go," she rasped. "I'm sorry. Tell everyone that I'm sorry. Herm is right."

"Herm Ivaros?" I said as her eyes shut and her grip on me went slack. I stared down as her fingers opened. Her lodestone glinted dully in my hand.

I jumped, startled when Benedict touched my shoulder. "Ah, Petra?" he said, his expression empty as he stared at the shell of the loom and the gaping hole to the empty vault. "Is that what I think it is?"

"Oh, Darrell," I said, throat thick with an immovable lump. She was gone.

"Petra? I . . . ah. We need to go," Benedict said, and I stood, tears spotting my face as I laced her lodestone around my neck. I took a breath to yell at him—my words faltering.

Behind him, a shadow swirled up through the broken tile. My chest clenched as I saw it soak into Marge then rise up through Benedict's coat like a wraith wearing Marge's image. Stringy hair, dead eyes: it was a rez. That fast, Marge was a rez. *From shadow, not dross?*

"That's shadow," I said, scared when the rez's eyes opened. It wasn't Marge behind them.

"No kidding," Benedict said as I stared at the rez, shuddering when her eyes met mine . . . a hint of intelligence in them. I slowly took up that stick. "Why is it risking all this dross?"

"Help me with Darrell," I whispered, loath to leave her to become a rez. "Now, Benny," I practically hissed, and then I froze as the image of Marge collapsed back to her coat-covered body to leave a sinuous, snakelike shadow staring at me. *Is it the one I trapped?*

I fingered the stick in my hand, knowing it didn't have enough dross in it to hold off a determined attack. "Benny, run!" I exclaimed, staff in hand as I bolted for the wall of the pit.

As if my movement had been a trigger, the shadow came at us. A high-pitched wail raked across my thoughts, spurring me on. Frantic, I hit the wall behind Benedict and began to climb as a cold tendril touched my foot. I slipped, pain a sharp jab as a broken brick gouged my hand. Blood flowed, and I struggled for a handhold. Panicked, I turned to the floor of the loom. The shadow was down there and it was growing, feeding on the dross inactivated by Marge's rez.

"Move your tiny ass, Petra!" Benedict bellowed. He was already over the edge, and I threw the silver-shod stick over him with a grunt. Benedict ducked and swore, and then he was yanking me up and over the top. Gasping, he rolled to his back and panted.

Immediately I scrambled up to peer down over the lip. "Shadow spit," I whispered, and Benedict rolled to his knees beside me. Together we knelt on the dusty tile of the first-floor hall and stared down at the shadow as it slowly dissolved back under the rubble. "Did it touch you?" I said, breathless. "Are you okay?"

"I'm fine," he said with a shudder, and I lurched to my feet. "You were the last one up. You okay?"

My knees were wobbly, and as I fought back the tears, I gripped the stick I'd found tighter. It was my dad's. Darrell's lodestone made a heavy bump around my neck. Pulse fast, I turned to the sound of sirens and shouting people. "No," I whispered. "I'm not."

15

⌇

OOD SAMARITANS AND DUST-COVERED GRADUATION ATTENDEES BLOCKED THE street, filling it with noise as the firemen tried to funnel everyone who could walk into the park, where hospital volunteers took their names and phone numbers to better find their loved ones. A second line of people in dresses, suits, and jeans had formed to move rubble, and a handful of graduating premed students in dusty robes had set up a triage under the paloverde trees, their ranks swelling as more students and their families alike came to help.

The wounded were beginning to make ominous knots and clusters, holding their injuries or staring vacantly. Even as I watched, the dean of the medical school flagged down the campus police, her face creased as she pointed, detailing what she could make available to the emergency personnel.

Phones were still clearly down, and it was noisy and chaotic in the early evening dusk. Everyone was moving, the uproar reminding me of an ant mound with a stick jammed into it. I looked up, squinting as a chopper from nearby Tucson hovered, taking it all in for the ten o'clock news. "He needs to land," I whispered even as the firemen began frantically waving him off, not, as the pilot probably figured, for privacy but because the chopper was kicking up the lingering dross. There was a good chance it might bring the helicopter down.

"Grady?" I heard shouted, and I spun. "Oh, God. Grady!"

It was Kyle, and my heart jumped when I saw Jessica at his feet, dazed but okay.

"Come on," I said as I tugged Benedict into motion. "It looks like mostly minor injuries. We need to find out what happened." *Ashley,* I thought, blinking fast. She'd been in there. Probably on the stage. Most of the worst off were in suits and dresses, not robes, and I checked my phone as we crossed the street. Still no cell service, and I wondered if I should leave my name with the hospital staff.

Jessica was white, shaky, as she huddled under a gray blanket, an untouched bottle of water in her hand. Kyle stood over her, wild-eyed and frightened. "She's hurt," the young man said as we closed the gap. "Why won't anyone help her? There are ambulances right there! All they did was take her name and give her a blanket and some water."

"Kyle, there are lots more people hurt worse than me. I'm okay," Jessica said, patting his hand.

"How is this okay!" he yelled, and I scuffed to a halt, that over-grown staff from the hall in my grip. "This is your fault!" Kyle shouted, turning his anger to Benedict. "Grady said your spiky shit wasn't safe. I helped Ryan move samples of it into the loom this afternoon, and now it's busted. You did this! You and that spiky shit!"

"Hey!" I shouted as the young man lunged at him, fists swinging wildly.

"Knock it off! Both of you!" Jessica protested, trying to stand when Benedict lurched clear, tripped on a chunk of rock, and fell right on his butt.

"Stop that!" I grabbed Kyle's wrist, yanking him away before he could kick Benedict. Sullen, Kyle jerked from me, his face creased in anger. Jessica tugged at his hand, coaxing him to come sit with her. "We don't know if it was his fault." I lowered my voice, glancing at the nearby campus police. They hadn't noticed us, but they would if Kyle kept swinging at Benedict. "What's the official story?" I almost whispered.

Jessica licked her lips, her brow furrowed in pain as she held her arm. "Nog says to tell everyone that the university's research reactor blew, and when the reactor's coolant water was dumped into a deep fissure, it set off the earthquake that damaged the auditorium roof and part of Surran Hall."

"Nog is okay?"

She nodded. "We were right at the doors." She looked at her leg ruefully. "I hurt my arm when I fell in the stampede. Nog is helping get people out."

Jessica lifted her gaze to the auditorium, but my attention lingered on the Surran building, the entire corner spread out over half a block in every direction. *Nog is alive.* Knowing the old man was okay made my breath come easier.

"Blaming it on an earthquake will work until they do the forensics." Sullen, Benedict got to his feet and rubbed his already scraped palm. His brow was furrowed and the first inklings of guilt pinched his eyes as he took off his bow tie and shoved it into a torn pocket. "I know what Darrell said, but inert dross couldn't have done this. It goes against all physical properties for it to spontaneously expand. If it blew, something forced it."

"Darrell?" Jessica blurted, her gaze darting across the street to the rubble near Surran Hall. No one was over there, all attention focused on the auditorium. "Is she okay?"

The lump in my throat thickened. "She and Marge . . ." I started, then couldn't say the rest.

"Oh, no." Jessica's eyes welled as her hand found mine.

Benedict's gaze dropped to his hands, scraped and bloodied. "I . . ." he started. "They're trying to clear a way past the dross pool," he said, then strode off, heading for the fire trucks.

"Petra?"

Blinking fast, I tried to shove the pain down to deal with later. Jessica gave my hand a squeeze, and suddenly unable to stand, I sank down beside her. The memory of Darrell's last words echoed in my mind, and I shoved that pain away, too.

"Petra, did you have a chance to talk to her?" Jessica said softly. "Was it Benedict's inert dross?"

"Of course it was. It's the only thing that changed." Kyle glared at Benedict, watching as he joined an assembly line removing rubble. His suit was dirty and his hands were gray with blood and dust, making him fit right in. I knew he couldn't see the dross. I thought that made him braver . . . even if it might be his fault.

The inaudible demand of a bullhorn was harsh, and my attention shifted to the sudden drone of a small generator to power the triage station. *The sun will be down soon,* I thought, then took a slow breath.

"Darrell said she and Marge were passing dross samples past a shadow when the vault went," I said, voice flat. "She thought the tight molecular structure of the inert dross explosively expanded when exposed to the high-dross environment of the vault."

My brow furrowed and I fought to keep my breath even. Two sentences to explain why she was gone, her and Marge both.

"It reverted?" Kyle said, the hatred in his voice sounding wrong from someone so young. "Became active again?"

"Not exactly." I brought my attention back from the rescue workers. They had brought in dogs, and I was glad Pluck was safe at home. "That might not have been nearly as destructive as what did happen. Their molecular structure shifted to match their inert activity level. All of a sudden, and all at once."

A small sound escaped Jessica. "They exploded," she said, reminding me that she had the experience to teach if she wanted. She should've been given the chance to be a Spinner, not me.

"Like a bomb," I whispered, though it was unlikely that we would ever know how much damage was caused by the explosion and how much was from the sudden onslaught of bad luck breaking beams, shorting out electrical work, and so on.

"How?" Jessica said, almost breathing the word. "That's not how the physics work. It would take energy to push it into changing. A catalyst."

Benedict had said the same thing, and a twinge of guilt hit me for yelling at him. "I don't know. But there was nothing down there but dross." Several thousands of pule-tons of it.

"Then it *was* his fault," Kyle said, and I stiffened. "This was your fault!" the kid shouted across the street to where Benedict was helping move rubble. "You stupid, arrogant *fool*! This is what your dumbass ideas get you!"

"Kyle!" I stood, flushing. Drawing attention to Benedict might not be a good idea.

"Daniel, Naide, and Len were working graduation!" Kyle shouted, and heads began to turn. "I was in there. Half the school was in there!"

"And they're okay," Jessica soothed, trying to get him to calm down. "They will be all right."

But people were looking at Benedict, and a widening circle of silence grew around him. He was being recognized, and not in a good way. Not anymore.

"Kyle." Jessica took Kyle's arm, pulling his attention to her. "If it's Benedict's fault, he'll be held accountable. Stop shouting. Please." Her gaze flicked to the news chopper, and Kyle seemed to collapse, frustrated and angry.

"I have to go," I practically whispered. "Darrell told me to find Herm."

"Ivaros?" Jessica said as Kyle turned, hatred lingering in his eyes. "What for?"

I fingered the stone around my neck—a Spinner stone. *Darrell's stone.* The lump in my throat thickened. I had to talk to Herm, for me as much as for Darrell or St. Unoc. "If he really can use dross to do magic, then maybe he can draw it back?" I guessed. "She told me to find him. That he'd know what to do."

"Why would he fix this?" Jessica's brow pinched. "He ran the last time a shadow break threatened. No one even knows where he is."

"I do," I said as I checked my phone again, breath catching. "Texts are back up," I added, and immediately Kyle and Jessica reached for their phones. Ashley's text came in first, and I felt a knot of worry ease as I read, **I'm okay. Talk later.**

Me too, I wrote, hitting send and then adding, **Benny is with me. Go home. Lev is worried. Be careful.**

"Ryan is in the park," Jessica said in relief, her eyes on her phone. "He's pulling together the sweepers."

"Great. Good," I said, my head still down as I found Herm's thread, adding, **I have to talk to you. Your place. Now. P.** "Tell him Darrell sent me to find Herm. I'd tell him myself, but he'll probably want to come with me, and this guy is like a paranoid ghost. I doubt Herm will show if Ryan is there." Finishing my text, I hit send.

Kyle's attention snapped up from his phone. "Your dad . . . I thought you hated Ivaros."

My gut hurt as I closed my phone and tucked it away. Herm had been watching me for ten years—taking the blame for something my dad might have done. Why? Factor in the money gifts, the silence, the almost paranoia-like attention to isolating himself, and the answer was obvious. He was protecting me. *It wasn't Herm; it was her dad . . .*

"I do hate him," I said. But I wasn't so sure anymore, and I fingered Darrell's lodestone. "And when this is done, I'll go back to hating him. But Darrell said he'd know what to do. I'm going to find out what that is."

My eyes narrowed on Benedict as he began to edge away from the gathered mages, all angry as they shot accusations and questions at him. But it was the man in a dusty suit jogging to the cluster of old men and women before a fire truck that tripped my warning flags. *Sikes?* I wondered, recognizing his tall, lanky height and his shock of black hair. Immediately I reached for my phone as I looked for Ashley. *Find one, find both . . .*

"I don't know," Benedict said, voice faint from the distance. "It shouldn't have happened. Regardless, I'm not the one who put three months of samples into the loom!"

That's right. Blame Darrell, I thought as I tried to refresh my messages, but the icon just spun and spun and spun.

"You think Darrell did this?" someone exclaimed, and Benedict turned on his heel and walked off.

"You can't go alone," Jessica said, her eyes tracking Benedict as well. "Herm is a wacko, and a Spinner to boot. You'll never get him to talk to you, much less help. You don't want to take Ryan, fine, but you need someone."

It wasn't as if I could tell her Herm had been sending me money for a decade, and I winced, torn, as Benedict struggled against the incoming flow of people. The only path they left him was through dross, and the idiot was picking up drifts like they were spiderwebs.

"I'll go with you," Kyle blurted, and a sliver of alarm found me.

Herm had said to trust no one, but there was one person I could trust, even if he annoyed the hell out of me, and I jerked when someone threw a chunk of brick after Benedict. It clattered against a parked car, and Benedict walked faster, pace stiff. It was simply good luck that he'd gotten out of easy reach of a spell.

"I'll take Benedict," I said, the need to leave growing. Ten to one that Benedict was headed for his stalled car. *There's a good idea.*

"Benedict!" Jessica exclaimed, and even Kyle looked doubtful.

"Why not? He's a mage. He can do magic," I said, suddenly twice as wary—but not of Benedict. Sikes was following him, slowed down by a white-haired man in a suit and a frazzled-looking campus-police captain. We had people in the police force just like everything else, but there was no telling if the captain was a mage or simply a quick way to get Benedict in cuffs.

"Hey, ah, Kyle," I said, sure now they were after Benedict. "You think you could toss a chunk of dross at that generator? I need a distraction to get Benny out of here."

Kyle's expression shifted to an ugly hate. "I'm not helping him," he said bitterly. "This was his fault."

My eyes narrowed. "That's right. You're not helping him. You're helping me."

"But this is his fault!" Kyle exclaimed again, and I took his elbow, pulling him closer, anxious to be away. Between the older man and the captain being detained to answer questions every six steps, Sikes wasn't making good progress.

"And he will be held accountable," I said in a hushed voice, and Jessica nodded. "But not by a mob and not when the world is watching." I hesitated, letting the noise and the flashing lights take precedence. "Darrell thinks Ivaros can help," I whispered. "She told me to find him, and I need a mage. I've known Benedict for years. Do it for her, not for Benedict."

Kyle glanced at Jessica, then pushed away from me, his expression twisted. "You owe me, Grady," he said, and I exhaled in relief.

Benedict had begun to put space between himself and Sikes, but it still felt as if my tiny window to act was closing. "Big-time," I said as I pulled him closer and gave him a hug. "Take care of Jessica."

"Don't I always?" Turning, he jogged off.

"Wait for my signal!" I added, and he waved a careless hand.

"I don't like this," Jessica said as I crouched to give her a quick hug. She'd be okay, though, and I felt an upwelling of gratitude as I gave her another quick squeeze and straightened.

"Me either. But to tell you the truth, I think I have the easier job. I'll text you when I know what's going on. Tell Ryan that a shadow is still in the loom. There's too much dross for it to stay, but . . ." My throat closed, and the rest of my thought choked to nothing. There was dross, but there might also be rezes, and rezes meant inert dross, and that gave shadow a refuge.

"I'll tell him," she whispered, her brow furrowed as she huddled under her blanket. "Be careful."

"You too." I turned. Stick in hand, I broke into a jog, dodging the hazy puddles of dross to reach Benedict before Sikes could. The staff felt utterly useless without the other two, but I couldn't simply toss it away, and then I realized that the mere sight of it was opening a way. Faster now, I dodged past cars parked in the middle of the road and knots of people taking videos and imagining the worst. I slowly gained on him, and my pulse hammered.

"Benny!" I shouted when I got close enough, and he jerked to a halt, sweaty curls swinging as his gaze found me as if pulled on a string. Fear crossed him, but it was for me, not him. And then it was gone. Something in me hiccuped, and I shoved it away to deal with later.

"What do you want?" he muttered as I came even with him and we started forward.

"Keep walking. Don't look back," I said when he twitched. "Campus police are after you."

"They think I did this on purpose, Petra," he said, his eyes holding guilt—panic, maybe, that this was his fault. "They want to put me in jail. They say I've been radicalized. They think I'm a separatist mage. That I blew up the vault on purpose. That's stupid. How does blowing up a vault help the separatists take control of mage society? It doesn't!"

I looked behind us to see Sikes and that old man. The captain had been detained, and even as I watched, the old man leaned against a light pole, exhausted. Sikes was clearly peeved, and the captain motioned for him to go without him. Half a block back, Kyle had reached the generator, standing there with a ball of dross. *Thank you, Kyle . . .*

"Benny, you might be a clueless elitist, but you're not trying to take over the world," I said as I hustled us forward, looking for a quick way into the shadows. I never understood separatists and their goal to rule the world through magic—which was stupid. How do you overpower a group who outnumbers you a thousand to one, magic or not? Clearly they had a plan, but how they got from point A to point B without breaking the world had never been explained to me. They didn't like sweepers or Spinners. That much was clear.

"I can't go home," he said as he stomped down the sidewalk. "There's no way off this campus. It's in lockdown. They think I did this. On purpose!"

"Okay. Listen. Kyle is going to pop the generator. We'll have three seconds to duck out of sight. You need to lie low, and I need to find Herm Ivaros."

"What, you think I'm going to be your dog sitter while you find a dross-eating lunatic?"

He was bitter, but I knew it was fear. "No, you're coming with me," I said, looping my arm in his. "I know where Herm Ivaros is, or will be. Whatever."

"Petra, I know what Darrell said, but he's a raving lunatic." Benedict's brow furrowed. "The man isn't going to help. He's going to pop some corn and kick back to watch. A no-vault, dross-using society was sort of his mission statement. He might be good with dross, but if you try to force him to gather it up, he's going to summon shadow and kill you like he did your dad."

"I don't think he killed my dad," I whispered, praying I was right, my heart aching that I might be. "And he's not going to kill me. Not after paying my tuition." I snuck a glance behind us. "I don't need your help. I am trying to get you out of here."

Benedict glanced behind us as well, pace quickening. "Ashley said your uncle paid your . . ." He hesitated. "Um . . ."

"He's not my uncle," I said impatiently. "I told her that to explain the envelopes of money every quarter."

Benedict sighed. "Okay. He's not going to kill you, but he's not going to help, either."

"Well, let's give him the chance to say no." My heart pounded. "And you really need to get out of here. Ready?"

Not waiting for an answer, I turned to give Kyle a nod. The young man nonchalantly tossed the dross under the thrumming generator and walked away.

Three . . . I thought dryly. *Two* . . .

The generator made a thunderous pop and stalled, and for a moment it was easy to see who had military training as they were the ones on the ground. Everyone else was pointing their phones.

Grabbing Benedict's arm, I shoved him into a nearby shop front, and we were gone.

16

ACCORDING TO HIS TEXT, HERM WANTED US TO MEET HIM JUST OUTSIDE ST. Unoc in the old industrial park. My apartment was on the way, and I'd thought it worth the risk to stop in and load up on water and food bars, not to mention hook up with my and Ashley's bikes. Benedict's car was a known, and it had always been easier to get around St. Unoc via the bike paths.

I'd given Lev the address because I didn't trust Herm and wanted someone to know where I was. Leaving Pluck with Lev had been the hardest thing I'd ever done.

Grabbing the bikes and heading to the old industrial park had been the plan, but Benedict had flatly refused to get on the lightweight, twelve-gear, pink bike with the market basket that I had helped Ashley pick out. Unfortunately the fat-tire desert bike that he'd borrowed from Lev was a big-box special, meaning it looked masculine and tough but was a piece of crap, made doubly so because the chain had stretched and kept slipping off. Which it promptly did again when Benedict bumped from the bike path to a cracked, empty street.

"This bike is a piece of shit!" Benedict shouted, his pedals spinning madly as he angled to the shoulder.

"Yeah?" I coasted to a halt, a rush of heat finding me when the wind of our passage died. Sun setting or not, it was still hot out here. Getting off, I propped my bike against a signpost. "I told you not to go into the smaller chain ring. Keep it in the large ring in front, and use a larger gear in the back. The third cog will give you a similar gear ratio without giving the chain so much play."

Benedict stared, his right eye twitching.

"Don't touch the left shift lever," I amended, and he grimaced.

"Then why didn't you say that?" he muttered.

Annoyed, I crouched beside the bike. "I don't have the tools to take a link out," I said as he held the back wheel up so I could spin the pedals and put the chain on. It was the third time since we left my apartment, and I was about ready to toss the bike myself. "Besides, I think we're almost there. Spin it," I added as I angled the chain back into place.

Benedict did, the whir and tick of the wheel dying to leave only the familiar *kic-kic-kic* of a cactus wren in the early evening. Faint in the distance, the roar of a trio of jets intruded. Closer but unseen was the hum of traffic. It didn't take long for city to turn into desert.

Benedict searched the horizon, his sweaty brow furrowed as he found the jets, but I wasn't worried. I'd seen Tucson's police hunt for fugitives, and it was invariably a noisy chopper with a spotlight, not jets zipping overhead.

"Thanks," Benedict said as I straightened from the bike, and I handed him a water bottle, since Lev's cheap-ass bike didn't have a bottle cage. He took it, clearly fatigued as he cracked the top and slammed it. For a moment, we stood unmoving, him drinking, me staring at the vestiges of St. Unoc's forgotten, ugly industry of an earlier time. The man wasn't out of shape, but it was obvious that sustained cycling wasn't in his wheelhouse. Rubble had left a grimy film on his dress shirt, and his hard-soled shoes were scraped beyond salvage. A thin track of water slipped down his neck as he drank, his Adam's apple bobbing.

It was peaceful here, but the ride out had been nerve-racking. Some places had power, others didn't. The lingering dross was settling into fender benders, blown transformers, streetlight outages, and stupid, freak accidents. Even better, the sun would be down soon. My eyes were more comfortable at dusk than noon, but even I had trouble seeing dross in the dark.

"I, ah, thank you," he said when he finally came up for air. "Not just for the water."

Silent, I glanced over the abandoned industry park. "You can't make anything better when you're in jail."

"I misread the room. Badly," he said, then added, "Ah, how much farther?"

"My phone says we're on it." I squinted at my phone—*Thirty percent*—then at the messy tangle of iron rising from behind a rusty sheet-metal fence. Even the sunset couldn't make it look pretty. "This might be it," I said, worried about my battery. I'd been thinking of water, not a phone charger, when I'd given Pluck a hug and walked out.

"A junkyard?" Benedict said, clearly unhappy.

I shrugged and went back to my bike, not bothering to get on. I could see the gate from here and it looked as if Benedict could use the walk.

"So Lev is a mage," Benedict said as he pushed his bike even with mine.

"Obviously."

"He looks military. How come he's not on base? Is he a ranger?"

Mage militia? I glanced at Benedict, squinting as flickers of sunlight broke through the rusted fence to flash against him. We'd long had an overseeing council of mages and Spinners who worked to keep everyone's standard of behavior within acceptable guidelines. Occasionally a reprimand or extensive cover-up was required, and the militia's rangers were there to enforce the council's verdict. "No, but good guess on the military. His mundane tour ended a few years ago, and he sort of hung around. He works the night desk at one of the hotels." *And I left my dog with him,* I thought, missing Pluck.

"Huh." His pace evened out as his tight muscles eased. "Probably a good fit for him. Ashley and him dating?"

"Depends who you ask," I said, wondering if this was jealousy I was seeing.

"That the vault blew was not my fault," he said, giving me a clue as to where his thoughts really were, and I sourly eyed him.

"Your inert dross is a bomb in high-dross zones," I said, and he flushed. "They need someone to blame, and it's not going to be the trashmen, no matter how much they bitch about us. They need us. They don't need you." Now that his process was shown to be faulty, that is.

Expression closed, Benedict silently pushed his bike down the road to the distant gate.

Left to myself, my thoughts turned to Pluck. I was worried about him, feeling guilty for having left him with Lev. Ashley, too, weighed on me. She said she was fine, but still. A decade of dross had flooded the campus, and though the auditorium could be fixed, lives had been lost or changed forever. I knew how that felt.

But the real problem had yet to even be recognized. Benedict's inert dross might have been the catalyst for ten years of dross flooding the campus, but it was everyone's fault. They kept making it. We kept shoving it in the ground. There had to be a better way.

"Petra, can you slow down?" Benedict said breathily, and I pulled up short. I'd forgotten he was there.

"Sorry," I said, waiting for him. His brow was pinched and his face red. He looked ridiculous out here in what was left of his suit, pushing a fat-tire bike down a service road, his bow tie shoved into a pocket and his dress shoes trashed.

"A junkyard?" he said as we found a gap in the fence, the pavement falling away to a dirt road. The rusting sheet-metal fence stretched to either side, stopping nothing.

"Looks like it." I squinted, disappointed.

"Are you sure this is it?" Benedict asked as we pushed our bikes into the yard and past mounds of rusting metal. Plane housings, tank treads, and other military trash bumped cheek to jowl with dented washing machines, car frames, and wicked-looking farm implements. There was even an old tractor. "It looks like a pit," he whispered, brow furrowed in concern.

"Well, what did you expect?" I said, hot in the setting sun. "He's been living off the grid for ten years."

"Yeah, but this is the same guy who has been sending you money every quarter." Benedict grimaced, clearly hot and sweaty in what was left of his white shirt and black slacks.

"Makes me wish I hadn't given so much of it to the ASPCA," I whispered as I unslung that oversize staff and used it like a probe to make sure there weren't any scorpions or snakes soaking in the last of the earth's stored heat.

Slowly the heavy machinery gave way to old metal cabinets and rusty fencing rolled up and forgotten. An abandoned hot tub full of white jugs practically glowed in the fading light. A trailer shack stood in a cleared area, solar panels fixed to the secondary roof someone had built over it. The adjoining carport was full of even more junk. But I knew we were in the right place when I saw the big trap made of three twisted I beams propped up like a tripod.

"We're here," I said, disappointed as I noticed not a hint of dross lingered under it. It had been cleaned, recently by the look of it.

"Mmmm." Clearly unconvinced, Benedict slowed, gaze on the dilapidated trailer.

"You think he's here?" I said as I propped my bike against the rickety wooden steps and peered in through a filthy window.

"Petra, I don't think anyone's been here for years." Benedict stayed where he was, too tired to move.

That clean trap said different, and I went up the two detached wooden steps to the filthy metal door. A surprisingly sophisticated panel was set beside it, a green light winking. *Henry. Right.* "And that's why there's an electric lock?" I said, trying the handle to no avail.

Benedict propped his bike next to mine. His sigh was heavy as he sat on the lowest step, his back to me. "You're an expert on locks, then? A master of air magic, perhaps? Going to put your hand right through the door and unlock it from the inside?"

That was unusually catty for him, and I gave him a sidelong glance. "No need to be nasty," I said as I looked for a control box. "He told me Henry would let me in," I mused. "I don't think he's talking about his cat."

I cleared my throat. "Hey, Henry. Petra Grady, sweeper first-class."

The green light shifted to amber then back to green, but the door didn't unlock. It had heard me, though, and a quiver of angst went through me.

Benedict turned on the step, his weary expression twisted up into question. "Henry?"

"It's what we call the computer in the loom. He's not on their system, but I bet it works the same, since Herm told me it would let me in."

He turned back around, his wide shoulders hunched. "I suppose we could bust a window."

"We don't need to bust a window," I muttered.

"Maybe the power is out?"

"The power is not out." Frowning, I stared at the door.

"You could text him for the code."

"There is no code. It's voice activated," I said, getting annoyed, and then I winced, realizing what I'd done wrong. I wasn't officially a sweeper anymore. "Ah, hey, Henry," I said, sort of embarrassed, and the green light shifted to amber. "Petra Grady, Spinner third-class."

This time, the panel chirped happily and the heavy lock in the door made an audible thump as it disengaged. *Son of a beaver biscuit . . .*

"Whoa, wait up." Benedict twisted on the step and stood. "You're not a Spinner," he accused as I opened the door and a wave of cool air rolled out over us.

Air is on, I mused, doubly sure we had the right place now. "Darrell made me her apprentice this morning." *And Herm knew it. Great.* "It's honorary. I don't have a lodestone," I said, my gut tight in a bitter, guilt-strewn heartache as I touched Darrell's stone around my neck. It wasn't mine, and no way in hell would I try to bind it. Not after I melted the last one to slag.

Nervous, I peered into the cool, dark shack. "You coming?"

Benedict stood at the base of the stairs and tucked in his shirttail, brow furrowed. "After you," he said. "He's your uncle."

"He's not my uncle." I went in, fumbling for the lights. We were far enough from the road that no one would see, and I flicked them on. Benedict scuffed to a halt beside me, his wincing sigh utterly understandable. The front room was a mess with an old couch, low coffee table, empty pizza boxes, and an unplugged TV in the corner. Flat, brown shag carpet, smoke-stained panel walls: there was even a dusty jackalope head. *Nice.*

"No offense, Petra, but your uncle is a slob."

I pushed past Benedict to check out the rest, flicking on lights as I went. "If you call him my uncle one more time, I'm going to shove that dross clinging to you right down your throat."

Benedict glanced at his arms, then me. "I suppose we can crash here for a few days. I'm going to find the bathroom."

Pace fast, Benedict hustled into a paneled hall, a whispered oath slipping from him as he pushed through the first door and practically slammed it shut.

"No, I'm fine. You first," I said as a sigh of relief sounded from behind the door even before a sliver of light showed from under it. "Dumbass," I muttered as I looked into the kitchen. Like the front room, it looked lived in. Pots and plates filled the sink in a jumbled mess, but I furrowed my brow as I realized they were clean—not rinsed and stacked, but clean.

That's odd, I mused as I looked over the small room. Clean dishes in the sink, empty pizza boxes and soda bottles overflowing the trash . . . kitchen table immaculate. My eyes went to the night-dark window, and suddenly uneasy, I flicked the overhead light off. *The table isn't visible from the window.*

"Benny?" He didn't answer, but my move to find him hesitated as my reflection in the window caught my attention. *Mother of cats, I'm a mess.* "Benny? You okay?" I said as I thumped down the hall, embarrassed.

"I'll be out in a sec . . ." filtered from behind the door, and I continued down the hall to find a tiny, low-ceilinged bedroom. The sheets were rumpled as if having been used, but the clothes hanging in the open closet looked as if they had been chosen at random for size and use. The TV wasn't plugged in here, either. Even the trash scattered around looked intentional. *Like it was staged.*

The floor creaked and I turned to see Benny in the hall shaking water off his hands. "The bathroom is weird."

"Like everything is there to make it look used, but it hasn't been?" I asked, and his eyebrows rose.

"No. It's empty. No shaver, no toothbrush, no towels." He winced. "No soap. I was hoping for a shower."

"No window, either, I bet," I said, starting to see a pattern. Where you could see in, it looked lived in. Everywhere else was empty.

Pulse fast, I spun on my heel to go back into the hall. The shack was a front. It wasn't big enough to have a hidden room. That meant a stairway.

"Was there a closet in there?" I said as I began rapping on the walls in the hallway.

Benedict stared, clearly at a loss. "What are you doing?"

"It's too cool in here for a junkyard shack," I said as I continued to tap. "I didn't see an air conditioner on the roof, but the air coming from the vents is cool."

"You're right . . ." Benedict drawled. "Ah, there is a closet in the bathroom, but it's locked."

Because that's not weird at all. I stopped rapping on the walls with my stick. "Show me."

Steps fast, Benedict eagerly shoved the door to the bathroom open. I pushed in after him, suddenly disconcerted as the room was tiny and he was already filling it. "Uh, sorry," I stammered, backing up into the hall again. He smelled like sweat and the desert, the scent plucking a chord I had thought long stilled.

"Why is he locking up his soap and towels?" he said, staring at the narrow door. He'd have to go sideways if it indeed opened to a stairway.

"Because it's not a linen closet," I said, and then louder, "Hey, Henry? Petra Grady, Spinner third-class."

The click of the lock shocked through me. Grinning, I punched Benedict on the shoulder.

Back hunched, Benedict pulled open the door, bumping into me and making my skin tingle. Together we pushed forward to see a set of metal stairs going down. The soft murmur of a fan droned, and a soft glow filled the stairs from below.

"Herm?" I called, straining for any sound, but there was nothing. "Herm, we're coming down!" I added. "It's me, Petra. I've got Benedict with me." I hesitated. "He's cool."

Benedict drew back from the door. "I'm cool, eh?"

A half smile quirked my lips. "Like a cucumber," I quipped as I edged past him. The stairway expanded as soon as I was past the door. Benedict was quick on my heels, and the silver-shod end of my found stick clicked on the wood stairs until they opened up into one big, house-size room.

"Wow." Benedict settled in beside me, his gaze on the multiple video feeds in the corner. It looked like a slice of NASA, and I winced when I recognized a shot of the front door amid the views of the main road and inside the house. I'd never even seen the cameras. If Herm had been here, he would have known it the instant we passed the metal archway.

"I take it back," Benedict said as he moved forward. "Your uncle is loaded."

"He's not my uncle." The bunker was cold, and I wrapped an arm around myself as I went to a rack of books against the wall. It was obvious that this was where Herm had been living, not the shack upstairs. A small kitchen took up one corner, the tiny table and grow lights over the herbs and succulents making it seem less basement. A plate, cup, and set of silverware sat in the drying rack; otherwise, it was tidy and clean.

A curtained archway led to a bedroom with two more video feeds. A second curtained archway opened to a workshop, both electronic and wood, and my lips parted as I recognized a full dross dispenser. There was a TV in the living room—this one plugged in—and an entire wall of books, both old and falling apart and new and still smelling of ink. "*The Fall of Camelot in the Twenty-First Century*," I whispered, reading the spine of one. *Philosophy?* I wondered, surprised as I spotted similar titles among the more practical volumes of dross physics and what looked like astronomy texts. *Deep Space Anomalies?* I mused as my attention landed on a lighted cabinet of trap sticks and their paired short-cords. None of them looked as nice as the one in my grip, but mine was pretty useless for catching dross; I only had the one.

"Petra, you might want to look at this," Benedict called, and I turned to the kitchen.

"What?" I said, beginning to feel uncomfortable at my curiosity. "Does he stock it with blood?" I asked, seeing as Benedict was staring at the refrigerator.

But my joke fell flat when I scuffed to a halt beside him. The faded olive door was plastered with newspaper clippings, performance reviews, cryptic notes written in a cramped handwriting, some yellowed with age, some brand-new. "Wow. What gives?" I said as I reached to finger a torn news article.

"It's you," Benedict said, and my hand jerked back.

"Me?"

Benedict plucked what was obviously a computer-generated printout. "He knew you made Spinner. Look."

I was more interested in the paper under it—dated eight years ago. "He knew when I made sweeper," I said, voice soft. I fingered the paper, blinking fast as I read Darrell's comment about me being able to see dross remarkably well. It was circled in what had probably been red ink, faded to brown now with time.

There was a loom memo from when I'd quit Dr. Brown to sweep for the loom. Another from Ryan noting my wand use and dexterity. A small stack of loom invoices were pegged under a ghost magnet, and I felt myself go cold as I realized they were all from when I'd brought in shadow. The newest, the one on top, was just a few days old.

"He's been watching me," I said as I saw Herm's cryptic note on the latest: *Contact Petra.*

I touched the phone in my pocket. He had.

"This is creepy," Benedict said, his brow pinched in worry.

"Yeah," I whispered, but my life wasn't on a bulletin board like a stalker, all spread out with red thread connecting all the points to try to figure out what came next. It was on the fridge, like a proud parent hanging up achievements, layer upon layer. Most parents take down the colored drawings when the spelling and athletic awards start coming in. Herm hadn't thrown a single thing away, stacking the new on the old for ten years.

Benedict shifted nervously. "Maybe we should go. He looks obsessed."

"He looks alone," I countered, my gaze going to the single photo on the entire fridge, one that had never been covered and was given the place of honor at the center top. It was of my dad, not old as I remembered him but younger. An unfamiliar man stood beside him, their shoulders touching as if they were friends. Their smiles seemed to say so. It must have been taken before I was born because my mother was there, too, slim and attractive in her shorts and tank top, her eyes hidden behind sunglasses.

The need to cover it up flooded me. Or maybe to steal it.

"Mmmm." Expression empty, Benedict pinned my performance reviews under the huge turquoise magnet before going to the small TV in front of the couch and flicking it on.

"He's got a satellite dish somewhere," Benedict said as sound filled the large open room. "It's set to the news." He chuckled as he sat down on the front edge of the couch, remote in hand. "Why am I not surprised . . ."

"Leave it there," I said, drawn to the TV by the terse chatter of an on-site reporter.

"The cause of St. Unoc's auditorium roof collapse and the adjoining destruction of a portion of Surran Hall is still being ascertained," the reporter was saying, his strong features sharp in the bright haze of a spotlight. "As you can see behind me, people are still trying to gain access to the deeper areas. The auditorium was at full capacity for St. Unoc's graduation, and though terrorism is not being ruled out, no one has come forward to take responsibility as the death toll continues to rise to twenty-three, with over two dozen being hospitalized and several hundred treated and released for minor lacerations and shock. It's hoped that the people currently listed as missing have simply failed to check in with rescue services, and the university is asking that all students and faculty contact campus police, using the outreach hotline at the bottom of the screen."

"They're looking for you," I whispered, and Benedict bowed his head over his clasped hands.

"Well, it's not as if they can flash my face and say I blew up the loom," he said softly.

I settled more certainly behind him, the back of the couch between us as the tragedy unfurled. The reporter continued to talk about St. Unoc's graduation as the camera panned to show the flashing lights and first responders. Temporary spotlights were aimed at several groups still shifting rubble. I felt a pang of guilt for having left and put a hand on Benedict's shoulder. People I knew were likely still down there: Jessica, Kyle, Nog, Ryan, all of them doing what they could. *And here I am, waiting for Herm Ivaros to come home.*

"Authorities are continuing to look for several people whose research might shed light on what happened," the reporter said. "The initial theory that a reactor dump into a deep fissure caused a quake has been dismissed, and now investigations are focusing on a possible explosion due to the mishandling of supposedly inert materials."

"Wow," I said, surprised. "That's really close. I would have thought the powers that be would want to keep as far from the truth as possible to help maintain the silence."

Benedict stiffened. "It wasn't my dross."

"Sorry." I gave his shoulder a squeeze, stiffening as Darrell's and Marge's university photos popped up as an inset, the tagline UNIVERSITY MOURNS underneath.

"Hey, I can't reach a tower," I said, gut hurting. "You mind if I go upstairs for a few minutes? I want to tell Herm we're here. I'll bring our stuff down."

"Sure," he said, his voice barely a whisper as he stared at the screen.

I turned away, my breath held as I refused to cry. I was glad that there had been so few deaths, but my heart ached. Darrell had been more than my boss. She had been my confidant and adviser, and all I had left of her was my memories and a stupid stone.

I stomped up the stairs, unable to stomach watching the candlelight vigil going on in front of Surran Hall. Moving fast, I stepped sideways through the narrow linen closet door, and then I stopped in Herm's tiny bathroom, staff clattering against the wall as I bowed my head and wrapped my arms around my middle. I could hear the reporter's voice, her words almost inaudible. "It wasn't your fault,

Darrell," I whispered, my mind lingering on how she had looked, the way she had pressed her lodestone into my hand, her pain.

I took a slow, cleansing breath. *It wasn't Herm; it was her dad . . .* Ryan had said.

My attention lifted, and I put a hand to my hair, eyes widening in dismay as I caught sight of myself in the mirror. I looked ghastly, and embarrassed, I worked my way out of the bathroom, my attention on my phone as I scrolled to find Herm's open message thread. I wasn't angry at Herm anymore, more confused. Had my dad caused the break? Had Herm taken the blame to protect me? It was obviously a new idea to both Ryan and Darrell. But Ryan had seemed excited.

Darrell had been scared, I reminded myself.

Uneasy, I flicked the lights off as I passed through the shack until I stood at the large, dust-caked window in the front room. Fingers cold, I sat between the torn pillow and the stack of empty pizza boxes, my phone's light bathing my face as I messaged Herm that I was at his place and did he mind if I cleaned out the fridge? I didn't want to come right out and say I was in the basement in case he was compromised—but he'd figure it out. *Uncle John's paranoia rubbing off, eh?*

I hit send, exhaustion slumping my shoulders as I stared out at the evening, not surprised that the light from the auditorium bounced off the night's haze to drown out the stars. The faint sound of a commercial filtered up through the ductwork, then went soft. There was only one bed down there, but I had no doubt that Benedict would take the couch.

The ping of an incoming message shocked through me, and I glanced down.

Ran into trouble but am on my way. I'm glad you're safe. This isn't your fault. Stay put until I get there. Sorry about the fridge. I can explain. I wasn't spying on you. H.

And yet my entire career at the university was stuck under magnets.

My fault? I wondered as I shifted to Jessica's thread. I wasn't the one who created a dross bomb disguised as a trash compactor.

"Hey, we found a place to crash," I whispered as I typed. "Let you know what happens tomorrow. Tell Kyle thanks."

I hit send, then stopped. A dog was barking, high and sharp. Excited. I could hear it through the walls. "If I didn't know better, I'd say that was Pluck," I whispered, then turned at a sudden thundering on the stairs.

"Petra!" Benedict shouted, the faint light from the hall eclipsing as he wedged his way through the narrow door. "It's Ashley," he blurted as he slid to a halt in the living room, arms pinwheeling as his shoes caught on the flat shag carpet. "Outside. She's on one of the video feeds. She's got Lev with her, and your dog!"

17

⁓

PLUCK?" I BOLTED OUT THE FRONT DOOR, WINCING WHEN I HEARD THE LOCK click shut behind Benedict. Standing on the steps, I made a sharp whistle. In the distance, the dog's bark became frantic. Louder was Ashley yelling at him to stay down, and I smirked.

"I'm pretty sure it's Lev," Benedict said when a car horn blew two long and a short as a small car eased into the drive. "He's the only one you told where we were going."

"Okay, but why did he bring Ashley?" I asked, coming down the steps as a big black shadow leapt from an open window of Ashley's little hatchback. I knelt, squinting in the headlights, as the happy dog slammed into me. And for a moment, my worry vanished as I staggered for balance and gave Pluck a hug. I didn't mind the slobber, and he danced and barked as I told him he was a brave boy, a smart boy. He was my good boy. He was okay, and a huge knot eased about my heart.

"Ashley?" Benedict asked as a door slammed and Ashley's curvaceous form and Lev's almost scrawny silhouette came forward into the car's lights. "What are you doing out here?"

"Oh, my God!" Ashley blurted, a flash of dross breaking to make her trip. Gasping, she caught herself and continued on, her sandal strap busted. "Dr. Strom. You really are here. I thought Lev was joking.

Everyone is looking for you. I told them it couldn't have been you who blew up the vault, but no one is listening."

"So I gathered," Benedict said, his smile tense as he rubbed his sore shoulder. "I'm glad you're okay."

"I never made it to graduation," she said, her gaze fixed on Herm's shack, even uglier in the bright headlights. "I ran out of gas. That's why I missed your presentation. I am so-o-o-o sorry. I was afraid to call you." Her eyes flicked to me. "And when the ceiling collapsed . . ."

My smile faltered and I stood up, my hand still on Pluck's head. She'd left me a text that she was fine, but how come she hadn't told me she was coming here?

Thick tail waving, Pluck went from one of us to the other, happy that his pack was again together. Lev seemed different out here in the dark as he scuffed to a halt beside Ashley, his casual confidence more sharp, his eyes moving a little faster as his gaze lingered on the horizon . . . the silhouette of scrap metal against the lighter sky . . . the roof of Herm's shack.

"Taking the bike path out was a great idea. I couldn't believe it when Lev told me you were trying to find Herm Ivaros," Ashley continued. "You really think that dross-eater can fix this? If you ask me, it was Ivaros who did it. He's a known separatist. Wants to rule the world." She hesitated, wincing at the shack. "Where are we?"

"You will not believe whose house this is," Benedict said.

Warning flashed through me. "It's the loom's," I blurted, and Benedict's eyes shot to mine. "A sweeper safe house."

Ashley wasn't acting right. The entire campus was in chaos, and she was out here? In her snake-unsafe sandals and her muscle at her side? And what about Sikes? His frustration as he chased Benedict through the street, how he had stood in Ashley's room as if he belonged, that Pluck treated him as a known friendly: I didn't like it.

"Hence the really big trap outside," I added when Benedict went silent in thought. "Darrell told me about it after the vault blew. Gave me the pass code and everything." No way was I going to tell them it belonged to Herm Ivaros or that he was my "uncle." I wasn't taking them downstairs, either, and I wondered if Benedict had shut the door. At least all our stuff was still upstairs. *Staff. Check. Left it in the bathroom.*

"Hey, ah, Ashley," Lev finally said, and my gaze dropped to the hint of dross clinging to his elbow. "I'm going to put the car under the carport. There's no reason for anyone to follow us, but Dr. Strom is wanted and your car is kind of obvious out here."

"Thank you, Lev. What a great idea!" Ashley exclaimed, her voice pitched as if we were at a bar and he'd offered to pay for drinks.

"I'll come with you," Benedict said as she handed Lev her keys, and the man hesitated.

"Um, sure."

"I'm so sorry for our argument about Dr. Strom's stupid job," Ashley said as they walked away, and I eyed her. *Stupid? We almost came to blows.* "It seems so petty now," she added. "The streets are so full of dross you can hardly move."

"I thought it would have drained to the desert by now," I said, tapping my leg for Pluck to come. He had a dross drift on his tail, and unlike Lev and Ashley, it wasn't his fault.

She shrugged, wincing when Lev hit his elbow on the car's door-frame and yelped. Swearing, he slammed the car door shut, and the sound echoed. "A lot did," she said. "The water drainage rills are full of it, but there are lingering pockets on the streets. It's going to take forever to clean it up. I thought you'd be at home when I got there. Oh, my God, I almost freaked, even with your text that you were okay. The militia rangers are looking for Dr. Strom. That's why I didn't text you. They monitor that stuff."

"They don't," I said, but immediately I began to wonder.

Pluck paced along beside us, nose to the ground, smelling every-thing. I reached the steps and sat down, reluctant to go in just yet. *How am I going to make sure that door to the stairs is shut?* Sighing, I sent my gaze to the red taillights of her car flicking to white and then nothing as Lev parked it under the carport. The interior light went on, but neither man got out and I wondered what they were talking about. *Us?*

Ashley hesitated for a moment, then sat down, her knees carefully together under her short skirt. It was totally inappropriate to give a presentation in, even under a graduation robe, and another warning flag went up. Uneasy, I pulled the dross off Pluck, the energy tingling hotly against my fingers until I balled it up and flicked it at the distant trap. Pluck's tail thumped as if the dog knew I'd saved him from who knew what, and I fondled his ears. *Shadow spit, why can't they pick up after themselves? It's not that hard!*

"Petra, what happened? It's like a bomb went off."

An image of Darrell flashed through me, and I walled my grief away. "Benedict's dross happened," I said, and her brow furrowed.

"Will you stop blaming him for everything?" she said, chin high. "There's nothing wrong with his inert dross."

"Until it gets in a high-dross zone and its molecular structure reverts to its natural expanded state," I said dryly. *Sorry about arguing with me, my ass.* "Darrell saw it happen." Which wasn't entirely true, but what else could it have been?

Ashley shook her head, hair swishing. "I've seen the math on this, and it wouldn't do that," she said. "Not unless it's forced. It couldn't have been Dr. Strom's dross. My money is on Ivaros. He was seen skulking around a few weeks ago. Probably planting a bomb."

"Benedict's spiky, inert dross was the only new variable," I said, throat closing as my grief welled up. "Can we not argue about it?" I added, voice going wobbly as I thought of Darrell.

Immediately Ashley softened. "I'm so sorry," she said as she tried to pull me into a sideways hug. I waved a hand to put her off, almost losing it when I saw the old, knot-decked woman in the motion.

"I'm fine," I said as I stood, suddenly frantic to have some space. "We should be okay here for the night," I added to include Benedict and Lev as they came back, both men looking closed and wary. "There's a bed in the bedroom and a couch in the front room."

"Oh!" Ashley said, truly surprised. "Okay. Um, Lev wasn't sure how long we'd be gone, so he brought something to eat. You hungry?"

Pluck's tail waved at the last word, and Benedict's gaze went to the military surplus backpack in Lev's hand. "I could eat," Benedict said. "I've never had an MRE."

I tried the latch, annoyed to find it locked. "What's an MRE?" I said loudly, then softer, "Petra Grady. Spinner third-class."

The door clicked open, and Ashley's lips parted. "When did you . . ." she started.

"This morning." I didn't want to talk about it, and I yanked the door open, gesturing for everyone to go in. The living room was dark, but the hallway was lit from the bathroom, and immediately Pluck went in, tail waving.

"But that means you can . . ." Ashley said as Lev hesitated, and it was Benedict who followed Pluck, clearly eager to get into the cooler air.

"Does it look as if I can do magic?" I said bitterly, my envious gaze going to her lodestone around her neck, glinting in the buzzing security light. *On her finger, in her ears . . .* I thought. God, how many lodestones did one person need? "Darrell died before she could tell me anything," I added. "It's a pretty useless designation at this point."

"I don't know. It got us in here," Benedict shouted from the hallway, and the light from the bathroom vanished as he came out with my staff, hesitating for a moment before propping it against a scored and stained wall.

Lev glanced at Ashley, then pushed past me, the bag in his hand rattling as he flicked on the living room lights. "Electricity works. How come you had the lights off?"

I stepped inside and turned the lights back off. "Because we aren't supposed to be here?" I said, but it really wasn't a question.

Finally Ashley came in, and I shut the door behind her. "Safe house? It's a pit," Ashley said, her gaze fixed on the pizza boxes.

"They're empty," Benedict said. "Clean. It's staged to look as if someone lives here."

"A slob, maybe." Ashley winced, her hands behind her back and clearly not wanting to touch anything.

"Mmmm." Lev set the canvas bag on the low coffee table and went to get the layout of the place, a happy Pluck in tow. "It's cool in here!" Lev called from the kitchen.

"Thick walls?" I said.

Benedict stood between the couch and the table, his gaze on Lev's bag. The security light coming through the window made him into a sexy shadow. "Lev, you mind if I get these going?"

"Knock yourself out," Lev said, and I could hear the fridge door opening and closing.

Benedict grinned. "There's only two. You want to split one?"

"Sure," I said, eyes on Lev when he came back out, moving through the shack as if looking for monsters under the bed. He wasn't dumb, and I prayed he wouldn't find the hidden door.

"Wow!" Ashley exclaimed as she stood in the archway to the kitchen. "It looks like it hasn't been touched since the sixties. Talk about retro."

Benedict took out one of the MREs and sat down. "Well, most of the metal outside is from the same era." Brow furrowed, he opened the bag, spilling several smaller, blah-wrapped packages and shuffling through them until he found the reheat pouch. "I need a glass of water."

Lev suddenly appeared in the hallway. "Looks secure. I'm starved."

"Tap okay?" Ashley said as she came out with four clear plastic cups, all of them icy and beading up with condensation. I stifled a sigh. Sure, ice water was nice, but I was willing to bet there were four new drifts of dross lurking under the counter.

"So what's an MRE?" I asked again as I gingerly sat beside Benedict. Eyes on the instructions, he reached for a glass of water, almost knocking it over.

"Meals ready to eat." Lev left the window, coming to sit at the table and open the second MRE bag. "Military rations. I got these before I left. They should still be good. Each one is enough for two in a pinch, but be careful. They'll stop you up faster than a pound of lard down your sink."

It wasn't exactly a nice visual, and I winced when Benedict poured a small amount of water into the reheating pouch and dropped it and a bag labeled PANCAKES AND LINKS into the original bag. Clearly a chemical reaction would warm them. A spell would be easier, but Benedict seemed to be having too much fun. And who was I to slight a no-magic solution?

"Pancakes." Ignoring the reheating pouch, Lev wrapped the entrée bag in a psi field and warmed it up in three seconds. "This one has coffee cake and M&M's. Ashley, which one do you want?"

"M&M's," she said after a slight hesitation, her eyes crinkling up the way I had seen them do when she was about to scam me for the last cookie in the bag.

I was pretty sure Herm had food in his bunker, but taking them down and trying to explain his fridge decor was not going to happen. Actually, now that I thought about it, I didn't even want Ashley to find out that "Uncle John" and Ivaros were the same person. *I have to make a call* . . . I thought, uneasy as I slid a cold glass of water across the table.

"So. Dr. Strom." Ashley inched to the edge of her chair, her knees carefully together and her expression hard to see in the dim light. "I am so-o-o-o glad you got out of there okay. Everyone is scared and trying to blame someone."

"Benedict, please." He shuffled through the remaining packets, pulling aside the one marked CAKE and setting it beside the M&M's. "I hardly think you need to call me Doctor."

"Benedict," she repeated, beaming. "I'll try."

I stifled an eye roll and took a sip of water as Lev opened his magic-heated bag of pancakes and links, breathing in the scent of warmed dough. Much to my surprise, the pancakes looked halfway decent, steaming as if they had just come off the griddle, not months or even years ago.

"It's going to take ten minutes this way," Benedict said. "Petra, you want the cake or the M&M's?"

A flash of memory rose, his youthful smile smirky and unblemished by worry or time as we shared a bag of M&M's in the art room. All except the brown ones, which we shot across the room at a target drawn on the chalkboard. That he used magic to propel them went without saying. He used the same magic to catch that rat that had escaped his lab's enclosure. Clearly he'd been practicing.

"I don't mind splitting them both," I said, and Ashley made a pointed huff.

"Sounds good to me," he said, our shoulders bumping as he opened the coffee cake and let me break it in two.

The cake was wonderfully sticky and sweet, but I wasn't sure I wanted to lick my fingers. Seeing my dilemma, Benedict opened up a second packet and handed me the napkin. "Not that I'm complaining, but why are you two here?" I said quizzically.

"The militia saw you leave with Strom." Lev ate his cake in three bites. "They think he blew up the vault, and now they think you helped him do it," he said around his full mouth.

"And because you brought him home first, they think I'm in on it, too," Ashley added sourly.

Lev downed about half his water. "And seeing as I'd rather be on the run than handcuffed to a desk explaining why we don't know where you are, we left." Rolling a steaming pancake into a tube, he began to munch. "'S good. Try the sausage links."

"Sorry," I said, and Ashley shrugged, poking at her pancake with a plastic fork. Pluck whined at her feet, and Lev frowned when she gave him half of her sausages. Ours were still warming up. Magic was faster than science. But I already knew that.

"I'm not a separatist," Benedict said hotly. "And my inert dross did not break the vault."

"I know!" Ashley exclaimed as she delicately nibbled her pancake. "It was Herm Ivaros. He's a filthy dross-eater who wants to take over the world. But they think Benedict is working with him." Her eyes rose to mine. "And you," she added, looking at me now. "Maybe me."

I'd already said I was sorry, and I watched, aghast, as Lev reached for his glass of water and downed the rest. It had taken him all of two minutes to eat. I hadn't even started yet, and I found myself wishing that Benedict had used magic to warm our meal up. This was taking forever.

"The pancake meal is my favorite," Lev said as he opened the syrup packet and drizzled it into his mouth.

"We can see that," Ashley said, then gave Pluck her last bite of sausage link. "So I'm thinking," the woman added, "if we can find Ivaros and turn him in, it will go a long way in proving that we had nothing to do with Ivaros destroying the vault. He already tried to break it once."

Lev rose, going to stand by the window with his back to us. "I still think finding him is chancy. The dude was exiled for using dross to do magic." Lev turned, clearly disgusted. "Why would anyone *want* to make shadow? And let's say we could find him. He's only going to sic shadow on us," he finished, visibly shuddering.

I felt a pang, and shoved it away. "Herm was never exiled. He fled to avoid charges." My fingers were still sticky, and I dripped some water onto my napkin and used it to wipe them clean. "Darrell sent me to find him. Said he could help." Actually, she told me to tell him she was sorry, that he was right. *About using dross?* I thought, confused.

Lev shrugged, his hands in his pockets and his silhouette looking slim and sinewy against the lighter darkness outside. "Using dross to do magic might be the only way to put that much dross back in the vault. But what about the shadow it makes?" His brow furrowed in worry.

"Yeah, well, once we have a vault of dross, you put the shadow in and get rid of it," Ashley grumped. Pluck was staring at her with his soulful eyes, wanting that last bite of her pancake. "Someone will have to make a new one." She hesitated. "You really know where he is, Petra?"

I looked up, not liking the hidden eager slant to her voice. "Ah, I might," I said, unable to look at her. "Benedict and I were going to go check it out tomorrow when things settle down."

"Excellent." Ashley tossed Pluck the last of her pancake and eased into her chair with the M&M's. "If we can bring him back to the university, he can take the blame for blowing up the vault, because it sure as hell is hot wasn't Dr. Strom."

Motions uneasy and slow, Benedict took the pancake and sausage packet out of the warmer. "I think it's finally done," he said, poking at it, clearly unconvinced.

I had a bad feeling that Benedict's dross was exactly why the loom had blown, and though making Herm take the blame had a certain appeal, Darrell had sent me to find the man to fix this, not be Benedict's scapegoat.

"Who cares if some Spinner has-been swings for it?" Ashley said, oblivious to what her words sounded like. "We're never going to know what really happened, either today or ten years ago."

Benedict's eyes flicked up to me. Suddenly I wasn't that hungry. "Excuse me," I said as I stood. "I need some air."

Ashley stared, eyes wide. "What did I say?" she asked, but I was already walking to the door. Ashley came across as an elitist dunderhead. I'd always looked past it, as it was clearly a result of her sheltered life. But this outright blaming someone else for bringing down the loom because she couldn't admit that it might have been Benedict's fault was too much to stomach.

"God, Petra. It wasn't Benedict's dross!" Ashley said, as oblivious as always. "Why not let the sicko swing? He got away with killing your dad. It's justice! And who knows. It could have been him. Oh, come on . . ." Ashley protested as I opened the door and walked out. "Pluck!" Ashley cried out, dismayed as Pluck lurched free of her grip and slipped out with me.

Frustrated, I thumped down the stairs and into the cooling desert. I had hated Herm Ivaros for so long. Ashley's idea to turn him in to save Benedict dug at me. Two days ago, I might have been right there with her, but now? Ashley was too eager for someone else to take the blame, gold-stamping Benedict and his process.

Angry and disillusioned, I picked my way through the accumulated junk, listening to the insects and the buzz of the security light over the shack in the nearly tolerable heat. My sweeper-sensitive eyes gave everything a sharp edge, even if the colors were washed out. An old car took shape out of the darkness, and I went to lean against the sun-warmed hood, my arms over my middle as I looked up at the dust- and light-faded stars.

Pluck nosed about, and I missed my staff as the thought of snakes and scorpions flicked through me. Sighing, I twisted to reach my phone in my back pocket. *Fifteen percent battery . . .* I thought, wincing as my night vision was ruined in a flash of screen glow. Squinting, I texted Herm, **Trouble on my heels. Stay away until I scrape my boots. P.**

I closed my phone out after making sure all my apps were off. I had to find a charger.

But a charger was truly the least of my worries. I didn't want Ashley and Herm to meet, not because she wanted to haul him in to take the blame for Benedict's mistake but because he was my past, and I didn't want to share it with her until I understood it myself.

"Damn it, Darrell," I whispered, wishing she was still alive, and the memory of her rose, still and unmoving, the pain of holding down that shadow gone. At rest.

Until a soft scuff turned me to see Benedict picking his way forward. A globe of light sat in his hand, and I cringed. Making a visible light made a hell of a lot of dross. I could see it spilling from his hand, the thin trail of haze just waiting to tangle his feet or snap his shoelaces.

Two bottles of water from my pack were tucked under his arm, and a plate from the kitchen was in his free hand. I waited for him, a little annoyed. It wasn't that I objected to magic in general, but what was I supposed to do with the dross?

"I didn't want your pancakes to get cold," he said when he got closer, the light in his hand glowing up onto his apologetic smile. "Maybe I should have used magic to warm it up like Lev. I've never used a chemical to heat food before. I thought it was cool."

Immediately I relented. The scent of the pancakes and sausage links didn't hurt, either. "Pluck, get down," I insisted as Benedict set the plate on the hood of the car, well out of Pluck's reach. "Smells good," I said softly.

I awkwardly rolled a pancake around one of the sausage links to make it easier to eat. Benedict took the other, doing the same. A sigh slipped from him as he turned to lean against the car as well, both of us staring at the sky. The moon was more or less full and had risen just before sunset. It would be a bright night.

The pancake was surprisingly good even without butter and syrup, and the link greasy, full of things that were bad for me. "Thanks," I said softly. "I shouldn't let Ashley get to me like that."

"Roommates can be difficult," he said, not addressing the real problem—which was him and his inert dross. But the man had brought me food, and I wasn't going to bring it up. Yet.

"I'll, ah, get that dross in a moment," he said as his light went out. "Put it in a water bottle once we empty one."

"Sure. Bury it," I echoed. Storing dross like that was akin to peeing in a soda bottle—nasty, but it would work. The bad luck it contained would likely dissipate before anyone found it. There had to be a better way, but at least it wouldn't be drifting around, snarling his sweat-stained curls.

Thank God the shower upstairs works, I thought. There was no way I was going to show Ashley the nicer one downstairs. Something was wrong, and I hadn't figured it out yet. I knew her low opinion of Herm was widely held—it might even be justified—but the smiles he and my dad had in that picture . . . The way Herm had set it front and center . . . Why had Darrell sent me to find him?

I needed to hear the truth from the man himself.

Benedict squinted at the sky as he ate, and I settled more certainly against the car, appreciating the silence. More stars were beginning to show now that his light was out, and I listened for the sound of jets. My phone was almost dead, and the lack of my music was irksome.

"Ah, how come you don't want them to see downstairs?" Benedict asked.

A sigh shifted me. "I don't know," I lied as I nibbled at my pancake-wrapped sausage. "Because we were invited, and she wasn't?" I hedged. "It's his home, and she wants to pin the vault breaking on him."

Benedict bobbed his head, his thoughts clearly on something else.

"It had to have been your dross," I added, sneaking a sidelong glance at him. "The only other thing in the vault was shadow."

Benedict turned to me, his eyes wide in the dim light. "That's right. She said there was shadow. I forgot. Maybe the shadow—"

"Whoa, whoa, whoa," I said, hand waving to cut him off. "Shadow avoids dross," I said. "Shadow didn't trigger the expansion. That would have killed it."

He leaned back against the car, thinking. "Shadow avoids active dross," he muttered. "What was in there was inert. And it did not simply expand on its own."

"So you say," I said lightly. "Shadow did not trigger your dross expansion." But he was right. The dross was inert. Maybe . . .

Benedict was silent, brow furrowed in thought. His light was out, but the dross he'd made wasn't dispersing, hanging about his feet like a cold fog in the night. It might eventually find its way to the trap at the front door, but I doubted it. Wiping my fingers free of the last of the grease, I reached for the short-cord wrapped around my hair. It was still frayed, and seeing his dross there gave me an idea. I could solve two problems with one task. It wouldn't use up all the dross, but it *would* minimize it.

Still chewing, I nodded at the drift. "You mind if I use that?" I said, and Benedict's gaze followed mine to his feet, the man clearly not seeing it. "I want to fix my short-cord."

He shifted his feet and the dross eddied up. "You want to use my dross?"

Leaning down, I dragged my fingers through the haze, the jolt of heat quickly vanishing to leave only a tingle of warning as I came up with a glittering drift. "Is that a problem?"

He leaned back, his expression hard to see in the dark. "No. Knock yourself out."

I almost smiled. Having spent all gym hour alone with him for three months, I'd knotted his dross before. He hadn't been allowed to take his lodestone to school, but like most teenage mages, he'd made a second one he kept hidden. And because I'd been sweet on him, I had obligingly picked up his dirty socks like a dutiful maid so he wouldn't get in trouble when too many accidents gave him away— at least to his parents.

The drift in my hand had quickly dulled to a hazy warmth, and I played with it, coating it in a psi field until the warning pinpricks dulled to nothing. "It doesn't mean anything. We're not going steady."

Benedict started, then eased into a chuckle. "That was a joke, right?"

I smirked, one shoulder lifting high in a half shrug. It hadn't oc-curred to me until just now, but mages were surprisingly limited, practically mundanes if they didn't have a lodestone, whereas I could ply my trade anywhere and anytime . . . and a feeling of satisfaction found me as I leaned back against the junked car and wound the torn silk about the rebelling dross. Without my hooks and needle, it would be more of a patch job, and the dross began to rebel in earnest as I finished the first anchor knot.

"What does it feel like?" Benedict said, and I flicked a glance at him, startled.

"The dross?" I moved four inches down the strand of silk, twisting it before making a second anchor knot. I wasn't sure if I should find an insult in his question or not. He'd obviously known other sweepers. But as he watched my moving fingers in a mix of horror and admiration, I decided he hadn't.

"No one in my family can do that," he said, gaze fixed. "At least not without getting a split nail or a wart."

I chuckled. "Who wants warts?" I said, and then, seeing as he was in earnest, my motion to knot the middle section slowed. "Tingles. Hot, then cold after I put it in a psi field."

Disappointment creased his brow. "That's textbook. I really want to know."

I shrugged as I pinched the two anchor knots to test their integrity. "When it's under stress, as it is now, and it wants to break, it feels a lot like putting your hands palm up under a hot, fast showerhead. Sort of a painful tickle."

He was fixated on my fingers as I made the first real twisted loop between the anchor knots. "And when it's not stressed?"

"Same thing. Only a little cooler and the tingles are spread further apart." The anchor knots were holding, and I spun the tail of the dross around the length of silk in my hand, felting them together. "It's hot until I wrap it in a psi field. That's why I use a wand so often. It insulates me from it." My thoughts went to the memo on Herm's fridge. He seemed to have thought that it was important.

Benedict watched me work for a moment. "I should have said this before, but I'm sorry about Professor Yanna. That was her, wasn't it?" He touched his hair. "With the beads?"

A flash of anger torched through me at the thought that he had reduced the amazing woman to her hair—but at least he acknowl-edged she was a professor. "Darrell?" I said, my throat closing. "Yes." Eyes on my work, I looped all the knots together with an angry fierceness. I was upset and my heart hurt.

"And the other woman?" Benedict said. "Was she a sweeper?"

I stifled the urge to snap at him. "Marge was the loom's second Spinner."

"I'm sorry." Benedict shifted back to the night and drank a slug of water. "I shouldn't have called them your guys. That was insulting. I knew they were your supervisors."

Which was kind of an insult in itself. They had been my friends, Darrell especially, helping see me through the loss of my dad until I found myself. I felt their deaths like a stab in the gut. "Thank you," I whispered, fingering the stone around my neck, then decided I should probably say something nice, too. "Ah, I'm sure your team is okay. Did you have a chance to check on them?"

Benedict's jaw tightened. He wasn't mad at me, though, and he slowly exhaled. "I did. They're fine. I never should have left them, though."

But you were mad and wanted to yell at me. I get it.

Benedict tilted his head and drained his water bottle. "I should probably get back," he said. "I only wanted you to have your dinner hot." He smirked. "Seeing as it took so long to get it that way. Lev is not dumb. He might find the door to the basement."

I nodded. "He won't get past it. It's not just the words, it's the person speaking them."

"True enough." Exhaling, Benedict made a large psi field, send-ing it out over the nearby junk field to gather what dross he could. It was exactly what I'd done to clear Sikes's dross from my living room, and I stifled a shudder when he drew it back and his field tingled against my skin.

"Did I get it all?" he said, holding the shrunken field in his hand, much as he had his light.

Bits of drift still lingered, missed. "Every last erg of it," I said, and he grinned, clearly relieved.

"I probably should have used my phone's light, but I'm almost out of battery and I don't have a charger."

"Me either. I'll be in in a moment," I said, and he nodded. "Thanks for everything." I held up the water bottle, giving it a shake.

The empty plate scraped as he pulled it from the car hood, and nodding, he turned and retraced his steps, shoulders hunched in worry.

Happy for some reason, I leaned back against the car and looked at the stars. I'd get the last of the dross he'd missed before I went in. Telling him he missed some seemed . . . pointless.

18

REACHED FOR THE FRUIT ON THE TREE, NOT KNOWING WHAT IT WAS, ONLY THAT I was hungry. I hadn't eaten in years, and the yellow, pear-like orb would be enough to keep me going. The warmth of the sun was hot even through the shade, its piercing rays burning where it made it past the delicately leafed branches. *I'm dreaming,* I mused as I stretched onto my tiptoes, distantly feeling the aches that the lumpy couch had given me.

But as my fingers grasped the golden fruit, the firm flesh grew spongy and the tender skin split to show a black rot within. Disgusted, I recoiled. With a sodden pop, the fruit hit the ground with a splat. My arm swung into the sun and fire pierced me. I stifled a cry, jerking deeper into the shade. Shocked, I held my scorched hand as the world past the shelter of the tree burned in a white light.

"You tried to kill me," a hissing gurgle whispered, and I spun.

"Darrell!" I jumped, only now seeing her sitting against the tree, much as I'd left her propped against her desk. Her form was ragged and indistinct; only her eyes and beaded hair held form as she rose— the motion far too supple for even Darrell's grace. "I'm sorry. I couldn't save you," I added, and her dark, green-flecked eyes fixed on mine. *Darrell had brown eyes . . .*

"You never tried to save me," Darrell scoffed, her gaze on the lodestone about my neck. It felt hotter than the sun against me, even as the stone flashed a cool green. "You would have me dead," she insisted, voice rasping.

I held my burned hand, retreating until the sun threatened to scorch my back. "I tried to save you," I insisted. It was my dream, and I'd be damned if I let myself be guilted into taking responsibility for her death. "There was shadow," I said, justifying my actions. "I had to leave."

Darrell lifted a thin, indistinct, smoke-fingered hand to the fruit. "Shadow," she said, her lips twisting as the fruit split and fell to the ground, ruined. "You fled!" Angry, she came forward, her hands fisted at her sides. "Are you a coward or simply a cretin?"

"I had to leave!" I backed up, crying out when the sun found me. "There was so much dross," I pleaded as the sun's claws raked me. "Darrell, I'm so sorry."

Expression grim, Darrell relented, her beaded skirt clinking as she retreated to give me room to inch out of the sun—but just. "And now that I have found you," she said bitterly, gaze upon my lodestone, "you leave me to starve in the sun."

I wasn't sure who this image of Darrell was supposed to be anymore, what my subconscious was trying to tell me. "Who are you? What do you want?" I whispered, and the sensation of icy daggers through my mind eased.

She was looking at the knotted cord about my hair in avarice. "Not a coward. A cretin," she pronounced with a bitter disappointment. "But no one else is listening. And unlike a coward, a cretin I can teach. You are a yeth. A foolish, ignorant yeth."

"Wow, rude much?" I said, but Darrell had extended her hand, a familiar, demanding slant to her eyebrows as she gazed at my knotted short-cord. Sullen, I loosened the tie and handed it to her for inspection.

"I'm still in the sun," Darrell said imperiously.

"So find some shade," I snapped. The world beyond the tree was a molten white, and I wanted to wake up.

Darrell's mood softened as she pulled the cord through her fingers, *thump, thump, thump,* until she came to the patch job. "I'll take that as an invitation . . . yeth."

"You're the yeth!" I shouted as she vanished, and then I started awake.

Breath held, I lay unmoving until I remembered why I was staring at the back of a nasty couch instead of my chest of drawers. I sighed, rolled over, and sat up, blinking as I looked out the uncurtained window to the junkyard. Everything was black and gold in the rising sun, beautiful, almost. I could hear Lev and Ashley in the kitchen, and smell coffee. Pluck was lying on my feet, his eyes morosely on mine, tail thumping as I gave him a pat. He'd taken up way too much room last night, but I hadn't had the heart to consign him to the floor.

Freaky-ass dream. Weary and feeling gross for having slept in my clothes, I shifted to sit on the edge of the couch and stare out the window, wondering how hot it was going to get today. It had been unusually cool the last few days, but June could easily hit over a hundred, if it wanted.

"Hey, Pluck," I whispered as I tucked Darrell's pendant back behind my shirt. It was almost black in the morning light, the color only hinting at green. "You want something to eat, jellybean?" I added, and the dog huffed, tail wagging as he lurched to the floor.

I was stiff, grimacing as I stretched for my pack and dragged it closer to paw through it for a food bar. The anxious dog pressed closer, but a frown took me when I found my short-cord instead. My repair had come undone and the dross had escaped. Again.

"Shadow spit," I whispered as I fingered the bumpy length of silk. Peeved, I glanced at the ambient-dross trap I'd set the night before using the chopsticks I'd found in a kitchen drawer. A faint shimmer skulked within it. The dross might be from my cord, but it was more likely from Benedict or Ashley. I had no idea what I was going to do with it, but it was better than leaving it to roll around the room like a dust bunny from hell.

"Back up, Pluck," I muttered as I dumped my bag out onto the coffee table to make sure the escaped dross hadn't taken refuge in it. The dog huffed as the food bars came sliding out, nosing a little too close. "You are not starving," I demanded as I shoved him back, but my bag was clean, and I stuffed everything but my short-cord away. I'd have to fix it again if for nothing more than to please my sensibilities.

Pluck made a sad whine, and I opened a bar and gave it to him one little nugget at a time. The soft sounds of Ashley and Lev in the kitchen were pleasant, and the big dog inched forward with each bite until he was almost on my lap. Relenting, I tossed him the last chunk. "Pirate," I said fondly as he scarfed it down and promptly trotted into the kitchen. Ashley's flirting rose into a fond cooing, and I smiled.

The need for the bathroom was becoming pressing, but my move to rise faltered when Lev strode out of the kitchen, giving me a casual "hey" before going down the hall and slamming the bathroom door shut. *Figures,* I thought as I eased back down with a sigh.

"You found coffee?" I called loudly, and Ashley laughed.

"Yep!" I heard the sound of a chair scrape and she came out into the living room with two mugs, a happy Pluck in tow. "There was some instant in the back of a cupboard."

"God, thank you." I reached for it with both hands, relishing the warmth on my fingers despite the bitter tang as it slipped into me, bringing me awake. Darrell's lodestone pendant swung free, and I tucked the black stone away before she could see it, not yet ready to deal with that conversation.

Somehow she was as fresh as the morning, clearly having had a change of clothes in her car previously packed for travel. She looked nice, but the crisply patterned shirt and tight pants seemed out of place amid the piles of jagged metal and old barbwire wraps.

"So if you had the bed, and I had the couch, and Benedict had the chair, where was Lev?" I said slyly, thinking two years of the man's attentions had finally paid off.

Eyebrows high, Ashley sipped her coffee. Her broken sandal strap flopped as she fidgeted. "Outside on the steps," she said dryly, clearly peeved. "Keeping watch."

"Oh." Not sure what to think, I glanced at the big plate-glass window and patted Pluck. "Had a really weird dream," I added as I pulled some tingling dross from the trap and rolled it in a psi field until it cooled, fingers flexing.

"I should check on Dr. Strom." Ashley shifted as if to rise.

"Darrell was in it," I said, continuing our conversation. The dross fought me, sending hot darts of threat into my fingers as I quickly knotted three ugly anchor knots. "I had to leave her there," I whispered. It rankled that her memory might sustain a rez, the very thing she had spent her entire life trying to minimize and eradicate. Shadow food.

Sighing, Ashley sank back down. "From what Benedict said, you didn't have a choice."

I shrugged as I looped the snared dross among itself and the silk, little darts of needles pricking when I bound it into a circular form. True, we had barely made it out, but it still hurt, and I studied the new knot to ensure it wouldn't work itself open. "Are you sure the math doesn't work?" I said, voice low. "The only difference was Benedict's inert dross and maybe that shadow I brought in. It couldn't have been the shadow. If it got free, it would have been destroyed. That's kind of the point to keeping that much dross in one place."

Ashley's lips parted. "There was shadow in the loom when the inert dross reverted? Well, there you go. It wasn't the high-dross zone that triggered it. It was the shadow."

"Ashley . . ." I started.

"Dr. Strom's process is perfect!" she said hotly. "Get off his case!"

"Ashley," I said again as she stood. "I'm not blaming him. I'm just trying to figure this out. Please?" But the idea that shadow could have done it was ridiculous.

Eyes narrowed, Ashley sat back down. Slowly the silence became comfortable, and I worked on fixing my short-cord, tugging on the knots to test its strength.

"Oh, my gosh," Ashley blurted, her voice hushed. "Is that a Spinner lodestone? I've never seen one close."

Startled, I reached for it, irate that it had swung free from behind my shirt again.

"It's Darrell's," I blurted. "She gave it to me for safekeeping." Right. Like I was going to tell her I was supposed to give it to Herm Ivaros?

"Oh." Ashley blew her breath out in relief, which was more than a little irritating.

"Trust me, I'm no Spinner," I said, my gaze going to the window. Benedict was out amid the piles of junk, arms swinging and pace stilted as he strode forward. "I melted the stone Darrell gave me to bind to into slag."

"Y-you what?" Ashley said, clearly shocked, but I was fixated on Benedict. He'd found a pair of jeans and an olive-green shirt in the back bedroom closet, and the casual look made him so much more . . . approachable.

A flicker of sensation dropped through me as he stomped closer. Flustered, I wrapped my twice-repaired short-cord about my mop, very glad that Ashley had let me use her shampoo and conditioner the previous night—even if I did smell like strawberries.

Benedict took the two wooden steps in one bound, and I smiled as he came in; Lev had fastened a piece of tape on the door, preventing the lock from engaging. "Coffee?" I said, lifting my mug in explanation. He was endearingly grumpy as he came to a halt, his hair tousled and a drift of dross on his heel. The need to pluck it off him growing—even as I told myself I wasn't his mom. He hadn't shaved that morning, and his jeans and casual shirt threw me; he almost looked like a sweeper on free-range duty, and I felt a flicker of foolish, adrenaline-based attraction.

"Maybe later. I want you to see something," he said, extending a hand to help me rise.

Something that is clearly outside. "Can I bring my coffee?"—as he hauled me to my feet and I stumbled, almost spilling it.

"Sure, whatever."

I looked at Ashley, thinking it odd she was just sitting there, an almost horrified expression on her face. "You coming?"

"N-no," she stammered. "I have to talk to Lev."

"Come on, Pluck," I called, and the dog happily ambled to my side as soon as the door opened. Benedict was already halfway down the stairs, and I took a hurried slurp of my coffee before hustling to catch up. "What is it? Rebar-toting mages out for your blood?"

"Not yet." He pointed, and we angled to the path winding between the old cars and tank treads. "I found a drone. I was going to take it out, but after seeing his setup downstairs, I'm wondering if it's Ivaros's."

"I wouldn't know, but I can take a look," I said, my unsettled feeling growing as he came to an abrupt halt.

"Well?" Benedict stared at a pile of junk. "If it's not Ivaros's security, then it's got to be the rangers'. The public isn't allowed to have drones that size."

"Oh," I said, surprised as I saw the saucerlike thing perched atop a stack of old cars. It was the size of a tire and black as the night.

"I thought I heard it fly in last night even through the closed windows. Something that big is noisier than a train. You think it's Ivaros's?"

"Maybe," I said when a little red light on it blinked and went out. *Crap, it's active.* "I'm going to guess militia. It can probably see the front door from up there. Think we should wave?"

"We need to get out of here." Benedict turned to the shack, his brow furrowed. "Before they show up."

Worry flickered through me. "I'm surprised they aren't here already. Maybe they think we will lead them to Herm."

Benedict squinted up at it. "It's going to follow us if we leave."

"Not if I short it out," I said as I estimated the distance. "I might be able to reach it from here." Benedict stared at me, and I shrugged. "Drop some dross on it, and it will blow. Too bad. So sad. Bad luck."

"That's nearly a hundred feet. You can hold a psi field that far?"

Some days are better than others. "On a good day," I said smugly as I focused on the black disk.

Benedict was clearly impressed. "I'll make you some dross," he said as he glanced at his ring glowing in the early morning light, and I swear I felt a warm tingle blossom between us where our arms almost touched.

"No, I'm good." I leaned to pluck that annoying drift from his foot. "Thank you," I chirped, and he groaned.

"Oh, man. I didn't even know that was there."

I gave Benedict a little smile before exhaling to create a modest psi field between my hands. But as I wrapped it around the dross, my brow furrowed.

The dross within my psi field felt different. It was tingling in complaint against me as always, but the usual hot flash of connection had not just muted but turned cold, almost frigid, as it rubbed against my thoughts in what slowly evolved into a decidedly pulse-like sensation. Curious, I pushed my hands together to condense the field, and the icy, pulsing pinpricks deepened, becoming faster until I pulled my hands apart.

"You okay?" Benedict said, and I nodded as I brought my hands together, then apart again, verifying the sensation. The closer my hands, the faster the icy wave stabbed at me. I'd never noticed it before.

"Yeah," I said reluctantly as I turned my attention to the drone and pushed my dross-holding psi field away. I'd directed psi fields thousands of times in the course of my career, but today, standing in the early sun of morning, I studied the wavelike sensation as the field settled over the drone. *Odd,* I thought, likening the feeling to that of the ringing of a slow, giant bell.

And then my frown deepened when I noticed a second, smaller pulse of tingles within my head, faster and out of sync with the first. It was uncomfortable, and I shifted my shoulders as the drift of dross settled within the drone, seeping through the cracks to the sensitive electronics. I wouldn't have to do anything but let nature take its course.

This is really weird, I thought as the dross slowly oozed into the machine. The tiny, almost unnoticed pulse behind my eyes was just like the first, but its different pace made an itching, irritating sensation. Grimacing, I exhaled and pushed my hands together as if I still held the field in the hopes that the initial sensation would shift.

But it wasn't the larger pulse that changed, and I made a small sound when the almost unnoticed wave behind my eyes shifted to match the first and, with a snap, merged.

"Thank God," I whispered, then jumped when the drone made a distant rasping *tink, tink, tink* and the red light went out.

"Ah, Petra?" Benedict said, but I was pleased. The odd ringing sensations were gone, vanishing with the dross. A ribbon of smoke leaked from the housing, and the black hunk of metal slowly tipped and slid down the stack of cars with a harsh clatter. Pluck went for it and I followed, wanting to make sure it was really dead. I'd used dross to short things out lots of times, but it had never felt like this before, and I massaged my palm, remembering the odd, twin echoes.

"We need to get moving," I said. "If it is the militia, they will send another as soon as they know it's dead."

But Benedict was staring at me. "How come you didn't tell me you could do magic?"

I froze, panicked almost. "Don't be silly," I said. But what I meant was *Don't be mean.* It had to be dross. That was all I could handle. That was what I did.

"You lied?" he said, eyes wide as he spotted Darrell's lodestone as it swung free. Again. "You're a Spinner! For real? I knew I felt magic. Petra, this is wonderful! Why did you lie?"

"I didn't lie to you," I said as I tucked Darrell's lodestone away. Nervous, I shifted the downed electronics, tilting the disk onto its side to estimate its weight. *Damn it all to hell . . .*

"Yeah?" Benedict inched closer. "I can tell the difference between active magic and breaking dross. It breaks on me enough. I should know," he said. "Darrell gave you her lodestone. I saw it. Why did you tell me it was an honorary position? Petra, this is wonderful!"

Somehow it hurt even more, and my chin lifted at the old pain. "Benny, I'm not a Spinner." Jaw tight, I whistled for Pluck and pushed past him. The drone could rot in the sun for all I cared. "Darrell gave it to me to give to Herm. They probably confiscated his before he ran away, and he's going to need it to fix the loom."

There was a clatter as Benedict hoisted the drone and scrambled to follow. "That is so weird. I would have sworn I saw your hands glow when you pushed them together."

My jaw clenched, and I wished he would stop trying to make me more than I was. It only left me miserable when I fell short of his ideals. "I'm not a Spinner." *And you are hurting me.* "We need to figure out how we are going to slip the militia. Ashley's car holds two, but I suppose we could empty out the back and make it work."

We came out from behind the last junk pile, Pluck trotting before us, tail waving as he headed for Ashley sitting on the stairs. Her lips parted as she saw us with that drone, and she stood, clearly excited.

"Oh, my God. You found a drone? You'll never guess what Lev discovered," she said, standing on the lowest step. "There's a bunker under the shack!"

Shit, I thought, hoping we hadn't left anything down there. Explaining why we hadn't told them about it would be . . . yeah.

"I thought you said he couldn't get past the lock," Benedict said softly, then louder, "You mean like a basement?"

"No, a bunker. With video feeds and everything," she said, her cheeks red in excitement. "Lev found a door in the bathroom when he was brushing his teeth. He never would have known it was there, but there was a TV going and he could hear it."

"Son of a bitch," Benedict whispered, but his face never changed, fixed into a fake, amazed expression. "A bunker? Are you kidding?"

In for a penny, in for a pound . . . I thought, reminding myself to be surprised.

Benedict dropped the drone at the base of the stairs. The black disk hit the dusty ground with a decisive thump. A buzzing whine came from it, and then nothing. "We need to get out of here," he said. "It's not scrap, it's militia, and if they know I'm here, they are on the way."

Lev pushed the door open and came out. Little drifts of dross had collected about his cuffs like dust bunnies. There was a new knot on his shoelace, and he was missing a shirt button. "Did Ashley tell you about the bunker?" he said, and then his steps faltered. "Whoa." He came closer, his gaze fixed to the drone. "Where did you get *that?*"

"Petra brought it down," Benedict said, a hint of pride marring his obvious concern.

"You took out a drone?" Lev crouched before it, seemingly both impressed and annoyed as he turned it over. "How? These things are like flying tanks."

I gave Pluck a little pat. "Dross. You'd be amazed what you can do with it tactically. Ah, we should probably load up. If we empty the back of Ashley's car, we should all fit."

"Dross did this?" As if not believing me, Lev felt along the carapace's underside until he found a lever and snapped it open. "If this is militia, I doubt that dross took it out." He lifted the carapace and tossed it aside. It hit with a crack of plastic, and I leaned to look: gears and levers, switches and batteries.

"These things usually have . . . yep." Lev poked at it with a stick.

"Multiple dross buttons to give it extra security. It would take a hell of a lot of dross to short this baby out."

My eyebrows rose. Mundane military training didn't cover magic countermeasures.

"And you know this how?" Benedict said as Lev stared into the whirring machinery.

"Because I trained for it." Lev stood. "The militia recruits from the mundane military. We have people knee-deep in the armed services like everything else, and there's a hidden program for mages, sort of a militia ROTC. I was planning on joining the rangers when I got out, but we had a difference of opinion." Lev turned to Benedict. "How did you bring this down, Ben? These things are nearly indestructible."

"I told you." Benedict gestured to me. "It was Petra."

Lev shifted to put his weight on one foot to look unconvinced. Beside him, Ashley was uncharacteristically silent. "Then that lodestone works?" he said, and I looked down, grabbing the lodestone and tucking it back behind my shirt. *Spider spit, stay there . . .*

"No." I flushed. "It's Darrell's. I brought it down with dross. Lots of dross."

"I saw her do it," Benedict said. "Maybe—"

Pluck's ears pricked and the dog stared as a little red light flickered on deep within the drone. It buzzed, a lens whining as it focused and shifted, making a quick three-sixty.

Lev grimaced. Earring glinting, he reached to touch the drone. My skin prickled at his psi field, and then he condensed it, flooding the drone with energy. The electronics melted with a sodden thump, and a plume of black smoke trickled up into the still air. Slowly the little red light went out, but it had seen us. All of us.

Ashley dropped back, her face ashen. "My car only holds two. Lev . . ."

Lev stood, his gaze still on the smoking ruin. "Ashley, I'm sorry.

If you go home now, you will be implicated with Strom and Ivaros. We all will."

"I'm not working with Herm Ivaros!" Benedict shouted, and a cactus wren *kic-kic-kic*ked back at him.

But at this point, it was all about appearances, and I gave his hand a quick squeeze as Pluck pressed into my leg.

Ashley scanned the brightening skies, a worried pinch to her brow. "Petra, we have to find Herm. They will never believe it wasn't us if we don't bring him in," she said, voice getting louder, more frantic. "I can't be arrested by the militia! Lev, how are we going to get out of here? They will recognize my car!"

A flash of irritation crossed Lev. "Will you relax? We don't have to take the car."

"Well, we can't stay here!" she exclaimed, and a thread of worry tightened through me.

"You want to wait until dark and walk out?" I suggested, but in reality I was surprised we didn't have a second drone over us already, and I peered up into the faultless sky. It was so quiet out here, you could hear a lizard fart.

"We can try the tunnel," Lev said, and Ashley made a scared-sounding laugh.

"Yeah, sure. Why not? We don't know where that goes!" she said.

I looked at Benedict, and he looked at me. "Tunnel?" I said for both of us.

"Where it goes is away from here," Lev said to Ashley, and the woman turned her back on him, arms over her middle, head bowed. "We can take the tunnel. It's a good plan, Ashley."

"What tunnel?" I asked again, and Lev gave Ashley a dark look before facing me.

"There's a tunnel in the bunker. It has to lead out," he said, his expression pinched. "If the militia *is* watching, all they will see is us going into the shack," he added, this time to Ashley. "They won't suspect anything until we are long gone," he soothed. "We can still find Herm." His eyes rose to the piles of junk silhouetted against the bright sky. "Or we could stick it out here."

"Against the militia rangers?" Benedict said with a scoff. "Lev, you might know how to use your magic defensively, but I don't."

Lev frowned in annoyance. "It's not that hard. Point and heat. Boom."

He was talking about using magic to hurt people, and I felt sick.

"I'm not going to do that. I'll take my chances with the tunnel," Benedict said.

"Me too," I said. "We will shake the rangers if we're lucky, and it will keep us out of the sun if nothing else."

Lev looked at Ashley, and when she shrugged, he bobbed his head. "Tunnel it is." Lev tossed the carapace under the shack's steps, shortly followed by the drone itself. "We have five minutes. Pack your bag for foot travel. Food, water. Nothing but the essentials. Ashley, I swear, if I find shampoo in your gear, I will make you drink it."

"God, Lev," she grumbled as she stomped up the stairs. "You're not my mother."

Benedict shifted to follow, hesitating when I went to lock my bike to the stairway.

"You think you're coming back?" Lev said, and I snapped the lock closed.

"It's a three-thousand-dollar bike," I said as I stomped up the stairs, and he shifted out of my way.

I wasn't keen on taking the tunnel, but we had to get out of here. I couldn't stand against militant mages, and I doubted Benedict and Ashley could, either. Lev might.

Pluck's nails scrabbled on the wooden steps as he followed me inside. Water. I'd want all the water I could carry. And food bars. They didn't take up much space.

Ashley sat on the couch, staring at her pack dumped onto the coffee table to be sorted. "Wait until you see the bunker," she said, clearly distracted. "It's a loom safe house all right. The fridge is covered with loom memos and stuff. I even found a picture of your dad."

"Seriously?" Following her lead, I shuffled through my own pack, glad I'd kept the empty bottle from the day before and refilled it. Benedict stood in the threshold, peeling the tape off the lock as Lev headed for the hall, Pluck trailing behind him.

"Five minutes!" Lev said loudly, as if he was in charge. "We're not coming back!"

"What is a picture of my dad doing there?" I asked Ashley, pretty sure we'd left nothing down there to make my lie obvious.

"Yeah. It's kind of creepy." Ashley slung her pack on and strode to the bathroom. "Lev? I only have the one bottle. You got any empties to fill?"

Benny shut the door, satisfied when it locked. I hoisted my bag and shook down the food bars as he came close, his brow low. "I could use another bottle of water myself. We didn't leave anything in the basement, did we?"

I shrugged as I zipped my bag up, the sound harsh over Ashley's muted prattling from the bathroom. I'd seen her react to stress this way before, but this seemed extreme. "Once we get free from here, we ditch them and find Herm on our own. Bring him back to the loom. 'Kay? I'm not turning him in to take the blame for this. That's not what Darrell meant or wanted."

Uneasy, Benedict nodded and hoisted his bag over one shoulder.

"Petra?" Ashley leaned out of the bathroom. "Come on. We have to go. It's safe. Lev wouldn't let me down there until he checked it all out. He thought someone was still there because the TV was going, but it's empty. Promise."

Promise, I thought as I slung my bag over my shoulder, grabbed that tall stick I'd found in the rubble, and followed Benedict.

Lev was already halfway down the stairs when I got there, and my lips parted at the splintered door and singe marks. My best guess was he'd physically beat the door in when blowing the electronics hadn't worked. I exhaled, a twinge of unease finding me. *Just how well do I know Lev?* Not as well as I thought, apparently.

"Wait until you see," Ashley said, overly cheerful as she stepped sideways through the jagged hole and onto the stairs. "Come on, Pluck!" she called, voice high. "Let's check out the fridge for doggie treats!"

Pluck whined, fidgeted, and then stepped over the shallow lip to schlump down the stairs, lured by the promise of food. "That dog thinks with his stomach," I said, and Benedict smiled.

But it faded fast when Ashley called up for me. Giving Benedict a worried look, I started downstairs, the metal-shod stick ringing.

"Nice," I said as the air cooled. "No wonder the house is cool."

"That's not the half of it," Ashley said as I hit the bottom step and looked the place over as if I'd never seen it before. "Come and see this. You could live for months down here."

"I think someone did," Benedict said, bumping my shoulder as he went to the fridge. A sigh of relief slipped from him when he opened it, and I stifled a smile when he began filling his bag with bottled water.

"Petra?" Her color high, Ashley shoved a picture under my nose. "That's Herm with your dad? Right?"

I took the picture, staring at my dad's face, remembering it. "Yeah," I said softly, wondering why Ashley hadn't noticed that everything on the fridge revolved around me. "They were friends." Until they weren't and my dad died. The need to talk to Herm deepened. "Hey, um, the militia will find that door if they come investigate. Shouldn't we get out of here?" I could not put the picture back, and I jammed it into my pocket. "Lev?"

"In here!" he called from the workshop, and Benedict closed the fridge, motions fast as he zipped his pack closed and hoisted it. "Let's move!"

Benedict stomped past Ashley and me, his shoulders hunched and clearly worried. "It had better be a long tunnel," he said. "Coming out amid the junk won't help."

"Anyone find a flashlight?" I asked as I followed him and Ashley, my steps slowing when I saw the large, rough-hewn hole gapping where the pegboard had once been. The worktable, too, had been moved.

"Ah, flashlight?" I said again as they clustered before the dark hole, Pluck's tail drooping. The floor was dirt, and the walls were dirt. Two-by-fours held up a plywood ceiling, but I had a bad feeling the wood was there more for looks than to hold anything. "Um, my phone is at ten percent. I am not going in there without a flashlight."

"Relax." Lev put his hands together, a light forming between them as he drew them apart. "If my stone runs out, Ashley has enough lodestones to hold a light for a week. That woman hoards stone like a freshman."

I flushed in embarrassment. Of course we had light. All I had to do was follow along behind them and pick up the trash. *God, Grady! Can you be any more stupid?*

"I do not hoard stone," Ashley grumped, but she had at least four on her that I knew of.

"And you're sure you can find Ivaros?" Lev asked.

I nodded, my grip on my stick tightening. "Darrell gave me his last known," I lied.

Lev's eye twitched, and then he started down the gentle incline. "Let's go!"

Ashley balked, staring at the black hole. "I don't think I can do this," she said, and I felt a surge of sympathy as I eyed the plywood ceiling.

"It can't be that long," Benedict said cheerfully as he draped an arm over Ashley's shoulder and pushed her into motion. "It will be fine. You'll be eating dinner in Tucson. Promise."

"Sure, if the back door opens," Ashley grumped, and then the two of them were gone, blocking Lev's light.

I patted Pluck as he leaned into me, the dog clearly not liking the tunnellike hallway, either. "You're with me, bean," I said, and the dog whined, tail waving. "Let's go."

19

"IF I HAD PROBLEMS WITH ENCLOSED SPACES, THIS WOULD REALLY FREAK ME OUT," Lev said, his voice echoing as he strode forward, a thin ribbon of dross spilling like fog from the light in his hand. Ashley and Benedict were ten steps ahead to keep clear of the mess, and Pluck slunk at my heel, clearly not happy. I had ignored the dross Lev was creating until Herm's raw-hewn escape tunnel merged into a large, city-maintained drain. The dross would likely sit in Herm's earthen tunnel undisturbed, breaking on rock and rats. Mostly harmless. But here . . .

Sighing, I ran my too-tall stick along the smooth cement floor, gathering Lev's waste like cotton candy. If I left it here, it might damage something important. It wasn't a lot, but what the devil was I supposed to do with it?

"At least it's not smelly," Lev added, continuing his soliloquy. "I don't think I could handle traipsing through a sewer. This has got to be for rainwater."

"No graffiti," Benedict said from up ahead.

"That's good, right?" Ashley's voice echoed. "We won't run into anyone."

"Sure," I said from the back of the line, but to me, no graffiti meant a locked gate.

"Shouldn't we at least see the end by now?" Ashley added. "We've got to have gone nearly half a mile."

Are we there yet? I thought sourly when no one said anything.

I jumped, startled when Lev's light went out.

"Hang on. Let me," Benedict said as a clear, bright light blossomed in his hand to show the worry lining his face. "Lev ran out is all."

"I need to make a larger lodestone." Lev scuffed to a halt beside them. "I didn't expect to be down here this long."

"Give a person a little warning, will you?" Ashley accused. Her arms were wrapped around herself as if she was cold, but the furrow in her brow seemed born of anxiety. Or anger, maybe. Benedict lifted his glowing psi field high with a forced nonchalance, shifting to the side of the tunnel for Ashley and Lev to take point. Clearly distressed, Ashley linked her arm in Lev's, her prattle filling the tunnel as she called for Pluck and the dog happily joined her.

I exchanged a worried look with Benedict, motioning for him to start forward, leaving me to sweep up the dross.

"The farther we go, the better, right?" he said as he turned away.

I sighed at the thin trail of dross spilling along the floor like breadcrumbs behind him. "I am not the shadow-spit trashman," I whispered as I decided there was too much on my stick and ran a hand down its length, pushing it off and into a ball. A flash of heat from the dross shocked through me, my fingers tingling until it cooled in my psi field. Annoyed, I flung the balled dross back up the dark tunnel for someone else to deal with. Militia rangers, maybe, if they were following us.

Almost in response, Darrell's lodestone pulsed into sudden, chest-cramping cold. Alarmed, I grabbed the pendant, surprised when a cold, green light leaked through my fingers.

Don't they have a manual for this thing? I thought as the glow around my fingers faded. It was as if the stone had reacted to me throwing the dross away, and I dropped it behind my shirt, shivering at its cold feel. The stone wasn't black anymore in the fading light from Benedict's hands, but a pale green. *Swell.*

"Petra, I'm getting that bad feeling again," Benedict whispered, his pace slowing until I came even with him.

"Yeah?" More dross than his light should account for drifted about his feet, and my eyes flicked to the ceiling, drawn by a thin wisp of dross eddying down from a crack in the smooth cement. *What the hell?* "Ashley? What's the dross look like up there?" I shouted as I pulled Benedict clear of it. Great. Dross always went for the lowest point, and we were pretty low. Chances were good it was the vault's release trying to settle, and with my luck, it would get worse before it got better.

"It's thick!" she called back, and a second light blossomed in her hand, held high. "Oh, my God! It's coming in from the ceiling. You want to come up here and work point to get rid of it?"

No, I didn't want to go up there and get rid of it. I had nothing to put it in. But my words to tell her to push through and deal with the fallout faltered when a flicker of distortion rose up from the floor between us and Ashley's increasingly faint chatter. It wasn't dross. It was shadow.

How? I thought in panic as I grabbed Benedict's arm and pulled him back a step. *Shadow spit, we have to get out of here!*

"It's just like the feeling I got down in the . . . Oh." Benedict's voice cut off as his gaze fixed on the shadow as its hazy nothing coalesced into a foggy snake. Curled up into a tight ball to avoid the dross spilling from both the ceiling and Benedict's hand, it sent up a little cobra head, weaving as it oriented on us. It was between us and the way out, and I didn't dare call to Ashley as she prattled on about "that damned dross snarling her hair." She had Pluck, and I wouldn't risk him running back to me. Not now.

"Is it here because it's dark?" Benedict whispered, not scared nearly enough.

"I don't know. All sorts of dumb things are going on," I said bitterly. *It's not after my hair tie, is it?* I mean, I'd been wearing the thing for eight years, though admittedly not in city tunnels that had never seen the light of day.

I drew Benedict back a step and smacked the butt of my staff between us and the shadow. Tail flicking, the shadow worked to stay clear of the dross. *Why is it even down here?*

"Ashley? Grab Pluck. We got shadow!" I called.

"Shadow?" Lev said, the usually unflappable man clearly jolted.

"Are you kidding?" She sounded almost angry, and I glanced at her silhouette, having to squint. "Petra, I don't have any shadow buttons!"

"I'm good! Keep going!" I shouted as I lifted a foot for the shadow button I still had wedged in my laces. "If there's a locked gate at the end of this tunnel, go open it. Benedict and I are going to be running as if hell is after us at the count of three."

"Oh, shit," she whispered. Grabbing Lev's arm, she whistled for Pluck and dragged Lev into a run. A sudden light bounced against the smooth walls as Lev's voice rose high over Ashley's demands, but she was right. They needed to get out. I could handle this.

I am going to have to.

"Okay, back up to the wall. Give it some room," I said to Benedict, my eyes fixed on shifting haze as I fingered the smooth disk. "Shadow will always go for the low-hanging fruit first. I'm going to throw it a shadow treat, and then we both run. Watch the ceiling for the dross spilling in. Ready? Three, two, one," I whispered as I flicked the black coin back the way we'd come. "Go!"

Benedict jerked as the shadow raced past us, following the cheerful ting of the coin hitting the wall.

We ran. Tingling sparkles of dross hit my face, flashes of heat falling from the ceiling like lava. More dross puffed up from our steps. Ashley had been right. The tunnel might be rising, but we were running through a dross flow. *God, please let there be a way out.*

And then my heart jumped as the ceiling ahead of us cracked, the sudden sound absolutely terrifying. Benedict sprinted forward. I lurched to follow, skidding to a halt when a sheet of distortion billowed out and down like a volcanic vent. Dross spilled in from above to fill the corridor. *Shadow spit . . .*

Face cold, I looked through the haze at Benedict, a globe of light in his hand. A rising haze of dross eddied about his ankles as more spilled down. I was on the wrong side of the crack. Sure, I could handle dross without it breaking on me, but this much? A drift was painful until I wrapped it in a psi field. What was spilling down to fill the corridor would burn like wading through fire, and I backed up, feet tingling in pain as I gathered my nerve.

I'd never touched that much dross before. And it was only getting worse as invisible flames dripped from the ceiling to roll like storm clouds along the top of the corridor.

"Petra, we have to go!" As if oblivious to it, Benedict held out his hand, right into the downpour. Dross spilled to either side to create a tiny slip of clear space. It gave me an idea, and inhaling, I made a psi field to push the dross away. It worked, and I dove through the temporary safe space, slamming into Benedict and almost sending us down.

"You okay? Why did you stop?!" he exclaimed as he stood me up, and together we ran. We were past the vent, and the skin above my shoes burned from the dross filling the tunnel.

"Go, go, go!" Benedict shouted at the hint of daylight, and then we both yelped, pushed forward when a thundering crack sounded and the tunnel behind us completely collapsed. I still had that stick in my hand, and it hit the walls as I struggled for balance, but it was Benedict who kept me on my feet and moving forward.

He'd dropped his light, and when I turned, I felt my face pale. A wave of dross was rolling toward us like a dust storm, filling the tunnel. *Benedict . . .* I thought, terrified. I'd survive it—obviously—but it was going to burn like hell.

And then I staggered, shocked when something hit my mind.

Shadow . . . Oily and cold, it numbed my sight and hearing, overwhelming with a self-righteous anger and need. It saw me as clearly as I saw it, and my mouth went dry as Benedict dragged me forward. Shadow had followed me through my psi bubble and was fleeing the dross flood. It couldn't stay in the tunnel and had nowhere to go but into one of us. Into me.

"Petra!" Benedict yanked me up, and I blinked at him, trying to focus.

Not Benedict, I thought desperately. "Sh-shadow," I slurred, and he dragged me toward the glimmer of light and the sound of Ashley's shouts as Lev tried to break the grate at the end.

The shadow was clawing to find a way into my mind. The stone about my neck flashed hot, then cold, and I drove the icy presence away, sealing Darrell's stone and my mind in a protective psi field. I couldn't walk, and it was only Benedict who kept me upright as I fought to keep it at bay.

"Go," I panted, trying to move my feet, but it was as if my legs were made of lead. Ahead, dross pooled at the ceiling like smoke from a fire. Beyond it, the honest light of the sun beckoned, just out of reach. I couldn't move, that shadow holding me paralyzed as we fought for control while Benedict pulled me toward Ashley's triumphant shout. The grate was down.

Benedict lurched, and I gasped as he pushed us out into the world. I fell and rolled, my hip and shoulder exploding into a sudden pain as I hit the hard-packed sand. Adrenaline scoured through me. My focus sharpened as the heat soaked in and drove the icy sensation of shadow away. Eyes closed, I sucked in the air, coughing out dross as my hands clenched into packed sand. We'd made it out. I was alive.

Pretty sure . . .

"What the sweet hell was that!" Lev shouted angrily as he stood by the broken grate.

I sat up, bleary. My legs were burning, and I scooted away from the dross pouring from the mouth of the tunnel, curling like smoke from the top of the broken grate before the sun hit it and it sank. Eight-foot-high, vegetation-encrusted banks rose up, settling us into a sunbaked, hot stillness. It was noon, maybe, and the rumble of thunder made me shudder. The shadow was gone, and still I shook, cold as I fumbled for my bag and stick.

"We need to go," I whispered. Obviously I'd shoved that shadow from my mind, but it had to be here. The tunnel was a deathtrap of dross.

"Petra, are you okay?" Benedict asked, bent double around a rough cough. Dross festooned him, and I rubbed my eyes, immediately wishing I hadn't when grit stung them.

Ashley waited just behind the opening and watched, a frustrated anger pinching her eyes as if she was going to blame me for the collapse.

Lev stood on the floor of the wash, dross eddying past his feet like a heat mirage. It was a good bet that none of us were seeing the same thing as dross pooled at the door like a heated oil slick, but it was obvious that we were in trouble as the cement around the grate began to crumble. *That's how the ceiling gave way* . . . "Why was there shadow down there!" Lev shouted, white-faced and sounding betrayed. "There was enough dross to kill anything!"

If I didn't know better, I would say the man was afraid. Lips twisted sourly, I pushed the dross off me, the heat of connection jolting. "The tunnel ran under a dross pool," I muttered. "Probably created when the vault collapsed. It ate away at the ceiling until it broke through. That's why they line the vault with glass." Ticked, I flicked the ugly stuff into the flood, not caring who it broke on. *Is that what it's like to be a mage?* I wondered. *Uncaring and unconcerned?* "We need to get moving."

But my attention snapped up at a low growl, and I froze.

"Oh, no . . ." I whispered when Lev spun, the man swearing as he dropped back almost to the tunnel. Eyes wide, he held a glowing hand out, his lodestone earring brilliant with the sun.

A bear of a dog stood stiffly before Ashley, his fur black against the green of the sedge clinging to the side of the wash, his shaggy fur dripping a foul stench. A low growl promising violence rumbled up from his chest, and his teeth were bared as he stared at her.

"Please, no," I whispered, my heart breaking as Benedict tried to drag me away and up the wall of the wash. It was Pluck. The shadow had been driven out of the tunnel as much as we had been. The light was too much for it. It needed to be in something or it would perish. I had forced it out of me, and it had gone into the next best thing. Pluck.

"It's shadow!" Lev shouted, the usually confident man panicked as he shifted his feet to find his balance. His lodestone earring was glowing, channeling the light of the sun, as he sidestepped to get Ashley out of his line of sight. His horrified gaze never left Pluck. And it had to be Pluck. Or it had once been him. He had gone shadow, and my heart broke.

"Lev, don't!" I demanded as the shadow-dog lunged at Ashley, teeth snapping. "He's gone shadow! You're only going to kill him. Stop!"

Ashley recoiled, screaming as she slipped on the side of the wash and went down.

I lurched forward, breath catching at Pluck's sudden yelp of pain. "No!" I exclaimed, a hand outstretched as Lev's field hit Pluck and the dog collapsed, sliding to a halt before Ashley. Horrified, the woman scrambled to her feet, staring at Pluck's motionless form.

"What did you do?" Benedict shouted. "Petra could have gotten it out of him!"

The glow about Lev's earring flickered and went out. "Back off, lab rat!" he said, face drawn and hand shaking. "Grady said it herself. The dog went shadow. There was no saving him."

Ashley backed away, staring down at Pluck. "H-he went shadow . . ." she said, eyes wide as she looked up at me. "Pluck wasn't supposed to die."

No shit. Throat closed, I limped to Pluck. Or at least what Pluck had become. The huge monster of fur and teeth wasn't moving, his eyes open and lips pulled back to show unnaturally long teeth. There was no blood, no gaping hole, and I guessed that Lev had cooked his heart, wrapping it in a psi field and setting the blood within it to boil like a microwave.

But then Pluck's paw twitched, and my heart broke a little more. We weren't done yet.

I'm so sorry, Pluck. He was a good dog. He didn't deserve this.

Jaw clenched to hold back the tears, I shifted to stand between Pluck and Lev. Pluck wasn't a spider. He was a thinking creature capable of love, and it would take a moment for the shadow to figure him out. Thirty seconds, maybe. "Benedict, take Ashley up the wash, will you?" I could have used the help, but the woman was a mess.

Lev exhaled, clearly shaken. "Don't everyone thank me at once," he muttered.

"Now!" I said as Pluck's chest moved.

Benedict's anger shifted to understanding, his expression going blank. "Let's go," he said as he lured Ashley into a reluctant, halting step. Lev, though, didn't move, and I stood beside Pluck not knowing what I could actually do. No bottle, no more shadow buttons. All I had was a silver-shod stick.

"You're going to bury him?" Lev said. "Seriously?"

"You need to shut up!" I shouted in heartache. "This wasn't Pluck's fault!"

I jerked when Pluck snorted, and the three of them turned, eyes widening as they froze.

"Ashley, get out of here," I said, simply wanting them out of the way as Pluck began twitching. Stick in hand, I twirled it to build up some momentum. This was not going to be easy—on the heart or the head. "Congratulations, Lev. You killed my dog, but the shadow is still in him. Back off so I can drive it out. Otherwise, this starts up again."

Pluck spasmed, ending the motion by lurching upright. Lips pulled from his teeth, he turned to Lev and growled.

"I killed it!" Lev was pale as he fisted his hand. "What the fuck!"

"Don't!" Benedict exclaimed, but Lev punched out at nothing as he yanked on the sun, channeling the energy through his stone and into Pluck. I fell back, horrified, an arm over my face as super-heated blood and flesh splattered me. Pluck barked savagely, and I looked up as Benedict dragged Ashley away. Lev stood there, staring as Pluck grew even larger, dripping more blood than he could possibly hold.

"How do you kill it?!" Lev shouted, and I lurched forward to smack my stick on Pluck's hindquarters to get his attention.

The shadow-dog spun, his low growl finding the pit of my being. His chest was gone, exploded outward from a second blast of super-heated energy. The cave of him was empty and gaping, and I refused to cry.

"I'm so sorry, Pluck," I whispered. The dog held five times the shadow that the spider had, and just the memory of that much in me made my mouth go dry. I couldn't handle that much shadow. I shouldn't be able to handle any at all.

Pluck . . . I thought as I jabbed the butt of my staff at Pluck. "Get out!" I shouted, and he barked, twisting to bite it as it thunked into his shoulder. "Get out of my dog!" I demanded.

And then Darrell's lodestone cracked into a mind-numbing cold, stealing my breath away. I dropped back, my hand fisted about it, scared as a tendril of shadow rose like an evil mist from Pluck. It was leaving him. Voluntarily. Shadow wouldn't do that unless it had something better to settle in. *Me?*

"No . . ." I whispered, backpedaling as the lodestone went cold, drawing the shadow from Pluck with the quickness of a whipcrack. Panicked, I tried to stop it, but it was too fast, and with a little ping of recognition, the shadow was in the stone.

Strings cut, Pluck collapsed.

No . . . I had time for the single thought, and then I gasped, my staff clattering into the earth as I staggered away with my arm over my face. The sky flashed white and the sun's heat burned. Crying out, I dropped to kneel on the packed sand, my eyes hidden. My pulse hammered, and for an instant, I wondered if I'd gone shadow.

But the wrongness that had tried to take me over when I had touched the shadow-driven spider was not there, and I shook, cold, as the lodestone swung before me. Frost had covered it. It burned my hand as I caught it. Fingers shaking, I wiped the frozen condensation away. It was black. The stone was utterly black.

My fingers sprang open, and the pendant swung free as cold emanated from it. *My God, it's holding shadow.*

"Grady?" Lev called, and my head snapped up.

"Don't touch me!" I said, a hand out to keep him back as I scrabbled for my long stick and used it to lever myself upright. My pulse hammered, and my chest burned as the lodestone bumped into me and swung away. Hunched, I flicked the hair from my eyes. What had once been Pluck was at my feet, still at last, oversize and reeking of a foul musk. Chest tight, I sent my eyes to a nearby cactus as a cactus wren sang. The world was washed out, shimmering in heat, and my skin was on fire—except for my fingers.

The stone is holding shadow, I thought again as I stared at the pendant in my grip. The cold was beginning to ease and the frost was gone. The sky, too, had regained a faint blue, and the silver edging the trees was gone. But the stone was still black.

"Back off," I practically growled at Lev, then sent careful tendrils of my psi energy about the stone. If it held shadow, I could sense it.

My lip curled as the chained shadow foamed and sizzled against my mind, but the stone held it all, and my mind remained untouched.

Sweet mother of cats, I think I broke Herm's lodestone, I thought, knees going watery.

Scared, I took the stone from around my neck. The cord whispered through my fingers like snow, and I stared at it.

But as I pooled the stone and cord in my hand to throw it into the tunnel, I hesitated. The stone held the shadow like a bottle. It was safe. It was a Spinner's lodestone. Maybe this was what it was supposed to do, sort of a protection like dross cords and knotted silk. Throwing it away suddenly seemed like a mistake. Herm probably knew how to get the shadow out.

Fingers shaking, I watched the dross ooze from the tunnel as I strung the lanyard back around my neck. The stone bumped against me, no longer cold, no longer hot, but still black as sin. The sky was again blue, and the shadows under the paloverde trees were just shadows.

And Pluck, I thought, my heart breaking as I looked down, *is still dead.*

20

"S IT GONE?" LEV DEMANDED, HIS FACE WHITE. "I THOUGHT IF YOU KILLED THE host, you killed the shadow."

"So you cooked my *dog?*" I yelled, my emotions raw. "I could have pulled it out of him, you stupid ass!" Throat tight, I dropped down beside Pluck on the sand, my fingers smoothing his blood-matted fur. "You were a good dog," I whispered, tears spilling from me. "You didn't deserve this."

"Petra?"

Benedict's shadow fell over me, and I blinked up at him, not caring if he saw my misery. Ashley was nearby, slumped in exhaustion, her feet clearly sore from her fashion slip-ons rubbing a hole in her ankle. Beside her, Lev looked almost angry as he punched his phone, texting someone.

"Petra, I'm sorry, but we have to go," Benedict said. He held his hand out, his reach for me hesitant. "Ashley says the dross is still leaking from the tunnel."

It had slacked off, though, and I gripped the ruined stone, angry as I laboriously got to my feet. My stick was cool in my grip, and blinking, I tried not to cry over Pluck. I wanted to bury him, but there was no time and the ground was as hard as cement, even if it was sand.

"You were a good boy," I said, eyes welling as I worked Pluck's collar off, my gut clenching at the flecks of blood on it. *Lev, you are a fucking bastard.*

Tears joined the water as I used one of my precious bottles to rinse his collar and tags, then shoved Pluck's wet collar into my pack. The *kic-kic-kic* of a cactus wren was a lonely sound as I stared down the wash at nothing, trying to find myself.

My gut hurt. There was a big gaping hole in me where Pluck had once been, the heartache raw and exposed to the world. My fingers touched his tags and my eyes closed.

Benedict's hand on my shoulder slipped away and his attention swung to the faultless blue sky. "Do you hear that?"

"Hear what?" Ashley said, her voice a little too nonchalant as she edged toward Lev.

"That's a drone," Benedict whispered, head up and lodestone bright as he pulled me to the edge of the wash. Yelping, he let go of me to slap his arm. "Something bit me!" he swore, then he gasped, staring at the brown-fletched dart stuck in his biceps.

They'd found us.

"Ashley, run!" I shouted as Benedict's eyes went unfocused and he began to sway. I scrambled to catch him, easing him to the rocky soil as I squinted at the line the ravine cut against the bright sky.

"Go!" I exclaimed again, hunching over Benedict as soldiers in desert camo boiled out from behind the cacti to stand at the top of the wash, lodestones glowing as bright as the sun from their hands and big-ass military-style guns in their grip. Ashley and Lev didn't move as they yelled at us, and scared, I raised my hands, standing with my stick held high when a few slid into the wash. Benedict was down, but Ashley and Lev were not.

Actually, Ashley seemed kind of relieved. And Lev . . .

My lips parted as Lev went to shake hands with one of the men, his pleasure obvious.

Eyes narrowed, I squinted at the tall man, trying to see past the helmet, boots, and tight-fitting fatigues. If it hadn't been for his lode-stone bolo, I might not have recognized him.

Sikes? What the hell?

"Whose idea was it to go through that tunnel?" Ashley said, looking almost comical in her broken sandals, shorts, and sunglasses, her pack at her feet and surrounded by men in desert camo. "There was fucking shadow in there. Lev had to fry my dog!"

Pluck is my dog, I thought, confused, and then I jumped, adrenaline flashing when two soldiers went for Benedict. "Hey! Back off!" I shouted, lurching forward when one of them rolled Benedict over with his foot and Benny groaned.

And then I was on the ground, my breath huffing out when someone's knee found my back. "Get off!" I rasped, face hot where it touched the sand. "You're burning me!" I wiggled, chin lifting when he wrenched my arm behind me. I took a breath to yell, and then I froze, panicking when an icy sensation swirled up from my lode-stone, angry and cold. *Oh, God. Calm down,* I said to myself, but the shadow heard me, rising higher as if in rebellion.

"Jeck! Kid gloves!" Lev called, and the pressure on my shoulder eased. "She's just a sweeper. She can't hurt you."

Stop! I screamed into my mind, this time to the shadow. I was afraid to move, and I held my breath, not believing it as the cold sensation in my mind eased . . . then vanished to leave a silky, sulky taste in my thoughts. My pulse hammered as a shudder rippled over me. The shadow taking refuge in Darrell's lodestone had listened. It. Had. Listened.

"Don't move," the man holding me down said, and I yelped as he jerked me up to sit on the hot sand. Someone kicked my staff away, and a third pulled my pack off, wrenching my arm in the process. Two men were dragging Benedict to the flat sandy bottom. I started to get up and the guy watching me shook his head, the glow about his lodestone ring shifting to a warning red.

I sank back down and tried to figure this out. We were surrounded by men in desert camo, rifles ready and dressed too hot for the sun baking down. They had guns and lodestones. But there was no insignia on anyone. Who the hell were these people, and how come Ashley and Lev knew them? It wasn't the militia. Was it?

"Ashley?" I rubbed my sore shoulder, but she never turned, ignoring me as she slammed a pink power drink in the thin shade she'd found.

"Lev?" I tried instead. He at least heard me, and the man's ears went red as he handed Benedict's bag to a thin guy with a shaved skull. His usual confidence was back, but I'd seen his fear. "What's going on. Are you militia? Did you sell us out to the mages?"

The man standing over me actually laughed. "Give me the lodestone, or I dart you and take it."

I stared up at him, my hand clenched around the cold stone. They already had my pack and stick, but this was different. "If this comes off, the shadow comes out," I lied, afraid to unclamp my hands around Darrell's pendant even as little darts of icy cold prickled against me.

Lev turned at that, not a hint of guilt on his face. "Grady, give it to him," he said, sounding tired. "The shadow is gone."

My gaze went to Benedict. Two people in desert camo were crouched over him, talking softly as they took his vitals with a military precision. "You can't use it," I said when I decided they weren't making anything worse. "It's a Spinner stone."

"Then you won't mind giving it to me," Lev said, hand extended. "Seeing as you really aren't a Spinner."

No, I wasn't a Spinner, and yet I was still loath to let it go. But the man watching me made his lodestone glow in threat and I uncramped my hands, feeling its loss already. I could sense the shadow pressing on my mind, demanding something from me. *Stay put,* I thought as I reluctantly took it from around my neck, and I swear, a new flush of cold stabbed my fingers when I gave it to Lev.

"See, Jeck? That wasn't so hard. And no one got hurt." Lev jiggled it in his hand to gauge my reaction before dropping it into a pocket. "Phone?"

Jeck tightened his grip on his rifle, clearly eager to use it. If I didn't hand it over, he'd simply take it. Frowning, I pulled it from my pocket as I gave Jeck the stink eye. "Who are you, Lev? And don't say you're just some guy down the hall looking to score a date."

"And wand," he added as a trickle of sweat rolled down his neck.

I squinted up at him. "Seriously? All it does is collect dross."

"Lev, we're ready to move Dr. Strom," a young man in a battered cap said, and Lev nodded, grimacing at the interruption.

"Wand," Lev insisted, and I handed it over. A faint smile found him. "Ashley?" he called loudly, and the woman turned. "You know her password, right? Get her phone charged up. Ivaros's location is probably in it somewhere."

Oh, no. Herm . . . I thought, suddenly panicked. They weren't after just Benedict but Herm. Who the hell were these guys?

"You got it!" Ashley said, her high voice cheerful. But her confidence faltered when her gaze landed on Pluck.

"You're giving Benedict and Herm to the militia?" I guessed, and Lev blinked, startled. "You are a real hero, Lev. You know that? How much are they paying you?" Shadow spit, I was a fool for trusting him, but Ashley? She didn't need money.

Ashley limped forward, awkward on her busted sandal. "Oh, my God. She thinks we're militia." Hand extending, she took my phone, sniffing at the dead screen. My wand, I noticed, had gone into Lev's pocket with the Spinner lodestone. "It's a lot simpler than that, Petra," she said, clearly unhappy with the soldiers beginning to cluster around Pluck, poking at him.

"So tell me. I'm not going anywhere," I smart-mouthed. But if she wasn't militia, then what was she? *Who are they?*

"Two years!" she exclaimed, arms over her middle as she glanced at Pluck. "Two years I worked with you and lived with you, to find that dross-eater, and when it finally pays off, they still can't see the big picture." Her gaze darted to me, the anger back. "Typical."

I felt my face burn. Two years? Had her friendship all been a lie? "Find who?"

Lev looked up from his phone. "Ashley," he said, his warning clear.

But Ashley leaned in over me, her strawberry-scented hair falling forward as she smiled. "I was trying to find Ivaros, sweetheart. And you were the only one he was talking to." She pushed back, her expression ugly as she watched Benedict being hoisted over the rim of the wash. "Uncle John. Seriously?"

Suddenly the conversation between her and Sikes in her room made a lot more sense.

"Ashley." Lev looked up from some paperwork a soldier was showing him. "You need to shut up."

"Why?" Ashley's chin rose. "She's going to do everything you ask her to, because if she doesn't, Benedict is going to take the fallout and she has a crush on him. Which I think is hilarious. What would he want with a sweeper? I mean, really . . . Besides, we have his process. That's all we need."

Anger was a quick wash tempered by fear, and I stood, careful not to make any sudden moves when Jeck took notice. "You're a separatist?" I said, aghast when I remembered her words around the dinner table. My eyes went to Lev. "You've been *spying* on me!"

Lev shrugged as if unconcerned, but I saw a hint of unease as Ashley chuckled.

"I have." Ashley grasped Lev's chin and gave it a little shake. "Lev is my backup. Keeping me safe."

"I am not your bodyguard, and we are not risking Strom," Lev said, but it was to Ashley, not me, and I stiffened when the soldiers clustered around Pluck began to laugh.

Neighbor down the hall, my ass. He was a separatist, and he had been spying on us for two years to find Herm. *Not us. Me.* "Hey, leave my dog alone!" I shouted, and Sikes turned from where he'd been giving instructions.

"You!" Sikes exclaimed, his raspy voice harsh from tobacco, and both Ashley and I jumped. "Get away from that dog. You don't know where the shadow went!"

The soldiers scattered. Mollified, Ashley recovered her aplomb, tugging her short shirt down over her midriff in what I recognized as a nervous tic. "We don't need Strom," she said, a mocking smile on her face as she watched me for my reaction. And yet they had hauled him out of here. Maybe I should be worried that I was still down here. In a wash. In June. *Maybe I need to become useful . . .*

Sikes came forward, sweat dripping from his leathery skin as the dark pits of his eyes looked me over—and found me lacking. "If Strom can figure out what triggers his inert dross to explode, fine, but my goal is and has always been Ivaros."

The sun beat on me, but I couldn't move, hemmed in. "The math doesn't work out," I said, hearing in it an echo of Ashley herself.

"It does if you have the catalyst." Sikes's gaze went to the top of the gully as more men gathered to look down, rifles in hand. "Get her out of the ravine. It's as hot as hell down here."

Relief was a quick wash as the soldiers began to work their way out. I glanced at Pluck, my chest hurting. "You think you can use this? Control it?" My voice was getting loud, but I didn't care. "Make a weapon out of it?"

But of course they did. They were not mage militia. They were radicalized separatist mages. Destruction was kind of their goal; taking over the world was easier when it was falling apart.

"Sikes, you are not thinking big enough," Ashley said, her high voice rising into the perfect blue. "Strom's process is far more than a bomb. Can't you see that?"

Steps slow, I followed Lev to the wall of the wash. They were separatists. Ashley and Lev both. *Shit. I'm in trouble.*

"I'll tell you what *Dr. Strom* invented," Ashley almost crooned when Sikes ignored her, her awkward mince because of her broken sandal almost comical among the sweating combat-dressed men. "He invented a process to take sweepers out of the equation. You want Herm because he's a filthy dross-eater, an abomination, a threat to mage superiority. But he's not the problem."

She really believes this stuff? I mused as Sikes reached the top of the cliff and looked down at her. The sun caught his bolo lodestone, winking cheerfully, but the man was hot and overdressed . . . and he looked frustrated. "What's the problem, Ashley?" he asked sarcastically.

The woman beamed, extending her hand for him to help her. "The problem is the sweepers," she said, and Sikes hauled her up. "Get rid of them, and you have everything. You'd have it already if they weren't sucking the strength out of you. Week by week. Year by year." She smirked. "Invoice by invoice."

Squinting, I scuffed to a halt, only halfway up. She was touting the very thing I'd been worried about, but hearing it come out of the mouth of a separatist, it had a different rhetoric. *Who the hell have I been living with?*

"Get Grady topside!" Sikes shouted, and I jumped, surprised when Lev reached back for me.

"You're a part of this?" I said as Lev wiggled his fingers for me to take them. It was obvious why they hadn't drugged me, irritating, even if I was thankful for it. *No threat, huh?* They thought I was helpless, and at the moment, I was halfway willing to show them otherwise. "You seriously want to rule the mundanes? You want to use Benedict's faulty procedure to destroy the peace we have lived in for thousands of years?"

Lev grabbed my elbow and yanked me up with a painful strength. "Watch your step, ma'am," he said, and I tugged free.

But I was out of the wash, and I appreciated the quickening breeze as I took in the six thugs facing toward St. Unoc, rifles and lodestones ready. Six more faced Tucson. Between them, parked on the desert dirt among cacti and sedge, were two Hummers, their backs open, engines on, and air going. Benedict was in one, our stuff in the other. Nervous, I licked my lips. *Too many guns, too hot a day,* I thought. I couldn't simply kick someone in the shin and run.

The loss of my phone and what Ashley might text to Herm was bad enough, but strangely it was the lack of the lodestone that hurt. That, and they didn't care about my rights or due process. I was in a military zone of their making . . . and I was a statistic. "You are a lying little bastard," I said as the remaining soldiers loaded up, and someone chuckled. "I trusted you, Lev. You are a piece of work, but Ashley is shit," I said loudly, and Ashley flipped me off, laughing as she swung into the front seat and angled the vents to her.

I forced my hands to unfist, anger a slow burn. Yeah, she had lied to me, but everyone lied to me. *I picked up that spill two days ago. That's not my dross. I did the dishes yesterday. You, too, can be a Spinner, Petra.*

"Be good and give me your wrists," Lev said, and I scowled at him. Like I had much choice? Grimacing, I obediently put out my hands, silent as he put a pair of cuffs on me. Leaning close, he whispered, "Because you are not just a trashman."

I stared, not sure what he was saying as the faint wrinkles around his eyes bunched. He had been terrified when Pluck went shadow . . . and I had captured it. I might be in cuffs, but I was stronger than him. "I'm not taking you to Herm."

Lev nodded. "When he finds out we have you, he'll come to us. Vehicle. Move."

I had nothing to say. Two people reached for me, roughly hauling me up and in. "Lev," I blurted, trying not to step on Benedict as I was pushed to the back. "Lev!" Hands shoved me down, and my wrists were locked to the seat as the wide tailgate shut.

"I'm riding with Ashley," Lev said. Giving the Hummer a thump, he walked away.

And then we drove off, leaving my dog to the unkindness of the sun and time.

21

*P*RETTY LIES AND FAIRY TALES, WRAPPED IN SOILED FLAGS. BLACK COIN SEEPS, LIKE *poison creeps, and balance found will fail."*

Jimmy Tross's "Black Coin" was tinny through someone's phone, the man's low, expressive voice cheapened by the tiny speaker. But I could hear his rich voice in my memory, and I closed my eyes, finding three and a half minutes of respite as we jostled down the desert twin track to nowhere.

The steel on my wrists felt heavy, and the cold stares from the people surrounding me were anything but pleasant. Most were a good deal younger than me, and I knew how easy it was to be stupid at that age. Following orders only caught ninety-five percent of the mistakes. *Yeah. Let's give that a lodestone and a sense of entitlement,* I thought, my eyes opening when we turned onto a paved road somewhere between St. Unoc and Tucson.

I missed Pluck, and I missed my phone, and I missed my sticks, but oddly what I missed the most was Darrell's lodestone—even if there was a shadow trapped in it.

I swayed, shoved upright by the soldier next to me when we took a sharp turn and the Hummer pulled into what had probably once been an elementary school, coming to a quick halt in the drop-off zone. Only now did the people around me begin to talk, the rough camaraderie slanting to the cruel as they hauled Benedict out like so many groceries and strapped him upright into a wheelchair.

"Hey, what about me?" I called, shaking my cuffs when they wheeled him away. But no one seemed to care, and I sank deeper into the dim interior as Jimmy's singing grew faint and then was lost. Slowly the *kic-kic-kic* of a cactus wren became obvious, and I searched the sunbaked lot until I found Lev talking with two older men in fatigues. He totally looked the part of a separatist. Finally the two men walked away and Lev lurched up and into the back with me.

"Can I have my stick and stone?" I asked as he unlocked my cuffs.

"No, they might break my bones," he said with a chuckle, his lodestone earring glinting.

"Oh, you're funny." I rubbed my wrists as he got out and stood waiting for me to join him. I hesitated at his hand stretched to help me down. Benedict had been wheeled inside, and I disliked that we'd been separated. I had no idea where Ashley was, and frankly, I didn't care. *Two effing years . . .*

Ignoring his hand, I made my awkward way to the edge of the Hummer and scooted down. My feet hit the pavement hard, the jolt going all the way to my skull as I found the sun. Squinting into the hot wind, I placed myself using the surrounding mountains. "I'm not helping you find Herm," I said, and he shrugged, that stupid half smile on his face.

"Finding Herm is not my job. Keeping Ashley safe is." Head twisting, he indicated the big twin front doors that everyone had gone in through. *Last little ducks.*

"Yeah?" I lurched into motion, eager for a little air-conditioning. "That why you joined? To keep *Ashley* safe? She doesn't even like you."

Two men I hadn't even noticed had fallen in behind us, and Lev gave me an odd look. "The feeling is mutual," he said, gaze flicking to them and back.

"Then you joined because you think that mages should rule the world?" I mocked, and he flushed. "Sorry, Lev. I liked you better when you were an idiot who joined to keep Ashley safe."

Lev scuffed to a halt before the institutional glass doors. "Not all separatists want to rule the world. That's ranger propaganda. Most just want to find and prevent weavers."

A wave of blessedly cool air washed over me as he opened one. "Weavers?" I muttered. "Seriously? I know you outliers believe in all sorts of oddball things, but weavers?"

He was silent as he followed me in, the rims of his ears reddening, and I sighed. "Okay," I finally said. "Why do you want to find weavers?"

Lev glanced at my escorts. "Weavers create shadow when they use dross to do magic."

"You think Herm is a weaver?" I said, but he didn't answer, and I remembered how freaked out he was when shadow had taken Pluck. I'd never seen the man upset before, and he'd been afraid. Shoulders slumped, I looked over the low-ceilinged lobby. It had never been proven that dross misuse was where shadow came from. Blaming the lethal stuff on a mythical magic user had seemed harmless—until they started labeling people as such.

Ashley's chatter was obvious among the more sedate voices in the hall, and my lip curled when I spotted her. I had trusted her. I had *liked* her—and it had been nothing but a lie to find Herm Ivaros. *She must think I'm an idiot,* I mused. *Uncle John, indeed.*

Annoyed, I strode down the asbestos tiles and ugly white walls beside Lev, intentionally shifting my pace so it wouldn't match his measured, clicking steps. I'd seen enough pointed rifles and glowing lodestones today to blunt my concern for them, and the faded outlines of hummingbirds and cacti on the walls made me feel as if I were being taken to the principal. Dross littered the corners, and I had yet to see a trap—which sort of went along with a supremist group bent on dominating the very people who kept them safe.

"Hey, I'd really like my stick back. It belonged to my dad." Which might not be true. It might have belonged to Herm.

"Not happening."

"And Pluck's tags. And that lodestone. Sentimental value," I added, and his eyes flicked to mine, brow high. "Darrell gave it to me."

"So you can lie. I was starting to wonder."

"Unlike you, who don't seem to know how to do anything but," I said caustically. "This is illegal." I glanced at the two men behind me. "You are illegally detaining me."

"Through here. Let's get this settled." Lev took an extra-long step to reach a set of glass doors and open them. My pulse quickened as I went into the office area and studied the multiple desks behind a long counter, staffed by men and women in fatigues and olive tees. It *was* the principal's office.

"Sit." Lev pointed to a bench outside one of the real offices with four walls and a view. Benedict was already there, still unconscious and parked beside the bench as if waiting to go in. The people we passed watched us with a wary confidence while they worked on their laptops and sipped their coffee, but I thought they looked odd in their military fatigues as they printed up propaganda and plans to overthrow the government. I guess. I didn't actually know what they were doing, and I tried to find some dignity in my jeans and sweat-stained shirt.

"There's water if you want it." Lev nodded at the single-use water bottles stacked beside Benedict, and my thirst redoubled.

"Wow." I sat, anxious for him to leave so I could crack one open. "Thank you *so* much."

Lev's eyebrows rose at my obvious sarcasm. Smirking, he left me there and went to talk to the man sitting at a desk just outside the door. After a moment, the man rose, giving the door a cursory knock before escorting Lev in. Voices rose, muted, and the door shut.

Immediately I snatched up a bottled water, snapping it open and downing it, breath held and throat moving. Shadow spit, I was thirsty.

"Ow . . ." Benedict whispered, head hanging. "Why am I in a wheelchair?"

I came up for air and slid closer. "Oh, thank God. Benny? Don't try to get up," I said as I undid the chest strap and took his hands in mine. The white skin around his ring finger looked wrong, and I covered it. "Relax," I added when he groaned, a shaky hand going to his brow. "You'll be okay. You want some water?"

"What happened?" he rasped. "Last thing I remember is that shadow . . . and then a dart in my arm." His fingers went to his shirt pocket to find it empty. "My ring is gone. Where are we?"

"Separatist camp?" I gave his hand a squeeze, and his bleary eyes found mine. "Ashley is one of them." *Two fucking years . . .* Anger sparked in me. "So is Lev."

"What do they want?" Benedict blinked, clearly trying to focus.

"To weaponize your inert dross," I said, still burning over Ashley. "That and Herm Ivaros."

"Why do they want Ivaros?" His gaze rose, and he looked around, finally seeing things. "He's a Spinner, not a mage."

"They think he's a weaver."

Benedict made a rude snort and reached for a water. "Weavers don't exist."

"Yeah, I know," I said as I cracked open a bottle and handed it to him.

But what if they did? *He's a filthy dross-eater, a threat to all mage rule. Get rid of the sweepers, and you have everything,* I mused, remembering what Ashley had said. Herm wasn't a weaver, but what if he had learned how to use dross to safely power magic? If mages could use dross, the need for sweepers and Spinners would drop, but I failed to see how that would promote the separatists' agenda of mage rule.

"Lev is a separatist?" Benedict rasped, a shaky hand rubbing his temple.

"Yep." I sipped some water.

"Well, screw that. I was starting to like him." Benedict slammed the last of his bottle. For a moment he was silent, his attention on that pale ring of skin around his finger. "Why are we sitting outside a principal's office?"

I shrugged, watching the people do their thing.

"They took my wand," he said, eyes roving the desks and busy people. "My dad gave me that wand for my high school graduation."

"They got my stuff, too." *My phone. Pluck's tags. Darrell's lodestone. Lev, if you damage that stone . . .* All I had left was my short-cord. Like that was any use.

"I'm sorry about Pluck," he said.

It was the last thing I had expected out of his mouth, and I shot a glance at him. "Me too," I said, keeping it neutral. "Thank you for pulling me out of the tunnel."

He took a breath, and I could hear it shaking when he exhaled. "I don't think I've ever been so scared. Damn, it was almost as if that shadow was alive. Did you see it look at you?"

I nodded, remembering how Lev had totally freaked. Maybe he was the smart one here.

Benedict sat in his wheelchair, his head bowed over his knees. "You don't happen to know what they gave me, do you?" he asked. "I can hardly move."

"Sorry. No." My attention lifted at the squeak of the principal's door, and I sat up as Lev came out and beckoned for us. "Can you stand?" I asked, not wanting the two men escorting us to get any closer, and Benedict nodded and got to his feet. Motions shaky, he took a step, only to have his legs give way.

"Benny!" I shouted as he crashed into a desk, scattering papers and knocking the pencil holder over. Pens rolled and bounced, and he pulled himself upright, red-faced and embarrassed.

"Sorry! I'm okay," he said as he scooped up the papers and tried to set things right.

"Are you sure?" I asked as everyone in the room hesitated to watch.

"Fine," he muttered, a defiant glint in his eye, and then I jerked back, startled at the sudden feel of a psi field settling over us.

"Drop it, Strom," one of our escorts said, lodestone gleaming. "Or I drop both of you."

The entire room had gone silent. My pulse hammered as suddenly everyone filing papers or on the phone became a threat. Benedict hesitated for half a heartbeat. "Take it." He raised his hands, and there was a heavy thump as a glass paperweight hit the floor. Eyes wide, he nudged it from him with his foot.

My lips parted. His legs hadn't given way. He'd faked it to get a chunk of glass.

Lev smirked, a wry expression on his face as he scooped it up and set it back on the desk. Someone chuckled, and like magic, everyone returned to work as if nothing had happened. "Are you going to behave?" the smaller man said as he stood before Benedict in an obvious threat.

"Sure," Benedict muttered, but my shoulders didn't ease until the psi field evaporated. A memory flashed through me of Benny on the playground, his smooth, youthful face tight in anger as he shoved a kid down for having smashed a butterfly. The day had ended with him sporting a bloody nose. He wasn't afraid to take chances, and as we scuffed to a halt before a frosted-glass door, I hoped I was as brave.

"Nice try," I said as I leaned toward Benedict.

"I wasn't going to do anything," Benedict said softly. "I feel naked without a stone."

I totally understood, and I wondered where my stick was.

Knees wobbly, I followed Benedict into a cement-block-walled office. Well-tended cactus gardens lined the window facing the parking lot, and the ticking of a sun-activated, rifle-toting bobblehead marked the seconds. An attractive rug in desert browns, reds, and purples tried to hide the ugly cement floor, the flat fabric scrunched where someone had shoved an indulgent chair into a corner. Two chairs sat before the old metal desk. Sikes sat behind the desk, the leathery-skinned, tobacco-stain-fingered man smirking as if he'd eaten the canary and cat both.

"I don't think this is his office," Benedict said as he studied him.

"It's Sikes," I said, remembering that they had never met. "Ashley's leash holder." Because there was no way I would believe that he was her career counselor anymore.

Sikes chuckled at that, the tall, supercilious man finding agreement with me. My gaze flicked to the bookcase behind him. Benedict was right. The pictures of two kids and a woman among the thick tomes didn't fit his almost gaunt spareness. Neither did the rug or the greenery. He was borrowing someone's office, and I wasn't sure if that made me feel any better or worse. It was hot in here, all the windows facing the sunbaked parking lot. By the lengthening shadows, we weren't too far from sunset, and my stomach growled at the faint scent of spaghetti.

"Sikes," Lev said in greeting, his next words cutting off when Ashley shoved open the door and walked in, looking smart in a clean set of fatigues, the heels on her new boots clicking.

"Hey, Sikes," she said, smug as she gave me a dry look. "I told you I'd find Ivaros."

Sikes frowned as she took a chair at the back of the room. "We don't have him yet."

The woman smirked, her foot bobbing to show off her boots. "We will."

My chest burned. Her combat gear was window dressing, everything that made her look a part of the team, but nothing there to save her life in a pinch. Her multiple lodestones glinted from her fingers, her ears, and around her neck, and I wondered if she had them all because in her heart, she'd been scared living with me.

Two years pretending to be my friend, I mused, remembering the opened envelopes, her interest when Herm had broken his silence and contacted me. *Tell me when he comes in, and I'll take you both to dinner.*

My hands fisted in my lap. I'd thought it odd that a mage had wanted to room with me, but I'd overlooked it because it had made me feel special that she might see me as a person, not a trashman. Turned out I was even less. I was a means to an end.

Pissed, I shifted my glare from Ashley to Lev as he settled in behind me and Benedict. *At least our escort stayed in the hall,* I thought. The room was getting crowded even as Sikes's aide left, closing the door and shutting out the office noise.

Silent, Sikes eased back into the ergonomic chair. "Dr. Strom. Ms. Grady," he said, his tobacco-rough voice and Texan accent bracketing a far more reasonable tone than I would've expected. "Have a seat."

Lev remained standing behind us as Benedict and I gingerly sat in the chairs before the desk. A chill ran over me as the air-conditioning kicked on, and my stomach rumbled again. "You have no right to hold us," I said, and Sikes's lips quirked.

"Obviously," he said, a cruel bite to his tone. "Dr. Strom." Utterly confident, Sikes leaned forward, his long, sun-scarred fingers laced atop his borrowed desk. "Let's get right to it. Your new process to create inert dross has a few bugs. I'd like to help you fix it."

Benedict glanced at me, clearly surprised. "Ah, yes?"

"His process is fine," Ashley said from the back of the room, and Sikes gave her a look to shut up.

"My best have been over your theories," Sikes continued. "I will admit we're as stumped as you as to what triggered the explosion that broke the vault."

"There are better ways to use Dr. Strom's process than twist it into a bomb," Ashley said, and Sikes cleared his throat, clearly tired of her theories.

"Fix it?" Benedict questioned, clearly not yet ready to admit that his dross had anything to do with the vault explosion, all indications aside, and Sikes's attention flicked back to him.

"Fix it," Sikes echoed. "How long do you think it will take to figure out how to make your dross explode again? Upon command?"

My chin lifted. "You can't make Benedict's inert dross into a weapon."

"It already is!" Sikes shouted, his bolo lodestone winking.

"It is not a bomb," Ashley said, her high voice pleading. "If you would simply—"

"Enough, Ms. Smyth," Sikes interrupted, and I shifted to see Ashley clenching her jaw in anger. "Dr. Strom, you brought down an entire auditorium by accident. Utilized properly, your process can take out communications, transportation." He smiled, his sun-damaged face wrinkling up in what looked like a rare smile. "All blamed upon an accident by the mundanes."

In it to find weavers, huh? I thought, looking at Lev. *Want to put an end to shadow, mmmm?* They were after mage supremacy. That was it.

"If it happens once, it can happen again," Sikes said as Ashley's foot bobbed antagonistically. "Preferably under controlled circumstances. What do you think triggered it, Dr. Strom?"

"Nothing," Ashley blurted. "It was an anomaly. It's perfect just as it is."

Sikes's eye twitched and his lips pressed. "Do I need to remove you, Smyth?" he said, and Ashley huffed.

"Dr. Strom?" Sikes prompted, and Benedict rubbed his eyes, clearly at a loss.

"I don't know," he said, and I began to wonder if he was starting to believe he had a part in the auditorium's collapse. "Maybe the high levels of dross?" he added, voice uncertain. "It could have been the shadow that was in there with it. Either way, there's no way to safely reproduce it."

"Would you like to?" Sikes pushed back in his rolling chair. "Full lab at your disposal. Unending supply of money to play with. What do you say?"

Benedict's lips parted, his eyes holding a near horror. "I'm not going to help you make a bomb."

Sikes smirked, his gaze flicking to me. "I think you will."

Anger was a slow burn. He was threatening me. Or at least he was looking at me, which was pretty much the same thing.

"Sir," Lev said, and I jumped, having forgotten he was there behind me. "I did not leave the military to make bombs. I joined to stamp out shadow and those who create it."

"I'm with Lev," Ashley said quickly, but the very way she said it almost turned it into a mockery. "We all want the same thing. A continuation of mage superiority. That's what Strom's procedure can give us. As is. Without warping it into something it isn't. With it, we won't be bolstering up sweepers' egos or wallets anymore," she added, voice fast as she tried to get it all out before Sikes told her to shut up. "We can take care of our dross ourselves."

"You don't need Benedict's procedure to do that," I interrupted. "You can take care of your own dross already. You simply choose not to."

"Enough!" Sikes shouted, his raspy voice harsh, and I stiffened when one of the security detail in the hall opened the door, did a quick visual, and then quietly shut it. Sikes was staring at me when I turned back, and I blanched at the hatred in his eyes.

"Petra Grady. Spinner third-class," he said, somehow making it an insult. "Congratulations on your advancement."

My gaze flicked to Ashley. "Sweeper. That lodestone you took isn't mine."

Sikes bobbed his head. "Sweeper. I agree. How long have you known Herm Ivaros? Will he behave himself, I wonder, if he finds you under threat? Turn himself in to us?"

"Probably not," I smart-mouthed, then thought better of it. It might be the only thing keeping me alive. "You seriously think he's a weaver?"

I had said the last with a laugh, but I was the only one who thought it was funny. Okay, sure, he had been touting that you could use dross to do magic, but a weaver?

"I don't even know what that means," I added to break the silence.

"It means he uses dross to make shadow," Lev said, which sort of went along with how my dad had died.

"It means," Ashley said, her tone imperialistic, "that he has the potential to be stronger than even a mage."

Which will really piss off the separatists, I mused.

Sikes cleared his throat to demand everyone's attention. "It means he is to be eliminated."

Whoa. Like dead? Okay, I didn't like the man, even if he had been sending me money for the last ten years, but to kill him because of what he *might* be able to do?

"Ivaros isn't a weaver," Benedict said softly, his face ashen. "He used dross. Okay, bad life choice. But if you call up shadow, you usually end up dead. It sort of takes care of itself, doesn't it?"

Sikes stared at him, his leathery, wrinkled face empty.

My pulse pounded. "I'm not going to call him, so forget it."

His smile ugly, Sikes pulled open a drawer and took out a phone. "Technology makes us vulnerable. You should be more careful where you leave your things."

"Hey, that's my phone," I said as I recognized the screen saver.

"Smyth? Password?" Sikes demanded, and my eyes narrowed as she practically flounced to him, her olive-gray fatigues, her shiny boots, and the cap atop her silken blond hair making her into a joke. Her blue eyes met mine before she typed in my password, and I stared at her, remembering giving it to her so she could call Pluck's vet.

Sikes pulled my phone closer and Ashley peered over his shoulder as he scrolled. "Ah," he said, studying the screen. "He wants to meet tomorrow. At three. Are you free, Ashley?"

"I've got nothing planned," she said, and something in me sort of snapped. Yes, I'd never met the man. Yes, I'd spent my entire adult life avoiding him. Yes, I had hated him, blamed him for my dad's death and taking him from me far too soon. And maybe that was why I burned now, ready to do whatever it took to keep Sikes from finding him. Herm had been there after my dad had gone, even when I had told him to go away. He had been there.

A soft, pleased sound escaped Sikes as he gazed at my phone in his hand, typing with one finger. "You have texted him that you will see him at three at your favorite coffeehouse," he said, his eyes flicking up to find mine as he set my phone down. "Thank you for your service, Ms. Grady. It is much appreciated. I'm sure he will be most cooperative to keep you in good health when he realizes we have you. Lev, you and Ashley see to it."

Lev shifted awkwardly behind me, boots scuffing. "Sir."

"With pleasure!" Ashley reached for my phone, her motion hesitating when Sikes put his hand on it. "Ah, thank you for the opportunity to see this to the end," she added.

I turned to Benedict, shocked to find myself almost panicking. I had hated Herm for so long, but he had been there even if I had tried to ignore him. He had given me a place to go when I needed it, and he had answers I needed to hear.

"Sir, Ivaros is already labeled a subversive." Lev winced as Ashley went to the door and stood waiting in a huff. "Killing him isn't necessary when all that's needed is to take away his source of power. Giving him to the mage militia will allow me to gain their trust and take away Ivaros's power, both."

Sikes opened a folder on his desk and began reading. "Our movement doesn't need to gain anyone's trust," he said, and Lev visibly deflated. "And as there will always be dross, there is no way to take his power other than killing him, as we have killed all his kind for thousands of years."

Lev's lip twitched. "Kill his kind, sir?"

Sikes looked up. "What did you think we were going to do, Evander? Once there are no more weavers hidden in the sweeper population, there will be no more shadows. Isn't that what you want?"

"Sir . . ." Lev started, and Sikes waved him off.

"We're done. I'm sure Ashley will pull the trigger if you are squeamish."

"I am not squeamish. But I don't kill people who pose no threat."

"Come on, Lev!" Ashley said brightly, looking sickeningly naive in her fatigues. She opened the door and the security escort came in.

"Put them in a cell," Sikes said to his aide, and a cold feeling slipped into me. "The bunker, not here."

I stood, pulse fast. Benedict rose as well, his hands empty and his eyes wide.

"We will discuss your future later, Dr. Strom. And yours, Ms. Grady." Sikes hesitated, and I balked when his gaze found mine. "I don't agree with Ashley's cockamamie belief that only by killing all the sweepers can we destroy the latent weavers slumbering in your population. Sweepers will always have a place in our society. Most of you already know where that is." His thin lips twitched. "But a little reeducation is good for the soul."

My gut clenched when the security detail gestured for us to leave. "Out of the crapper and into the sewer," Benedict muttered, and I inched closer to him.

"Sikes." Lev fidgeted, unwilling to leave. "Killing someone for what they can potentially do is not why I joined."

"Then why did you join, Mr. Evander?" Sikes said, clearly exasperated. Ashley was long gone, and it was clear the man wanted to get on with his day.

"To put an end to shadow, sir."

"That's what we are doing." Sikes looked up, a sun-damaged hand motioning the security detail to move us out. "That is what we have done for millennia. You are dismissed, Lev," he added calmly, clearly done with it.

"Yes, sir," Lev said darkly, and Sikes's eyes narrowed in annoyance. "Grady, this was not my intent," Lev said as he turned to me.

And yet here we were: no lodestones, no sticks, no options.

"Out, Evander!" Sikes bellowed, and Lev gave him a salute so sharp it could cut ice, turned, and walked out. It suddenly struck me that Lev was the only person I'd seen adhere to any sign of respect, a remnant, probably, of his time with the mundane military. Everyone else seemed to think the loudest barking dog was the leader.

The noise of the office filtered in along with the sound of Lev's boots as he jogged after Ashley . . . and then my expression blanked as I looked at the two guards.

"Move," one said, lodestone winking. "Out and to the right."

Panic wound around my heart, squeezing. It was falling apart.

22

SAID, 'MOVE,'" THE NEAREST GUARD DEMANDED AS SHE REACHED FOR MY BICEPS.
I jerked away, and her ruddy expression hardened. "Now," she added, clearly content to let me walk on my own as long as I kept moving. Chin high, I strode out into the open office.

Benedict was right with me, his face pale and his wide shoulders hunched as he came even. Together we wove through the small maze of desks and into the hallway with its empty awards case. "Where are you taking us?" Benedict said when we found the cooler air of the hallway.

"The ranch," the woman behind me said, and then softer, to her partner, "Marty, is transport out front yet?"

"On the way," he said, and Benedict met my eyes, his brow pinched with worry.

We both jumped at the sudden harsh beeping of a building-wide alarm, and the woman marching us forward glanced at her watch. It was one of those tech-rich jobs, and she immediately relaxed and gave me a look to keep moving. Frankly, I was surprised she could keep it running, with the amount of free-range dross around. It had to be insulated.

"What we got, Fisk?" Marty asked, and the woman, Fisk, apparently, scoffed.

"Fire alarm," she said, sounding annoyed. "It's a glitch."

"The wiring in this place sucks," Marty complained.

Benedict shot me a glance, but there was no hope in it. Wiring, they said, but it had probably been dross. This place was a sty.

"Outside," Marty said. "I'm not going to stay in here and wait with this racket."

It was no skin off my nose, and I stiff-armed the metal and glass door with the belligerence of a thousand teenagers. I scuffed to a halt on a faded number three, feeling as if I was waiting for my dad to pick me up after school. *If my school had had armed guards,* I thought sourly as the bright lights of an approaching Jeep glittered in the hazy twilight.

Benedict and the security detail stood close, rifles in hand, lodestones obvious. The sun was setting behind a thick bank of clouds, and the upper skies were a breathtaking pink and blue. The stored heat in the pavement billowed up, the come-and-go warmth fitful in the breeze.

"Ranch, huh?" I asked as an odd, unsettled feeling crept into me. I knew the desert bike paths like some people knew the bus schedules. The sun was almost down, so once they depleted their lodestones, they would have . . . rifles. *Think, Petra.*

"Ah, Petra?" Benedict said softly, and I followed his gaze to a small man running toward us from a side door, laden with a military backpack and what looked like my stick.

"Is that Lev?" I whispered, recognizing the bad haircut and the awkward lope.

Like a returning tide, my anger blossomed. Spies. Both of them. And yet, there he was, gaze furtive, breath easy as he slowed to a halt before our security.

"Glad I got to you before transport arrived," he said, not at all winded from the short run. "There's been a change of plans, and the idiot who tried to cut the fire alarm took out communications. Sikes wants them to submit to preliminary testing before going off-site."

Fisk studied her watch, tapped it, and sighed. "No one told us."

Lev made a "yeah?" gesture as he glanced at the building behind us, the alarm still hooting, everyone ignoring it. "Like I said, communications are down."

"Why do you have her stick?" Marty asked, and Lev sighed. He hadn't bothered to look at me yet. As if I was nothing. *Or because he's up to something?*

"Sikes thinks *she* might be sandbagging," Lev said, eyeing me. "He's ordered a full workup, and that includes seeing what they can and can't do with their weapons."

Weapons? I thought, surprised. I suppose I could hit someone with it, but that was nothing compared to lodestone magic and rifles.

"I need to verify it," Fisk said as a black four-door Jeep squeaked to a halt before us.

"The ranch, right?" the driver said, not bothering to get out, and Lev's eye twitched.

Fisk frowned. "We seem to have some question about that. The fire alarm took out the Wi-Fi. Can you radio back and confirm?"

"Yep." The driver leaned back in and reached for his radio.

My pulse hammered.

The instant the driver's attention shifted, Lev reached behind his jacket. "Ben!" he shouted, and Benedict jumped, scrambling to catch the glass paperweight coming at him.

"Down! Now!" Marty yelled, and I gasped, disoriented when Fisk shoved me to the pavement. The flat of my arms stung and my breath whooshed out when a knee hit my back.

"Hey!" I exclaimed, puffing to get my hair out of my eyes. Ben stared at the glass ball in his hand in confusion . . . then whipped it at Marty.

Marty ducked. His lodestone flashed, energy visibly spilling from it in a bright haze, shaped by a tight field even as the driver scrambled out of the Jeep. He got all of one step before Lev grabbed the driver's shirt and swung him around to slam headfirst into the side of the

Jeep. Dazed, the driver dropped to the pavement and sat against the back wheel, stunned, as the glow about his lodestone ring flickered and went out.

Up to something . . .

"I thought you had made it into a lodestone!" Lev said, clearly miffed.

"In three seconds?" Benedict said. "Inside a building? Where's my ring?" He backed from Marty's advance. "I need my ring!"

"Incoming!" Lev shouted, and I ducked at a pop of magic, cowering when a hazy glow of energy coated us like an aurora. My breath whooshed out—it felt as if the earth reached out and grabbed me, crushing me flat . . . I was caught like an escaping rat.

And then with a flash of pure light, it was gone.

My lungs rebounded. I twisted, heaving up from under Fisk and knocking her to the ground. Marty's attraction spell had hit her, too, and she looked pissed, one hand reaching for her pistol, the other in a fist, lodestone ring gleaming as she sat up.

Still on the ground, I kicked her fist to shift her aim as she formed her psi field.

"Just keep pissing me off, you stupid sweeper!" she shouted when her spell went askew, the energy wasted. The sun was down. Her stone was empty. Sure enough, she aimed the pistol at me, and I kicked her again, sending it skittering across the parking lot.

"Grady!" Lev shouted, and I tossed the hair from my eyes, hand going out to catch my stick as he threw it at me. Silky and smooth, the rod of wood iced into my hand, and I swung it at Fisk. Rolling, the woman retreated.

"Put the stick down!" Marty yelled, his glowing fist shifting from me to Benedict and back again. "I won't tell you twice!"

Lev shoved the bound driver to the pavement, his gaze roving. "Grady, you want to stop that from being an issue?"

I followed his attention to Fisk staggering toward her pistol. I scrambled up and ran at the woman, shoving her down before smacking her pistol with my stick as if it were a hockey puck, sending it spinning into the scrub at the edge of the lot. The woman's expression became ugly, and with a soft intake, she came at me instead.

"I'm good!" I exclaimed as I danced clear. Her lodestone was spent and her gun was gone. "Benny needs his ring!"

"You will all knock this the fuck off, or I will shoot!" Marty shouted.

The pop of the pistol shocked through me. I had an instant of clarity. Benedict was okay, but faces were at the window. This was a crappy jailbreak. We had to move. Now.

"Looking!" Lev upended his bag and shook it.

A bright ting of sound rang out, and I watched, unbelieving, as Darrell's pendant hit the pavement and rolled. I froze . . . and something in me seemed to hiccup.

Fisk's fist slammed into my gut in my second of distraction. Dazed, I stumbled. "Wait . . ." I rasped, unable to breathe. But no one heard me.

I shuffled forward, fending off Fisk as the black glass rolled across the hot pavement, and I took another hit in the gut when my knees found the pavement, fingers stretching. Someone was yelling for me to put my hands up, but I had one thought and nothing else mattered.

Mine, I thought as I snagged the silken cord and dragged it closer . . . only to gasp when someone pulled my head up by my hair. Pain struck, and then I stiffened, unable to breathe as a black wash of tingles poured through me, ripping every hint of warmth from my body. My blue-tipped fingers froze on the hot pavement, and my skull pounded in an ice cream headache.

And then the pain was gone as a terrified scream echoed against the flat of the desert.

"Lev, get back!" Benedict shouted. "Don't let it touch you!"

Bleary with cold and pain, I sat up.

It was shadow. The glass in my hand glinted with a pale, clear light; the dark black stain was gone. My hand shook in a cold agony, but I couldn't drop the pendant, and my heart seemed to stop when the woman's screams for help choked to a dim muffle. Shadow poured into her open throat, forcing itself in. Convulsing, the woman fell to the ground.

"Fisk!" Marty cried, horrified, as he ran to her.

"Don't touch her!" I shouted, but it was too late, and a flick of a glinting shadow rose like a heat shimmer from the shaking woman, smothering him in an icy nothing, winding its way to his nervous system and cutting his strings.

I jumped when Benedict touched my shoulder. "Get in the Jeep."

The shadow had come out of my pendant. I was sure of it, and I froze in fear when a hazy ribbon rose from the two downed guards, little sparkles of gold catching the last of the light as it condensed into a thick snake, coiled around them as if they were prey. It was looking at me, and I trembled when two eyes formed and opened, gold and glowing.

There was a sliding rasp as Lev dragged the driver from the Jeep. "Good God. Where did that shadow come from?" Lev said, eyes wide.

"Petra, you got any dross buttons?" Benedict whispered.

I couldn't take my eyes from the weaving snake orienting on me. "Go," I said, afraid if I moved, it would follow. An image of Benedict withering under shadow took me, and I gathered my courage. *Not Benny. You will not have Benny.*

"Go! I'll be okay!" I exclaimed, one hand outstretched to the black snake, the other reaching for my hair tie. I didn't have any shadow buttons, but I had inert dross in my knots. *I am a sweeper. This is my job.*

Benedict's grip on me tightened when the snake's green eyes

shifted brown to match Pluck's . . . and then we both jumped when it slithered into the desert and was gone.

My hand dropped, and I stood there, unbelieving. At our feet, Marty took a heaving, shuddering breath. *My God, he's alive. They both are.*

But people were coming out of the building and we had to get out of here.

"Stay back. All of you!" Benedict shouted, voice harsh beside my ear. "Or I will explode your fucking hearts in your chests!"

He had finally gotten his ring, and I blinked at him, bleary with confusion, achy with pain. My head lifted when an air-raid siren wound itself into a terror-inducing wail, and the approaching people hesitated, unsure where the new threat was coming from.

"Get in!" Lev revved the engine as the new alarm sounded. I tore my eyes from the two people on the ground. *They're alive . . .*

"All personnel," came loud over the speaker. "Code D at the gym. Code D."

I turned to Benedict, thinking we had failed . . . my eyes widening as a flicker of power iced up from the building. "Benny?" I whispered, and he turned to follow my gaze, jerking as a boom of sound exploded upward and out, taking the roof of the gym with it.

Fire licked at the edges, and then a roar of heat. The gym was on fire.

"Let's go!" Lev said again. "That's me. I set it as a distraction. We need to move!"

Benedict handed me my stick. One hand on my arm, he dragged me to the Jeep and pushed me in. Cries for help came from the building, and everyone jumped when another boom of heat and sound echoed in the desert.

Behind us, Marty slowly sat up, groaning.

More than alive, they are okay, I thought in wonder. They had survived shadow, but a sick feeling bent me almost double as I peered out the window. I had been talking to Benedict. I had told Benedict to go, that I would be okay—but it was the shadow who had listened and fled.

This was undoubtedly the worst day of my life, and I started when Benedict lurched in beside me and slammed the door shut. His hand found mine, his grip tight.

"You two had better be worth it." Lev put the Jeep in motion, his eyes flicking from the road to the rearview mirror and back again as he floored it. "I blew my damned cover for you!"

My knees were wobbly. The stone in my hand was tingling, but it was a warm tingle. The shadow wasn't in it. *No, it went into the desert when I told it to leave.*

"Three years!" Lev said, smacking the Jeep's steering wheel. "Three years of listening to these idiots spout their bullshit. Three years of biting my tongue."

Benedict shifted to look out the back window as we bounced over the curb and made a beeline for the nearby road. My pendant was glittering a pale green, and his fingers shook as he took the lanyard from my fingers and laced it over my head. The stone settled against my chest with a sensation both full and empty. I blinked, trying not to cry as he told me without words that this was okay. That I was okay.

And it *was* my pendant. It wasn't Herm's, or Darrell's. It was mine. There was a new understanding in Benedict's pinched, worried expression. I might not be able to do magic—but I could command shadow. I was more deadly than shadow itself. *If I lived long enough to learn how to control it.*

"And don't get me started on your roommate!" Lev stomped on the gas, and I clutched at the door as we bounced through a narrow wash and Benedict hit the ceiling.

"Nothing wrong with staying on the road, Evander," Benedict complained as the ride smoothed and we careened into the dark. Dusk was beginning to gather, but the world would be bright to my sweeper-sensitive eyes as long as he kept the headlights off.

"Hey, ah, don't take this the wrong way," Benedict said. "Why are you helping us?"

Lev's worried gaze met Benedict's through the rearview mirror. "Haven't you been listening? I'm not a separatist."

"Yeah. Right," I muttered. "Lev, stop the car. Stop it! You're getting out. Now!"

But Lev didn't slow down. Didn't even take his eyes from the dusky road. "I'm a ranger in the mage militia," he said, and Benedict's lips parted as he finally got it. "Inserted into this ugly little cell of hate to keep track of them. If the separatists want to kill Ivaros that badly, we need to know why." Lev shifted the mirror to look at me. "I'm sorry, Grady. I couldn't tell you, but—"

"It's need to know, right?" I said, not sure I believed him. "And you really expect me to—what? Take you to him? Why would I do that?"

"Because I think they want him dead because he can stop them," Lev said, adding a sly, "I couldn't get your phone, but if you know his number, you can use mine."

"Oh, my God. Look at that," Benedict whispered, and my argument faltered when I followed Benedict's pointing finger out the back window. The entire school was on fire, as if the very air had been turned to gasoline fumes.

"I may have overdone it," Lev said, and I spun back to him. "I really hate those guys, and I had to get you out. Ashley wants you dead, but Sikes thinks you can lead them to Herm. When she finds out she missed again, she'll—"

"Whoa!" I interrupted, braced against the Jeep as we bottomed out on the road. "What do you mean 'missed again'? Okay, I admit she's fallen into a bad crowd, but kill me?"

"She is trying to kill you," Lev insisted, eyes again on the road. "That tunnel didn't collapse of its own accord. She weakened the ceiling. She wants you dead, Grady, and I'd appreciate it if you told me why. For the last two years, she was perfectly content using you to find Herm. Now she wants you both dead and Benedict on a pedestal."

Pluck wasn't supposed to die, I remembered her saying, and a twinge of guilt found me as I took Benedict's hand, scared. Now that I thought about it, she had been acting funny before we all went down there. Scared. Angry. Determined. *Homicidal?*

"She saw Herm's fridge," Benedict said, but I didn't know what difference that would make other than it was kind of stalker-creepy. "Your shadow saved you twice now."

"Wait. What?" I said as Benedict's gaze went to my lodestone pendant. He'd seen the shadow come out of it. Frightened, I let go of his hand and pushed to the corner of the Jeep.

"It saved you," he said as if it was a fact, a big, scary fact. "In the tunnel, and now."

I took a breath to protest, yelping when Lev slammed on the brakes, swerving wildly when the road in front of us suddenly erupted in a gout of sand and broken pavement.

"Hold on!" he shouted as we careened, and I clutched at Benedict, bracing as the Jeep threatened to tip over. Lev overcorrected, and then we slammed into a narrow wash.

The engine cut out and I froze as little pings of dust and stones rattled on the roof.

"Everyone okay? Get out!" Lev shouted, wrestling with his door. "Get out and run! That was magic! The vehicle is an energy sink!" he added as his door finally sprang open. "It will attract magic like a lightning rod."

My door was stuck, but Benedict kicked his open and dragged me out. I snagged the bag and the long stick at the last moment, and then we were scrambling up the wash and away, only to skid to a halt beside Lev. An identical black Jeep was coming to a tire-hiccuping stop amid the cactus beside the smoking crater.

Shit, I think Lev is right, I thought. Ashley was behind the wheel, her lips pressed together in an annoyed anger I usually only saw directed at telemarketers and baristas who got her order wrong. The shattered road smoked behind her, probably taken out by superheating the rock under it. Behind her, an oily smoke billowed into the air where the school stood. Sirens were faint in the still air, but here, we were alone and apart.

Ashley got out. Her new fatigues were torn and her hair was mussed. Stray drifts of dross lingered at her feet like disobedient kittens to snag her stockings when she wasn't looking. She limped closer and stopped, taking off her scratched sunglasses and tossing them into the cacti.

"I won't let you hurt Petra," Benedict said, his hand outstretched in warning. His lodestone glittered white against his hand, energy already glowing warm in his grip in a psi field. It was after sunset. He probably had a few good pops in his ring . . . and then he'd be helpless until he could recharge his stone.

Knowing it, the woman laughed, the sound cold and bitter.

"You wouldn't hurt a fly, Benedict. I saw you choke with those guards," she said.

I laid a hand on Benedict's arm, lowering it. The woman always had more than one lodestone. Once, I'd thought it had been vanity, or maybe a petty dig that she could do magic and I couldn't—but now I wondered if it was a little more sinister than that. The blast that took out the road would have depleted any lodestone, but she was too confident to be tapped out.

"Or better yet, walk your too-smart ass over here," she added. "Your process gives you a place in the new order of things. You don't have to agree with us to profit from what we do."

Oh, God. Lev's right, I thought as I glanced at him, the small man standing with his fist tight to his middle, ready to blast her with everything he had. I could feel the psi fields forming, latent power crawling over my skin like ants.

"Don't do this, Ashley," Benedict said, brow pinched in worry. "I know you don't want to hurt anyone. Let us go. I might be tapped out, but Petra isn't."

Yeah, watch out. I'll hit you with my dross-filled stick, I thought sourly.

"Petra?" Alarm flashed over Ashley, quickly smothered. "You knew?" she barked at me. "How long have you known? How long!"

How long have I known what? But her necklace pendant was glowing, and Benedict pulled me back a step when she grasped it, light leaking from between her fingers.

"Yeah, she knows," he said, bluffing, as it was the only thing seeming to keep Ashley on the far side of the crater, and I eyed the new dusk for somewhere to hide, something to throw at her. Anything. *Did he think I was going to sic shadow on her?* I mused, horrified at the memory of the screams of the guards.

"Ashley, don't!" I exclaimed when her pendant flared into a white light, little streamers of energy curling out and away to spark in her hair as she took it in her hand. "Please!"

"Down!" Lev shouted as a white light shot from her with a sharp crack.

It was headed right for me. *The little bitch is trying to cook me from the inside out!*

And then I hit the ground when Lev slammed into me. A tickling of energy rippled over me, like dross trying to break against my skin, and I looked up, realizing Lev was using a psi field to block Ashley's magic.

The twin forces wove and sparked around us, finally dying away to nothing. He'd nullified it, meeting her energy with his own. Ashley howled in impatience, digging in her pocket for another stone. Crowing in success, she held aloft a second lodestone, her eyes fixed on Lev and me. I felt her field form, prickling like the sun, and I cursed the day I had taught her how to make one that big.

"I'm out . . ." Lev whispered, expression grim. "If you're going to do something, now would be a good time."

"Me?" I said, freezing when I realized Benedict had come up behind her, his expression grim. His intent was obvious, but I didn't see how . . .

"No!" I shouted, a hand outstretched in warning. "Benny, no!"

Ashley spun, the energy hazing her hand going right into Benedict's chest.

"Benny!" I exclaimed as the man dropped, groaning. I lunged, jerked back by Lev as Ashley danced away, her own face ashen as she stared at Benedict struggling to breathe.

"Look what you made me do," Ashley said, and something in me snapped.

Eyes narrowed, I shook Lev's grip off me. "That was a mistake," I intoned. Pissed, I stepped forward, stick in hand, not caring if she had any lodestones left or not.

"You think I meant to do that?" Ashley said, pointing to where Lev was helping Benedict slowly get to his feet, pale and shaken. Relief filled me, threatening to turn my knees to water. "That was your fault," she added. "Pluck too."

"Mine?!" Furious, I shifted to put myself between her and Benedict. Lev had him. He'd be okay. Maybe I could make a field of my own. Right in her throat. Stop up her windpipe and suffocate the bitch.

"Petra, I'm fine," Benedict rasped, but he was holding a hand to his chest and he looked pale as he hung in Lev's grip. "We have to get out of here. More are coming."

My attention flicked to Ashley's Jeep, then ours, its radiator steaming. A beeping horn was faint on the cooling breeze, and I followed the noise down the road to a set of bobbing headlights. A white pickup truck was careening full-tilt through the dark toward us.

"You really think I'd be out here without reinforcements?" Ashley said, but it was coming from the desert, not the burning separatist camp, and she began backing up to her Jeep.

I suddenly realized the truck wasn't stopping. It was aiming for her!

Ashley ran, diving into the scrub to avoid being hit when the truck slammed on the brakes. Gravel popped and scattered as the dingy white truck drifted a hundred and eighty degrees around me and rocked to a halt.

"Get in!" a masculine voice shouted, followed by a crazy hooting laugh as the door to the white pickup was flung open. "Grady, get your ass in here!"

I lurched forward, face cold as Lev shoved me into the front seat and slammed the door shut. Ashley was shrieking, arms spread wide as she stood on the road's shoulder, the sheen of a thousand tiny needles catching the truck's headlights.

"Benny!" I reached for the door, and then I drew back at the twin thumps of him and Lev hitting the truck bed. He had my stick and pack, but it was Benny I was most worried about. "We're good! Go!"

I put a hand to the dash when the man floored it, tires spinning as he aimed for Ashley.

"No!" I yanked the wheel, and Benedict cried out as he rolled across the truck bed and slammed into the low wall.

Arms pinwheeling, Ashley fell into the cacti again. When I glanced back, she was standing in the road, trying not to move as she screamed bloody murder.

"That wackadoodle is a little schizy," the man said, his cheerful voice as gravelly as the road he turned onto. "I hope that doesn't come back to bite you on the ass. Most good deeds do."

"It will. She's my roommate." Pulse fast, I studied the man in his worn overalls and thick boots. His grimy black baseball cap was pulled low over his face, and a full stubble glinted in the lights from the dash. Thick, arthritic hands gripped the wheel with an obvious, painful strength, and he let go of the wheel so he could stretch one. Most of his hair was gray, but the short cut about his ears had some black at the nape. Weathered, sharp eyes traveled over me, then the men in the truck bed, before coming back to me, his gaze lingering on the stick in my tight grip.

"Roommate. Yeah. And you wonder why I emailed you. We need to talk," the man said, and I felt my expression empty.

It was Herm.

23

HERM'S EYES WIDENED AS HE SAW THE LODESTONE AROUND MY NECK, GLITTER-ing with a bright green emptiness. "Hey, that's my old lodestone!" he added, reaching for it.

Instinct kicked in, and I pushed to the far side of the truck as Benedict shoved the window between us open. "Hands off!" he shouted raggedly, and Herm drew back, scowling.

"It's Herm," I said flatly, and Benedict's jaw dropped.

"*That's* Herm Ivaros?" he said as he pulled his arm out of the window, clearly unimpressed, and Herm's frown deepened.

My grip around my pendant eased. I didn't know what to think. I mean, I wanted to talk to him, but my dad was still dead. I'd been running on the belief that I could set aside my anger for the good of our society and get the vault repaired. Now I wasn't so sure.

Herm's grip on the wheel tightened. The truck began to labor as the needle on the dash crept up to ninety-five mph. I felt ill going that fast in the dusk, but I stared right back at the old man when he turned his piercing gaze to me. I'd never known my mom. My dad had been my entire world. And this jackass who had just saved us from Ashley was why he had died.

I took a slow breath, exhaling my anger. "I didn't send that text to meet you at the coffeehouse. It was the separatists," I said flatly. "How did you know where we'd be?"

The truck began an ominous ticking, and Herm eased up on the gas. "Separatists have been watching you for the last six years," he said, his somewhat rheumy gaze on the side mirror to check behind us. "I've been watching them for ten." A sly smirk quirked his lips, and then it was gone. "So tell me, Petra Grady. Is it good luck, or bad, that we met on the road?"

"It's my luck," I muttered, and he chuckled.

"Thank God you got yourself out. I'm down to passive dross annoyance without a lodestone. Speaking of which . . ."

"This is not yours," I said, holding the green stone, and he eyed me sourly.

"Congrats on making Spinner. Can you use it?" he asked pointedly, and I warmed even as the memory of downing that drone rose high. It had been dross, hadn't it? *Oh, God. What if it wasn't? Benny had said he felt magic . . .*

Benedict wedged an arm back in through the window again, his face filling what was left of it. "She's working on it," he said, his expression pained.

Gratitude was a quick wash. I didn't know why I felt so possessive. By rights, I should give him the stone, help him fix the vault, and forget all of this ever happened. But as I fingered the stone and let it fall to rest against me, I wasn't sure forgetting was a possibility anymore.

Herm looked past Benedict to Lev wedged in a back corner, pensive and quiet. "I did not get you free of Sikes to give you to the militia. You know he's one of them, right?"

"I do now," I said, wishing he would slow down. We were among the sage and armadillos, and going this fast was stupid. Not to mention the *schinky-clink* in the engine was getting worse. "He helped us escape," I said, and Benedict nodded.

"Yeah?" Herm clenched the wheel. "For whose benefit?"

Lev perked up, clearly having heard. "Hey, I'm just trying to survive, here!" he shouted over the wind.

"Mm-hm." Herm sped through the night. "I'm not letting you take her, soldier boy. Let me hear you say it or I'll stake you out for the coyotes."

"Stop it, both of you," I said, and Lev ran a hand over his stubbly chin. "Nobody wants me. I'm a means to an end, and seeing as that end is driving the truck, I think it's a moot point."

Herm squinted at me. "I know why they want you. Why do they want Wonder Boy, here?"

They didn't want me. Not really, and I shrugged. "They think Benny can militarize his inert dross into a bomb."

The old man's bushy eyebrows rose. "That's right. You've been working with inert dross. I've seen your theory on how to make it invisible to shadow." His eyes flicked to Benedict. "They put some in the vault, didn't they. And something triggered it into expanding."

"A week ago, I would have said no." Benedict resettled himself with his face by the window, a flicker of pain marring his features. "Maybe."

Herm's lips quirked. "A mage broke the loom. Figures." He glanced at me. "I thought you might have done it. You and your shadow."

I scrunched into the seat, silent. "I don't know what you are talking about."

"Good. You can lie." Herm turned his attention to the dusky road as we jostled along. "Your dad was too proud to lie. Maybe you will survive."

"Petra had nothing to do with the loom breaking—" Benedict started, pained and raspy.

"Something triggered it." Herm slowed, turning the lights off as he took a sharp right and drove onto a dirt twin track. The engine's complaint eased, but the hot-engine light was starting to flicker. The silhouettes of scrubby cacti lined the way, easier to see now that the truck's lights were off. *Abandoned cattle ranch?* I wondered as we went so slow that no dust was raised, or at least not much. The moon had come up when the sun went down, and the entire desert was glowing now that the truck lights weren't trying to compete.

"I don't know, Benny," I said, worried. "Maybe that shadow I brought in had something to do with it. It was the only other thing in the loom when it blew."

Herm's gaze came up from the narrow two-track. "You didn't kill it?" he said, his wonder obvious. "It's still alive? Have you been feeding it?" His expression lightened. "You have! Where is it? Why isn't it in your stone?"

"I–I . . ." I stammered, remembering the shadow burrowing to get to me through the loom's glass, and Herm guffawed.

"Let me guess," he continued, voice knowing. "You brought in a shitload of shadow. Really hard to catch. You had to bend a few rules."

My lips parted and I touched my lodestone where the shadow had once been. "How . . ."

"That shadow went for you, and you put it in a psi field like a stray wisp of dross," he said, and Benedict gasped.

"No," I said, shuddering at the remembered feel of the shadow in me. *Bound? To me? It can do that?* I thought, scared.

"You bound that shadow," Herm said, pointing at me with an arthritic finger. "And it's been following you ever since. Does it know you abandoned it, or does it think that you planned the entire vault-breaking incident?"

"Shadow doesn't think." I shrank closer to the door as my thoughts went to that dream where Darrell berated me. It had been a dream, hadn't it? I wanted to look at my lodestone but was afraid to. The shadow that had taken Pluck had gone into it. What if it was the same shadow I'd put in the loom? Had it followed me down into the tunnel? Something had taken the knots out of my old trap tie.

And what about Ryan's words when my ear had been pressed against the door to the loom? He said the shadow that I'd caught had responded when I'd melted that lodestone ring. Maybe Benedict's inert dross was entirely safe. Maybe my shadow *had* triggered the explosion to escape the loom and survive. *My God. What if Herm is right?*

Benedict's brow furrowed in question and worry. "Petra?"

I felt ill, and I stared out at the moonlit desert. "I don't know," I whispered, and Herm harrumphed. "I don't know," I said, louder. "But he's right. I think it's the same shadow that's been dogging us."

"Ha!" Herm barked, and I jumped. "There's a reason dross feels warm to you until you wrap it in a psi field. You're cooling it. Making it inert. Just what a shadow wants," he said, and I put a hand to my middle. "Maybe if we all had shadows to feed we wouldn't have so much dross lying around."

"You don't feed dross to shadow to get rid of it!" Benedict blurted, his face pale as he held a hand to his chest.

"Why not?" Herm said, and Benedict pushed from the window, speechless.

I hugged my middle, afraid I was going to be sick. All those people hurt. Millions of dollars in damage . . . My fault?

"Petra?"

Upset, I waved Benedict off. He gave me a nervous smile before easing himself from the window and slumping beside it, clearly still hurting. If I was turning dross inert with my psi fields, it would explain why shadow had chewed my sticks and eaten my dross knots. It made more sense than Professor Brown handing me a bottle of bad material. *Shadow spit. I'm a living, breathing dross button.*

Lev pushed himself from the back of the truck and wedged himself in where Benedict had been. "Grady, going to the rangers is a good option."

"Hey." Herm glared at him through the rearview mirror. "I did not save her ass from her wackadoodle roommate to give her to the wackadoodle mage police force."

"No one wants me, Herm," I said bitterly. "You're the golden goose."

Lev inched closer to the open window, his dark hair whipping in the wind. "It beats being murdered by radicalized mages."

Herm's face reddened. "I know your game, you little pissant, and you won't have her."

"She wouldn't be in a box. I bet I could get her an entire team," Lev said calmly.

A team to do what? "Hey!" I shouted, and they turned to me. "You all need to shut up before I give Herm to whoever offers me the most money."

Lev glanced at Benedict. "You don't mean that, do you?"

"He ran away when the vault cracked," I said, tired of being polite, and Herm's grip on the wheel tightened. "Left my dad to try to fix it on his own, and he died for it."

"That's not what happened," Herm said.

"Then what did?" I said, frustrated.

For a moment there was silence, and then Benedict cleared his throat. "Hey, uh, Lev. Could you help me into the corner. These bumps are shaking the hell out of me."

Lev's expression creased in annoyance, and then smoothed. "Yeah, sure," he said, moving slow as he helped Benedict away from the window.

I was silent, waiting as Herm stared out into the moonlit night and ran a hand over his thinning hair. "Your dad was not a sweeper, or even a Spinner, though that's what everyone thought he was," he started, and I quailed when his eyes met mine. "He was something else entirely. A weaver of shadow and light, of energy and dark matter. Like you."

"I'm not a weaver," I said, angry that he'd try to snow me with a "you are special" story. What orphan didn't secretly want to be the princess of a lost kingdom?

But Herm only chuckled, fiddling with the windows until the

wind wasn't beating the hell out of us. "You are, and please believe me that not a day goes by that I wish I had kept my mouth shut as your dad had wanted. Separatists killed him for the threat he was to their ironclad hold on our society." His focus went to the worsening road. "But it may as well have been me who stuck the knife in for my part in it."

I fidgeted, afraid he might be right, that he was lying, that he was telling the truth, everything. "I'm listening."

A soft grimace crossed him, not really a smile—there was too much heartache in it for that. "You know by now that shadow eats inert dross," he said, and I nodded, wondering how far back he was going to start this story.

"They get it from rezes," he continued. "That's why sweepers work so hard to keep the rezes free from dross. That, and rezes tend to scare people when they get enough energy to trigger a replay of the last moments of their life. But what most people don't know, especially Spinners, is that it's not always dross that brings them to life. It could be a shadow, desperately trying to connect to someone. Your dad believed that shadow craved the human psyche, thrived on it, and that subsisting on rezes was slowly starving them."

Which didn't jibe with the fact that shadows killed everyone they touched. *Except me. And the two guards . . .*

I licked my lips, glancing at the long stick beside me, then back to him. "Okay. What do rezes have to do with my dad?"

He was silent as he turned off the rutted road onto a smoother but even more faint two-track, slowing as green eyes reflected back at us from the scrub. "Back before you were born, I found your dad drunk and scared after what should have been a simple rez cleanout," he said. "The shadow he'd brought in had been vaulted, and no one begrudged him downing a bottle in the safety of the loom to try to forget it. I helped him home, listened to his soused ravings. He said that the shadow had been smart. That it had listened to him, and that they had made a deal, one that he broke when he destroyed it in the vault."

It was too close to what had happened to me, and I said nothing, waiting.

"I'd just made Spinner," Herm said. "Maybe my ego got in the way, because even after he sobered up, he insisted that shadow could be reasoned with. I honestly thought nothing of it until a week later he asked me to come over and he showed me."

"Showed you what?" I whispered.

Herm eased up on the gas as the truck began an ominous whine. "Shadow," he said, the amazement of the moment still in his eyes. "He touched it. Gave it a psi-wrapped chunk of dross. It looked like a bird. Acted like it, too."

"Inert dross," I whispered.

"Yep." Herm shifted uncomfortably, flexing his hand in a remembered hurt. "We figured that part out later by accident. I told him to stop. For a while I thought he had. Things got better. The nightmares eased and he found your mom. Settled down. Bought a flat. Had you." He smiled. "Lost your mom." His smile faded. "Grew distant again."

"He didn't stop, did he," I said. "With the shadow."

"No." Herm took a long, slow breath. "But I didn't notice. Eventually his shadow-handling skill got him a Spinner stone."

Like me. My hand rose to grip my lodestone protectively.

"It turned black shortly after he took possession of it," Herm said. "I didn't find out why until much later. Everyone thought he'd been given a bad stone, seeing as the color was off and he was never able to do magic. He thought he was a failure, and there was some talk that giving it to him had been a mistake."

My hold on my stone tightened.

"And then, overnight, he mastered it. Only he wasn't using light particles like every other Spinner," Herm said, his gaze finding me across the long seat. "He was using something else."

"Shadow?" I guessed. *Please don't let it be dross. Please . . .*

"In a manner of speaking." Herm fussed with the vents, a hint of guilt in him. "I often wonder what would have happened if we hadn't figured out that every Spinner stone in existence once held shadow. That it abandons it like a crab needing a new shell when it becomes too small for its awareness, leaving enough structure for a Spinner to bind to it."

I looked at the clear green of my stone, feeling the emptiness it held.

"Your dad wanted to keep quiet about it. Said it would upset the balance of mage power. But he had two new Spinner stones and they had to be explained somehow." Herm leaned forward, the light from the dash making odd shadows on him. "You have to understand that we forgot that it's shadow that makes a Spinner lodestone, forgot it so long ago that we don't even know when it happened." He stared at the moonlit desert, his mood unsettled. "Or perhaps more importantly, we lost the need to question why we lost the knowledge in the first place.

"I should have listened to him, not gone behind his back," he continued, his eyes holding more guilt, less pain. "I took the stones to the Spinners' guild. Told them everything except that your dad was involved. They were ecstatic. Said it was the find of the eon. Your dad, on the other hand, called me an egotistical prick and said I was going to end up dead. In hindsight, I can admit I was jealous. I didn't want to believe he was right."

"About what?"

Herm's shoulder lifted and fell. "He saw what it all meant more clearly than I did, or maybe his shadow had told him something. Whispers that a way had been found to bolster Spinner numbers were being bandied about. Even one found stone was cause for celebration, and they had two to explain. There was a meeting at the loom, and that's when the vault cracked."

The shadow eclipse when my dad died, I thought as my throat closed.

"Your dad wasn't there," Herm said, unable to look at me. "Me either, but half of St. Unoc's Spinners were. We lost them. All of them were capable of handling the leak, but they were betrayed, killed because of what they knew. Because of what I'd told them."

"It was intentional?" I asked, remembering being in class that day, the tense bewilderment when the news of the crack raced through the school . . . and then the awful knowing when the dean of the university knocked on the classroom door, the empty house I went home to, still holding everything that had been my dad. *Oh, God . . .*

"It was a homegrown mage attack," Herm said softly. "The beginning of the separatists, though they didn't call themselves that at the time. We had found the way to raise any sweeper who wanted it to Spinner status, and they were afraid what that would take from them."

"I don't understand," I said. "Why wouldn't more Spinners be a benefit?"

"Benefit to who?" Herm said bitterly, gaze fixed on the night. "Like the mages of old, those in power today knew there were probably hundreds if not thousands of weavers lost in the sweeper population, stunted because of a lack of stones. And if more weavers could be found, or if one made a multitude of Spinner stones with their shadow, the mages' hold on the Spinners and sweepers would be over."

My lips parted in anger as I figured it out. It was a power play, a grab for resources, a way to keep themselves on top and at the same time keep those who were their equal serving their needs in an engineered society. "They killed my dad," I whispered, glancing at Benedict wedged into the corner. I had to believe he didn't know even as he bought into the lie. But then again, we all had.

"Eventually," Herm said, voice wispy. "Everyone thought I was the weaver, and when I begged your dad to help me mend the vault, he refused. He said he was glad the vault was broken and that the time of storing our waste in a great big hole was done. He insisted that the only way to end the mages' entrapping servitude was to find

315

a balance of magic and shadow. And for that, shadow needed to be protected as it had once been, not drowned in a vat of dross."

Herm shook his head. "I didn't understand at the time. The thought of not having a vault was terrifying. I helped the remaining Spinners fix it, but your dad was there and shadow rose from him, angry. A few realized it was your dad, not me, who controlled the shadow. They attacked him. Surran tried to fight them off," Herm said, his voice going wispy.

"Surran, as in Surran Hall?" I asked, and he nodded, his eyes holding a soft pain.

"She—" Shuddering, he took a slow breath, his grip on the wheel tightening to a white-knuckle strength. "She tried to protect him. They killed her first, then your dad. He died."

He said it so matter-of-factly, those two words—two words that crushed everything that had made me happy, making parts of me harder, less willing to give: he died.

"And in turn, his shadow drove them all mad with its grief."

"It knows sorrow . . ." I whispered as I stared out at the black night.

"To this day I don't know why it didn't kill me. They found us within the new vault, your father and Surran dead and the only mage still alive mute with madness. I let them believe that I was the weaver to keep you safe, and then hid to give you a chance. A childhood. A life, maybe."

I didn't want to believe him. I'd hated him for so long. To thank him would be like sawing my arm off.

"Grady, I loved your dad as if he was my brother. Maybe I should have told you to run when I realized you were attracting shadow, but I doubt you would have believed me. I was worried they might be monitoring our communication." He ran an arthritic hand over his mouth in worry. "And there was always the chance that you might be just a sweeper."

I stared at him. *Just* a sweeper? But I was used to the sentiment and let it pass.

"I stayed away to protect you," Herm said, his expression pained in the faint light from the dash. "Maybe that was another mistake in a long line of them, but you *are* a weaver. I don't expect you to like me, but please allow me to help you as I should have helped your dad."

"Help me what?" I said, exhausted and worn-out by a hard-won realization.

Herm slowed almost to a crawl, the truck rocking as he crept over the rough terrain. "Find your way. Bring back the balance between magic and shadow as your dad wanted."

I put a hand to the dash to hold myself steady. *Bring back the balance?* "Darrell sent me to find you," I said. "She sent me with your stone to bring you back to fix the vault, not teach me how to master shadow."

Herm shook his head. "If she sent you to find me, it's because she knew I could protect you. Maybe help you figure this out. She was there. She saw, though she probably never gleaned all the truth from that day. You need solitude and a little structure. After you know what you're doing, you can return and try to change the world."

"I'm not trying to change the world," I said, angry. "I just want things to go back to the way they were."

Herm frowned as if I was being stupid. "Nothing is going back to the way it was, and why would you even want that? You're a weaver, Grady," he said as the road smoothed out again. "And now both the separatists and the mage militia know it. Let me teach you how to survive that."

I sat in Herm's truck feeling trapped. "I cannot believe this," I said as I flung a hand into the air. "I could have stayed home and eaten ice cream! My dog would still be alive!" But I hadn't. I had tried to help, and now my world was gone. Turning to the window, I stared out at the distant lights of Tucson and St. Unoc, feeling as if the night was going to swamp me. He said I was a weaver. A master of shadow. What I was, was a pariah! Who would ever want to get close to that? Not a sweeper. No one.

Lev stuck his head in the window, a worried expression pinching his brow. "Ah, we might have a problem," he said, and I followed his glance to Benedict wedged in a back corner, an arm wrapped around his chest. "Ashley hit him pretty hard. The militia has a medical—"

"We are not going to the militia!" I shouted, and Lev grimaced.

"Lev, I'm fine!" Benedict said, clearly not. "I just need some water."

"Should be some in the toolbox," Herm said, then he checked his watch and muttered something under his breath.

Lev pulled himself back through the window, and I lost them for a moment when he opened the toolbox under the window, ultimately coming out with several bottles. He handed the first to Benedict, then two to me. "Grady, I wouldn't let them put you in a cage. If you really are a weaver, we need to know what you can do. Magic when the sun is down? Never depleted? The militia can help Ben. Help you. No strings attached. You go anywhere else, and the separatists will find you."

No strings. As long as I do what they want. "Lev. Shut up," I said as I cracked the first bottle and gave it to Herm. Clearly disgusted, Lev went to sit by Benedict.

"Thanks," the old man said, and I grimaced, not liking that he saw more in the gesture than there was. "I am glad you got yourself out," he said as he slowed even more, eyes searching the scrub. "I haven't had a lodestone for nearly a decade. It makes me little more than a mundane without it."

"You mean a sweeper," I said flatly. "You can still touch dross."

Herm was silent for a moment. "I can still touch dross," he admitted. "You want to take the shovel out of my hand? I can't seem to stop digging."

I held my unopened bottle tight, angry. "You want your stone back," I said, surprised when he vehemently shook his head.

"Not when it's hosting a shadow. I can wait until it outgrows it."

He knows. I took a breath, catching my words when Lev looked through the window again. "Ben needs a hospital," he whispered. "Herm, you got a phone? Mine can't find a tower."

From the back of the truck bed, Benedict shouted, "I do not need a hospital!" He winced, hard to see in the fading light. "But I would appreciate knowing where we are going."

"A DIY shelter. This is promising," Herm said as he crossed a bridge spanning a deep wash, promptly taking an immediate right and looping around to go down into the wash itself. Eyes wide, I put a hand on the dash when he drove down the embankment and drove the truck right under the bridge and into one of the huge tunnels.

"What are you doing?" I said as he turned off the truck and the engine died with a pained rattle and thunk. Not bothering to answer me, he got out and went to lift the hood. Steam billowed up, and he retreated, his expression lost in the moonlit smoke.

"We're here until this cools off," he huffed, and Lev vaulted out over the tailgate. "They won't check the culverts for a few hours, and this one might not be on their maps. We can be in Phoenix before dawn. And from there, they will never find you." Herm's gaze flicked to the back where Lev was helping Benedict slowly out of the truck bed. "Should we be expecting a chopper in the meantime?"

"You should be so lucky," Lev said, one shoulder under Benedict's as he helped him to the side of the large stone culvert. "There aren't any towers out here."

Herm grinned, looking mysterious in the steam from the engine. "Yeah. I know."

"I said I'm okay," Benedict said as he shuffled, pained and hunched, but I had my doubts.

"We should make a fire," I said. "No one will see it if it's in the culvert."

Lev nodded, and leaving my stick in the truck, I got out. The scent of damp sand tickled my nose and I breathed in the night, feeling the cool relief of the open sky radiating the day's heat. A clutter of vegetation had collected at the mouth of the culvert, and Lev was already making a hearth of sorts. Benedict sat nearby, his back to a wall and his feet outstretched. "Harder than it looks," I whispered as I began to tentatively tug on a caught branch.

Lev stood from the rock ring and watched me for a moment. "I'm going to see if I can adjust that fan belt," Lev said. "You want a water, Ben?"

"No," Benedict said, and Lev gave his shoulder an encouraging smack before going back to the truck, his voice high as he asked Herm if he had a flashlight. Yeah, I probably wouldn't want to waste my lodestone on a light, either.

"You think he can fix the vault?" Benedict asked, and I yanked on a water-smoothed stick until it rasped out of the tangle.

"Yes, but he won't," I said, frustrated. I dropped the stick and reached for another. The sensation of being trapped thickened. He thought I could make a new world order? Seriously?

"But there has to be a vault," Benedict insisted. "The dross has to go somewhere."

"Says who?" Herm said from the truck, clearly having overheard us. "Let it go, Grady. Someone else will fix the vault. You need to think about you right now."

I frowned as Herm and Lev bent back over the open hood of the truck. My world had imploded. Nothing was familiar, nothing would ever be the same, and the only person who could put things right wanted me to walk away from even the chance of bringing it all back together, to hide in the hope that I could learn to use what my dad had left me.

We were free of the separatists and had found Herm. Too bad I wasn't impressed.

24

T HE CROWS HAD FOUND SOMETHING, PROBABLY AN OWL. THEY WERE HARASSING it mercilessly, and their harsh caws were the only sound in the temporary cool of the predawn morning. Groaning, I rolled over and pulled the ratty truck blanket over me. The cold of the culvert was an uncomfortable ache. Our original idea to leave at midnight had been quashed when the truck wouldn't start. I hadn't cared as Phoenix hadn't been my intention in the first place.

Regardless, sleep had been fitful if at all, but the last thing I wanted to do was wake up.

"That lying son of a bitch! Petra? Petra!"

I jerked fully awake, everything aching as I sat up. Benedict was standing over Herm, the older man slouched as he sat with his back to the culvert. Bleary-eyed, Herm blinked as if coming out of a stupor.

"You were supposed to be on watch!" Benedict exclaimed, pale but clearly better than he had been last night.

"I did my watch." Herm rubbed his thick stubble and glanced over the cold fire. "Lev was taking the a.m."

Benedict's attention went to the brightening haze of the coming dawn past the culvert's round O of an opening. "Lev is gone."

"Gone?" A wash of adrenaline scoured through me, waking me up better than a belly-buster supersize coffee. "Are you sure? His pack is still here." I threw the blanket off me and stood, my gaze going to the truck still parked behind us. "Maybe he went to find a tree or something."

Clearly disgusted, Benedict stomped to the edge of the culvert and peered up at the crows, his silhouette sharp against the predawn sky. "We have to leave before he reaches cell range. He's a militia ranger. And I am a trusting fool. And you are an old man."

"Hey!" Herm shouted, but I was feeling kind of stupid myself. Giving Lev a watch hadn't been the smartest thing, but I never would have guessed he'd leave, walking through the desert to find his people.

Tired, I sat at the cold fire ring and dragged Lev's bag closer, to find that he had left us all the food bars and all but two of the bottled waters. "I'm glad you're feeling better, Benny."

Benedict turned as if surprised, a hand to his chest. "Yeah. I guess I am."

"Okay." I levered myself up, tired already. "Let's go. We can eat as we walk. Maybe we can catch him on the road before he reaches cell range."

Benedict looked past me to the truck. "We'd have a better chance in the truck. It's going to get hot in about an hour, too."

"Sure," Herm said. "We find Lev, and he calls down an entire squad on you. Again. Don't think I didn't see what he did to you outside my escape tunnel."

"You saw?" I looked up from brushing the dirt off me. "Why didn't you help us?"

Herm widened his eyes. "Guns? Lodestones? What do you think I am?"

I exhaled. *Indeed.*

"Forget Lev. We have one shot at this. I say we aim for the mountains." Herm looked out of the culvert, his gaze on the nearby hills. "The farther up we go, the cooler it will be."

"Do what you want," Benedict said. "I'm going to try to get the truck started."

"The one that Lev 'tinkered' with all night?" Herm chuckled. "Grady is right. We need to get moving. Mountains, then the coast."

Benedict leaned over the engine, studying it. "Lev didn't want it to start," he said, voice distant. "He marooned us here. Whatever he did, I can undo."

The chance that we could drive out of here was worth the twenty minutes it might take, and as the thought to find a tree of my own grew, Herm heaved himself to his feet. A hand held to his back, he shuffled to Benedict stretched over the long-cooled engine, tired, travel stained, and frustrated in what was left of his presentation best. A wisp of dross clung to him like a hazy heat distortion, and I winced when it broke and he hit his elbow on a chunk of unyielding metal. Swearing, he shook the pain from his arm and bent over the engine again.

"Try that," Herm said, pointing, and Benedict poked at the engine with a screwdriver.

"I'm tired of bad luck," I said as I went to stand at the edge of the culvert, searching the predawn sky for any sign of a chopper. But in all honesty, I should have expected Lev to do something . . . unexpected. Good God, the man was a cliché.

"It's not bad luck. It's your luck." Herm tapped at something under the hood.

Benedict glanced up at him. "You call this good luck?"

Herm shrugged. "No, I called it Grady's luck."

"That looks okay," Benedict said softly, then louder, "Okay, I'll bite. What kind of luck does Grady have?"

Herm pushed back from the engine, the stubble on him looking worse for the early hour. "She escaped the separatists, good. Only to have her roommate find her, bad. But the explosion told me where you were, good. Lev left in the night, which I think we can all agree is bad if he shows up with the militia, but it is good if we slip away and lose ourselves."

Too many ifs. "I'm not running away with you," I said, and Herm's eye twitched. "I'm going back to St. Unoc."

"Grady's luck is delphic," Herm continued, his arms belligerently over his chest as he glared at me. "Hard to understand until it's in the past. And even then it's confusing. Just like her."

Benedict leaned deeper over the truck, groaning. "I don't see anything good here."

"Me either," I said, ogling his backside. Sighing, I ambled over. I had been so worried about him last night. Now I felt silly. The chirling call of a roadrunner filled the silence, and I smiled as I remembered Pluck chasing the wily birds.

Oh, Pluck, I mused, and suddenly I was trying not to cry as the heartache threatened to swamp me. I missed him, and I blinked fast, sniffing everything back, shoving it down to deal with later.

"You think you can get it to start?" I asked as I scuffed to a halt behind them. The crows continued to harass whatever they had pinned down, and I wondered if they'd give up once the sun rose.

Benedict glanced at me, and when he pushed himself off the engine, I handed him the food bar. "Thanks. If I can figure out what he did to it. I don't think he broke it, maybe pulled a plug or something." He took a bite, his gaze going to the bright circle at the end of the culvert. "What is with those crows?"

"Not a clue," I said, startled when one dropped to land at the edge of the culvert.

"Shadow!" Herm exclaimed, and I gasped, backpedaling. It wasn't a crow but shadow standing on the hard-packed sand. The thing looked like a huge bird, wings at least six feet in spread, nearly touching the sides of the culvert. They dripped a hazy, viscous slime, hissing when it hit the dry sand to evaporate into an oily smog. Wings spread, it fastened a black eye on me and hopped forward. Toward me.

"Holy crap!" I shrieked, pushing Benedict behind me. "Stay back!" *Where's my stick!*

"I knew it!" Elated, Herm nevertheless scrambled to put distance between him and it. "You do have a shadow. It's been in that lodestone before, hasn't it."

My pulse hammered. Benedict had a hand on my shoulder, and I gripped the stone about my neck as the memory of the shadow downing those two military thugs ran through me. "Once or twice." I stared at the ugly form. "But how do you know it's mine?"

The ugly bird cawed, a spine-shuddering croak that echoed in the still air.

"Well, mostly because it's just standing there." Herm slowly peered over the truck at it, his brow furrowed. "I've only seen a bound shadow take a form. Your dad's looked like a bird."

"Yeah, well, all I've ever gotten before was a snake." I warily pushed Benedict backward. My stick was in the truck. I had nothing to catch it with. But it wasn't moving, simply sitting there staring at me. "This is new."

Herm made a soft sound, and the "bird" clacked its bill at him. "The sun is coming up. I'm guessing it wants to take refuge in your lodestone. Give it some psi-wrapped dross and maybe it will take shelter there."

"It's not a pet," I said, frightened. "It's shadow!"

Herm shrugged as the "crow" folded its wings. A black mist drifted from it, glowing an oily silver in the brightening light. Head cocked, it squinted at me with an almost human eye and hopped into the shade of the culvert.

"Is it getting smaller?" Benedict whispered, and I shivered at his breath on my ear.

"Your dad said shadow is always the size it needs to be." Herm came forward a step, and the shadow-crow turned, whipcrack fast, clacking its beak in threat. Chuckling, Herm stayed where he was. "Nasty thing."

I wasn't sure if he meant its attitude or how it appeared, because the shadow construct was awful. Oily skin showed in bare patches, bumpy with erupting feathers. The beak was a dirty white, and the claws were knobby and blistered.

But when it turned back to me, its bad attitude eased and it crooned a soft chitter. My pulse hammered, and I forced myself to stand my ground as it hopped closer. The feathers it left behind evaporated in a pearly smoke.

"Wait," I said, suddenly panicked. The thing had shrunk to the size of a small dog, but it was still coming right at me. "Oh, God. Stop. Stop!"

Chortling, the shadow-crow halted. Benedict's held breath came out in a whoosh, and I suddenly felt silly. His hands were clenched on my shoulders, and my pulse was fast.

"It's listening to you," Benedict said, his gaze riveted to it, not in fear but curiosity.

"It is, isn't it," I said. "Good ugly bird," I crooned, only a little sarcastically, and it cocked its head at the cawing crows, sending them packing with a harsh call of its own. The sound seemed to crawl over my skin, and I stifled a shudder even as I felt a ping of what might be . . . recognition?

"It won't hurt you," Herm said as if he did this every day. "You're its weaver."

Easy for him to say. But Benedict was watching, and feeling unreal, I held out a fist as if it were a stray dog, perversely attracted to it. I mean, it was the baddest of the bad, and it looked to me?

The shadow-bird eyed me, then Benedict. I took a step closer, dropping my arm when it hissed.

"Give it some dross," Herm said again, and I frowned. With two magic users and no trap, there was certainly a lot of it around.

"Go make yourself scarce," I said flippantly, then jerked, nearly falling into Benedict when it spread its wings and took off in a leap and a push, flinging itself at me. Half snake, half bird, it skittered over the ground like a disfigured, lame rabbit until it reached me and slithered up my leg.

"Get it off!" I shrieked, panicking as it vanished into my front pocket. "Benny!" I shrilled, afraid to move as a cold vibration hummed against my leg. It was In. My. Pocket. And I was scared to death.

Benedict stared at me, eyes wide, his hand outstretched as if he was going to reach right in and pull it out. It would kill him, and I backed away.

Herm, though, was laughing, and I hated him for it as I stood in the shade of the culvert and shook, afraid to move, afraid to wrap it in a psi field and force it out. Just . . . afraid.

"Get it out of my pocket," I whispered, and Herm cleared his throat, motions slow as he came out from around the front of the truck.

"It likes you," he said. "I'm not messing with that." He hesitated. "Which begs the question, how many times have you let it into your mind?"

"I haven't," I said quickly. But I had, and I shifted uneasily as icy pinpricks stabbed me.

Eyebrows high, Herm sipped his water and waited—staring at me.

I glanced at Benedict, then my pocket. It was odd. The thing had been the size of a vulture, and now it was a tiny lump, cold and prickly. "Um, once before the loom fell, once when Pluck died." I took a breath, eyes fixed on Benedict's. "Yesterday, when we escaped the guards."

Benedict's lips parted and I shrugged, scared. The lump in my pocket was making waves of prickles. "You could have gone shadow," he said, pale.

I felt sick as I recalled how the shadow had tried to burrow through a crack in the loom's glass to escape. And then how it hid in the bottle when Darrell had exposed it to the dross behind the loom's door. I should have stopped it right there. It was intelligent even if it was deadly. *And it was mine?*

Herm made a grunt of satisfaction when I nervously touched my torn, knotted hair tie. It had eaten the dross out of my stick, too. *And then there was that dream . . .*

"You were the anomaly," Benedict said, and I bit my lower lip, embarrassed. "It wasn't something in the new labs or that the shadow had figured it out. You were moving dross through the calibration tube with your psi fields, not the dross magnet. The dross was inert before I froze it." His focus went distant. "That's why the lab shadow went point on it."

"That's what makes her a weaver," Herm said cheerfully. "A weaver of shadow and light. Go on. Bring it out." He smirked, looking at my jeans pocket. "I dare you."

Dare me, huh? But the cold spot of nothing had dulled, and as Benedict watched in near horror, I awkwardly reached in, gasping when something chill wrapped around my fingers. Pulse hammering, I drew my hand out, staring at the black haze of a snake twined about my fingers.

"Oh, my God!" Benedict exclaimed as he backed up to the truck, but I couldn't look away from it, the tiny wisp of shadow in my fingers rising as if responding to my fear. Like a tiny cobra, it coiled upward, hood spread as it hissed at Herm, the sound like branches scraping against a frosted window.

"Maybe you should try to relax," Herm said, and I exhaled, my breath cutting it to ribbons that melted back as fast as they split.

"It is so small," I said, stifling a shudder as the thin, icy black snake wove around my fingers. My skin itched, aching with the cold of it, but the faint pressure in my thoughts seemed . . . warm.

Herm inched forward with a new wariness. "Don't ever call yourself a sweeper."

He's scared, I thought, and the snake finally stopped that weird noise. I stifled a shudder when its outlines vanished and it melted into a chill puddle of black in my palm. Pulse hammering, I spilled it back into my pocket. *It came to me . . .*

"We need to get out of here before Lev shows up," Benedict said.

There was a new fear in him, but it was for me, not of me. I think until that very second it had all been a maybe, a theory. Now it was real.

"Phoenix, then as far as the money will get us," Herm said, and I shook my head. Oh, I'd admit that had a definite appeal: the claustrophobic shelter of a car, the mindless nothing of a trip, seeing no one but fast-food attendants and maybe someone at a gas pump. The world would make sense as I lost myself among the mundanes, hiding from them and my own people alike.

But the thought of Jessica and Kyle . . . Ryan was still alive. The separatists and militia would both be dogging my trail—and hiding was not how I wanted to live.

"I'm not running," I said, and the puddle of black in my pocket sent a wash of cool through me. "You ran and they made you into a pariah. I'm not going to live like that."

"Haven't you been listening?" Herm said angrily, a sharp look cutting off Benedict's protest. "Grady, once your friends find out what you are, they will fear you. They will slander your name and discard what you've done. The truth will never be known. They didn't make me a pariah because I left. I left because they made me a pariah."

"My friends will understand and I am not my dad," I said as I dangled my fingers into my pocket in the hopes that the shadow would stop its cold prickling against my thigh.

"No, your dad was smarter," Herm said bitingly, and my eye twitched. "You need to go into hiding from mages and mundanes alike until you understand how your magic fits in. I can keep you safe until you know how to live off-grid." He hesitated, his anger easing as he saw my hand in my pocket. "You don't even know how to use that stone around your neck. Let me help you, or you will find yourself in a militia lab with four walls and a door that never opens."

Frustrated, I stomped to the fire and yanked that tatty truck blanket up. "Herm, I am not going to run away and hide, and if you don't understand or at least respect that, I will shut you out of my life and figure this out on my own." I snapped the dirt from the blanket, angry at the world. "But you're right about one thing. Show me how to use my lodestone. I'm going to need it if Lev and his diamond-lodestone earring come back."

Scowling, Herm leaned back against the truck, his arms over his chest. "What, so you can go off half-cocked thinking you know everything? I'm not teaching you shit."

Benedict sighed as he tinkered with the engine. The blanket wouldn't fold, and I finally wadded it up and tossed it into the truck bed. "Tell me how to use this thing, and maybe I'll have a chance," I said.

Herm eyed me, his expression unreadable as the rising sun spilled into the wash. My gaze flicked from him to Benedict as he went to sit in the front seat, one foot on the running board as he turned the key. *Whir, whir, click.* Nothing.

"You said you wanted to help me?" I said. "Teach me how to use it!"

Silent, Benedict got out of the truck and hung himself back over the engine block.

I waited, breath held, as Herm pushed up from the bumper, mood bad. His shoulders shifted in a sigh, and then his head lifted. "Fine. We can try," he said flatly.

Benedict's gaze flicked up as I drew the pale green stone from behind my shirt and set it on my palm. My pulse hammered and my knees went watery.

"It took your dad six months to figure this out," Herm said dryly. "But I'm sure you'll pick it right up. Step one. Put a psi field around it as if it were a stray dross drift. It's green, so your shadow is in your pocket, but it probably left some energy to play with."

"Psi field. Check." And as I settled my thoughts within the stone, I decided *something* was in there. A faint pressure pushed on my skull, and cold spiked against my fingers, like a fast-moving, icy spray. "Got it," I said, the pinch of time making me impatient.

"Really?" A flicker of unease crossed his brow, and then he banished it. "Okay. What you are feeling is not the sun's energy. It's energy shed by shadow. Dark matter."

"Dross?" I said, horrified, and Benedict's eyes met mine from over the truck's engine.

"Not dross, dark matter," Herm said. "Dark matter isn't the opposite of light or the absence of it, either. Think of dark energy as having its own identity, its own properties that are in opposition to those that light possesses."

"Okay," I said as I thought back to my utterly useless but required Intro to Physics.

"This is how your dad explained it," Herm said, his mood beginning to ease. "You know that light is made up of particles that move in waves."

"Sure," I said, not remembering that at all.

"Mages use the wave part, Spinners use the particle, and dross is created when the two are separated." He hesitated until I bobbed my head. "Dark matter is neither a particle nor a wave. It exists without mass or weight of any kind that we can measure, and here's the kicker. Unlike light, it moves instantaneously. It's already there. It's always there, like gravity or time." He glanced at the pendant in my hand. "But it only collects in enough abundance that you can use it where shadow has lain."

I didn't think he meant the shadow cast by the sun but real shadow. But still . . .

"If you think you're up to this, then try heating it," he challenged me as he set a half-empty water bottle down just outside the culvert. "The dark matter is already there and waiting. The longer your shadow lingers in the amulet, the more is available. When there's too much, it avoids the stone and you either use some or get a new piece of moldavite for it to reside in."

Unsure, I glanced at Benedict. He wasn't even pretending to fix the truck as he wiped the grease from his hands and watched. I felt myself warm in a coming embarrassment. *Heat the water,* I thought sarcastically, my tingly hold on the pendant tightening. Doubt flickered about my resolve, but Herm was staring at me as if expecting I would fail. Sighing, I turned my attention to the plastic bottle.

Grip tightening, I shrank my psi field until it was inside the pendant. The pinpricks of ice against my mind redoubled, and in my mind's eye, I could see the open latticework of the green moldavite glass. Feeling frosty and remote, I let the chill wash over me, stifling a jerk when the rise and fall of a prickly sensation found me—like the ringing of a slow, giant bell.

My breath caught. It was the same feeling that I'd felt in the junkyard.

"With enough practice, you might notice a pulse-like wave," Herm said, and my eyes opened, elated. "Your dad said it was the echo of creation, rumbling like thunder against the edge of the universe. The stone amplifies it. The more dark matter it contains, the stronger the sensation."

Hot damn, this is real, I thought as I soaked in the soul-stirring rise and fall.

"With a few months of practice, you might sense a second wave of energy, smaller than the first," Herm said as my eyes closed.

"I feel it," I said as I soaked in the twin, tear-welling sensations: the first echoing against the back reaches of the universe, and the smaller bouncing against the inside of my head. It was my psi field, its song half a step out of alignment with the universe.

"You do, huh?" Herm chuckled, thinking I was faking it, and I smiled. I couldn't help it. "Okay. Bring the ringing of your psi field in line with the universe and you can tap into the dark energy your shadow left in the stone and use it."

Like I did with the drone, I mused, and I slowly exhaled, not breathing to slow my pulse and bring the soul-shaking sound of creation in line with the homey, smaller echo of it in my mind. As before, I knew exactly when they met, and I began to breathe again when the pinpricks of ice in my hand evened out. A faint, vibrating sensation both cool and warm lay in my thoughts. I looked down. My hands were sparkling with darkness. The energy of the universe was mine.

"My God, Petra, you're doing it," Benedict whispered. "Like you did with the drone."

"What drone?" Herm said.

Smirking—and I swear to God that I was—I pushed my energy-enriched field from my hand, sending the darkly sparkling energy to envelop the bottle as if it were a stray drift of dross needing to be captured. This . . . I knew how to do, and exhaling, I let go of the energy, willing the molecules to vibrate faster as if I were a living, breathing microwave.

And then we all jumped at the sudden pop, and the bottle sent a jet of superheated water straight up in a miniature geyser. Startled, I lost my hold and my psi field collapsed.

"Hot damn! That sucker went thirty feet!" Benedict shouted, elated. "Petra, I told you that was magic!"

I couldn't move as Benedict grabbed my shoulder and gave me a sudden and startling hug. He pushed back almost immediately, his eyes going to the empty, sagging plastic bottle, then the glittering pendant in my hand. I was tingling where we had touched, and I could hardly breathe. I had done magic.

"What the effing sweet hell?" Herm said, looking betrayed as he picked up the bottle. "You knew how to do it. Why did you make me go through all that if you knew?"

"Because I didn't," I said. "I mean, I did it once by accident," I added, and Herm stood, hunched and worried as he tossed the mangled plastic into the truck bed.

And then I flushed. *Shadow spit, I did magic!* Expression emptying, I looked for the dross. But as I scanned the drying sand, there was nothing. "Ah, where's the dross?"

"There isn't any," Herm said sourly, still trying to find his aplomb.

"Dross is the waste product of light. You used dark matter, and the waste from that *is* light."

"Light isn't a waste product," I said, and Benedict gave me a fond punch on the shoulder before going to try the key again. *Whir, whir, whir, clunk, brumm, sputter.* He was getting closer.

"It is," Herm said. "Just because we like it doesn't mean it isn't waste. It's a by-product of the sun's nuclear furnace." His lips twisted. "And probably another reason mages are willing to kill you to keep it quiet," he added. "Weavers turn their trash into energy. Mages are the other way around." Clearly concerned, he leaned under the open hood. "Ben, try turning it over while I'm adjusting it," he added softly, and Benedict handed him the screwdriver. "We need to get out of here. Now."

"I overdid it," I said, and Herm made a waving, frivolous motion as if he were swatting at flies. It reminded me of Darrell, and my chest hurt.

"Only because I didn't tell you to sever your connection before releasing the energy," he said, focus on the engine. "It will take practice. You can regulate how much heat you create by how much dark matter you allow your psi field to take in. You sensed it, yes?"

I studied the pale green stone in my fingers as Benedict turned the key, getting better results than before. "Sort of," I said, remembering how it had felt . . . the pinpricks of energy changing to a perfect, cold hum.

"Good." A faint hint of worry creased Herm's brow as he tweaked something. "Don't try to make a light by burning oxygen in a free-floating psi field yet. Unless you want to burn the hair off your head." He came up and gestured for Benedict to try again.

And wonder of wonders, the sad *whir, whir, click, click, click* turned into a choking *brumm* of noise.

"We got it!" Benedict shouted, elated as sound filled the culvert. "Thank God. I wasn't looking forward to walking out of here in the heat," he said loudly.

Herm shut the hood and gave it a pat. "Lev tampered with it. I never dreamed he'd pretend it was busted to maroon us here." He hoisted his pants up, brow furrowed again. "Grady . . ."

"I'm going back to St. Unoc," I said as I upended the bag Lev had left into the bed of the truck. Food bars and water bounced, unheard over the noise of the truck, and I tossed the bag back into the shadows. I wanted nothing that belonged to him. Nothing.

Silent, Herm scuffed to a halt beside me. I ignored him, feeling my gut clench. "You really think you can show your friends that you can control shadow and not have them freak out?" he said, more lip-read than heard, and I nodded, pulse fast.

Herm sighed, glanced at the truck, then me. "Then I will come with you."

My pulse jumped. "Thank you," I said, then gave Herm a hug— as if he was my uncle.

Herm jerked, surprised, as his hand patted me softly on the back. "Why?" I said when I let go, and he shrugged.

"I'm tired of being alone and watching you from the outside," he said, as if embarrassed. "I promised your dad I would help you, and if this is what you want to do, I will be there. Maybe with two of us, we will be harder to silence."

Benedict scuffed forward, his brow furrowed. "You drive. I'll be in back."

"Me too," I said as I grabbed the edge of the bed and pulled myself in. "Hey, you want to draw straws to see who's going to clobber Lev if we find him?"

"The main road can't be more than a few hours' walk up." Benedict's expression was pinched as he swung himself in and settled in a front corner. "With some good luck, we'll catch him before he hits cell service."

Herm's expressive face folded into wrinkles. "Ah, if I'm driving, we're taking the back roads into St. Unoc. The less I see of Lev, the better."

"Fine." I settled in the corner opposite Benedict, jumping when Herm slammed his door shut.

"If we can get to St. Unoc, we should be okay," Benedict said, having to nearly shout as Herm slowly backed the truck out into the new sun.

I smiled up and nodded at him, but my confidence had faltered. A lot could go wrong in a day, and with my luck and a pocketful of shadow, it probably would.

25

THE SUN WAS BARELY ABOVE THE HORIZON, NOTHING BETWEEN IT AND US BUT millions of miles of dust and a thin layer of atmosphere. The heat was already palpable even with the wind whipping about in the back of the truck bed. Benedict sat wedged in one corner, me in the other. His scruffy stubble was clearly bothering him. I didn't feel very daisy-fresh myself. It was too windy to talk, and I'd been eyeing a wisp of lingering dross drifting about the truck bed, swirling in the eddies and threatening to latch on to one of us.

It was irritating the hell out of me, and I finally stretched to reach it. The small drift prickled against me as if wanting to break, and as I rolled it in a psi field, I decided the familiar sensation was a lot like the one I got from dark matter before bringing my psi field and the universe in alignment.

I'm making it inert? I thought as I shifted to drop it into my pocket. Benedict's eyes darted to mine, and I shrugged at the stab of cold prickling against my fingers. That I had made the dross Professor Brown had given me for my final exam inert made more sense than him giving me bad dross. Ten years . . . How could I not have figured it out? Was I really that oblivious, or was it truly that hard to parse out?

"It's okay, Petra," Benedict said, his words hard to hear over the whipping wind.

"What's okay?" I said, embarrassed, and he glanced at Herm before levering himself up and scooting closer.

"Whatever is bothering you," he said as he settled with his shoulder almost touching mine. A thought flickered through me: a memory of him yelling at me from the street, drunk and angry that I had walked away from him. I'd be worried, but I was probably the first person to have ever done that to him. He hadn't been abusive, just . . . frustrated and not knowing what to do with the anger.

"Are you worried about that shadow of yours?" he guessed, eyes scanning the road behind us for a dust trail.

"It's in my pocket, Benny," I said, sounding more angry than I had intended. "The entire mage society thinks it's deadly, and I don't know why it isn't trying to kill both of us."

"Can I see it?" he asked, and my lips parted. "I mean, if it can come out in the sun."

He wants to see it? I took a breath, held it, then let it go. "I don't know," I said, my brow furrowed. "I should probably find that out." I hesitated. "What if it attacks you?"

"It could have done that a hundred times already." Benedict's expressive eyes pinched. "If you don't think the sun will hurt it, I want to see it."

I honestly didn't know. It had sought me out when the sun rose that morning, and the sun had been down when it had attacked the guards at the separatists' base. But the sun had been up when it had left Pluck's body to find shelter in my lodestone.

"I can try," I said, then reached into my pocket, stiffening at the mind-numbing cold tingling along the bones of my hand all the way up to my skull. Shivering, I sent a psi field around the shadow and the sensation eased. My eyes flicked to Benedict's, and at his nervous smile, I gathered it up, jittery and unsure.

"Here goes," I said as I carefully withdrew the black coil of smoke, careful to keep it in the shade of the cab. The shadow felt like oil and water as I spilled it from hand to hand, sharp and spiny, both softer than fur and colder than iron in winter. The sensations ebbed and flowed, strengthening as the shadow began to anticipate the motion, a head forming, rising up as if questioning what I was doing. "Sorry," I whispered, stilling my motion, and the shadow coiled about my fingers, tightening its grip as if it appreciated the warmth of my hand, and coalesced into a more certain shape. "Shadow spit, it can't still be hungry. I just gave it a dross wisp."

Benedict's lips quirked. "Shadow spit? You swear cute."

"Yeah, well, you try using the big words when an entire school system adopts you." I'd been eighteen, but everyone had treated me as if I'd been ten. 'Course, I had acted as if I was ten for a while.

The shadow continued to haze and sparkle, sending little darts of want into me until I plucked another errant drift of dross from Benedict's sleeve, rolled it in a psi field, and cautiously extended it.

In a sinuous, scary-fast motion, the shadow-snake flung itself at it. Little darts of ice stabbed into me as it engulfed my fingers and the dross both, and I stared as wide wings formed, shifting to cover the dross like a bird over prey. Little glimmers of light flickered amid its absolute depths, and I held it aloft, studying it as it was occupied. "Huh. Let me know when you want more, okay?" I said, not expecting an answer. "Stop eating the dross out of my hair tie."

Benedict chuckled as the sated shadow collapsed into a puddle in my palm, where it sent pulses of oily pinpricks into me. "It doesn't seem to mind indirect light."

"Yes, well, I'm not going to force it into the sun." I gazed at the puddle of black, wishing it would go into my pendant instead of my pocket.

"Do you believe him? About what happened with your dad?" Benedict asked.

I glanced at Herm through the thick truck window. I had closed it when we had found the main road, and the older man's expression was worried as he peered up through the tinted glass looking for choppers or drones. "It sounds right," I said. "More right than what they teach us."

Benedict, too, scanned the cacti and paloverde trees, his brow furrowed. "I agree. You sometimes never know why people do what they do. Not even at the end. It's like your luck, both good and bad all wrapped up in one." His gaze landed on me. "I can't see shadow in you at all, only the light. I never thought I'd be glad to be so blind."

There was a little drift of dross caught in his hair, and I plucked it free, wadding it up and stuffing it into my pocket to lure the little shadow-snake back into hiding. Sure enough, it followed it, skating an icy path down my arm and vanishing into my pocket, where it cramped my side in an ache of cold.

God, why aren't you parking your chilly ass in that lodestone? But I knew why. Probably. It wanted a larger stone. Unfortunately there was only one place I might find a better one other than at Tucson's yearly rock and gem show, and it was half-buried in rubble.

"Herm's story fills in a lot of gaps," Benedict said, his voice an encouraging neutral. "And I've always believed that weavers once existed. That's where I got my idea to try to inactivate dross on a large scale. It was said that that's what weavers did. They made dross safe." He took a slow breath, staring at my pocket. "As scary as it is, I've seen nothing that disputes that."

That didn't sound so bad, but I doubted the reality was that simple. There had to be more if the mages of old had been so bent out of shape that they had tried to commit genocide on an entire demographic of their own kin.

"Herm thinks I can direct shadow," I said. "Do you have any idea how dangerous that is?"

"Yes." Benedict eyed the horizon. "But you aren't shadow."

"Benny . . ." I protested as the wind blew the hair into my eyes.

"You aren't shadow," he said, and my eyes dropped to his hand when he took mine in his.

"Still . . ." I said, not sure why he had taken my hand but not about to pull away. "What if he's lying to me?" I whispered. "What if I'm really using dross?"

Benedict glanced at the closed window between Herm and us. "I don't think he is. Herm needs you. I heard him say it. He doesn't want to be alone, and whereas that might sound like words, it's something no one wants to admit. Especially when it's true. I think he sees you as the only person who might forgive him for what he's done."

"You think I should trust him?" I asked, voice faint, and Benedict's lips quirked.

"Hell no. But as you might have noticed, I'm a lousy judge of character." He took his hand from mine and scrubbed it across his bristles. "I can't believe I offered Ashley a job. Twice."

"Yeah, well, you weren't taking rent from her for two years," I muttered as I fiddled with my laces. They were dusty but intact, unlike Benedict's dress shoes, which had seen enough breaking dross to leave them in tatters: toe box torn, laces in knots, lizard scat stuck in the crevices. "I just want to go back to St. Unoc." I brushed the dried sand from my shoe, trying to remember if I had *ever* had to scrape dog doo from my sole. "Fix the vault if it's still broken. Survive. Help the remaining sweepers come up with a cover story that would convince the world that we don't exist."

"That's what, week one? What then?" he prompted, and I drew my knees to my chest and held my legs to myself.

"I don't know," I said softly, not having thought about it before. "If they don't drive me out, maybe let Herm try to teach me something. He probably knows more about weavers than anyone."

Benedict made an encouraging noise, and I turned my attention to the desert as civilization began to show again. "If they kick me out, I wouldn't mind a little traveling around," I said, smiling. "I've never been out of St. Unoc much. Dad had work, and after he died, it was all I could do to keep the flat. I'm not complaining, but it seems that everyone at St. Unoc comes from somewhere else. They all have stories. Favorite restaurants I'll never see, experiences I can't relate to."

I glanced at Benedict, then back to the horizon. Blocky, institutional-size buildings were dotting the landscape. They were at a distance now, but they would get closer. "Herm seems to know what he's doing. Who knows? Maybe I could find a few weavers hidden in the sweeper population. It's probably the only way I'm ever going to get a date again."

"Are you kidding me?"

Benedict's voice was full of amazement, and I looked up, shocked at the look in his eyes.

"Petra, you are the most frustrating, annoying, wonderful woman I've ever met. The light I see in you . . . It's amazing. Why do you think I asked Ryan to assign you to my project?"

Asked? More like demanded, I thought, then, *He likes me?* "You can see light in me?" I asked, and his lips quirked.

"All the time," he said shortly. "From the day I saw you on the swings, pushing higher than anyone else. I should never have ignored that the dross you touched had gone inert. Maybe if I had slowed down, listened, found out why the lab's shadow triggered on the dross you touched, the vault wouldn't have blown and we wouldn't be on a road at six thirty in the morning avoiding mage rangers."

I managed a thin smile, but it faded fast.

Eyes down, Benedict made a soft sound. "I wish I was more like you."

"Me?" I pulled the wind-whipped hair out of my mouth, dumbfounded.

He nodded. "I'd give up magic in an instant if I could see dross. Then maybe I wouldn't need so much help."

His gaze was fixed on the horizon, and I suddenly wondered if

I'd read him wrong. Maybe the perceived slights were actually him being angry with himself.

A muted thump on the window jolted through me, and I looked to see Herm trying to slide the window open. Benedict leaned to help shift it, and Herm turned to us, glancing back at the road as he shouted, "This is as close as I want to get the truck into town!"

I studied the heavy industry almost cheek by jowl with low-cost housing. I knew exactly where we were, and I leaned into the window. "There's a jump-off to the bike path down that road," I said, pointing. "We can park. Walk in from there on the surface streets. Campus is about a mile from here."

"In the sun?" Benedict said, squinting at it.

"In the sun," I affirmed. "You can do anything Lev can do."

Herm turned onto the smaller road that I had pointed to, truck slowing. "I'm just glad we didn't see the little shit," he muttered, following the signs to the Gulbert Wash bike path.

"We can park there," I said as I scanned the small lot with its glorified stone-walled outhouse. "Fill up the water bottles." I hesitated, a new need arising. "I could use the restroom."

"Me too," Herm said, his gaze suddenly intent as he took the first parking spot available, spinning the truck around and coming to an unsettlingly fast stop. The lack of wind made the sun feel that much hotter, and immediately Herm got out, slamming the door to the truck as he made a hunched beeline to the restroom. There was only the one, and I slumped, resigned to waiting.

Or at least as much of a beeline as he could, I thought as I watched him follow the paved walk weaving through the planted cacti and desert-themed outdoor art.

The silence was numbing after the constant wind, and I awkwardly inched to the back of the truck bed to get out. Benedict vaulted over the side of the truck, his muffled groan making me smile as he reached for the tailgate and lowered it for me.

"Thanks," I said as I got out, and he bobbed his head, his gaze on the whoosh of the nearby traffic. The main road wasn't busy, but it was positively dead here, with only a few parked cars with empty bike racks.

"You knew about this," he said, making it more of a statement than a question.

"You say that like it's a secret." His lodestone winked cheerfully from his ring, and I tucked my pendant behind my shirt. "Yeah," I added when it was obvious he was waiting for more. "I'm out here every weekend when it's nice."

"It's hot," he said, eyes still on the road, and from the restroom came the distinctive sound of a flush.

"Well, I wouldn't be out here now," I said, and Benedict's gaze flicked to me.

The bang of the restroom door was loud. I grabbed a couple of empty water bottles from the truck bed and pushed into motion. "Be right back," I said, and Benedict nodded.

It felt good to be moving, and I swung my arms as I walked toward Herm.

"A mile?" the older man asked as the gap closed, and I nodded.

"You could call an Uber," I suggested, and Herm's face split into a wide grin.

"Ahhh, that just might be worth the risk." He touched my arm as I went by, giving me pause. *He needs you,* Benedict had said. "I'm going to get stinky," Herm complained, his words going faint as he continued on to the truck.

I was smiling as I went into the oversize restroom. Calling it an outhouse wasn't accurate, but it was close. It had plumbing and a sink with a sign assuring the user that it was potable water. It had to be locked at night to keep it from becoming a mini-apartment for the desert homeless, but that was a small price for the city to pay to keep the cyclists peeing where they were supposed to.

But my smile vanished when I looked in the cracked mirror. "Oh, my God!" I whispered, a tentative hand reaching for my lank curls. I had cozied up to Benedict looking like this? My hair was in lank ringlets and there was dirt on my cheek. I didn't even want to think about my jeans. I'd never wear them again. Embarrassed, I washed my face, not caring that the soap smelled like cheap disinfectant.

I left a bottle in the sink to fill as I used the bathroom, needing a little extra time after two days of uncertainty and food bars. I wasn't surprised when Herm beeped the horn for me to hurry up. "I'm coming!" I shouted as I washed my hands, knowing he couldn't hear me in my little eight-by-six concrete-block sanctuary but yelling all the same. "You're going to want this water about ten minutes down the road," I muttered as I filled the second one and capped it.

But my annoyance evaporated into disbelief when I heard the engine race, gravel popping as the truck peeled out.

"Benny?" Adrenaline was a painful wash as I lurched to the door. My mouth dropped open as Herm and Benedict bounced back onto the road and took off in a squeal of tires, a familiar militarized Hummer in hot pursuit.

My pulse hammered. *Benny* . . .

26

BENNY AND HERM WERE GONE. I HAD NO PHONE, NO IDEA IF ASHLEY AND SIKES
had caught them. All I could do was walk into town and locate
someone from the sweepers' guild to help me find them. I stuck to
the bike path and washes all the way into St. Unoc, trying to stay out
of the sun and the eyes of everyone. I could have tried to thumb a
ride, but I was in full paranoia mode and slogging in the heat was
preferable to the fear of flagging down the wrong person. Besides,
every time I got too hot, I simply dangled a hand into my pocket,
shocking myself with a cold dart of angst and winter. And the shadow
was angsty. I could feel its agitation at the edges of my thoughts every
time I touched it.

"Oh, thank God," I whispered at the sight of the next walk-
through culvert and some cool that did not come with a side order of
shadow-based apprehension. I'd been among buildings for the last
ten minutes, and though I could hear traffic overhead, down here on
the hard-packed sandy trench with the trash and dross wisps, the air
was dead and still.

The sudden darkness felt like heaven, and I stopped just inside to
lean against the comparatively cooler wall of the culvert to crack the
top of my water, slamming it down as I peered out at the world and

placed myself. I knew where I was, and with a feeling of worried satisfaction, I dangled my hand into my pocket for a little relief.

"Hey!" I yelped as the shadow curled around my wrist, deadening my hand in a sudden cold. Pressure pushed on my palm as if it wanted something, and for a moment, I let it turn my hand into an ice cube. The shade probably felt good to it, too.

"You hungry?" I breathed deep to bring in the faint scent of fast food on the rising wind. "I am. Let's see what the last mage left for you."

The shadow curling up about my wrist rose like a little cobra as I scanned the dusky tunnel for dross. It was harder to spot in my sun-blinded eyes, but I sent a psi field ranging about until I found a pinprick tingle, balling up a small drift to give it.

The little snake flung itself on it as if starving, and a faint hint of satisfaction curled my lips up as I held it in my palm, painful stabs of energy jarring me. "What have I become?" I whispered as the hazy snake flowed through my fingers, shifting from hand to hand until a weird tickle against my brain told me it was happy. Happy. The shadow was happy.

"I am such an idiot," I said, bringing it to my eye level and searching for something looking back at me. My sight narrowed, and the sound of traffic became muffled. In an odd, uncomfortable sensation, oil and water fizzed through me.

"Is that you?" I mused, cupping the shadow more surely.

And then I gasped, stumbling deeper into the tunnel's darkness when a memory surfaced of me trapped amid a burning hot mist.

My back hit the cool wall and I slid to the sand as I stared at the shadow in my hand, pulse pounding. It wasn't my memory. It was the shadow's. The very air had been on fire, and in a sudden shock, I realized it was a memory of the vault.

I blinked, unable to breathe as it shoved into my mind a memory of it desperately seeking refuge in a spiky ball of inert dross. The dross had been twisted into a nightmare of wrongness, unable to be consumed or decay. Satisfaction poured through me as it remembered shifting the dross back to its malleable state; a triumphant glee when the energy released blew the vault apart, allowing it to escape; its pain as it hid in the rubble; and then its wonder when I came back, almost as if I had put it in the vault with the intent that it should break it.

None of it was my memory. It wasn't my satisfaction. It wasn't my righteous anger, my confusion, my disappointment that it had all been an accident and that nothing more than chance and a foolish yeth had freed it. It was the shadow's.

"Oh," I whispered, face cold as I slumped against the grimy wall of the tunnel. Benedict's dross might have been the bomb, but my shadow had indeed triggered it. And it had done so to survive me putting it in the loom.

Horror crossed me, and I held the shadow closer, the reality of the pain I'd put it through not sympathy but a memory. "My God. I'm so sorry," I whispered, and the little snake cocked its hooded head at me. "I didn't know," I whispered as little wisps of shadow tingled coldly against my fingers. "I didn't know you could feel."

The painful pinpricks jabbing my hand eased. My shoulders slumped, and then my grip spasmed as an icy knife sliced into my thoughts. *Now that you do, you still want to remake that hell?*

A heartbeat too late, my psi field rose at the assault. Shuddering, I flicked the shadow off my hand, where it hung in the air until drifting to the ground. I got to my feet, shocked as I put a still-tingling hand to the wall for balance.

It had been in my mind. I'd heard it. But even with my confusion, one thing was very clear. There was no way I could allow the vault to be remade. It was a veritable hell.

"Sorry," I whispered, staring at the shadow as it coiled itself into a sinuous shape at my feet. "Um, you sure you don't want to go into the lodestone?"

But it didn't, so I carefully picked it up and dropped it into my pocket. My pocket shadow.

"Most people find puppies or kittens," I said, talking to myself as I readied myself for one last push into the sun. "But no . . . I find a shadow."

The heat was oppressive as I stumbled out of the culvert, beating at me as I took a footpath up the embankment to the adjacent bike path and back into the city proper. Nothing was certain anymore. My entire life was a crapshoot. I didn't know when I was going to eat or where I was going to sleep, or the lengths the militia or the separatists would go to find me—and with a final heave, I lurched out of the wash and onto a city-level bike path.

It was like being reborn, covered in sweat and grime as I came up into the light and motion. The heat was a hot wave, and I began to walk the sidewalk, head bowed. I knew where I was, but everything seemed different. I felt watched, alone, hunted.

Until I realized that everyone was ignoring me. I looked like a homeless person, and no one wanted to see me lest they feel compelled to do something about it. No wonder the free-range sweepers liked dressing this way.

To my right, the Lance building rose high to cast a small shadow on the street. Traffic was light, and everything seemed normal despite the gap in the skyline where the auditorium once stood. *Normal, except for the dross,* I mused as I stopped to wait for traffic. It was everywhere. Like a herd of giant dust bunnies, it drifted down the street to pool in the low spots or under benches until a gust of wind or car pulled it into motion again.

Grimacing, I drew a drift from the crossing sign before it reached the electronics and shorted it out. Immediately a spike of want stabbed my leg, and I stuffed the ball of bad luck into my pocket with that shadow. Either the sweepers were not picking it up or the mages were letting it roam free. I didn't know which would be worse.

Prickly and cold, the shadow seemed to wind its way around my chest, and I stifled a shudder as the back of my ear went cold. It was *on* my *shoulder,* and I was afraid to look lest I find something staring back at me from an eyestalk.

Clearly the shadow was shunning the Spinner stone around my neck. Herm said they outgrew them, and I started down the street to the broken auditorium in the hopes that I could find someone at Surran Hall. If I took the roundabout way, I could stop at my apartment for a shower, though they might be watching my place. I knew I would be.

My pace faltered at the pop of a two-way, and I eyed the two guys at the corner across the street. They were just standing there even though the light had changed—studying everyone. *Short haircuts, identical boots. What the hell are they doing wearing boots in this heat?*

"Out of the frying pan," I whispered as I turned and walked the other way, stiffening at the soft chirp of a car's tires. The Lance building was two doors down. If I could make it there, I could slip out through the service door in the back where the dross pickups were.

I glanced behind me, kicking myself when I made eye contact. They'd noticed me.

"And into the fire," I finished as I wondered how much energy my shadow had left in my stone. My pulse hammered, and I straightened, finding a more sure pace. Tension singing in me, I boldly pushed into the revolving door and strode in.

My God. I thought it was bad outside. Eyes wide, I took in the glittering haze under the lobby's tripod trap. Hazy dust bunnies gathered in the corners and under the lobby chairs. A whirl of it rose up in the draft of my entrance, and I slid out of the way as it drifted to the door. It was a sty in here, and my nose wrinkled as the wisp of shadow clinging to my neck shrank down as if in fear. "I won't let it touch you," I whispered, thinking it odd how fast I'd gone from terrified to protective.

Only then did I turn to the street. "Shadow spit," I whispered, cold in the blast of air-conditioning. One had remained at his post, but the other was following me.

"Petra Grady!" a relieved voice rang out, and I spun, biting back a yelp when the shadow dove for my pocket and hid itself again.

"Thank God you're here. I was beginning to think no one would come."

"Mark." Immediately I angled to the heavy man, sublimely aware of the soldier approaching the door. "Yes. I'm here. You got some dross to pick up?"

He took a breath, voice faltering as my eau de culvert washed over him. "Ah, yes," he said as we headed for the elevators. "We haven't had a regular pickup in two days. I told them it was an emergency, but no one has come since the loom broke."

"Well, let's take care of it." I hammered at the elevator button. But it didn't open, and he followed my attention to the man following me. *Ah . . . shit . . .*

"Damn militia," Mark said, smirking as the man ran smack into the revolving door. The dross had caught in the mechanism and it wouldn't open. "They've taken over the streets looking for Dr. Strom," he continued, waving the man off as if to say I was expected. "You haven't seen him, have you? He and Herm Ivaros are the ones who blew up the vault. They are separatists. Can you believe it?"

The last had been whispered, and I frowned. "They are not, and that's not what happened."

Mark turned, eyebrows high. "No?"

I shook my head, and then my luck turned even better as the man from the street raised his hand in acknowledgment, turned, and walked away. I exhaled, slumping, as the elevator chimed and opened. I got in, not caring where we were going.

"You have been busy?" Mark said, his nose wrinkling as the door closed.

My hands were shaking, and I hid them. "In a word." I pressed into the corner, embarrassed. "Hey, you don't happen to have a shower here that I could use, do you?"

"Sure." Mark glanced at my filthy shirt and pants. "I heard the loom was damaged when Strom, ah, when part of the auditorium's roof collapsed. You don't know when regular pickups will resume, do you?"

Two of the loom's Spinners dead, hundreds of injured in the hospital, and he was worried about regular pickups? "Sorry, no." The elevator opened, and I waved for him to go out first into an empty hall. The elevator was air-conditioned, but nothing could cut the smell of two days without a shower.

"I'm so glad you're here." Mark's dress shoes clacked as he swerved from side to side down the corridor, avoiding the hazes of dross as if they were potholes. "We had to close it off."

I followed him, frowning when I realized where we were. *Third floor?* "Close what off?"

"The entire building," Mark said as he used a key to get into the back office area. The door opened, and the faint prickling in my pocket turned into a painful stab. *What the hell?*

"I had to send everyone home." Mark flicked on the lights and strode into the empty offices, utterly oblivious as I jumped, my hand slapping my pocket when the shadow pulsed with cold . . . and then slithered to the floor to wind its fast way through the abandoned desks and chairs to vanish under a familiar door like a wisp of evil dross.

And that's when I heard it. Someone was sobbing, her heartrending gasps of misery drifting into the faint hum of the air-conditioning like a dream.

"The rez is back? Already?" I said, stifling a shudder. *Damn, had it only been five days?*

"It's worse," the man complained. "You can see it now. Her. I can't be expected to keep a clean building when there are no pickups. We have a contract."

I nodded, not knowing what he thought I could do without my sticks. "I'll take a look."

"I don't care what it costs," Mark said. "You need to get it out."

I couldn't care less about Mark's contract or the rez. My shadow was in there. I couldn't walk away. "Ah, can I have the room?" I asked, and he nodded.

"No one in or out," he said, clearly relieved. "Unless the building is on fire."

"Great." I put a hand to the door, pulling back at a hot twang of energy. "Ah, this might take a while. I'll call you when I'm done. No charge on this."

"Good. Great. Thank you." He turned and started back the way we'd come—fast.

I didn't have a phone but wasn't planning on calling him, and I eased the door open.

Darkness pooled in the office, like a black hole sucking in light. I flicked on the light, hesitating as the expected glow seemed halved almost. A faint hint of it reached the corners of the room, but the center, where the desk sat, was still in darkness. Even the clicking of the servers seemed muffled, and I scanned the room for my shadow.

"Oh," I said, brow furrowing when I saw the rez huddled under Dr. Tyler's desk, sobbing.

Worried, I crouched to study the apparition so full of dross that she had a clear form and shape. What light hit her made dappled patterns as it glowed through the strands of hair that had slipped her topknot. One shoe on, the other gone, she huddled as if beaten. "This can't be good," I whispered, wondering where my shadow was . . . until I remembered this was where I had found it.

That it might have abandoned me hit me hard and I stiffened. "Shadow?" I whispered, and the woman under the desk sobbed all the harder. "Shadow! You can't stay here. Someone will find you!"

But the rez continued on, the empty pattern replaying over and over, impossible to change, doomed forever to be this way.

"Where the hell are you?" I whispered. But then I froze when the image of the crumpled woman shuddered and her 1800s dress became clear and in focus right down to her slipper-like shoe. Blinking, she stopped crying. Suddenly my shadow was the last thing on my mind as the ghostly image turned, black eyes focused as it found me. *Holy shit, it's awake.*

"It was my fault," the woman whispered, and I shuddered. Her four words seemed to pulse over me, making her somehow both more solid and see-through.

But she was talking to me, and I had to do more than stare at her. Cold cramping my gut, I licked my lips. "What was your fault?"

The woman began to cry, great big tears plopping onto her knees and turning the carpet beneath her damp. "I didna move quick," she practically moaned. "I deserved to be beaten."

"No one deserves to be beaten," I said, and the woman slumped, her bun falling apart to send glints of blackness into the corners of the room where the light still reached.

"I do," she said, and then she screamed, cowering. The sudden sound sent a shock through me, and I stared, horror-stricken, when a silvery blood began to seep from her head and shoulders. A rip ran across her back, and her pale skin erupted in welts and raw edges. *My God* . . .

"I'm sorry!" she cried, pressing back against a wall that no longer existed. "Please!" she begged, and then she screamed again, the fear-driven sound hitting the pit of my soul as she tried to cower, jerked upright by nothing I could see.

The woman hung there, shaking, struggling. Her dress became dirty, and her hair wild. "Please no, please no!" she wailed, her terrified eyes finding mine. And then she collapsed in a crumpled pile, her dress torn about her shoulders, one shoe missing.

"I couldna breathe," she sobbed, confessing to me. "I deserved to be beat. I shouldna have bit him, but I was so scared. He was hurting me." And then she looked up, her fear turning my stomach. "No. No! Please no!"

Again she cowered, and more marks appeared, each one heralded by a cry of pain. Slowly she grew still, her soft sounds of misery even more distressing.

"And then he locked me under the floor," she said, her hair about her face as she huddled. "He wouldna let me out. I promised I wouldna tell, but he left me there. I said I'd tell my husband that I fell down the stairs, and he called me a *whore!*" She sobbed the last word, as if it meant everything, a death sentence.

Sick at heart, I inched closer, my knees on the dirty carpet. "I am so sorry," I said, and then I blanched as her skin went a sparkly white and her eyes were suddenly not there. She was decaying before my eyes, and my stomach turned as a sour scent of rot rose heavy.

"The police came, and my husband," she said, her words hard to understand as her tongue had become thick and soft. "I shouted, but he couldna hear me." Shoulders bowing, she hid the ruin of her face and cried.

He couldn't hear her because she was dead. "What's your name?" I said, and her outline became more solid.

"Irene." Her eyes re-formed and her dress knitted together. "I'm Irene McNash."

I nodded and inched closer. "Irene, I'm Petra, and the door is open. You can leave. Your husband can't find you, so you need to go find him."

"I can't!" she wailed, her skeletal fingers hammering at a floor that had long since rotted. "He locked me in here. I miss my babies so much. They are so beautiful."

"The door is open, Irene," I said again, and her expression emptied as if in shock. "Find them."

"It's open?" she said, her hope rising high, scrubbing out the welts and bruises.

"It's open," I said. "You can go. Take my hand. I'll help you through it."

She stood, standing beside the desk as she brushed her skirts whole and touched her hair into order. "I can't. I'm so filthy."

I smiled. Not sure what I would feel, I reached for her. We both started as our fingers met, a shiver of power trilling through both of us. Irene stared as if only now seeing me. "You are beautiful, Irene," I said, and suddenly she was whole and mended, right down to her missing shoe. "Go find them."

"Oh," she said, head tilted and smiling as if she could see the sun. "Oh, look! It's so beautiful. Oh, my babies! John? John!" she called, and then I jerked my hand away as if stung. Cold. She'd become cold.

But when I glanced up from my fingers, she was gone.

"Damn," I whispered as a chill ran through me. Where she had sat under the desk was my puddle of shadow—fat and sassy, oily almost. One eye opened in the middle, finding me.

Relief filled me, and then annoyance that I'd been scared it had left me. "You can animate rezes?" I said, then jumped, swallowing back a cry of surprise when the shadow moved, darting forward to quickly spiral up my leg. I stumbled back as cold cramped my chest as it vanished into my lodestone.

I froze, pulse hammering. A warm vibration shifted from the pendant to me, and I dared to take it in hand. The stone was utterly black, a faint, cold tingle pinching my fingers until I wrapped it in a psi field and the shadow seemed to settle with a satisfied hum. It had expended enough of itself that the stone fit it again. Or at least that was the theory I was going to go with.

"You are amazing. I didn't know you could do that," I whispered as I eyed my pendant. "Is that why you were here when I found you? Were you trying to set her free? Or were you just soaking in the inert dross she was giving off?"

A pleased buzz of cold thought muddled through mine. Irene had become scary-sentient while holding shadow instead of dross, the typical mono-thought gaining enough depth and memory to resolve the imprinted energy and set it free. Set her free.

Content, I tucked the pendant behind my shirt, my smile fading at the sudden argument on the other side of the door. There was only one way out of the office. *Shadow spit.*

THREE KINDS OF LUCKY

"Grady!" someone shouted, and I started.

"Webber?" I called out, immediately flinging the door open. It was Webber, the free-range sweeper looking odd in a pair of jeans and lightweight shirt instead of his usual suit and tie. Terry was with him, also having shunned his rags for jeans and a polo shirt. Mark stood between them and the door, clearly trying to keep them out.

"It's okay. I've got it," I said, and the building manager dropped away, relieved.

Webber strode forward, pulling me into a quick hug, eyes bright. "We've been trying to find you! Jessica said she'd seen you, otherwise, we would have thought you were in the auditorium. Where have you been?" he said, and I found I could still smile.

Jessica and Kyle hadn't told them I'd left to find Herm Ivaros, and in a sudden wash of self-preservation, I was loath to tell them myself. "You wouldn't believe me if I told you," I said, then gave Terry a sideways hug as well.

Mark shifted from foot to foot, uneasy. "They showed up a few minutes after you. Did you get it? Is it gone?"

"Um, yeah." But I had no jars of dross, nothing to show for it but a fat, happy shadow hiding in my lodestone.

"Damn, Grady, where have you been?" the free-range sweeper said again, beaming. "The militia is asking about you. Did you know that?"

"I, ah, yeah," I said, plucking my filthy shirt. "That's why the, ah, disguise. I ducked in here to avoid them, and Mark told me the rez had flared up. I figured if I cleaned it out, he'd let me use their shower."

"Same old Grady," Webber said. "See, I told you she hadn't gone to the dark side."

My smile went stiff. *Dark side?* "So, hey, I'm really glad to see you," I said as we began a slow movement to the hall. "Have you seen Dr. Strom? We were on our way into town and we got separated." My voice faltered as the expressions on their faces went closed. "Oh, God. Is he okay?"

"You're with Strom?" Terry asked, his voice cold. "Kyle said you left the auditorium with him."

"Ye-e-eah," I said, and Webber's eyes narrowed. "He was at my apartment when it happened. Is he okay? Last I saw him, he was hightailing it down the road in a, ah, white truck." I took a slow breath, shoving the anger of Lev's betrayal away. "I know what I said before about his process, but if it was his inert dross, something triggered it. It wasn't his fault."

Terry reached for me. Startled, I took a step back. "Are you with them?" he asked again.

"There is no 'them,'" I said, jerking away when Terry reached for me again. "Hey! Knock it off. I told you it wasn't Benedict's fault." No, it was mine. "Have you seen him or not?"

Terry's chin lifted. "We saw him this morning. Briefly."

My relief was short-lived. "Is he okay?" I said, not liking Terry's aggressive attitude. "Where is he?"

Webber studied me, his expression empty. "Herm Ivaros was with him. Did you know that?"

I froze. Getting caught in a lie would put me in a militia cell, but telling them the truth might get me there faster—even if they were my friends. "Uh, I did," I said, and they exchanged grim looks as Mark shifted uneasily. "Darrell sent me to find him to fix the loom."

"She's one of them," Terry said as Mark gasped, and Webber's brow furrowed.

"She said Darrell sent her to get him," Webber said. He'd always been the more coolheaded of the pair. "Are you saying that Darrell was a separatist?"

"Maybe Darrell didn't know," Terry said, then he lurched forward and grabbed my arm.

"You need to let go of me," I said coldly, the only thing keeping me from smacking him being Webber's protest. That, and the icy tingle of my lodestone.

Mark smiled nervously. "Hey, you're all clearly busy. Can I sign an invoice or something?"

"I said, let go of me," I repeated, trying to tug free.

"Terry, knock it off," Webber said, clearly unhappy. "She is a sweeper. She's not going to side with the separatists. If Darrell sent her to get Ivaros, there was a reason."

Terry reluctantly let go, and the cold in my chest dove deeper, becoming an ache. Mark exhaled, sounding more relieved than I was. "Petra Grady isn't involved in this mess," he said forcefully, but seeing as his beliefs were based solely on the fact that I was clearing his office of a rez, they rang false.

"Sorry. I'm a little twitchy." Terry gestured for us to move to the elevators. "The militia has put the entire campus under martial law. A group of separatists have holed up in the damaged auditorium. They are making a stand. Destroy the militia and anyone else who gets in their way."

Mark's chipper steps faltered. "Oh, my God . . ."

I forced my jaw to unclench. If Sikes had Benedict and Herm, that was where they would be. "How many?" I said, and Webber's shoulders eased at the anger in my voice.

"We don't know exactly," Webber continued. "But I'm with Terry. If they can make a separatist stronghold in St. Unoc, others outside the city will join them. This is a problem."

Hence the sweepers refusing to pick up their mess, I thought, eyeing the dross eddying in the corridor. "You think?" I said as we found the elevators. "There is an entire mundane military base to our south. We're, what? Maybe thirty thousand? And only half of that is mage. Why are they doing this now?" But I knew.

"See," Webber said, giving Terry's arm a smack. "I told you she wasn't with them."

Terry grimaced, clearly not convinced. "Then why did she go looking for Ivaros?"

Mark's eyes were round as he hit the button to call for the elevator, and I eyed Terry, tired and wanting a shower. "Darrell said Herm could help fix the vault. That's it. Benedict was helping me find him. Neither one of them are separatists."

"Knock it off, Terry," Webber said as the elevator opened. "Grady is the last person to want the mages in charge. We need to get back to the loom."

"Loom?" I questioned as Terry held the door and we all filed in.

Webber nodded. "Temporary setup in the old records building. You can get cleaned up. Eat. Ryan will want to talk to you."

"He's okay?" I said, elated, and the two men nodded, their silent, nervous exchange worrying me. But as I got in the elevator, my worry grew, not lessened.

When I'd left, Benedict was being blamed for breaking the vault. I knew he hadn't done it, but he'd shown up with Herm Ivaros, and though I believed that the old man wasn't a separatist, no one else would.

My lodestone was cold through my shirt, and for the first time, I was glad it was there.

27

'D ONLY BEEN TO THE SMALL, TWO-STORY RECORDS BUILDING ONCE, WHEN I'D
needed an affidavit after my dad had died. The low-slung adobe
building had originally been a residence, the huge cacti and pink
gravel placing it as part of old St. Unoc before being converted to light
commercial. The tiny drive off the four-lane street could hold maybe
three cars if it hadn't been full of pallets of empty dross bottles. There
was a park to one side and a miniature golf course on the other.
Across the busy road were trendy restaurants and bars, a touch of
modern for the otherwise laid-back area.

Head bowed, I paced the cracked walkway to the door, wanting
nothing more than air-conditioning, something to drink, and a
shower. *In that order,* I mused as Terry opened the elaborately gated
front and the scent of rice and beans tickled my nose. My stomach
growled and I turned to the heavenly smell coming from a small
kitchen. The ceilings were low and the tile on the floor was exquisite.
The front desk in what had once been the entry hall was empty, but
I could hear someone playing Ping-Pong and the muted murmur of
a TV.

"Let's talk in the back office," Terry said, and I hesitated until he
pushed past me to take the lead. Like I knew where the back office was?

The records building was the university's original loom, abandoned when the associated vault under the park had become too small for the growing school. Much like a firehouse, there were living quarters upstairs, and with the kitchen and game room for meetings, it was an obvious choice to set up operations. Best of all, it was clean. Not a hint of dross anywhere, and my shoulders relaxed.

"I thought they'd closed this place," I said as I followed Terry into a claustrophobically narrow hall and past the living room turned game room. Stacks of supplies lined the hallway to make it a tight fit, especially for Terry.

"They did," Webber said. "Even emptied the vault. There's nothing here but records."

"And most of them are upstairs." Terry glanced over his shoulder at me, his bulk taking up most of the hallway. "The vault is sound, though, and we've begun to fill it back up."

"Seriously? It can't possibly hold—" I started.

"It's to destroy the encroaching shadow," Terry interrupted, his expression grim. "A good dozen people died in the collapse, all potential rezes. Ryan says if even a small fraction become active, they will pull in every desert shadow for five hundred miles." He took a slow breath. "Even with them sitting over what's left of the vault. It's like an open dross pit down there."

"Oh." I wove past a stack of bottled water, worried as I held my lodestone. I had gone from scared-to-death to protective in mere days. I wasn't going to question it.

Webber touched my shoulder and pointed to a small yellow door at the end of the hall. "Starting a more permanent vault will have to wait until the militia routs out the separatists."

"They are making a bloody mess of what's left," Terry muttered as he went in.

I scuffed to a halt inside the room, squinting at the bright light coming in through the large patio doors and spilling across the colorful tiles. The backyard was walled, empty apart from an ancient lemon tree growing in the lumpy earth that might have once had grass on it. I could hear a mockingbird through the closed glass door, and the covered patio with its cool tile and soot-blackened chiminea would have been pleasant under other circumstances. The air was cranked back here, almost chilling.

"Akeem?" I questioned as I unshouldered my pack.

"Missing." Webber sat in one of the chairs in front of the antique desk, his narrow frame shifting in a sigh. "Presumed dead. Ryan made it. Maybe you can get him to talk."

"I thought you said he was okay," I said as I studied the pleasant office and wondered who it belonged to. A floor-to-ceiling bookshelf took up the wall behind the desk. Abstract knotted-wool art hung on the walls between painted desert landscapes done in purples and oranges.

"That depends on your definition," Webber said. "He just sits there, rolling that damn eight ball from one end of the table to the other."

I felt my expression blank. "He's here?" I said, jumping when Terry reached past me and shut the door, his smile mirthless.

"Not at the moment. Webber, why don't you find Ryan?" he said, but it wasn't a question, and Webber got up, almost apologetic as he edged past me and back out into the hall.

I stood, arms over my chest, as Terry settled his bulk behind the desk as if he owned it. I had never much liked the man, always griping about something or other. He'd come up a few years before me, and that he was still pulling free-range dross from the quad probably rankled.

At least he had been. Now it looked as if he was setting himself up to run the place.

"So you're clearing the streets of dross?" I said, forcing my voice to be light as I eased into the room and sat. The thin cushion felt like heaven after sleeping in that culvert, but I couldn't seem to get comfortable. "It's okay to use Benedict's procedure to minimize it. It wasn't his fault it exploded. Something triggered it." I flushed, not wanting to explain it was my shadow.

Terry leaned to put his meaty elbows on the desk. "You sure you want to cover for him?"

My gaze jerked back from the dusty, ornate metal chandelier. "I'm not covering for him. It's safe. We found out what triggered it."

"Which is . . ." Terry drawled.

"Ah, shadow?" I forced my hand to stay in my lap instead of gripping my lodestone.

Terry's eyebrows rose, his doubt obvious. "Shadow. In the vault. Right." He sighed and leaned back, glancing at the closed door. "Dross destroys shadow."

"Inert dross doesn't, and it didn't happen in the vault. Darrell said it happened in the loom." My hand crept up to my lodestone in guilt. I had tried to destroy it. I almost had. "This is not Benedict's fault. And he's not a separatist. Do you have a phone I can use? One quick call can settle this."

Terry was staring at me, and I let go of my pendant. "That's right," he said, his voice tight in envy. "I heard Darrell made you a Spinner." He leaned back. "Because you're good with shadow. Just like your dad."

Suddenly I was uncomfortable being alone with him in the back room. "Um, it was Ryan, actually." I forced my hand open and showed him the pendant. The stone was solid black, but by his cursory interest I knew he didn't have a clue that it held shadow, and my tight jaw eased. "I think he jumped the gun, seeing as I haven't really bonded to a stone yet. This is Darrell's. She gave it to me to . . ." My breath caught, and my throat tightened. "She gave it to me so it wouldn't be lost," I lied. "I can't use it."

Which was also a lie, but I wasn't going to admit anything at this point.

Terry nodded, his relief almost palpable. "That's too bad. We could use another Spinner."

"Terry, I need to talk to Ryan," I said, and then turned as the door opened. "Kyle!" I exclaimed, jumping to my feet. Webber was behind him, a bottle of water in his grip. "My God, I'm so glad to see you," I said, throat tight as I remembered how I'd left Kyle and Jessica outside the auditorium. "Is Jessica okay?" I added as I tugged him into a hug.

His skinny arms went around me, giving me a tight squeeze. Worry was a hint in the back of his eyes when he let go, and my joy faltered.

"Is it Jessica?" I said, and he flicked his gaze at Terry behind the desk.

"She's fine. We're all okay," he said, but that his hands still held mine said different. "She's at home, resting." Again he looked at Terry, his smile vanishing. His message was clear. Jessica was fine; the problem was Terry.

"Good." It was a tiny word to the relief I was feeling. "You don't know where Ryan is, do you? I have some news."

Terry cleared his throat, and I swear Kyle flinched. "Ryan hasn't been much use lately," the large man said. "You can tell me."

Kyle licked his lips, feet shifting nervously. "I'm glad you're back. I'll find him," he said, then darted out of the room before Terry could do more than take a breath.

His steps faded fast, and then the slamming of the front door rang through the house like a memory given sound. Terry was waiting when I turned around, and with Webber slowly closing the door to the hall behind him, it suddenly felt like an interrogation. *Relax, Petra,* I thought, as a memory of Sikes sitting at a desk that wasn't his came drifting up, unwelcome.

"Ah, sure." Uneasy, I resettled myself in the chair, feeling twice as dirty as I took the opened bottled water that Webber handed me. "Thanks." I drank half of it in one go, gasping for breath when I came up for air. "I really need to find Benedict. Can I borrow a phone?"

Terry tapped a pencil against the desk. "Why?" he prompted.

"Because the separatists are trying to force him to militarize his new process," I said, and Webber made an audible gasp. "They have a base outside of town in an abandoned elementary school." Or at least they had until Lev blew it up. Maybe that was why they'd moved into town.

"The one that burned down yesterday?" Webber said, aghast. "It's still smoking. That was you?"

I winced, not sure how much I wanted to say. "Ah, I think it was breaking dross, actually. Benedict and I escaped when the alarm went off."

"Escaped." Terry eyed me in ugly disbelief. "You were there trying to find Herm Ivaros, perhaps? A known separatist."

"Ah . . ." I stammered, only now seeing how that had sounded. "Herm is not a separatist, and neither is Benedict. That the loom broke was not his fault. Shadow triggered it."

Terry was silent. Accusing.

"You seriously think I'm in on this?" I said, my knees starting to feel wobbly. "I went to find Herm Ivaros because he's a Spinner. We need him to help fix the loom. I took Benedict with me because I needed mage firepower to bring him back if he still had a lodestone and didn't want to come."

"Curious that," Terry said, grating on me. "You knowing where Herm was."

I took a breath and let it out. "I knew where he was because he's been pretending to be my uncle, and when the loom broke, he wanted to meet. He helped us escape the military. He's not one of them."

"Your Uncle John is Herm Ivaros?" Webber said, staring at me from his chair. "The guy who paid your tuition? Bought you a three-thousand-dollar bike?"

I flushed. "He's not really my uncle, and I bought that bike on my own," I said. But in actuality, he found me. The distinction was important, but it wouldn't help my case.

"Hey," I blurted as Terry exchanged a knowing look with Webber. "It's not me or Herm or Benedict that you need to be worried about. It's the wackadoodle separatists holed up in the auditorium who are the problem. I need to talk to Ryan."

But Terry only sat there, as if he had any real say in the matter.

"Terry," Webber said, his soft word jolting me. "Maybe I should set up a meeting tonight so Grady can tell everyone what she knows. I'd like to find out more about shadow triggering Benedict's inert dross. We can handle shadow. It might give us a dross bomb if nothing else."

Shit. "Okay, I'm done here," I said as I stood. "Let me know if Ryan shows up. I'll be at my apartment."

Terry rose, lurching to get around the desk and skidding to a halt in front of the door. I froze, my eyes narrowing on the big man. "Terry, get the hell out of my way."

"You really expect me to believe that Darrell sent you to find Herm Ivaros?" he said bitterly. "I was there to sweep up when the loom's seal broke in 2014. Darrell hated Herm."

My hands ached, and I glanced at the glass door to the backyard. "Hate takes a back seat when you need help fixing a problem," I said. Webber had stood as well, slowly moving to get between me and the sliding door. "Stop treating me like the enemy."

Terry's brow furrowed in frustration. "Herm and Benedict are working together, and probably you, too, though I don't know why. We found them, and when they refused to come in, Benedict blew the street apart and they both fled."

My lips parted. "He what?" I said, shocked, and Webber nodded, confirming that he was telling the truth. "Why? Is he okay?"

"You're worried about Benedict?" Terry barked. "Benedict is a separatist! He wants to put mages in charge of us, and the mundanes, and everyone. Herm is helping him. It's his original agenda. He's the leader of the separatists."

"Are you nuts?" I exclaimed, remembering the disheveled man cackling as he tried to run over Ashley.

Terry's eyebrows went mockingly high. "This is what I think," he said. "I think Benedict intentionally took out the loom and filled the streets with dross. Made it seem like an accident, then went to join up with Ivaros."

"The separatists are trying to *kill* Herm," I said. "Not because he can further their agenda but because he can end it!"

"And that's why Benedict blew up the street and fled. I think you and that dross-eater Ivaros are together. He's been sending you money for how long? For what? To spy on us? To put Strom in a position where he could blow up the loom? He asked for you specifically."

"And I quit!" I shouted, then winced. Quit after a scathing report about it being dangerous. My lies were destroying my truth.

"My God," Webber whispered, and I reached for my lodestone, holding it.

"Benedict's inert dross broke the loom," Terry continued. "*You* helped him escape. He returned with Herm Ivaros, a known dissident, and harmed two sweepers while trying to evade us."

"That's not what's going on," I said, head shaking. "Terry, I'm trying to help."

I jumped at the light knock at the door, my expression easing when I saw Nog, looking odd in jeans and a short-sleeved tee instead of his uniform of rags. The slow, steady man's confidence was paper-thin and his eyes were haunted.

"Whoa," the older man said as he came in. "What's with the ugly faces? Grady, it's good to see you."

I reached for him, desperate for some understanding. "Nog, thank God," I said as I took his hands. "I am so glad you're here. Where is Ryan? Terry is talking crazy."

Nog's smile looked pained, and I dropped back when his hand hit my shoulder, almost pushing me away. Worry pricked my brow. Nog was wise but not fast, and even though he had seniority, Terry's anger might have railroaded over him, as it clearly had over everyone else. *Ryan, where are you?*

"She's with them," Terry said, and nervous, I inched away from Nog, too.

"I'm *not* a separatist. Nog, where is Ryan? I need to talk to him."

Nog ran a hand over his chin. "He's having difficulty dealing with his recent losses."

Terry pointed at me, his expression ugly now, as if he no longer had to pretend. "She admits that she went to find Herm."

"To fix the vault," I said, weary now. "Darrell sent me. He can help with this."

"You are lying!" Terry shouted, his face turning red. "Herm would rather die than fix the vault. He's here to make sure we don't make another!"

Nog pushed at the air as if trying to slow him down. "Terry, relax. Grady is not a separatist."

My God, Terry had gone absolutely nuts. "Look, I need to find Benedict," I said. "He can explain everything."

"Forget him, Grady," Terry said, still between me and the door. "Lines are being drawn between those who want to rule and those who have the guts to resist them. Which side are you on?"

"I'm not on anyone's side," I said, but they wouldn't believe me.

Nog hunched, his eyes pleading with me. "Our concern is that if the separatists continue to exert their dominance, the mage militia will respond. We can't afford a public show of magic power."

I felt cold, and I backed up until I hit the desk. "They wouldn't dare."

Nog shrugged. "If they can militarize Strom's dross, who knows?"

Heat flashed through me, then cold. My hand rose to find my

pendant, and icy prickles stabbed at me, demanding action. "I don't believe what I'm hearing," I said, breathing out a chill breath. "Benedict's dross only expands under shadow. Prevent that—"

My voice cut off as I realized what I was saying.

Oblivious, Terry uncrossed his arms. "Which side are you on, Grady? Up to now, I would have known. Or perhaps I didn't know you at all. Maybe you like being treated as if your sole existence was to pick up after someone who thinks they are better than you."

"I'm not on anyone's side. I just want to find Benedict and Herm," I said. *Stay in there,* I thought at my shadow, my grip aching with cold. *Oh, God, stay in there.*

"I've heard enough." Terry motioned for Webber to come forward. "I don't know whose side she's on, but it's not ours. Get Darrell's lodestone. Lock her up."

"Hey!" I shouted, fist tightening about my pendant. But I did nothing, shocked when Webber grabbed my biceps, wrenching my grip from my pendant and holding me still as Terry took it from around my neck. "She gave that to me. You can't do that!"

"This is all circumstantial," Nog protested as Webber held me firm. "Why would she be helping the separatists? She's a sweeper!"

Terry's expression was ugly as he looked up from my dangling pendant. "Put her in the closet. We'll figure it out later."

"Terry!" I exclaimed as Webber tugged me off-balance. "I'm trying to help!"

"Make sure it's locked," Terry added, and I tried to spin, caught between two men.

"Guys, don't do this," I protested, shoes skidding on the tile as they propelled me into the hallway. "I haven't done anything wrong. Let me talk to Ryan. Damn it, let me go!"

Terry's sudden cry of fear cut through my protest, and we froze, the open door to the empty closet staring at me.

"What the fuck is that!" Terry cried out, clearly scared. "Webber!"

"Hold her," the tall man muttered, but I couldn't move, heart sinking as Webber let go and jogged back to the office.

"Holy shit!" Webber said as he stood in the hall and gaped. "Don't touch it. You got a dross button?"

"Yes," Terry said, and my expression fell. "But it doesn't want it. It came out of her lodestone."

Son of a bitch . . . I had been outed.

My pulse hammered. Gasping, I brought my foot down on Nog's instep. The man howled, letting go to dance back. I gave him a shove, slamming him into the wall in the tight confines. I bolted for the front door, every fiber of my being focused on that tiny scrap of light. If I could reach it, I could escape. Find Benedict. Fix this.

"Get her!" Terry shrilled, and then I groaned, fire striking the back of my skull.

I stumbled, hand outstretched as I hit the wall and fell to the floor.

"In the closet. Now!" I heard, but I couldn't focus. Dazed, I felt myself dragged back down the hall and shoved into the closet. My head lolled up as they slammed the door.

I was in darkness.

The memory of Irene crying against the door flooded my mind, and I tried to get up, failing. My head felt as if it was exploding, and I couldn't see straight.

"I'm trying to help," I whispered, but they couldn't hear me. Someone was shouting on the other side of the door, but the words didn't made sense, a garbled nothing.

"Even the Wild West had laws," Nog was saying. "You can't know that she brought that shadow in with her."

"She's in league with Herm Ivaros!" Terry shouted. "How much more proof do you need! Where is it? Where did it go?"

"Terry," Nog pleaded, but their voices were going faint, and I rested my forehead against the door, a careful hand going up to find a wet lump amid my hair.

I began to shiver, starting when a warm tingling found my foot and began to steal higher. It was my shadow. Terry hadn't caught it. Inch by inch, I felt it settle over me like a blanket, warming me from inside. I knew I shouldn't let it, but my head hurt, and I was cold, and I couldn't stay awake.

Finally, I gave in and let the darkness take me.

28

_____

SOMETHING WAS PULLING ME, A PRIMITIVE, BACK-OF-THE-BRAIN NEED TO BE somewhere else. It gnawed at my muddled thoughts, the only certainty in my confusion. I was trapped: to move meant peril—more power, less self. I didn't want to become anything other than what I had found myself to be by accident and chance. I was vulnerable, reliant upon a lesser force for my safety. _And that lesser force is an uncouth, ignorant yeth._

I knew they weren't my thoughts banging about in my mind, but the emotions of frustration and anger were so close to what I was feeling that they struck a chord. That is, except for the ignorant yeth part.

Groaning, I opened my eyes to find myself slumped in the corner of a glass-walled room. The vault was to one side, the sweeper lounge to the other. In sudden horror, I realized I was _in_ the loom. A shock so sharp it should have woken me jerked me upright and I sat with my head inches from the ceiling.

But I was asleep, dreaming, and so I only sat on the floor of the loom and pushed against the thick glass, searching for a crack, a way to escape. I could sense shadow, not dross, on the other side of the wall luring me to join with it, become more by becoming less, but I couldn't let go of who I was, and so I turned to the sweeper lounge and hammered on the glass wall.

"You don't want to be more?" Darrell said, and I spun, terrified to see that the wall between me and the vault was gone. Darrell stood amid the shadow untouched, inky waves curling up and around her like a lover playing with her beaded hair. "Accept me," she said, and bewilderment joined my fear. "Leave everything. Become."

"You're not really Darrell," I said, and she sighed, waving a hand in dismissal as I'd seen her do a hundred times before.

"That doesn't mean I can't be useful," she answered, a sparkling black haze dripping from her fingertips as she reached into the darkness behind her and drew Irene from it as if from a bath. Shadow spilled from the woman like water to reveal her scrubbed clean by death, a baby fussing in her arms. Cooing, Irene smiled at me, her eyes burned-out and empty pits.

I recoiled, retreating until the glass wall of the loom pressed against my back.

"If you don't like her, then perhaps this image?" Irene said, jiggling the baby boy in her arms such that his swaddling clothes shifted gray and vanished only to thicken about him again. "It's time to become something else. I ache for it."

"I'm not ready to die," I said, remembering that blow to my head, and the two of them laughed.

"No, not die," Darrell said. "Shadow isn't death. It's everything that isn't. Take it. Claim it. Let me help you."

"You're my shadow . . ." I whispered in sudden understanding. And then I jumped when something thumped against the glass wall. I turned, hope igniting through me as I saw Benedict. Weary and filthy in his tattered presentation best, he hit the glass with a chair, trying to free me. Behind him stood Herm and Ashley with a flippant disregard, uncaring even as Benedict lifted the chair again with a desperate need.

"No, wait!" I shouted, patting the glass to tell him to stop. If it broke, the tide of shadow behind me would flood forward, killing him.

Expression torn, he lowered the chair. "Come out!" he shouted, his voice muffled. His hand pressed to the glass, and I met it, feeling his warmth through the four inches between us. "Grady, please! Don't do this. I can't follow you if you do this."

"Leave her," Herm said gruffly. "She's where she belongs."

Ashley stepped forward, her nails chipped and her hair misstyled, dross clinging to her like pus. "Get her out of there, Benedict. She's too afraid to become. She's just a sweeper."

I'm a weaver, I thought, eyes narrowed at Ashley's attitude. Then I jumped when Benedict slammmed his fist against the glass. Cracks appeared, the spiderweb lines lighting through me.

"Grady?" Darrell called, and I spun to her. Irene was gone. The shadow in my mind knew the woman from the 1800s was not a good lure. "You're not a Spinner. You are a weaver. You are the difference. You can't hide from it. You *are* it. Shadow is the yin to the mages' yang, and the mages have lied. They tried to destroy shadow so light will prevail, but they've only hurt themselves. Accept what you are. Bring back the balance of shadow and light."

"I don't understand," I said, then pushed into a corner, wide-eyed when Darrell took a step forward and was suddenly in the loom with me. *She's in here with me!*

"Stay back," I said, cowering as the gut-roiling scent of decay filled my nose. "Get out!"

"Why?" she said as shadow boiled up behind her.

"Go away!" I shrieked, kicking out, and she crumbled into a pile of white bone and knotted cords.

I had to get out of here. Benedict hammered at the glass. More cracks spread and grew, but it wasn't enough, and I turned my tear-wet eyes to see that Darrell's bones and knotted dross skirt had dissolved. A streaming, hazy shadow was spiraling into a new shape. I pressed into a corner, wishing I could wake up. Benedict was trying to break me free, and I could not wake up!

A green eye took shape in the swirling, gagging reek, focusing on me with an eerie, angry intensity. *What is it that you want?* echoed in my thoughts, and I sobbed, boiling silver tears spilling from me to spot my hands. I was trapped in this nightmare, unable to move. Ice filled my head, and it hurt. It hurt so bad.

"I want to go *home*," I said, hearing a catch in my voice. "I want to sit on my balcony with a cup of hot coffee and Pluck at my feet and look out on a world that makes sense. I want tomorrow to be different but recognizable. I want the dross and shadow back where they belong and everything normal again."

The green eye became brown, soft hints of gold highlights glinting in it. *Dross back where it belongs? Perhaps. But shadow? No. And your wants won't ever be realized without trust. I will try trust. You ignore logic even as you speak it to others. But when was luck ever logical, and you, Grady, are the wielder of luck, good and bad and delphic.*

"Trust?" I said, blinking fast when the shadow that had been Darrell grew. Hazy and cold, a monstrous form filled the loom, pushing me deeper into the corner. Shaggy hair erupted from pus-filled welts, bursting as it shook to send splatters against the glass that hissed and welted the surface. I hardly breathed as a heavy-jawed head turned to me.

It was a dog. Sort of.

"Pluck?" I said, and the dog's lip curled up in a threatening growl to show broken teeth.

"Petra!" Benedict hammered desperately at the glass as Ashley and Herm laughed.

But growl or not, it was Pluck, and needing something to pull me from this nightmare, I held out a hand, inches from his decay-black teeth. Spittle dripped from him and he stank of rot. His fur was matted, and where it wasn't, it was falling out. There were great gaping tears in his ears, and his claws were long, digging into the stainless-steel floor of the loom to leave smoking gouges.

"Oh, Pluck," I said, recognizing him even under the taint of shadow. "I miss you."

The monstrous dog gave a huff that was pure Pluck, and the choking scent of deep decay wafted forth, sending a shudder through me.

"No, don't," I said as a half-rotted tongue lolled out, and I shoved him away before he could lick me. Ice cramped my hand where I touched him, but nothing more. "Sit," I said, and he dropped. His eyes fixed on mine with an unreal intelligence even as he obeyed.

Fear dropped down my spine. It wasn't Pluck. Pluck was never that obedient.

I would offer you a form that is both useful and pleasant, but this is what you trust?

I hunched, breath hissing at the alien prickles of thought echoing in my mind, and with that, I snapped awake.

For one panicked moment, I thought I was dead, but being dead would be more comfortable. My head was an unreal ache. Nausea clenched my gut and I shook with a harsh thirst. I sat up, sliding until my back found the corner of the stuffy closet. Knees to my chest, I pressed the heels of my hands into my eyes and wished the pain would go away. Ice picks in my brain would be less painful.

"Sweet mother of cats," I whispered as my nightmare flooded back. I'd dreamed I'd been in the loom, shadow on one side, my life on the other. Darrell and Irene made demands of me that I couldn't understand. Benedict, Ashley, and Herm had been unable to save me.

"Oh, Pluck." I shuddered at the memory of his shadow self. "I really do miss you."

And then I gasped as the blackness of the closet became solid and a huge, shaggy head lifted from my feet.

"Holy shit!" I cried out, pulse hammering as I pushed away, crying out again in agony when my already spinning head hit the back wall. Dizzy with pain, I struggled not to throw up. My hand was out to keep the shadow at bay. That is, until it touched me and a dark, electric zing cramped my hand and I jerked it to my chest. Cold. It was so cold.

"You're . . . real," I whispered, and it snuffed disparagingly, a low growl rising from it like distant thunder. "I thought it was a dream."

The monstrous thing sat up with the sound of scraping claws, and I cringed, pushing deeper into the corner. The snake and bird were gone. It was a dog, sort of, if dogs were pony size and stank of muck. It shed a black haze, almost glowing in the dark of the closet. Its teeth, where not black and decaying, were wickedly numerous, and it hadn't yet stopped growling, even as it stared at me with brown eyes . . . eyes that reminded me of Pluck.

Slowly my pulse settled. "It wasn't a dream," I whispered, and the low rumble stopped. "Was that you?" I asked. "Were you in my thoughts?"

In answer, the dog sent its lumpy, half-bald tail curving around its massive paws. Wisps of shadow trailed from it like smoke or fog, and I wasn't sure I was really seeing it or if it was projecting itself into my mind.

"You're that shadow that's been following me, aren't you," I said, and the dog's eyes seemed to glitter green, focusing on me with an angry intensity. A prickling began at the bottom of my mind, rising. I could feel it in me, fizzing like oil and water, and I stood, panicked. "Stay out," I said firmly, recognizing the feeling. "You stay out of my mind. I'm not letting you in."

Shadow Pluck lifted a lip and growled.

"Stay out," I said again, reaching to fondle his torn ears, and the dog relaxed, no less angry, but at least he'd quit grumbling. "Why do you have to look that ugly?" I added, and Shadow Pluck huffed, pulling away and filling the far corner as if to say it wasn't his fault.

But my headache had become almost tolerable, and I gingerly felt for the doorknob to give it a rattle. "Hey! Anyone out there?" I called, and the shadow dog made an eerie, nails-on-blackboard groan. "I need a bathroom!" I added, ear to the crack.

But there was only silence, and I slumped against the door, listening to the muted sound of a distant TV.

Sick at heart, I eyed Shadow Pluck. No light made it into the closet, but I could see him as if we were under a full moon. "You're in my mind?" I asked, and the dog made a neutral huff. "Can you get us out of here?"

Again the neutral huff, but it gave me an idea. Screwing up my courage, I ran a hand down his neck to grasp a haze of smoke and pull it free.

"Okay?" I said when the dog fastened a sharp eye on me, and when he did nothing more, I stared at the wisp of shadow in my hand. "You I will let in my mind," I said, sending a psi field about it as if it was an errant bit of dross needing to be captured.

The dog made an eerie growl as the curl of shadow roiled against the confines of my control. Again the feeling of prickly icy bubbles rose up. This time, I let it in, and the shadow splinter fizzed against me, rough and smooth, its blackness turning gray as it bumped through my thoughts. It was too small to have a will of its own and was utterly open to my suggestion.

My headache is gone, I thought as I spilled the shadow splinter from one hand to the other. "Break the lock," I said as wings of smoke and gossamer spread. With one push of its lacy, not-there wings, it took to the air until it plastered itself against the doorknob.

Shadow Pluck whined, the awful sound scraping through me like dirty ice.

My eyes squinted at the sudden, uncomfortable prickle of dross breaking, and then the lock snapped with a dull *thunk*. Pleased, I reached for the splinter, only to have it evaporate.

"It's gone," I whispered. The winged snake had used itself up in breaking the lock.

Apparently unconcerned, Shadow Pluck nosed the door open. A dim shaft of darkness painted the tile in shades of gray, and I followed the dog into the dark hall, blinking and holding my middle against the lingering nausea. A faint light glow and the sound of conversation told me someone was up front. *The sliding door,* I thought, turning to the rear office.

"Please, please, please . . ." I whispered as I eased the door open, my shoulders slumping as I found the room dark and empty. A gray glow illuminated the backyard to throw the rest of the office into shadow. I could go out the back sliding door and over the wall. No one would be the wiser. *Can it be this easy, or is it a trap?*

"Petra?" came a low voice, and I spun, pulse fast as I grabbed Pluck's ruff. It slipped through my fingers like a fog, and the shadow lunged at the desk.

"No!" I shouted, and Pluck skidded to a halt. Lip pulled from his rotting teeth, the shadow growled, the low sound rumbling like thunder in the night. But he had stopped, and that's all that I had wanted.

"Ryan," I said in relief, and the man pushed himself up from the desk and into the light coming in through the sliders. Pluck's growl rose in pitch, eerily high. Oil and water streamed through me, and I walled off the shadow's demand to *kill the keeper of the vault.* "Pluck, sit," I said, horrified at the images of madness lifting through me, and Ryan's eyes widened.

"That's Pluck?"

"More or less. I said, sit!" I demanded as I struggled with Pluck, and the shadow-dog made a pained-sounding cough and sat, his head even with my waist. It was an odd mix. He could clearly make himself as solid as he wanted. Or maybe it only seemed that way. Finally the enormous shadow-dog went still, his putrid breath washing over us with each pant. Relieved, I glanced at the hallway when the TV went to a commercial, then eased the door closed. My escape was right there, but I couldn't leave. Not until I talked to him.

"You did it, Petra," Ryan whispered, gaze riveted to Pluck. "I knew you would."

He seemed tired, haunted, and my elation at finding him faltered. "Knew what?" I asked.

"You learned how to master shadow," he whispered, and a cold chill found me.

I haven't mastered shadow, I thought, then jumped, startled when

Pluck bumped his head under my hand, his ice-cold nose sending sparks of unaligned energy rubbing against me. Okay, maybe I had, and as I tried to form an answer, that icy bubble of oil and water began to rise up through me again. It was Pluck, and I shoved him from my mind. And it was *him*, not *it*. The moment I'd begun identifying the shadow as Pluck, he had become my dog.

I said, sit, I thought firmly, my shoulders easing as the prickly sensation fled to leave a blessed warmth in its place.

"I failed your dad," Ryan said, voice soft with regret. "I didn't want to fail you, too."

"Herm told me everything." *At least his version of it.* "Why didn't you?"

"I wasn't sure." Ryan smiled, but it looked broken. *He* looked broken. "Do you want your dad's long-staff?" He turned where he sat, and my pulse leapt when he took it from where it leaned against a bookcase. "Benedict dropped it when he fled. I've got your lodestone, too."

Pluck whined as I reached for both, taking first the staff, then the glittering green lodestone as he lifted it from around his neck.

"I told them a Spinner had to hold it or it would fill with shadow," he added ruefully. "I'm glad Darrell gave you hers."

"She told me to give it to Herm." My shoulders eased as the smooth length of worked wood filled my grip, and Pluck's rotting tail shifted back and forth as I looped the pendant over my head.

"That was an excuse." Ryan shuddered as he looked at Pluck. "You wouldn't have believed her if she told you."

I wasn't sure I believed it now, and I had a slavering dog from hell at my heel. "I need to find Benedict," I said, and Ryan seemed to slump. "None of this is his fault. He's not a separatist, and neither is Herm."

"I know. Last I saw him, he was running from them, not us. Terry had it wrong. But I think the separatists got them both. Try the auditorium," he said, unusually listless. "Can you use it?" His gaze was on my lodestone, and when I hesitantly nodded, his attention went to the night. "Everything is going to change," he whispered.

"Terry is nuts," I said, worried about Ryan. "Why are you letting him do this?"

Ryan watched Pluck pant, streamers of black stars escaping the dog. "They won't follow him for long."

But they shouldn't be following him at all, and I propped my stick against the desk and crouched before Ryan, studying his lined face. "The militia wants to militarize Benedict's procedure," I said, but his gaze never lifted from the shadow-dog. "It wasn't his fault the loom broke."

"That's going to be a problem, yes," Ryan said, seeming not to care. "I haven't figured that one out yet."

Tired, he scrubbed a hand over his eyes, and I stood, torn. *Do I leave him here, or take him with me?*

"Everything is going to change," he whispered again, and my eyebrows rose when he reached out to try to coax Pluck to him, dropping his hand when the shadow-dog flicked a ragged ear and a sparkling haze hit the wall like pus and hissed into an evil smoke. "Herm bought you as much time as he could," he said, his voice at least regaining a sliver of strength. "You survived our bumbling attempts to wedge you into a square hole if nothing else." His attention landed on the still-smoking wall and winced. "I don't know what I was expecting. Petra, I'm sorry if this is a burden. I had no clue that your dad was the weaver. Everyone thought it was Herm."

Burden? I put a hand on Pluck, and cold ached through me. "I have to go. Can you walk?"

"Sorry about leaving you in the closet." Focus again distant, he lost what agency he had. "I thought it better until you woke up."

"Ryan." I knelt before him again and made him look at me. "Come with me."

The fatigued man blinked. "No. You need to leave St. Unoc. The separatists know what you are now. They will kill you to stop you from changing things, like they killed everyone else who tried. Like they killed your dad. They know if shadow rises, light will fall. They will fall."

"That's not how shadow and light work. One shouldn't overpower the other. It's a balance. They broke it. I'm fixing it."

Ryan's gaze dropped to his open hands. "They will kill Herm just for knowing the truth. I think they're waiting, hoping you try to free him. I'm sorry. You don't deserve any of this."

But a separatist army and our own militia were drawing lines in our streets, and what I deserved or didn't deserve didn't play into it. "Ryan, come with me. It's not good for you here."

"I'll only slow you down." He pushed back into the darkness. "Terry is loud, but he's a minority. I can do more here. You can trust Kyle and Jessica, but, Petra . . ." He grasped my hand, drawing me closer, and Shadow Pluck growled. "None of them know yet. None will believe. Be gentle when you tell them. They're going to fear you. Even Kyle."

I followed his gaze to Pluck, hackles raised as he stared into the night. "Are you afraid of me?" I whispered, scared of his answer.

"No," he said, forcing a smile. "Yes," he added, and his grip slipped from my hands. "You are the change, Petra, and that frightens people even without some scary-ass, pus-dripping dog who can drive people mad. I'm sorry."

I glanced out the sliding doors and into the night. Pluck stood at the door, head up and tail stiff, looking so much like my dog wanting to go out that it hurt. "Can you do something for me?" I said as I took my stick in hand. "Will you tell Kyle about weavers? That they are real. Don't make me do it."

Ryan nodded. "Go. I'll tell them you were gone when I went to check on you. Your shadow scared the piss out of Terry. I could tell them that you sprouted wings and flew off, and he'd believe me."

"Thank you." I gave his shoulder a squeeze, wondering how I had become the stronger of us. "Wish me luck."

Ryan reached after me. His hand was cold, but Pluck's thoughts in mine were colder, and the man jerked when the dog scraped one claw against the tile in threat. "Be careful," he whispered. "They will kill you if they can. You're only one person, and they have killed thousands over the years."

A smile quirked my lips. "They have to kill my shadow first."

He ducked his head, a rueful chuckle escaping him. "That they do." Sighing, his gaze went to the backyard and the sound of a low-flying jet. "This is a mess."

Truer words had never been spoken, and stick in hand, I pushed the sliding door open and walked out.

29

PLUCK OOZED INTO THE NIGHT BESIDE ME, AS DARK AS MY MOOD.

"This really sucks," I whispered as Pluck pushed his decaying, misshapen nose into my hand, nudging me toward the wall. Ryan was standing at the glass when I looked back, and I gave him a wave before using the lemon tree to vault myself to the top of the wall and then over.

My feet hit the ground in a back alley and I froze, eyeing the two men standing in a puddle of light at the corner. They were watching the house but hadn't seen me.

I pressed into the wall and pulled Pluck to me, chunks of his hair falling out as I gripped his ruff. *Oh, my God, this has to stop,* I thought, shaking the horrid mess off me and watching it dissolve into a heavy mist and vanish. "Are we going to be dodging separatists all the way?" I whispered.

Pluck made an annoyed huff. His tongue lolled around his broken teeth as he put a paw on my foot.

I stiffened as ice seemed to shock through my veins, and I yanked my foot out from under his not-there paw. He wanted into my thoughts. "Can't you talk?" I said, and he huffed as if I was stupid. "I'm not letting you in my mind. It hurts," I said, and he lifted his nose, telling me to go deeper into the shadows.

I didn't move, and he headbutted me. There was no weight

behind it, but I stumbled back from the icy cold that slammed into me. "Knock it off," I whispered as I caught my balance, but he had already shifted to sit in the faint moonlight where I had been, his doggy eyebrows high. "You want me to stay here?" I guessed, and he lifted his nose in an obvious yes. Maybe it had been a mistake not letting him take Darrell's form.

I gestured for him to have at it, and he gave me another one of his huffs and trotted off, his feet never touching the ground, wisps of shadow drifting from him like stray moonbeams. Shadow Pluck clearly had an idea, but letting him into my mind to tell me what it was wasn't going to happen.

I jumped at a sudden crash, sliding deeper into the shadows when the two men went on alert. Flashlights played over the parked cars, and a black haze dove for the night. *Pluck?*

Ice prickled against my calves, and I spun to see the dog behind me. *Move. Now.*

His thought was like a knife in my mind, and I fended him off, suffering even as I put a hand through his shoulder for balance. Winter froze me from the inside out, and I made a psi field about my mind as my head cracked like ice. *I have no mass,* came his thought. *Why do you keep trying to touch me?*

I blinked, dizzy. I wasn't sure if it was because of him in my mind or a concussion. "I don't know. Maybe because it would be easier if you did." I took a slow breath, trying to find my balance. "The auditorium," I whispered. "Can you run vanguard for me?"

Black ice bubbled and fizzed against my mind, softer than before, and I let it, surprised when my headache eased until he trotted into the darkness. His pace quickened, and I almost lost him when he darted between two parked cars.

"It's the other way," I said, pointing, and a low growl rumbled through me as his eyes shifted from brown to green. My side went numb with cold when he knocked into me to get me moving, and I danced away, almost tripping on the curb.

"Fine, the long way," I whispered, giving up. But the chill from him was making my head feel better now, not worse, and I dangled a hand into his shoulder, little wisps of shadow playing about my fingers like fur. Either I was getting used to him, or he was learning how much I could handle; the ice daggers in my brain were almost tolerable now, and my pace slowed when I began to see flashes of light flickering under abandoned cars and in the corners. *Is that . . . dross?* I wondered, startled when Pluck huffed an agreement.

Shocked, I pulled my hand from him. The brightly glowing drifts vanished and my headache slammed back into play. I reached for him again, sighing as his cold thoughts bubbled through mine and the dross glow under the cars returned. It was obvious what was going on. If I let him lay gently in my mind, I could see the world through his eyes. And the world through Shadow Pluck's eyes was a fairyland of lethal, burning dross.

"This is amazing," I said, and a little band of black haze wrapped itself about my wrist, easing the pain even more.

I'd always had good night vision, but through Pluck, the cloudy skies and full moon were an unearthly mix of luminescent grays and golds. A brilliant haze bounced against the clouds to the south, far more than the full moon could account for. Dross. It still lingered at the auditorium.

It was easy to find my way through the curfew-empty streets and avoid the white-hot flame that dross had become. Each block left me feeling better, and a flicker of appreciation warmed our shared thoughts; he was impressed that I could touch dross with impunity. Grateful, almost?

And then his thoughts icing mine vanished. "Ah, Pluck?" I whispered, scuffing to a halt when the light from the dross drifts went out and the night dulled. He was gone. "Pluck?" I called softly, then jumped when my foot went icy cold.

"There you are," I said in relief, but it was only a wisp of him, fizzing through my mind with no clear words, only emotion. *Here,* it seemed to say, and stick in hand, I followed, my shoes silent on the cooling sidewalk surrounding the quad. The sharp tingle led onto the watered grass, and the air became stifling under the paloverde trees. And then even the tingle vanished.

"Pluck?" I whispered, spinning when a voice broke the stillness.

"Grady . . ."

My lips parted at the hazy, not-there shape sitting at the park bench, little rills of darkness spilling from it. It was a rez, and it knew my name.

"Grady?" the slurred call came again, and I put a hand to my mouth, gaze riveted to Darrell's beaded hair dripping shadow and smoke, curling about her wide hips. It was Darrell. She wasn't alive. She was a rez. Again.

"Shadow spit," I whispered, cursing Pluck for bringing me here. I didn't have time for this. Sure, I wanted to free her, but maybe it could wait?

That was when I saw Pluck sitting next to her, and I frowned. If Pluck wasn't animating her, then who was? Or better still, what was she doing here? The loom was across campus.

"How did you get here?" I whispered, not expecting an answer, and the apparition carelessly waved her hand, little rills of energy spilling from her fingertips like living dross. The gesture was familiar, and I jerked as if punched.

"Who's to say?" she said listlessly, her sightless eyes staring at me as her hands knotted a strand of shadow and dross. "No one told me there were rules. I was tired of being in that pit. You can't grow roses underground."

It had her memories, and it hurt. "Pluck, are you doing this?" I said, and the shadow-dog made a huff, shaking himself to make little wisps fly free, before trotting forward. *Okay, it's not Pluck.* "I don't understand. Rezes can't move. Darrell died blocks from here."

You are correct, Pluck thought as a tendril of shadow wrapped around my ankle, his icy words rubbing like razors against my mind. *A desert shadow animates her, and with that, the rez possesses movement and a borrowed reasoning. The construct left its creation place, driven by the shadow's need. It's looking for something. I thought I could commune with it, convince the shadow to abandon the shell it had taken, but it's confused, clinging to the Spinner's memory, unable to understand why she doesn't respond. What you leave behind when you die, a shell though it is, it is a lure we can't resist. A cold blanket on a colder night.*

I didn't know how to feel about that, and I faced the rez and gathered my resolve. It looked like Darrell, and it acted like Darrell. If anyone saw it . . .

"Darrell, you need to let go," I said, and the rez laughed, rills of soot falling from the bitter sound echoing across the park as its beaded hair tinkled like broken glass.

"I can't let go," it said as it stood, envy and avarice in its shadow-held eyes. "Help me. I can't let it go!"

This was shadow speaking, not the memory of Darrell, and I backed up to the street, stick in hand and worried as Pluck wound a possessive coil about me. "This was a mistake," I said as the night brightened into a fairyland of dross. Pluck fizzed against my thoughts, his emotion a turmoil of guilt and fear. Fear for him. Fear for me. I was fairly sure I could fend off an unbound shadow. I'd try if it made one move toward Pluck.

"I can't let it go!" the shadow-animated rez shouted again, eyes sparking, and I stumbled onto the sidewalk as it reached out, searching. If one shadow had been drawn from the desert, there were likely hundreds, all of them craving contact. Terry had been wrong about a lot of things, but he was right about this.

"I'm sorry. I can't help you," I said. "Go back to the desert."

"I can't," the image of Darrell wailed. "I can't let go!"

My face went cold from more than Pluck pressing into me as the rez writhed in a memory of pain. Pluck shook in fear, not only for me but for himself. *Run,* he thought. *It's half-mad. It wants to smother me to take you for itself. Your mind will be torn to shreds before it remembers how fragile you are.*

"Help me be free of this. Please!" the rez begged, and I retreated, mouth agape as it began to disintegrate, the memory of flesh turning into a heavy smoke. "Please," it begged, dissolving to a hazy memory, and still the shadow could not let go of what remained of Darrell.

It knows not itself. Go. Pluck shoved me, his icy headbutts pushing me farther down the street. But I turned, aghast, when an eerie wailing rose. It warbled higher than any voice, piercing and carrying a pained acceptance and longing. No sound like that had ever passed a human's lips. It was the shadow, aching for release even as it clung to a half memory of what it craved.

The feral shadow's pain and misery echoed in the curfew-empty street, and I set a hand atop Pluck's shoulder, braving the ice pick of heartache and guilt stabbing through me. Guilt? He felt guilty?

"Pluck?" I whispered. "Why can't it let go? It's only hurting itself."

We all went mad when the mages killed our weavers.

"They . . . When?"

Pluck's substance faltered, his definition falling apart as he pushed me farther away from the sound of the rez railing at time and tragedy. *Yesterday,* he whispered, the single word shattering into thousands to drift like midnight snow through my mind. *It feels as if it just happened, but that's not true. It was so long ago that the lies the mages told about us have become the truth. We are now all indiscriminate killers.*

I stopped right there in the street, kneeling to bury my hands in his oily ruff, forcing him to look at me until his eyes vanished and he dissolved, leaving me holding nothing but a chill haze. "You are not. I'm touching you now."

That's why I dare to hope despite all I've seen. A single green eye bubbled up from the ball of matted fur. *Shadows will come. Have* come. *They sense the loss of the vault and will seek revenge for their lost weavers. Perhaps if they find you instead, standing between them and the hell the mages want to create anew, they will find a way to heal.*

Behind us, the rez finally went still, the sudden lack almost more disturbing than its keening. "Pluck, what happened?" Ice frosted my skin, and Pluck shrank to a black puddle. "Pluck?" I called, frantic, but he was there in my mind, reluctant, confused, bitter, and resolute.

There was a balance of magic and mage once, he thought, and I rested a hand within him, my fingers going numb as his regret and guilt rose high in me. *A balance of shadow and light. It was imperfect, but it held. Mages used light and left dross in the wake of their magic. Weavers cooled the dross, and through shadow, left light when they did their spells. But there's always darkness, and the power of the mage is chained to the day. Jealous, they began a great lie that shadow was evil. Weavers learned to hide, and shadow faltered. But it wasn't enough, and whenever a weaver was found, both mage and mundane killed them, leaving their bonded shadow to grieve and anger.*

"That's horrific," I whispered, breathless as his brittle heartache seeped into me.

Where there had once been a whole, there was half, Pluck thought. *Less, perhaps, and when the final weavers were found and destroyed, the mages turned their attentions to us, beginning a lie that we turned into a truth, for in our loss, we learned how to kill. But we learned it too late, and now, even those who might hear us are deaf. They fear us, fear what we have become. A putrid, revolting thing to be destroyed.*

My own guilt rose high, and I gathered the puddle of black to me, trying to coax it into a shape with my cold-cramped hands. "Pluck, who knows this? Who is covering this up?"

A snakelike head rose, drooping and listless. *Once, all the mages. Now, no one remembers it all except us. The mages' lie has become a truth as we fight to survive, killing anyone who finds us, as to do otherwise leads to our death, our voices silenced.*

I offered my hand, and he slowly wound up and around until I had him again. *I thought when you gave me cooled dross that you had survived the mages' purge—that you understood. Your fear hurt. How you saw me . . . I didn't understand.*

"Pluck, I didn't know." But my words seemed pale beside his overwhelming grief.

We had names once, drifted through my thoughts.

I licked my lips. The need to be moving was growing and I stood. "What was your name?" I whispered, feeling as if I gathered winter to my chest when I pulled him close. If he couldn't walk because of grief, then I would carry him.

I don't remember, he thought, but the thaw in my hands told me he was lying. My throat closed, and I shifted him higher. I felt inadequate, overwhelmed by the guilt that I had tried to kill him not once but several times. Obviously I wasn't trying to kill him anymore, but calling him by my dog's name seemed wrong at this point.

What have the mages done to us? I thought to myself, but I think Pluck heard as he began to slowly find his form—even as his emotions of gratitude and shame grew thick in my thoughts. Against all odds, he had found what he needed in me, and he felt guilty because his kin still languished in pain.

"You okay?" I said as he sifted through my hands and found the pavement.

Not answering, he shook himself as if coming out of water, his oily, matted fur flying from him in a spasm of relief to leave smooth skin. A wickedly intelligent eye fixed on mine, and he flicked his ear of the last of it and stood before me without fur, his black skin silky and his body trim, sharp ears pricked. Wisps of his self furled to hide his feet, and the faint scent of rot that clung to him . . . vanished. He was still a hound from hell, but now he was . . . elegantly fierce, not putrid.

"How?" I said, and the dog who wasn't a dog shrugged.

I am what you think of me, he thought, and a lip lifted in a doggy smile. *The world sees me as you do.*

And I no longer saw him as a scary, life-ending, holy-shit shadow-dog with pus-matted fur and rotting teeth. Actually, now that I thought about it, his appearance had been steadily improving, and I wondered what he might look like tomorrow.

Lips quirking, I reached to touch him, then withdrew. He wasn't a dog to fondle his ears and tell him he was a good boy. Not to mention that I didn't want him to know my thoughts at the moment. Mages had systematically murdered all the weavers to end the shadow that gave them their strength, then began another campaign of lies to find and destroy shadow itself. Worse, they'd stunted potential weavers to the fringes of society as sweepers, tricked into collecting the very thing that would destroy the shadow that might free them.

No wonder shadow killed the mage or sweeper who forced it out of hiding.

"I am so sorry," I whispered as we left the puddle of light and slipped into the warm darkness.

A cold tendril wound around my wrist. *You are not responsible. No one alive is.*

But I felt as if I was, and as the night again became alive with dross, I vowed that no one would make a new vault to destroy shadow.

"Pluck, I will fix this. I swear, if I make it out of here alive, I will fix this. We have to find a balance of shadow and dross again. Nothing deserves to live that alone."

Pluck's head rose, and a cold, muscular thigh pressed into me, numbing my entire side. *It is what I desire. It is all I desire beyond keeping you alive. Now that I have found you, I can't decide between the two. I fear that no one is strong enough for this task. I won't ask it of you. I cannot ask it of you. I fear to lose you.*

Only now after seeing the shadow caught in Darrell's rez did I understand what I meant to the shadow, and I rested a hand atop his shoulder, no longer afraid of the cold fizzing against my thoughts. It was more than cooling dross for him to become stronger with. It was more than me having magic. There was a symbiosis here of dark and light. Of weaver and shadow.

"I think we can find a way without either of us dying," I said. "Not alone, though. We're going to need help." Help, yes, but I was starting to think the sweepers' guild might not be able to look past the "shadow bad" thing we'd been fed our entire lives. I needed Herm and Benedict more than ever, and I looked at the underside of the clouds over the auditorium, glowing as if the moon had come to earth.

"Light!" someone shouted, and I yelped, cowering at the white-hot spotlight slamming into me.

Shit. It's Terry. I spun, my stick raised in threat. "Back off, Terry! You try to put me in a closet again, and I'm going to smack your head through a wall!"

"Grady, it's me," a calm, familiar voice said from the blinding light, and my panic shifted to something more enduring. It wasn't Terry. It was Lev. "Let me explain before you go off half-cocked. I've been watching you since you left the park. If I had wanted to dart you, you'd be down by now."

They will cage you, echoed in my memory. I took a breath, dizzy from the quick turn. In one smooth motion, I spun my dad's stick in a show of hit-your-ass. The light was blinding, and I grabbed my lodestone when it thumped into me, tucking it behind my shirt. It was black. Pluck couldn't take this, so he had fled into it.

"Stay the hell away from me, Lev," I intoned, and from the dark, someone chuckled.

"I'll be damned," came a whisper, and then louder, "The light worked, sir. The shadow took refuge in the lodestone as you said."

Stick in hand, I turned to the sound of grit under a pair of boots. If they were going to abduct me, I was going to leave a few bruises this time. "I said no. You left. End of story."

"That was smart to leave the bag at the culvert," Lev said, and I shifted, squinting at the dark outline he made against the light. There were others behind him, how many, I couldn't tell, but I could hear them. "I wasted the afternoon executing an extraction on an empty tunnel." He scuffed to a halt at the edge of the light. City-camouflage fatigues and an unslung rifle were bad enough, but he also had that lodestone winking from his ear. "Where are Ben and Herm?"

Wary, I let the butt of my staff touch the ground. "Sikes took them," I said. "You want to turn that light off before they find me? I don't have time for this. I'm trying to save the world."

"Aren't we all." Lev stood there, his somewhat short, backlit silhouette reminding me of Peter Pan for some reason. "That shadow going to stay where it is if I douse the light?"

Like I knew? But I nodded, and Lev made a motion, and the light clicked off, effectively blinding me for a moment.

"I didn't know Sikes had Ben. I'm sorry about that," he said, his expression hard to see with my light-stunned eyes. "Maybe I can help. Shadow doesn't scare me."

I chuckled, knowing that was a lie. "Yeah. Right."

Lev handed his rifle to someone behind him and inched closer. "Fair point, but I grew up around people capable of dealing out death and having the restraint to not use it. Shadow is merely the latest toy." He hesitated, weight going to one foot, as if convincing himself of that. "Give me twenty minutes to send my team to do a decent recon for you."

"Why would you do that?" I scoffed, my knotted guts easing when my fingers went cold and Pluck was beside me again.

"Because we are going to do one anyway." Lev came a step closer, halting when Pluck shook his head to make his ears smack in a threatening popping sound. "Because my superiors don't care if Sikes kills you," he added, "and I think that's a grave injustice. Not just for you but for our society as a whole. Twenty minutes. That's all I want."

I bit my lower lip, gaze going to the faint glimmer of lodestones from the dark as my eyes adjusted. *Shadow spit, there are like twenty people there.* "And I should trust someone who doesn't care if I live or die because . . ."

"Because if you want the noisy toys, you gotta play with the noisy boys." Lev smirked to look like the devil himself before he sobered.

"Right now, Nodal—he's my superior—is convinced that you're Sikes's paper dragon, a figment of imagination that fuels the separatists' fundraising and bolsters their rolls. No real threat. But I know you." Lev put a finger to his nose, eyes glinting. "I have watched you for two years. I might not know *what* you can do, but I know what you're willing to do to save what's important to you."

I said nothing, my grip on my stick tightening to a white-knuckle strength.

"Right now Nodal thinks you're a joke," Lev said.

"Because I'm a trashman." My face burned, and at my heels, Pluck prickled and fizzed.

Lev inched closer, until the light evened out and I could see his worried, intent expression. "Petra, you are a weaver. You and your shadow will either change everything or get killed as every weaver before you was, your dad included. I'm trying to give you some options."

"I'm not joining the militia," I said, and Lev put up a hand for patience.

"Hear me out. There's no way in hell that you will be able to go back to your life, yes?" Lev glanced at Pluck. "If you don't willingly attach yourself to a larger group who can protect you, you will end up in a cage."

"So where's my option?" I barked, grimacing when someone laughed from the dark.

"The option comes in wrangling an agreement from Nodal while he's blinded by his own prejudices." Lev smiled, his deviltry easy to see in the dim light. "He thinks you're a paper dragon, but I say you are a sleeping one. Afterward? When he sees you awake? You won't get nearly as much freedom and will pay for it with more of the same."

I understood what he was saying, but I wasn't going to join the militia, and I glanced down at Pluck as my fingers dangling in him went icy cold. "Why should I trust you?"

"You shouldn't. But *I* trust *you*." Lev idly looked at his fingernails. "Not to mention that Nodal is half a thought away from bombing the auditorium with mundane technology to get rid of the separatist threat."

"Bomb . . . ?" Panic iced through me, mirrored by Pluck's fear when he saw me ready to bolt. Good thing he hadn't opened with that, or I'd be gone already.

"No one wants to bomb a city structure," Lev said, far too calm for my liking. He was manipulating me, and I hated it. "But what choice do we have?"

I licked my lips. "Give me until dawn. I'll get them out."

Lev grinned. "Yeah. I know. But you gotta talk to Nodal first," he said, gesturing for me to go before him into the dark. "I've got a Jeep a street over. Sikes won't do anything until sunrise and he has the sun to back him. That's your cutoff. Proper intel and outfitting will make the difference between success and failure. I can get that for you. And after you kick some separatist ass, Nodal will see how valuable you are and protect you."

My shoulders shifted in a sigh as I sent a careful thought into my lodestone, and the icy memory of Benedict being darted flickered coldly through both Pluck and me. *Sweepers exist to destroy shadow,* bubbled and fizzed in my thoughts, and I stifled a shudder. *Locked you in a closet. Perhaps our salvation will come from an old enemy.*

Pluck was more trusting than me . . . but I wanted to believe. "You screw me over, Lev, and you will find out what it's like to touch shadow."

"Yes, ma'am."

There was a nervous titter as I pushed into motion. I could talk to anyone for twenty minutes. And then I was going down and, as Lev said, kick some separatist ass.

30

M Y HEADACHE HAD RETREATED TO A DULL THROB, AND I GINGERLY FELT
through the soft bandage to the tender lump. A professional
dressing wrapped my elbow, and several more covered my scrapes.
According to the medic who had checked me over, I had a concussion,
and I'd been told not to go to sleep until tomorrow night. Right. As
if I'd ever sleep again.

I didn't know where Lev was. He'd given me a soda and a couple
of cookies from someone's MRE before escorting me by Jeep from
their makeshift medic station to a newly commandeered ranch just
outside St. Unoc. The sun would be up in a few hours, and I was
getting antsy.

Cookies. As if I am a little kid to be bribed into good behavior, I
thought, even as I brushed the crumbs away. But they were shortbread, and I'd almost be willing to set aside my antagonistic tenden-
cies for shortbread. Sighing at my own foibles, I sat in the front seat
of a Jeep and drank my fizzy pop. The medic had given me a pair of
dark glasses to help with the glare from the huge lights turning night
to noon, and I wished I had my phone; "Sunglasses at Night" would
do wonders for my mood.

"Stay in there," I whispered when a feather of gray eddied from
my lodestone to play in my drink's effervescence.

"Ma'am?" the escort sitting beside me asked, and I gave him a salute with my soda.

"Trying not to burp," I lied. "Stay in there."

"Burping is an underrated art form," he said, then belched.

I smiled thinly, my eyes going to a hazy drift of dross eddying down the stone stairs of the sprawling ranch house. The area was rife with it, and I sighed as the distortion settled on the last step like an errant cat waiting to trip someone.

With an odd, mental hiccup, the distortion on the step blossomed into an eye-hurting glow. A sudden cold spike jammed itself into the base of my skull, and like magic, the night was alight with dross. It was my shadow. He wanted to talk.

They are organized, he thought at me, the cold spike easing as he felt my discomfort and eased up. I took another gulp of my pop, eyes watering. I'd been cooling my heels for over an hour and I was just about ready to walk off. The sun would be up soon, and with that, any advantage I might have would be gone.

I jumped when my escort's radio crackled, and he took up the receiver and told them to go ahead.

"Nodal is ready for Ms. Grady," a masculine voice said, and my escort glanced at me.

"Confirmed. Bringing Grady in." He clicked off the radio and motioned for me to get out.

"It's about time," I muttered as I wobbled to my feet, my balance iffy. *Concussion. Right.*

That dross was still there on the stairs, and I edged to the side to avoid it when three militia guys in khakis noisily stomped across the covered porch, the large trunk in their care clearly lighter than when I had seen it brought in.

"Mind the dross," I said as I passed them on the stairs, and they scoffed as if I was being overly cautious.

My pace slowed as I entered, the activity far more than what I would have expected. To the left was the living room, clearly a temporary communications hub staffed by young men and women in jeans and civilian fatigues. A set of uncarpeted stairs led upward, and I could see a stone and tile kitchen beyond it at the back. Additional lighting had been brought in, and the glare cut right through my glasses. Someone had set up a trap in the corner, and it was overflowing with dross, the distortion waver making my lip curl and fingers itch.

"To the right, ma'am," the man escorting me said, then he turned at the heavy thump from outside. The handle of the trunk had snapped and the two men were loudly blaming everything but the dross that had done it.

I felt out of place, nervous as I entered what was clearly a dining room: dramatic blue-and-silver wallpaper, blue tile floor, subdued lighting, and the longest mahogany table I'd ever seen.

"Wait here, please," the man said. "Master Ranger Nodal will be along shortly."

"Sure." I propped my stick against the table and dragged a chair out at the head of the table. The overlapping conversations from the front room were pleasant even as they made me uncomfortable, and I eased myself down slowly to hide how much I hurt.

My lodestone swung free, and I grasped it. *You'd better be right about this,* I thought, and my fingers went numb with a spiking cold. Grimacing, I let go of my lodestone only to jerk my foot up at a hot tingle of dross, pulled across the floor by the dross in my staff.

"This is taking too long." Anxious, I pulled the haze from my foot and rolled it in a psi field. *Hey, you want this?* I thought, stiffening at a sudden thump of cowboy boots in the hall. It was Lev and an older man, and I flicked the inert dross away as they came in.

I could feel my shadow's attention follow the hazy distortion as it rolled into a corner and merged with another drift. Maybe Nodal should engage my services as a sweeper, because this mage-only party was a freaking mess.

Nodal, because that was who it had to be, was in worn jeans and a plaid shirt. He looked casual next to Lev's surplus fatigues, but his confidence more than made up for it, putting him at the top of the dog pile. His ebony-dark hair was straight and cut close to his skull, and with his spare, tall frame, weathered dark skin, and wrinkles, he looked like a cowboy. His holster was empty, but there was a lodestone on his belt buckle. All he needed was the hat. *Hispanic? American Indian?* I mused as he took his glasses off and studied me. He belonged to the desert, though. That much was obvious.

I gave him a neutral half smile. Dross clung to him, but it was clinging to everyone.

"Petra Grady, this is Master Ranger Nodal," Lev said as I stuffed my frosty lodestone behind my shirt and stood. "We aren't big on formality, so it's either Master Ranger or Nodal, but not both."

Master Ranger. Right . . . "Nodal," I said, bobbing my head instead of meeting his extended hand. Nodal took that well, smiling as if he approved. "It's been over an hour. Lev said twenty minutes."

Eyebrows high, the older man gave Lev a sharp look, and Lev sort of shrugged. "Reconnaissance took longer than expected, sir," he said.

"Grady." Nodal motioned for me to sit. There was a folder in his hand, and I stared at it. I'd give a lot to know if it was about me or the promised information about Sikes.

"Did you see Benedict and Herm?" I asked, and Lev nodded.

"They are restrained, but okay."

My relief was a quick flash, and I shifted uneasily. *Tick-tock.* "I need to go."

He says your yeth is secure, iced up through me, and I jumped, surprised. *I want to see how master rangers feel about shadow.*

He's a mage. He will want to kill you, I thought back even as Nodal pulled a chair out and sat about halfway down the table.

"You're here. If I don't give you five minutes, Lev won't ever let me forget it," the older man said as he put his glasses back on and flipped the file open.

My loom ID photo was front and center. The file was about me.

A quiver of angst rose and fell. Both Lev and Nodal had lodestones, and all I had was . . .

You have me, the shadow almost purred through my thoughts, icy and sure.

But a lifetime of fear was hard to let go of, and I didn't sit down. Showing Nodal my slavering shadow-dog probably wasn't a good idea, and my head hurt as Pluck simmered at the back of my awareness, getting every ugly, worried thought that crossed my mind. "I need to go," I said again as Lev settled in beside the open archway. "I've wasted too much time already. I have to extract Benedict and Herm before Sikes kills them to get to me or you bomb the place."

His rough fingers sure, Nodal flipped through the file, studying my life. "Of course. Sit down, Ms. Grady."

"*Before* he kills them or you bomb the place," I said again, and Nodal looked at me from over his glasses.

"Of course," he repeated, this time glancing at my chair. The dross he'd brought in was slowly pulling from his elbow, attracted to the drift I'd tossed into the corner. "Lev is of the belief that you have an uncanny control of a new kind of magic. Weavers?" His lips pressed and his brow furrowed. "I'm not devoting any resources to helping you in your vendetta—"

"It's not a vendetta," I said, and his eyes came up to mine.

"Let me finish," he said, clearly not used to anyone interrupting him. "I'm not devoting any of our resources to your vendetta until I'm satisfied you have control over what you carry and won't make matters worse." His gaze dropped to my lodestone. "I may be a mage, but I'm not ignorant of shadow, and I will not be taken out by friendly fire."

Control? I didn't have control over shadow, and I sank down into my chair.

"Thank you," Nodal murmured, his attention returning to his paperwork. His pen broke with a sodden snap, and he lifted his hand, staring at the ink staining it. Needless to say, the dross he'd brought in with him was gone.

"Me being here is not my idea," I said as Nodal made the mistake of trying to blot the ink off on his papers. "But if you could wait until I get Benedict and Herm clear, I'd appreciate it." *Yeah. Appreciate it.* It was the understatement of the decade, and I stifled an anxious quiver.

Unperturbed, Nodal set his ruined notes aside and focused on me. "You think you can liberate two men from a separatist group in three hours?"

"It was four when I got here," I complained, and Lev shrugged when I glanced at him. This was getting me nowhere, and I slumped sullenly into my chair, fingers rolling a quick staccato on the mahogany table.

Defined eyebrows high, Nodal wiped his fingers off on the rag an aide handed him. "Lev says you are a weaver."

Unease trickled through me, and I fought the urge to grip my lodestone. "Maybe someday, sir," I said, the honorific feeling odd coming off my lips, but I really wanted that intel and to get out of here. "Right now I'm simply trying to figure this out."

Nodal flicked a glance at Lev. "I've been given the impression you can control shadow."

"*A* shadow," I said. "Not all of them, and I don't really control him. It's more of a . . ."

Adviser, iced up through me.

"Partnership," I said, and Pluck bubbled and fizzed, his mixed opinion of me obvious.

Nodal glanced at his phone for an incoming message and set it screen-down. "Can I see it?" he asked, and Lev shifted uneasily.

"Um . . ." I murmured, thoughts of my paper dragon becoming scale and bone and needing to be caged.

"That's what I thought," Nodal said, sighing as if we were done.

"Give me my intel, and I'll leave," I snapped, and his eyes flicked to mine, a hint of ire in them.

"Sir." Lev inched closer. "I've seen it in action and she has more control than she's admitting."

Control me? bubbled and fizzed in an icy wash, pounding through my mind.

"I do not control shadow!" I shouted, hand clenched around the lodestone, fingers aching with the pulse of cold.

"Okay." Nodal stood and motioned for someone in the hall. "Put her in holding. I'll decide what to do with her later. We'll move forward on the auditorium as a warning to any more would-be separatists. What's our timetable on that?"

Damn it all to hell, it was a cage after all. "Benedict and Herm are in there!" I stood, panicked, as a second aide came in. But my chair caught on the tile, and as I fell backward over it, I felt the ping of dross breaking. Shrieking, I went down. My head hit the floor and I groaned. Ice exploded in my mind. Reeling, I tried to get to my feet and focus as shouts of panic erupted.

"Secure those fields!" Nodal shouted, but I couldn't look away from Pluck standing atop the table between me and the rest of them. Black haze drifted from him as he faced the two guards, Lev, and Nodal. A heavy fog dripped from Pluck's teeth, discoloring the table in a measured plop and hiss. Silky nails the size of my fingers dug into the polished wood to make it creak and snap. A sour, rank smell rose, but that was nothing to the threatening noise coming from him, the growl both low and high, like nails on a blackboard.

Shadow spit, the dragon is awake. "Pluck, stop," I whispered as I dragged myself to the table and clawed my way up. Psi fields were tingling over my skin in threat, empty of energy—so far. "I said, wait," I added as Nodal watched, his own lodestone gleaming as I put a hand on Pluck's muscular, smooth neck. Blessed cold soaked into me, dulling my headache.

"Knock it off, Pluck!" I exclaimed, desperate to nail this down, and a third eye bubbled up from his neck to look at me. "No one is going to touch me." I looked at Lev, who was grinning. He was the only mage in the room not holding a psi field. "Right?"

"Right," he said, clearly pleased.

Pluck finally stopped making that awful noise and he became solid enough that I could drag him from the table, sparks and smoke rising from where his claws dragged over the smooth wood. "Fry a friggin' frog fritter, will you just sit?" I was kind of embarrassed, and pleased, and a little humbled. And then I was scared as I remembered what might happen if I looked like too big of a threat. Benedict needed me. And Herm. Losing them was not acceptable collateral damage.

"As I said, Master Ranger, sir. Control." Lev curtly motioned for security to back off.

Nodal let his psi field dissolve, and I shuddered in relief as I felt it leave me. "We see your strength at last, Ms. Grady. Lev was right. I owe him an apology."

"No worries, sir," Lev said cheerfully. "I hardly believe it myself."

I licked my lips, head throbbing and feeling shaky as I struggled to keep Pluck contained. Most of him sat at my feet staring at Nodal, but little wisps of him were peeling off, threatening to drift away and manage some mischief. "Give me a second, will you?"

Nodal gestured for me to take the time I needed, gingerly sitting down as if to prove he wasn't afraid. He should be. One touch of shadow and he'd go insane. But he knew that.

"Knock it off, they aren't going to hurt me," I said, feeling more than a little awkward. And then I stiffened as a cold spike rammed into my skull.

I will not let you be shoved into a closet again, hissed into my mind. *I have to keep you alive, or I will never find the balance.*

"They aren't going to kill me," I insisted aloud, warming when Nodal eyed me in interest. Pluck wanted to keep me alive so he could find balance? "But if you ever see them coming for me again with those psi fields, do whatever you want," I added, and Lev smirked as Nodal's eyes narrowed.

The ice in my thoughts seemed to deepen. *I will do what I want, regardless. This was a mistake. I made a mistake. There is no reason here. Mages have not changed.*

Grimacing, I buried my hands in the shifting shadow of his neck and stared into his eyes. He had three of them at the moment: two were following Lev and Nodal, one was staring at me. It gave me the willies. "Coming here might have been a mistake," I muttered. "But walking away would be a bigger one. If I— If we can't stop Sikes, they will destroy the auditorium, scattering what dross remains over three states. You know what happens then? Everything goes back to the way it was: mages make dross, sweepers vault dross, dross kills shadow." I glanced at Nodal. "The only way we end this with no vault is to show someone that shadow can reason."

Sullen, the ice pick in my brain began to thaw. *That is my goal beyond keeping you alive.* The shadow in my hand seemed to thicken, pinpricks of ice stabbing me like diamond slivers. *If we retrieve your foolish yeth, they will understand that shadow can be reasonable and there's no need for a new vault.*

"I think it's going to take more than that, Pluck," I whispered. All I wanted was to save Benedict and Herm, but yeah, no vault would be nice. Feeling overwhelmed, I eased back to leave a single hand within his cold sphere of haze. The ice pick of his thoughts slid from my brain, and I took a slow breath. "I would suggest you stop trying to manhandle me," I said, and Pluck flopped to the floor under the table, little ribbons of shadow drifting up from him to evaporate.

Nodal leaned to squint under the table at Pluck. "His name is Pluck?"

I winced as Pluck lifted his head, pieces of him still sticking to the floor. "That's not really his name . . ." I started, then froze when Pluck stood, then shook himself to send little flakes of sparkling black into the air.

"Ah, that might not be such a good idea," I warned when Nodal reached for a drifting sparkle, then I jerked when an ice pick jammed itself into my mind.

It will not kill him, fizzed through me, quickly followed by a sheepish, *I want to meet him, and think I know now how not to kill everything I touch.*

"You want to meet him?" I said, and my hand atop his shoulder went numb from cold. My attention lifted from Pluck's green/brown eyes.

"Ah, sir," Lev warned as the man reached for one of the drifting flakes.

Like gossamer, it landed on Nodal's palm, and he jerked, his eyes flicking to me. "It's cold," he said, and Lev exhaled in relief.

"Pluck," I said in warning when the shadow padded forward to sit down before Nodal, looking like a sleek dog from hell, shimmers of green hazing his feet and tail and the top of his head like a mohawk. Nodal glanced at me, and when I shrugged, he put out his fist as if greeting a strange dog.

Please, please, please, I thought, my breath held as Pluck nosed it.

Nodal jerked, but his fist opened and he gave the shadow-dog a pat on the neck. "Pleasure to meet you, Mr. Pluck. How do you feel about the mages wanting to take over the world?"

I thought his tone rather insulting, but my sour smile faltered when the shadow-dog's lip curled and a twin growl and high-pitched nails-on-blackboard squeal split the air. Lev cringed, and a muttered "Holy Christ, what was that?" came from the other room.

Ashen-faced, Nodal withdrew, and the little drifts of shadow clinging to his fingers slowly evaporated. The man's mocking ease was gone, replaced by a wary respect. Maybe Pluck had overdone it.

"Okay. You proved your point. Get over here," I hissed, and the shadow dissolved into a thin ribbon that puddled at my feet. Little jolts of mirth and relief iced through me as a tendril curled about my ankle.

"Interesting." Nodal waved the faces in the hallway away. "I don't entirely trust you, Ms. Grady," he added. "But with Lev's assurance, I'm willing to see if we can work together. You and your associate."

Wise minds strive to the same conclusion, Pluck said, and I stifled a shudder when his icy thoughts slipped from mine.

"Wonderful." I was nervous and anxious to leave. "I could use the intel to get Herm and Benedict out of the auditorium before you bomb it."

Lev grinned and a flash of annoyance struck me. This had been his goal the entire time, and I'd walked right into it like a horse to water. Just my luck I was dying of thirst.

"You have until dawn." Nodal touched a second folder under the first. "Or rather, fifteen minutes before dawn. Then I bomb the auditorium whether you are still in there or not. There is no extraction. I'm not going to risk my people. If you go in, you're on your own."

"That is how I like it. *Sir.*" I hit the last word hard, frowning when Lev gestured for me to ask for more. "And if I rid you of your separatists so you don't have to bomb it at all?"

"I have a better chance of pink butterflies flying out my ass," Nodal said, his mirth vanishing when Lev leaned close and whispered in his ear. The older man's eyes shot to me, and a tired sound escaped him. "Seriously?" he mused aloud, and Lev nodded and eased back.

"I will not be put in a cage, Master Ranger Nodal," I threatened, my hands in fists to hide their tremor.

Nodal eyed Pluck, then me, in an evaluating silence. "If there is one thing that I have learned, Ms. Grady, it's that bringing down a more powerful force is not hard. It only takes timing."

My eyes narrowed and the haze of Pluck solidified into a lip-curled, aggressive dog. "Yeah?"

"But Lev insists that I am passing up a golden opportunity," he added, his hand shifting palm-side up as if asking for something. "I tell you what. If you rid St. Unoc of the separatist faction before I have to bomb the city, we can talk about making a place for you here tracking down and eliminating future separatist threats."

Lev nodded as I glanced at him, clearly eager for me to say yes. "'Eliminate.' You mean 'kill'?"

Nodal confidently lifted a shoulder and let it fall. "The ones who pose a threat, yes."

I shook my head, disgusted. "No. Just because Pluck is lethal, it does not follow that he is a killer. I know I'm not."

Lev ran a hand over his stubbly chin. "You aren't giving us many choices, Grady. If you can eliminate the separatist threat, you are dangerous, and if you can't, we still can't let you simply walk around as if you're a sweeper. You can either work with us or be contained by us." His thin eyebrows rose in deviltry. "But attached to the militia? Attached to the militia, you will shine, Grady. I promise."

A muffled curse slipped from me. Not just one trap but two, and I had stepped into them both. If I saved Benedict, I damned myself. If I didn't save him . . .

A sliver of panic iced through me, echoed by Pluck.

Take it. The whispering, ice-cold thought lifted through me like green fire. *If you do not stop the vault's construction, this is for naught.*

I took a slow breath, my eyes going to my dad's staff propped up against the table. My father hadn't raised me to be a coward, but I doubt he meant for me to be a killer, either. I was desperate to get Benedict free of the separatists, but the militia's price might rob me of my freedom as surely as any cage.

I bit my lip and looked at the night-black window. "Okay, but if I pull this off, I want Herm given a pardon and Benedict's name removed from any hint that his process helped destroy the vault."

Lev made a tiny fisted-hand pump of success, steeling his features when Nodal glanced at him, his attention drawn by the motion. "Someone has to be blamed," the older man said. "Blaming you makes it hard to remove you from the public eye."

My pulse hammered. I wasn't simply bargaining for my life but Benedict's and Herm's as well. "Shadow broke the vault. I'll take the blame," I said, then hesitated as a cold thought intruded, giving me a headache.

I wish to be free to search for weavers and amenable shadow, Pluck said, and I nodded.

"Oh, and, ah, I would like access to anyone who is good with shadow. I can't be the only weaver out there. We need to develop a more healthy balance of dross and shadow, and for that, we need weavers. There will be no dross dump in St. Unoc with the sole intent to destroy shadow."

Nodal beckoned an aide closer. "That's two things. For all that, I get a very close tie to you, Ms. Grady."

Again I looked at Lev. This was not what I wanted my life to be, but all things changed, and when they did, it was up to the individual to decide if they were willing to give up who they wanted to be to become who they needed to be to survive. Most times, it was an easy choice, and if I was honest with myself, there was no way I was going to let Benedict perish because I was afraid. The only real question was, would the outcome outweigh the cost? Because if this worked, my shadow magic might be more disruptive than the separatists.

Jaw clenched, I nodded my agreement.

"Well, all right, then!" Nodal rose and handed the paperwork to his aide. "Let's get you wired up and you and your associate to a Jeep, Junior Ranger Grady."

Junior ranger? I slowly stood, jumping when Pluck shrank to a tiny wisp and dove into my lodestone.

Shadow spit. I was working for the man—and I didn't even know how much I was making.

31

~~~

'M NOT SURE THIS IS GOING TO WORK." I EYED THE EARPIECE IN MY HAND IN DOUBT as the young woman in fatigues fiddled with the receiver.

"Yes, ma'am," she said. "It will allow us to maintain contact when you are in the city. Pop it in, and I'll get the audio adjusted."

I winced, loath to "pop it in." Still, I was feeling unusually professional as I sat on the front porch steps of Nodal's ranch-house encampment in the dark and waited for my escort. The emotion didn't stem from the half-eaten MRE at my elbow. It certainly wasn't from the clean jeans and black tank top smelling of someone else's fabric softener. It was my new boots, pure and simple. They were military surplus, and I didn't like them. I wasn't a mage to make war. I was a sweeper. I cleaned stuff.

Pluck was nothing more than a toxic shadow under the stairs at the moment, and my melancholy grew when he sent a wisp of self to wrap around my ankle. Even half expecting it, I jerked when his thoughts bubbled against mine like cold fizz and the night became bright with scattered dross. He was curious about the earpiece.

No, wait! I thought as a thin ribbon of him rose to touch it.

A piercing squeal burst from the receiver, and the woman jumped, swearing loudly.

"Sorry." I set the earpiece on the step between us, a thin trail of smoke eddying down from it in the glow of the porch light.

The woman frowned as she took it. "I've never seen them do that before."

"It's probably me," I said, one hand holding my shadow-laced wrist behind my back, and she smiled as if I was joking. I wasn't.

Frustrated, I sat on the top step and listened to the mockingbird singing his little heart out as the woman shuffled about in her kit for a new one. The need to get Benedict and Herm free before Nodal's deadline was gnawing at me. I didn't have any real interest in subduing the separatists apart from it making my life easier, but if Ashley was still among them, then I might find some pleasure in it.

And then I'll be a junior militia ranger. Ya-a-a-ay!

My attention lifted and I stood, eager to move when a Jeep came to a quick halt at the foot of the stairs. Its headlights illuminated a shaft of lumpy desert and I wondered how long the militia had been here—and if they were planning on making this a permanent show of force, a smaller but likely a deadlier threat than the mundane military base down the interstate.

"Tell you what," I said, taking my stick in hand. "Give me a couple of dimes. I'll call you when I'm done."

The woman looked at me, clearly not getting the joke. "Yes, ma'am," she said, standing when Lev stomped out of the dark, head down but pace eager.

"Is she ready?"

The woman made a soft nod of respect instead of a salute. We were probably considered in enemy territory, where a salute could be deadly. Or maybe they didn't salute in the militia. The only ranks I'd heard were ranger, junior ranger, and Nodal's master ranger. Like I knew?

"Yes, sir. No, sir. I'm having difficulty creating secure communication."

I thumped down the stairs, stifling a shiver when Pluck's tendril slipped from me and the night grew dark again. I paused on the lowest step, turning when the communications expert gasped. Pluck had manifested himself into that sleek, imposing dog and she had frozen, clearly not having known he was even there. But just as obvious was that she knew *what* he was.

Lev eyed him warily as Pluck loped down the steps. "I don't think anything electronic will last in St. Unoc," he said. "Too much dross."

I watched Pluck pass right in front of the headlights. Clearly his avoidance of light was a preference, not a need. I hadn't been sure until now, and Lev's eyebrows rose when the shadow-dog jumped into the back of the empty Jeep, the vehicle never moving as his massive outline landed in it, nails scraping.

"I guess we're ready." Lev gestured for me. "Load up, Junior Ranger Grady."

"You call me that again, and I'm shoving a wad of dross down your throat." I strode to the Jeep, feeling out of sorts and watched as I passed through the same headlights and dropped into the passenger seat in front of Pluck.

"Going to go all ronin on me, huh?"

I glanced at Lev as he settled himself behind the wheel. "You suck," I said sourly. "This was your plan all along, wasn't it."

"Not until you stood in front of your dog with nothing but a stick and demanded that whatever had warped your dog get the hell out of it." He smirked at me. "It's your fault."

My fault. Frustrated, I slumped where I was. Lev chuckled and stomped the Jeep into motion, sending me to grab whatever I could as we bounced over the lumpy yard to the drive. The sky was brightening to the east, and a quiver of angst tightened my gut. What the hell was I doing?

"I can take you to within a few blocks," Lev said loudly as we found the road and our pace quickened. "Any closer and we risk being detected, and I am under strict orders not to engage. I'll leave you there and you make your way in. Good?"

"Yeah, whatever," I said, stifling a yelp when Lev jerked the wheel and I caught myself against the door. My grip tightened on my stick and I pressed my feet into the footwells for balance, as he seemed determined to catch air at the top of every swale.

But the wind was pleasant in my hair, and I gazed up at the jets roaring overhead when the ride evened out and we found ourselves rolling down St. Unoc's main street. Pluck had shrunk down again, his outline holding only a hint of dog, a low lump of smoky locks furling in the wind of our passage. Seeing my attention on him, he sent a drift of self to curl around my wrist with the chill of the long dead.

I stifled my shock at his touch, my breath catching as the late night shifted. That fast, it may as well have been noon as each and every wisp of dross hiding in the dark glowed like a spot of reflected sun, lighting the night from the bottom up. It was everywhere, and I sent a silent thank-you to Pluck, his thoughts fizzing coldly into mine with hints of joy. Apparently riding in the car was a lot like flying, without the stress of finding the wind.

Ten years of magical waste made for a beautiful, fairylike sight, but it would take years to pick it up. *And do what with it?* I thought, resolving it wouldn't end up in a hole in the ground again. My grip flashed to the dash when Lev hit a chunk of pavement. "Can you slow down?"

"I thought you were in a hurry."

But our pace eased and I took a relieved breath. That is, until we turned onto Commons Street and what was left of the auditorium came into view. A bright haze hung over it like a second sunrise: reflected dross on the cloud cover, I was guessing. The entire city looked different here, the streets empty and quiet from the insanely early hour. Or late. I wasn't sure anymore.

"Check the bag on the floor," Lev said, and I glanced down at it. "I thought communication might be a problem given the issues inherent with so much free dross. We aren't going to help, but that doesn't mean we are abandoning you."

"Gee, thanks." I leaned to flip the bag open, shuddering as Pluck's touch pulled from me and the night grew dark. My eyebrows rose. It was a gun.

"I'm not using that," I said as I shoved the bag under the seat with my foot. "I told you, I'm not going to kill anyone."

Lev grinned, his white teeth glinting in the faint light. "As if I'd give you a firearm. It's a flare gun. Shoot it in the event you succeed so we know not to bomb the auditorium."

My sour mood softened. He thought I could do this. Maybe. "Thank you." This was different, and reassured, I took the surprisingly heavy flare gun in hand.

"You're welcome." He angled around a stalled car, then continued on, pace slowing as more stalled cars began to show. "My intel puts them at six. We left a drone atop what's left of the roof so we can watch you. They haven't moved from the stage. You'll find Strom and Ivaros there as well." He shook his head as if amazed. "They're all together. No sentries, which I think is stupid because there's a ninety-five percent chance they are waiting for you, so be careful."

"Thanks," I whispered, suddenly even more nervous. *Shadow spit. What am I doing?* "Ashley?"

"Front and center," Lev said, jaw suddenly tight. "And Sikes." He turned to me. "Don't beat yourself up about her. She's a piece of work. Take her out if you can."

He said that as if we were at war and she was collateral damage, not someone I had lived and worked with for two years, gone shopping with, made a birthday cake for. Yes, she had been lying the entire time to find and murder Herm, but I couldn't end her life for that, even if her opinion was, as Herm said, wackadoodle, and I felt my stomach clench.

"They're using mundane lights to preserve their lodestones, but someone has the hostages under a psi field. Oh, and there's lots of dross." He glanced at me, his grin wide. "I asked them to be detailed about that, but all I got was 'lots.'"

"That's fine." I licked my lips, suddenly worried for Pluck.

"The site has been declared clear of survivors and everyone has been accounted for. There's a cleared fire exit on the south side and I suggest you enter that way. I wish I had more for you, but no one is taking you seriously." His jaw clenched. "You're going to change that," he said, then cranked the wheel, spinning us into a tight circle and throwing me into the Jeep's door.

Ow, I thought as I pushed myself up and glared at him. We were two blocks from the auditorium, the street choked with dross-stalled vehicles. *South side fire exit. Check.*

"You don't talk much when you're ready to kick ass, do you. All meditative and calm."

Oh, if he only knew, and I nervously did a mental inventory. *Stick. Lodestone. Dog.* "What's to say? I win and I'm the militia's new toy. If I lose, I lose everything." Stick in hand, I got out, knees watery and breath fast. Pluck flowed to the ground as a haze, only the barest hint of dog showing as he trotted on nonexistent feet to the nearest dark shadow and out of the headlamps. Turning, he stared at us, his glowing eyes reflecting an eerie green.

"Grady, you're not a toy," Lev said as he sat there with his hands squarely on the wheel. "Or a tool. Or a weapon," he added. "You are the future. I believe that. After this, they will, too."

I took a breath to say something . . . then let it out. I wasn't sure there was going to be an after, and I turned away. The flare gun went to the small of my back and I stared at the broken auditorium, nothing but a black silhouette against the brightening sky. *It's going to be hot today.*

Uneasy, I began to walk away. "Good luck, Grady," he called, and my pace faltered. That was what my dad had called me: Good Luck Grady.

But I didn't turn, didn't acknowledge him, and he finally drove off. The sound of his engine quickly faded and Pluck padded from the shadows. He was larger again, and I rested a hand atop his shoulder so I could better see the dross. A shiver raced through me as his thoughts bubbled coldly against mine and the last of the night flashed into an electric vision of shadow and light. The ice pick of his thoughts in my brain was getting easier, and I took a moment to watch the light flicker like heat lightning over the auditorium. The need to find Benedict ran through me, and we stepped forward together.

32

THERE'S A LOT OF DROSS, LIFTED NERVOUSLY THROUGH ME AS WE TURNED A corner and the reflected light rising from the broken auditorium spread out under the bottom-lit clouds. Nodding, I sent my gaze deeper into the night. "A lot" was an appropriate term. Large drifts of hell hid in the shadow places between us and the broken building, too hot for Pluck to touch. The need to clean it up, make it safe, was hard to suppress, and I felt Pluck's gratitude.

"There's probably even more in the auditorium," I whispered. "Can you handle it?"

A green eye formed on top of Pluck's head, and I jerked my hand away. *I can keep you safe,* he thought, and I gingerly renewed my hold on him as the eye sank in and vanished.

Creepy-ass shadow-dog . . .

Pluck huffed, but I could feel his determination to keep me alive. It was humbling, and I felt a rush of protectiveness in turn as Pluck's thoughts bubbled and fizzed against mine.

The scent of broken brick and dust began to grow, and I picked my way through the rubble, using my long stick to catch myself when I lost my balance. Lev had said they had no sentries, but I knew the rangers at least were watching me. Great mounds of debris rose to either side, taking the place of parked cars. Silence quashed the usual night sounds. Pluck, though, just seemed to look better the closer we got until I wasn't sure what to make of him anymore, his pebbly smooth dark skin catching the glow of the occasional streetlight and his feet the size of teapots.

He didn't make a sound as I clattered and scuffed. Stray drifts of shadow slipped from him as he led me in past dust-caked cars and piled concrete. There were no mages, no ongoing rescue, but it was obvious by the cleared paths where they'd been, and Pluck and I walked between increasingly high walls of broken rock and rebar looking for the cleared fire exit and ignoring the DO NOT CROSS tape.

Until Pluck's gaze lifted, his pace faltering as he stared at the mound of rubble before us. Lev had said everyone had been accounted for, but people were still there in the dark, shifting wreckage.

And then my breath hissed in when Pluck's presence iced through me. They were glowing with dross. And if they were glowing, they were not real. They were rezes, ghosts chained to the spot of their death, far below the fallen roof.

"Are they dross or shadow rezes?" I whispered.

A fizzing, cold thought bubbled up through mine. *Shadow.* Pluck lifted his nose, snuffing great drafts of air. *I sense magic. Your yeth is likely at the center where the most dross is. And where he is, the rest will be. I'll find the exit for fire.*

"Benny is not a yeth. Wait. Pluck . . ." But he had already bounded off, leaving me to my duller night vision. The randomly moving rezes were harder to see without Pluck's sight, but I could sense them, and a shudder rippled over me as, one by one, the rezes paused in their patterned motion to stare as if considering following me into the darker reaches.

I quickened my pace.

Stick gripped tight, I followed the hazy wisps Pluck was leaving like signposts, gathering them up as if they were stray bits of dross. Each wisp made the night brighter, the dross more obvious.

I tried to be silent, but the ragged path hid dips, and I stumbled as I went, cursing every rockslide, every stone clink. "Pluck?" I called softly as I found a stairway leading down. It was Lev's promised entry, and I inched forward, leery of anything easy. Dross lined the corners of the steps, and I hesitated. Pluck wouldn't have come this way. It was too dangerous.

Here, fizzed into my thoughts, and I shuddered as my entire foot went numb with cold. It was Pluck, having shrunk down to the size of a small snake.

"Are you sure?" I said as the dross drifts suddenly glowed with an evil heat, and Pluck wound his way up my leg and then arm to perch upon my shoulder.

Down there, he affirmed as he draped himself over my shoulders, numbing them.

"Of course it is," I said, my thoughts going to the shadow-animated rezes searching the rubble. Feeling ill, I carefully inched into the stairwell lit by a lingering dross, moving quickly until I found the door at the bottom open and hanging from a hinge. I could hear angry voices, and my pulse quickened.

A low growl lifted from Pluck, odd since he still looked like a snake. Free of the dross-covered stairway, he dropped heavily to the moonlit, dusty carpet. My shadow vision flickered until an icy tendril wrapped around my ankle, and then I stopped, riveted, as the auditorium flashed into a burning dross light.

We had come out not at the bottom but somewhere halfway down. I hadn't realized it before, but the floor of the auditorium was underground. One side of the wide bowl had caved in like a fallen caldera, evidence of the blast. What had once been the ceiling littered rows of seats, and it was obvious that this was where most of the casualties had come from. The stage and podium looked fairly intact, but they, like the risers, were covered in dross.

As Lev had promised, six people stood atop the stage in an angry knot, flashlights and lanterns set to light the area. The heated argument and their ragged postures made it look like a postapocalyptic play scripted by Spielberg; everyone was talking at once, all trying to be heard.

Dross welled up from cracks in the stage floor, running like a river over the old boards to drift into the orchestra pit and make an ugly moat. If Pluck fell into it, he'd be burned alive.

"Do you see Benedict?" I whispered, and then a familiar, high-pitched harangue drew my gaze back to the stage.

"Ashley," I muttered, wishing I'd been wrong as she continued to rave, arms waving as she paced. The dross she was kicking up rolled over the new pumps she'd found somewhere, and her torn dress-up fatigues had been replaced with a matching black pullover and slacks. Her cactus-pierced skin was red and swollen where it showed, and her hair was pulled back into a severe knot to hide the ragged ends. Band-Aids decorated her hands and elbows, and the glint of a heavy lodestone ring shone from her thumb. Dross-torn and hurting, she nevertheless seemed determined as she gestured and shouted for the others to listen.

And then my heart seemed to stop when Sikes shifted and I saw two figures kneeling beside them under a wavering psi field. One was Herm, and though I couldn't see the face of the other, I knew the shape of those shoulders, the anger in that stance as he looked defiantly up at Ashley, his hair in disarray and his knees stuck to the floor with a mage binding spell. It was Benedict.

She's got his ring . . . Angry, I stepped forward, jerking to a halt when Pluck iced my feet. "They're here," I said, and a tendril of ice wrapped tighter around my wrist. For someone with no certain mass, he certainly had a way to stop me in my tracks.

Listen . . .

"I have to get them out of here!" I said, louder.

Listen!

His fear swallowed my next complaint. Unsure, I stood where I was behind the dusty empty chairs as Ashley faced off against a handful of angry mages. Under Pluck's touch, the clouds reflected the dross glow until it seemed bright as noon at the stage. More dross circled them, thicker than I'd ever seen. Either it was still welling up from the broken vault or they had been doing one hell of a lot of magic.

My eyes flicked to Benedict and Herm, stuck to the floor. *Maybe a little of both . . .*

"I'm telling you we don't need them anymore!" Ashley exclaimed, hitting Herm's thigh with what was probably a trap stick. "None of them. Strom's process negates the need for a vault. If we don't need a vault, we don't need Spinners or sweepers to man it."

My jaw dropped. She . . . she was serious? I'd thought that she was simply an elitist idiot.

"We have control of both populations," a confident voice said, and my lip curled as Sikes took command of the conversation. "There's no need to wipe out the sweeper population. Control the shadow, control the weavers, and everything else falls into place."

"Except you haven't done either," Ashley said, and Herm pushed himself up off his heels, awkward and slow as he fought the attraction spell holding him to the dross-covered stage. Sikes's ring redoubled its glow, telling me he was the one responsible for it.

"Kill me and get it over with," Herm said, his voice strong as it echoed from the half shell over them. "I'm not going to make a vault for you to drown shadow in. You are a cretin, Ashley. A no-talent hack! Grady has more ability in her one hand than you have in your entire body, and you know why? Because she's a weaver, and you will never be anything more than a mage!"

Expression ugly, Ashley smacked his ear with the stick. A cry of protest rose from the watching mages, and Sikes strode forward to take the staff, only to jerk to an annoyed halt when she threatened to hit him, too. Pluck pressed into my thigh to keep me from moving as Herm slowly righted himself and Benedict watched with a helpless, growing anger.

"You have no control!" Ashley shouted. "Shadow is gathering. It would be on us now if we weren't standing amid ten years of dross. You want a second shadow age?"

Unmoved, Herm sat back on his heels, blood dripping from his ear. "Why not?"

Furious, Ashley jabbed the stick at him, right into his ribs. Herm doubled over, groaning.

Sikes yanked the stick from her, immediately tossing it to hit the hard stage and roll to the edge. "Enough," he said derisively. "Your job was to find Herm, not plan strategy. If you want to help, go search the city to find enough Spinners to remake a vault we control. Once we have that, you can go on any vendetta you want, but until then, you will do as you're told."

Ashley glared at him, shaking. "I brought you Herm, and this is how you thank me?"

"You brought me a Spinner, not a weaver," Sikes said. "The weaver was right under your nose and you never saw her."

He said it to hurt her, and Ashley took the hit hard, her cactus-swollen hands shaking as she glared.

"I want two more Spinners before noon tomorrow," Sikes was saying, thinking he'd cowed her. "The militia is the least of my worries." The man smirked at Benedict and Herm, stuck to the floor under his magic. "If they could overpower us, they would have done so already. We need a vault. Now."

"Benedict's process frees us from the need of a vault," Ashley insisted. "We don't need sweepers to fill it. There's no reason to maintain a population that is hiding potentially hundreds of weavers, popping them like zits year by year when they show up."

Sikes slumped as if tired of it all, and Ashley flushed.

"There will always be shadow," another mage said, bookish and scared-looking. "We need a vault to destroy it. Curtailing the number of Spinner stones will suppress any new weavers. It has worked for thousands of years." He glanced at the other mages as if for support, getting a soft agreement.

"Are you blind? Everything has changed!" Ashley shouted, the heel of her pump catching on a floorboard to make her stumble. "We do not *need* a vault if we can make dross inert. There's no *need* for sweepers or Spinners to dispose of it. There will be no shadow if there are no weavers. It's time to end this farce and cull the waste."

"My God," I whispered, face cold. "Is she seriously talking about genocide?"

Ashley moved to stand over Herm, the man still hurting from her last strike. "But at least we agree on one thing. Grady needs to go." She hesitated, looking at Herm now. "Where is she?"

Herm tilted his head, blood dripping from his scalp as he stared at her. "I spent the last ten years putting her life before mine. I'm not giving her up now."

"Where did you hide her?!" Ashley shouted, frustrated, and Herm's hands twitched as he struggled to break Sikes's spell. But he had no lodestone and Ashley held Benedict's. "All this time, wasted. It was never you. It was her father!"

Herm settled back on his heels with a mocking surety. "Sucks to be wrong, doesn't it."

"Ashley, enough!" Sikes said, and the woman dropped back, pissed to the ends of the earth. "Ivaros," he added softly, his lodestone ring glinting as he turned to Herm. "Tell me where Ryan and Akeem are. I can see that your name is cleared."

Herm chuckled. "Like I care anymore."

"I do not believe this!" Ashley said, but the mages had begun to dissolve into smaller knots, all talking. "We don't need sweepers," she continued, ignored. "Benedict's process works as long as you keep it away from shadow. No sweepers, no Spinners, no weavers, no shadow."

"My God, Ashley. Get a grip!" Sikes shouted, and the surrounding arguments hesitated. "We are not wiping out an entire demographic who can handle shadow!"

"Yeah? Well, you already have," Ashley said. Angry, she gave

Herm a shove for the hell of it. The man had been expecting it, and he simply rocked where he knelt, dross eddying about his knees. "I'm not scared of shadow. I've worked with it before. It can be handled safely. Bottle it up and shove it in a hole. Done."

"She's really putting my 'don't kill your roommate' policy to the test," I said as I worked my way around Pluck and into the cleared aisle. "I've got this," I added, knowing the dross seeping up between the cracks in the stage was like living lava.

Grady . . . Ice coated my ankle, cramping all the way to my thigh. *I can't go with you. It's not safe.*

When had ex-roommates ever been safe? "I'll be okay," I said softly.

You can't kill a twelve-headed snake alone, you fool yeth!

But I was used to dealing with dangerous things alone, and the last tendril of him slipped from me as I walked away. The glow of the room dulled, and I blinked, pace faltering until my eyes adjusted. The stage was lit only by flashlights, and the dross was now a simple heat distortion—but it would still kill Pluck.

"Ashley?" I called, and they all spun, flashlights shifting to find me. "What the *hell* are you doing?"

I raised a hand to shade my eyes. The binding spell on Herm and Benedict wavered as Sikes saw me, then renewed. "It's her," Sikes said warily. "I told you she'd come."

Indecision colored Ashley's face for an instant, and then it hardened.

My heart gave a thump as Benedict's bowed head rose, his brow furrowed in heartache as I strode out of the dark, my new boots kicking up dross. "You aren't supposed to be here," he whispered.

And as Benedict's pain-racked, heartbroken eyes met mine, something in me flip-flopped. My pace faltered as I blinked, unexpected tears threatening. I was so full of emotion something had to give. I hadn't wanted it, didn't want it, but it was there, and I couldn't pretend it wasn't. I wasn't here to stop the vault from being remade. I was here for Benedict. That was it. That was everything. *Damn it, Grady. Your timing sucks.*

Herm's lips parted as he saw Pluck skulking at the outskirts, and I shrugged when understanding flickered over him. "You did it," he said softly, his pride obvious when I reached the stage's stairs. "I knew you would." Expression hardening, he turned his anger to Ashley. "Now you're in for it," he added, flicking his head to get the blood from his eyes. "Grady isn't a rising weaver. She's mastered shadow, and it's going to kill you."

Worry flickered over the faces of the surrounding mages, even Sikes. Ashley, though . . .

Her expression ugly, Ashley snatched the stick up from the stage and smacked it into Herm's ribs. Grunting, Herm went down, coughing when he breathed in the ankle-deep dross.

"Knock it off, Ashley!" I shouted, my metal-shod stick in hand as I jogged up the steep stairs. They were coated with dross, and I gasped, shocked when my footing gave way and I slipped. I fell, my chin slamming onto the top step. Breathless, I froze, eyes watering. It wasn't the dross. Someone had spelled me, and I was suddenly struggling to breathe as a foreign psi field settled over me . . . and squeezed.

"Get her lodestone!" Ashley crowed as two mages grabbed me. "She can't do anything without a lodestone!"

I dropped my stick to grasp my lodestone. Sikes darted forward to grab my staff, the tall man looking like a spider as he retreated. It wasn't his spell crushing my lungs—the ring on his hand was blazing, but it was to keep Benedict and Herm unmoving—it was Ashley's. Fingers pried at my grip on my lodestone, and I cried out when someone bent my fingers back, almost breaking them. "No!" I shouted as I felt the stone leave me, followed by the sudden snap of the lanyard breaking.

I went limp as they hauled me unresisting up into the light. Someone shoved me forward and I hit the stage between Herm and Benedict, my palms hiccuping against the hard boards. Gasping, I breathed in dross and coughed out stars as I knelt between them and cradled my floor-burned hands.

"Petra!" Benedict exclaimed, but my thoughts were on my lodestone. Ashley had it, but that didn't seem to matter as I inhaled to create a psi field and settle it about the stone in her hand. The ping of connection was like heaven itself, and I shuddered as the chiming of the universe found me, echoes of its creation hammering against the edges, expanding it with each pulsing ring. Dark matter rubbed raw against me until I exhaled and brought my soul in sync and the icy pinpricks vanished into a still point of strength.

A smile found me as my gaze touched on Sikes. I inhaled again, the tingling spikes of dark matter dissolving into an icy hum, and a green glow seeped through Ashley's fingers. What filled me was not dross. It was dark matter. It was the stuff of shadows. Ashley might hold my stone, but the energy in it was mine.

"Why is her lodestone glowing?" someone said.

It was too late. I sent my energy-singing psi field into Sikes's and Ashley's magic, breaking them both.

Ashley gasped, looking betrayed as I got up, lungs burning as I sucked in the air. Herm and Benedict groaned in relief as they found they could move. Sikes's ring glowed a dull nothing. His magic was spent until the sun rose. But then again, so was mine.

"Break it! Break the damn thing!" Sikes shouted, and something in me snapped.

"You little pissant," I whispered, lunging for the man.

"Petra!" Benedict exclaimed as I shoulder-plowed into the mage and we both went down, dross puffing up around us like invisible flame. The man bellowed in afront. Hands reached for me as he protected his lodestone, but he'd dropped my stick and I grabbed it, lurching to my feet and swinging its length wildly until they retreated.

"How dare you!" Sikes stumbled as the mages pulled him into their midst, his hand holding his lodestone as if it was his heart. "You'll never work in this city again, you hear me?"

I almost laughed, and I gave him a look telling him he was being stupid. But he already knew it, and he became even more angry as I spun my stick to clear the dross from me like cotton candy. Jaw tight, I moved to stand between Benedict and Herm as they slowly got to their feet.

"Why do you even want this!" I cried out, and the mages retreated farther as I flicked the dross from my stick into the dusty chairs. "What are you so afraid of that you have to control everything! Or are you so selfish that no one can have something you can't!"

Ashley snickered, calm as she stood beside a flustered Sikes, my depleted lodestone in her pocket and her arms crossed to hide Benedict's ring. It was linked to him, so she couldn't use it, but I was sure she wasn't tapped out. She always had a spare. "The smart have always ruled the stupid, and Petra, you have been a fool."

I stopped twirling my stick and let the silver-shod end hit the stage with a dull thump. Dross eddied up, curling like toxic smoke before it settled. No matter how much I removed, more replaced it from the broken vault under us. "You all need to rethink this," I said as Herm and Benedict stood behind me, back to back. "I just had an unsettling conversation with the militia. You have until dawn to peacefully walk out of here." I frowned at Ashley as she twirled her lodestone on its chain, not believing I had been so blind. "I'm here for Benny and Herm. You can stay here and die, or you can come with me and sit your life out in a cell." Because at this point, I was hoping they would fight.

The mages looked at Sikes, his jaw clenched as he stared at me in hatred. "Take her," he said, but not one of them moved, afraid. I'd bested their magic, and unlike theirs, mine was potentially unlimited. *If I could get my shadow down here,* I thought, glancing at Pluck pacing the outskirts like a wolf around a fire. There was simply too much dross.

"You take one step toward us and I will draw shadow down on all of you," I said boldly. "You know it's here. You feel it. Look at him!"

Sikes's hands fisted as everyone's eyes followed my stiffly pointing finger to Pluck pacing a nervous arc in the chairs. My lips parted in surprise. Behind him, rezes had gathered amid the rubble, one here, another there, a silver light spilling from them where their skin was torn. More watched from the broken roof, their glowing silhouettes distorting the night sky. Their bodies may have been removed, but their memories remained, and shadow had joined with them, creating not mindless rezes but something different: rezes who could reason and move, shadows who might understand.

The glowing figures were drawing closer despite the dross eddying about my ankles and spilling off the stage like fog. As soon as Sikes remembered it was keeping the shadow at bay, he would call my bluff.

A soft touch on my hand made me jump, and I turned, lips parting as Benedict tugged me closer until our sides touched. "You weren't supposed to be here, Petra," he whispered, heartache pinching his brow. "We left so you could escape."

"Lev found me." I looked at his fingers in mine, feeling their warmth. "Gave me a chance to get you out before they blow this place up."

"You're serious? They're going to blow it up?" Herm asked, and I followed his gaze to the ragged rim of the auditorium silhouetted against the night sky. "Wait. Is that . . . Darrell?"

My hand slipped from Benedict's as I took in the familiar stance, the proud woman standing with her beaded hair clinking in the night breeze. "Ah, yeah," I whispered. "It's a rez. I found it in the park. It must have followed me here. Brought some friends." *Bad luck.*

"Rezes don't move," Herm blurted, and then he frowned. "Are you doing this?"

"No. She's animated by desert shadow," I said, heartache burning. "They *are* shadow. Rezes animated by shadow can move, think." *Kill?* I wondered, worried as I tried to count the glowing figures rising up around her, getting about a dozen. The lodestone around

Ashley's neck was glowing, but the real power lay gathered in the dark. I knew it was too much for me. One shadow I could handle. This many? Not so much. All of us were in danger, not just the mages.

"We are leaving," I said to the mages clustered in a tense knot, hoping that we still could. "You can come with me and get a hot meal in a cell or stay and get blown to hell. No meal on that flight."

"You think you can threaten us with your little stick, a washed-up Spinner, and a wanted mage-ologist?" Ashley took a step forward, arms swinging when her new heels caught on a crack and almost sent her down. The surrounding mages, though, were scared as they looked into the broken auditorium and saw their collective deaths.

"I'm not making you do anything, Ashley. Stay here. Please." Never dropping her gaze, I handed Herm the flare gun. "Get yourself and Benedict out of here. Pluck will get you past the rezes." *I hope.* "Fire into the air and the militia will get you out."

Yes, Lev had said to shoot it if I'd been successful, and if they left, I would be.

"I'm not leaving you with them." Benedict stared at Pluck standing at the edge of the light, Darrell beside him. More rezes were gathering behind them, dust on their rubble-torn finery, a silver essence spilling from them where rebar and stone had torn bone and skin. Their anger was obvious, all of them with the wisdom of the shadows, all of them knowing the truth of what the mages had done, all of them seeing in Ashley the same greed, the same need to dominate, that had robbed them of their weavers.

"Ashley," one of the mages said, clearly uneasy. "I'm not saying we give ourselves up, but we have to get out of here."

Sikes held out his hand and the man took a handgun from the small of his back and handed it to him. "You're right. No weaver means no shadow," Sikes said, pointing it at me. "We're done here."

My eyes widened, and I stumbled when Benedict grabbed my arm and pulled me close. Herm stepped between us, white-faced. Behind Sikes, the separatists scattered. But it was too late. The rezes had ringed us all, held in check only by the burning dross surrounding the stage.

Staring at us, Sikes almost laughed. "Move, Ivaros. I need you alive to fix the vault."

"We don't need a vault!" Ashley shouted, pissed. Expression ugly, she stomped over to Sikes and reached for the gun. "Give me that. I'll shoot all three of them."

Ashley with a gun? I thought. *Oh, that's not good.* And then suddenly the two of them were wrestling for control of it.

"Petra, run!" Benedict shouted, lunging at them both.

I gasped, dropping my stick when the gun boomed and something bit my thigh.

"No, no, no!" Benedict exclaimed, horrified, and I looked down at the blood seeping past my fingers. Fire burned and my heart raced as Sikes yanked the gun from Ashley's hand.

Oh, my God. Ashley shot me. Nodal was right. It wasn't hard to bring down someone with a lot of power. It just took timing. It didn't have to be good timing, either.

"Go," I said as I stumbled, falling until Benedict caught me. Sikes had it half right. No weaver meant no control. The shadows would fall on them. On us. "Get out of here."

"You shot her!" Herm shouted, his expression riven as they eased me to the dross-covered boards. I blinked, gasping when a huge, slavering black dog landed upon the stage between me and Ashley—howling in pain.

"Pluck!" I rasped, struggling to reach him as the dross billowed high and Pluck shrieked. The dross was burning him, engulfing him in an invisible flame.

Ashley stumbled away as the shadow's scream of pain rose to a high-pitched squeal, vibrating the air as it pushed the dross like the wind pushes waves. The mages scattered, lurching from the stage and into the rubble.

With an eerie keening, the shadow-animated rezes moved, falling on them like wolves upon scattered sheep, angry and looking to assuage the heartache from their lost weavers.

It hurt to move. I lay on the stage, my hand on my thigh going warm as my gaze fixed on Pluck. Tears spilled hot from me. Streamers of black ripped from him as the dross burned. Ashley stood frozen in awe as the dog writhed, refusing to move from between us. The fearful shrieks of the mages twined about Pluck's howls as the shadow-animated rezes fell on them, driving them mad, killing them down to the last. Later I might weep for them, but right now I didn't care. We were probably next. If not for the ring of dross, they'd be on us now.

"He's burning," I rasped, as I tried to push Benedict's arms from me, struggling to reach Pluck. "Let me go! He's burning!" I could make a psi field, turn it all inert, but then the shadow would fall on us. Drawn to it. To me. I could save Pluck—or save Benedict and Herm.

"Benny, let me go!"

Benedict pulled me close, cradling me, fighting to keep me with him. "I can't," he said, voice rough. "I won't. And I don't have to. I will fix this. It's my fault."

I stiffened. *With what?* Ashley still had his ring. The sun was down. He couldn't do magic. "Wait." I turned in Benedict's arms as I felt his psi field flood the stage with his will, and then farther, down into the vault. His reach shouldn't be that big, but I knew it was love that gave him strength—and fear twisted my gut.

"What are you doing?" I rasped.

"All this is my fault," he said again, grip on me tightening. "My responsibility."

"Benny, no!" I shouted. And then everything shifted as I felt him use the dross on the stage to turn every last wisp of dross within his reach inert.

With an unreal pop, the burning dross coating Pluck vanished. A hazy, not-there glimmer hit the stage boards with a pained whine as the hellish glow flicked out of existence. An odd patter rang like a brief rain as spiny marbles fell where drifts once hazed. The utter silence behind the pings and clatter was profound, and I held my breath as I felt every single shadow-animated rez recognize Benedict, what he had done.

And then, even more frightening, one by one, the rezes flickered and went out as they fled. Something had scared them.

A faint, eerie rustle rose as I felt a new, heavy presence lift its head and wonder at the world—until it put a name to its feeling. It was hungry.

"What did you do!" Ashley whispered, scared as she realized the encircling dross was gone.

Shadow, raw and untamed, surrounded us. Far below, a huge chunk of inert dross lay somnolent and still. The new shadow dipped a thought toward it, then turned away, a single eye forming to look at us from the dark.

A quiver shook me as the shadow animating Darrell flickered and vanished, fleeing the raw, feral power. A pained whine rose from Pluck, nothing but a hazy, fading memory. "Let me go," I whispered, terrified. If that shadow touched Pluck, it would kill him. That was why they had fled. It was too big. It would destroy us all.

"You fool!" Ashley raged, oblivious to the danger. "You turned it inert? That dross was the only thing keeping the shadow at bay! What if the shadows use it to trigger an explosion?"

But they were gone, and only one shadow remained, newly formed and ignorant of everything but its hunger. The stories were right. Using dross to do magic made shadow, and Benedict had used a lot of dross.

"Stop her!" Herm shouted as Ashley ran for the stairs, her pumps clattering.

Benedict's grip on me vanished as he lunged for her. I hit the boards, and with a singular vision, I crawled my way to Pluck. "Pluck," I rasped, and then Ashley yelped as Herm downed her.

"Where you think you're going, missy?" he said, and then Ashley's shout of anger rang out as Benedict yelled at him to get his lodestone.

I couldn't look from the hazy drift that had once been my shadow, my beautiful shadow, and as Benedict and Herm fought Ashley, I gathered the cold haze of Pluck to me the best I could. He was silent, not a fizz or bubble in my thoughts as I sat on the stage and tried to contain him. Pluck had died in my arms once before, and I couldn't bear it if he did again.

But he was only a hazy thought, and he kept spilling away.

Tears began to fall as I struggled to hold him. His presence became warm, and I wrapped him in more of my self, cooling him, smothering the dross fire that still burned him, burned us both. *You stupid, foolish shadow,* I berated him, heartbroken as I sat there, my leg aching and my bloody hands staining the gray wisps and distortions. *Why did you do that?*

Because you are mine, drifted into my thoughts, as soft as snow on a still, cold night.

My breath caught and my tears vanished. He was okay. He'd be okay. That is, if the shadow Benedict had created didn't kill us. Face wet, and hands holding a faint chill, I looked for it, a prickling pulling the hairs on the back of my neck high. It was still here. Waiting.

"She got away," Benedict said as he approached, and then his reaching hand drew back when he saw my hand, red and sticky, clamped to my leg. "But I got our lodestones," he added, and I jumped, startled when he set the pure green stone into my hand as if it would fix everything.

Maybe it can . . .

"Can you walk?" Benedict asked, his hand shaking where it touched my shoulder. "How bad are you hurt? The rezes are gone. We should get out of here before they come back."

"Ah, I don't think that's possible anymore," Herm whispered as he scuffed to a halt, his eyes on the empty chairs. "You made one hell of a shadow, Strom."

His lips parted as if only now realizing it. "I did what?"

I slipped my free hand into his and gave it a squeeze. "You saved Pluck," I whispered as he looked down, even as my heart ached at the coming cost of that. "Thank you."

"I'll lead it off." Herm's eyes were fixed on the swirling, black fog that was beginning to find form. "It's too big to capture. Not even with ten sticks and five weavers." His jaw clenched in grief and guilt. "It is my penance."

But as I felt the edges of my empty lodestone, I knew the feral shadow would not follow Herm. It was going to linger above the inert dross, stalking the streets. My streets. Unless I did something about it.

"Sure. Take Benny with you," I said as I pulled myself up using Benedict. I wanted them to leave, nothing more.

Benedict seemed to blink, shocked at my words. And then he saw me holding that empty stone, the clear jewel catching the moonlight to look like green water. Pale, he tightened his grip on me. "I made that shadow, and I'm not leaving," he said.

Behind him, the new shadow condensed, an odd keening rising like an ill wind. My one hand pressed my leg. It burned as if it was on fire. In my other hand, a small black shadow, curled in misery, lifted its head and hissed at the feral energy facing us.

"You both need to go," I said, and Herm's attention flicked to me. "That dross-made shadow needs to be contained or it will flood the streets."

"You can't catch that!" Herm said, aghast.

"I'm the one who made it," Benedict interrupted. "I'll catch it."

I blinked at him, seeing him as Pluck did, shining with light. "God, you're pretty," I said, and he seemed to blanch, thinking I had lost it. But I was seeing things clearly, more clearly than I ever had before.

"Grady, it's too big," Herm said. "We need to get out of here. Let the militia bomb the auditorium. Destroy it."

But all that would do would be to scatter the inert dross over St. Unoc, pulling in even more shadow. I felt Pluck silently agreeing, his thought bubbling like crushed ice through me until a whisper of an idea crossed my mind. I wasn't going to stuff it into a trap. I was going to lure it into a tiny stone and leave it there. Smiling, I touched Benedict's stubbled face, shocked at how warm he was. "Don't let the militia bomb the auditorium, okay? Promise me that."

"That is my shadow, not yours!" Benedict exclaimed, and then he yelped, shocked when I gave him a shove to the stairs. "I'm not leaving you, Petra!" he protested as he caught his balance, red-faced and determined.

"I'm sorry, Pluck," I said as I peeled the silky smooth snake off my wrist, little pinpricks of fear and anger stabbing me. "Keep Benny safe. Please."

I am not a babysitter, iced through me as I gave him to Herm, and then he was gone and Herm held him, my shadow hissing in anger at me.

"You are a damn fool," the old man said, then gave Benedict a push. "Run, you idiot. If anyone can do this, it's your girlfriend."

"I'm not leaving. Back off, old man!" Benedict swung at Herm, and the old man caught his punch, twisting Benedict's wrist into a painful hold. I spent eight glorious seconds watching Herm push Benedict to the stairs, one hand on Benedict, the other fighting a not-there snake.

Until a muddled need fizzed against my mind and I spun, jerking my foot free of a chilling haze. A snakelike head was weaving to orient on me—until it figured out how to make eyes and found me. Resolute, I studied the rising shadow. It didn't think like Pluck, didn't know pain, or sacrifice, or love. All it knew was hunger.

"I am the weaver who you will answer to," I said, my voice wavering as a thin tendril of ice touched my foot and drew back, sensing my understanding of it and knowing I would fight to keep my mind intact. "That's right," I whispered as I staggered, leg in agony as I marshaled a psi field. It had form. I could catch it like an errant drift. I had held shadow before.

But when my psi field touched it, the shadow turned and attacked.

33

MINDLESS, THE SHADOW DOVE DEEP INTO ME, SAVAGELY COATING ME IN ICE AS it rolled my soul and stole my warmth. I fell to a half kneel, one hand on my leg, the other catching myself against the floor. Panicking, I flooded it with warmth to push the shadow away. Sure enough, the shadow spilled in behind my hot thought, angry and wild as it dug deeper.

Fine. The hard way, I thought as I inhaled to set a field about the shadow. I could feel the shadow's surprise as I spun it into a tight ball, condensing it to a fraction of its size. Its strength, though, was the same, and its shock that I had captured it fizzed against me for an instant before daggers of ice stabbed at me.

My jaw clenched as I fought it. It was in my mind, trying to take control. I breathed in cold and exhaled ice as the emptiness of what lay between space filled me.

You will listen! I thundered, empty lodestone in my hand.

But it didn't, and I threw my strength against it, spinning it down to a hard knot once more. It fought like a whirlwind for its freedom, tearing at my mind and giving me flashes of its anger. It was like holding burning sand as I shoved my shadow-filled field into the lodestone.

Harsh hunger sent me reeling. My fingers went numb with cold, and I stared at the stone as it turned black and frosted. "Got you," I whispered as I felt the shadow pull from my psi field with a snap, filling the voids within the stone until it found the edges of its prison—and rebounded against me.

"No!" I shouted as it ripped through my protests and escaped, smarter now.

I gasped as I hit the stage, elbows stinging as a cold smothered me. It had learned I was a trickster and it swung round to tear at me with an icy vengeance. The second I had let go of my field, it had escaped to gnaw upon me anew.

I rose to my knees, sending my mind into the buffeting maelstrom once more, swirling my thoughts like a dross-cored stick to gather it up until the shadow chilled my soul. "You will listen," I whispered, then gasped, horror filling me as my psi field cracked from the shadow's cold bite and it escaped, slipping past my thoughts like an ill wind.

Groaning, I pulled the sparkling motes of my damaged field back to my soul to try to warm it.

But the shadow was there in my mind, waiting, and suddenly I was fighting to breathe.

"You little shadow-snot yeth . . ." I gasped, flat on the stage and shaking in a bone-numbing cold. If I was going to die, I was going to take this damn shadow with me.

Again I pushed my psi field from me in a heated wave of grief. It flooded from me in a golden wave, brighter than dross, brighter than the sun.

For an instant, the shadow hesitated, shocked by the warmth.

And then, it collapsed inward to my soul, eagerly taking my heat with it.

Agony sang in me. I breathed in shadow and choked out stars. Swamped and reeling, I poured my strength upon the shadow, swirling it into a twisted knot and refusing to let it go lest it find Benedict and Herm. *You will not have Pluck,* I rasped as I dragged that damned shadow back into the lodestone and felt my soul go cold from its anger.

If the only way to catch it was to die with it here, then I would.

And I held it, refusing to let it go as it fought against me.

I am so sorry, Pluck, I thought in grief . . . and then, suddenly, I wasn't alone.

The feral shadow screamed in frustration as it was plucked from my mind and spun into a confused knot. Something shoved my thoughts from my lodestone. I gasped as heat flooded back to me like the sun, burning where my soul lay exposed. I watched, my mind cradled as a thousand silvery ribbons ripped through the feral shadow like sunbeams. Cold poured around and over me in a wave, but I was cocooned, protected, as the feral shadow fought, each and every thought it had freezing to a somnolent stillness until it was suddenly struggling to stay intact.

Pluck? I thought in fear. Had he come back? The shadow was too big for him, and panic shook me.

Until I realized it wasn't one voice but many who bubbled and fizzed within me, warming my soul, telling me only a fool yeth tries to catch wild shadow. Weavers couldn't bring their fields cold enough.

But their combined voices could, and awe filled me as the desert shadows buffered and protected me. Their thoughts were my thoughts, and I felt tears prick when the touch of my soul reminded them of their own weavers long dead. Even as they poured their cold misery on the feral shadow, the shadows ached for their names and those who had given them to them.

Kneeling on the stage, I sobbed as their sorrow flowed through me, a debilitating pain clenching my heart.

"You still have names," I rasped, my focus blurry on my hands pressed to the oak floor as the feral shadow went sluggish under their combined presence, ripped apart and scattered. "I will find weavers for you. You will be cherished again. I promise I will find them. I can't be the only one," I breathed, finding it easier to bear as their grief slowed, assuaged by saving me as they had not been able to save their own weavers.

We do this for you, not us, one said as they began to retreat, oil and water fizzing through me until it was just me in my thoughts: my heartache, my pain.

My soul felt like a hard lump. The stone in my hand was still green and empty, and I dropped it, hearing the ping echo in the eerie silence. My fingers were stiff with cold, and I pressed my hand against the burning agony of my leg, gasping as the ice of my fist numbed the pain. Sore and feeling stretched, I looked up.

Shadows. My mind might be empty of them, but they were everywhere in the dimly lit rubble, waiting for me, aching for their weavers.

"Thank you," I whispered, and the one wearing the memory of Darrell dipped its head in understanding as pain pinched her eyes.

Petra! arched through my mind, and then I gasped, shocked when a shadow-dog slammed into me, coating me in a warm haze. *You're alive. How did you . . .*

"It was the desert shadows," I said as his thoughts fizzed warmly in mine. "They ripped it to shreds." Eyes closing in joy, I yanked him closer, burying my face in his neck, shaking as I realized I had done the impossible.

"Hey, you feel warm," I suddenly realized, and he pulled back, a wolfy chuckle rising from his deep chest.

No, you've gone cold. His thoughts fizzed and bubbled as his wolfy brow furrowed and his gold eyes pinched when he saw the desert shadows ringing us. They were still here, broken but surviving, and though not a single one touched me, I sensed their jealous pain as they saw Pluck and me together.

"I'm sorry," I whispered, and a bright flash of hope flickered under their heartache. They would wait for me to find them weavers. For a while. As long as the vault remained unmade, they would wait. "I will find what you seek."

Pluck stiffened as one of the shadows reached to touch me—then withdrew. One by one they flickered and went out to sink into the vault of inert dross.

"I will find them," I whispered, woozy as a sodden bang echoed over the broken city and I looked up to see a brilliant red flare arching across the brightening sky. It was Benedict, and I sat down to wait for Lev, just me and my shadow.

Lev was right. The entire world was going to change. I simply had to hold on.

34

THE SUN WAS HARDLY ABOVE THE HORIZON, AND THE WIND WAS ALREADY WHIP-
ping up from the desert. I relished the hot dry air lifting through
my hair as I sat on my narrow balcony with a blah mug of coffee.
Knees almost to my chest, I rested my feet on the railing and watched
the dust devils spin their way across the nearby parking lot. Traffic
was a distant shush of noise, and I smiled at the muffled head-banging
thump of a bass set too low slowly vanishing into the background.

Pluck overflowed the chair beside me, his pointy ears flat against
his skull in annoyance. The morning sun was almost on him, and I
reached to adjust the pink, oversize umbrella clamped to the railing.
The webbed chair with its cup holders and umbrella had once been
Ashley's. It went without saying that it was far more comfortable than
mine, but as I touched his wisp-draped ears, I decided he could have it.

You like the sun too much. Pluck's thoughts bubbled through mine
with a soft chill, and I pulled a small drift of shadow from him to use
to warm up my coffee. It wasn't even good coffee.

"You can go in if you want." I swung my lodestone from its lanyard in invitation, and he huffed at me, little streamers of frost chilling my hand. He knew I was joking. The stone was far too small.
Even so, he'd likely be hiding under my bed come noon.

The view out my balcony had changed little in the last few weeks.

It had been almost two weeks since the desert shadows had taken out the separatists' leaders, and though the world *seemed* to have gotten back to normal, I felt anything but. The initial separatist uprising had been quelled, and though Nodal was pleased they had been dealt with, he wasn't happy with my amnesia concerning what had actually happened to them or that they were dead. Ashley, too, wasn't talking, even after having been caught just outside the auditorium by Lev and his crew coming to pick me up.

Two weeks, and dross still littered the city, causing the occasional interruption in power or car pileup despite the university's sweepers out in force gathering dross and shoving it into anything they could find. Benedict's process had been hailed as a godsend, and after a couple of well-attended lectures, every mage with a class-three field or higher knew how to turn it solid. Whether they would or not was still up for debate.

It was keeping Benedict busy, officially free from any taint of wrongdoing. Nodal had been as good as his word. I was happy for him but feeling rather alone in my new understanding of shadow. It didn't help that my one and only attempt at going to the makeshift loom had been met with frightened stares and quick exoduses until I found myself standing in an empty room with the TV going. Kyle, Jessica . . . even Ryan was twitchy around me. Herm had been right, and it was frustrating.

I'd like to think that the reason everyone was avoiding me was because of the no-vault existence that the militia was enforcing, but as I glanced at the hazy distortion overflowing the chair, huffing at the sun creeping down the wall toward us, I knew my "in-house" exile in St. Unoc stemmed from another source. I didn't care. There would be no dross vault in St. Unoc. Never again.

It's hot out here, Pluck thought, nails scraping as he slipped from Ashley's chair.

"Hey, Pluck, I've been thinking," I said, my hand reaching to find him as little streamers of him drifted into the shadowed apartment.

Dangerous, he mused, and I ran my fingers over his skull, enjoying the darts of cold energy sparking through me.

"Would you rather be something other than a dog?" I said, uncomfortable with the idea that the world saw him as a dangerous pet.

Pluck huffed, clearly wanting to go inside and out of the heat. *I can be many things. This image is comfortable. You like it. It has little expected responsibilities and many opportunities.*

"Something that talks, perhaps?" I added, and he seemed to deflate somewhat. "How about a crow?"

I can talk, fizzed through me, a hint of annoyance slanting his ears.

"To other people," I added, and he shook, ears slapping to send little drifts of shadow to sulk in the corners.

Why would I want to talk to other people?

He set his head on my lap, looking mournfully up at me with his beautiful green eyes. The rotting, stinking image that he had once been was long gone. It had been formed by my fear, and now he was as pure and beautiful as life itself.

Your fool yeth is here, he thought, head lifting when I glanced over the balcony to the approaching sound of a Jeep.

"So he is," I said, stiffening at a sudden, thrill-based vertigo as I spotted Benedict in the open-air vehicle, the man appearing rested in his casual jeans and button shirt as he held on to the dash for dear life. The driver was in fatigues. I knew without looking that it was Lev, careening down the road to come to a body-jerking halt.

I smiled as Benedict made some muttered comment and got out. "Hi, Benedict! Lev!" I called, and his attention snapped up to find me. "Come on up. The door is open."

The door was always open. After the rumor mill had me summoning a three-headed dog to take out a dragon-shaped shadow, all my neighbors had moved out except Lev. We had the entire building, which had been more than a little annoying when Lev had a party last week and his music shook the windows for six hours straight. I'd been invited, but after an uncomfortable half hour, I'd left.

The auditorium, too, had been all but abandoned after the lingering desert shadows had shown a propensity to bring the university's dead back to life to go for an occasional walkabout. But I suppose it was better than not knowing where they were. And the shadows did a better job than the militia at keeping people out of the auditorium. Two weeks, and they still hadn't started fixing it. I doubted they ever would. Not with rezes popping up to scare the crap out of the workers. The official story was that the insurance company and the university were arguing over who was going to pay for the repairs. It could be decades.

"Hey, Petra. I brought breakfast." Benedict beamed up at me, a paper bag held high. "Danish okay?"

"Yummy. I'll get a second pot of coffee going," I said, smiling, and the man nodded, turning away at something Lev had said. Lev was in his fatigues, and I doubted this was a pleasure visit or to check on my gunshot wound. Overnight in a militia hospital with Pluck glowering under my bed had been more than enough for everyone.

Pluck pushed open the slider door and I followed him inside. Immediately the shadow-dog collapsed in the middle of the floor, his edges hazy and misty as he stared toward the hallway, green eyes glowing. Waiting.

"Be nice," I admonished, and a flicker of gold shot through his haze. Eyebrows high in speculation, I scooped up a glass left out last night and set it in the sink, wondering how my life put me here. Something in me fluttered as I heard their voices twining together on the stairs, and then they both went silent at their soft knock. I beamed as Benedict came in, smiling.

"Hi, Petra," he said, pulling up short upon seeing Pluck sprawled on the floor in an unsubtle, passive-aggressive threat. "How's your leg? You look good today. Lev wanted to talk, and I had a morning free."

"Things finally starting to slow down?" I left the pitcher under the tap to fill when his arm went around me, and I sort of leaned into him, giving him a careful sideways hug as my leg twinged. Hesitating, I looked at his lips. I wanted to do more, but I also didn't want Pluck and Lev watching what might be our first kiss. Benedict's thoughts seemed to be in a similar vein as his grip on my shoulder tightened and he pulled away with an obvious reluctance, the bag in his hand rattling.

"Slow, yes," Benedict said as Lev cautiously edged into the living room, his gaze on Pluck. "Ah, you want a plate under these?"

"I got it." I turned off the tap. "You want some coffee?"

"That depends." Lev collapsed on the couch as if he were still nothing more than my sinewy, rough-around-the-edges neighbor. "It's not that bitter roast Ashley bought, is it?"

Benedict inched out of the kitchen, a faint worry wrinkle pinching his eyes as he studied Pluck. The shadow-dog had oozed to the middle of the floor, his ear twitching in and out of existence.

"I threw it out weeks ago. Benny, go sit. He's not going to do anything," I insisted, grinning as I gave him a last half hug and rocked away.

"Right . . ." Benedict heaved a sigh, edging around Pluck with an obvious reluctance.

For a moment, there was a growing silence as I filled the percolator. I saw Lev after work more often than not, but this had the feeling of something else. "Hey, Lev. Kind of early for you to be home," I said, fishing.

"I'm working," he said sourly as he slumped deeper into the couch. "I got a promotion this morning. And it's your fault."

"Ah, you're welcome?" I said, eyebrows rising at the sweeper emblem next to his new insignia. The tiny button was almost lost, but it stood out to me like a beacon. "How is your advancement my fault?" I measured the coffee grounds, relishing the rich scent.

Lev looked up from my copy of *Knitting for Dummies* that I'd picked up last week. Yep, my nights were that boring. Jaw tight, he tossed the book to the table, the pop of sound blowing Pluck's haze into a drifting distortion until it settled. "I asked to be your superior, and because Nodal didn't want anyone between him and me, they made me master ranger."

"Seriously?" Benedict settled himself on the couch across from Lev. "Congratulations."

Lev shrugged, clearly unhappy. "Sorry," I said insincerely, and he sighed.

"It comes with a desk. The paperwork is a pain in the ass." He hesitated, eyes finding mine. "Ah, you got a minute?"

I set the percolator over the stove and got the gas going. "It's early. I've got five. But I'm not talking business over coffee." I leaned against the counter, arms crossed. Everything felt kind of weird, and I watched Benedict eye Pluck as he resettled himself, his foot almost touching the shadow as if to prove he wasn't dangerous—even if he was.

"I still can't get over being able to see him that clearly," Benedict said, and Pluck's eyes dissolved. Suddenly his head became his tail, and his tail became his head.

"You can touch him, too," I added.

I bite, iced through my thoughts, and I stifled a smirk.

"Hard pass." Lev got up and ambled into the kitchen. "I need the big mug," he said as he went to the cupboards.

"It's all yours." I shifted out of his way, and he exhaled, finding it. "What's on your mind, Lev?"

Benedict inched forward to the edge of the cushion. Breath held, he put a hand out to the puddle that was Pluck, his hand fisted as if meeting a strange dog.

Sure you don't want to be a person? This is going to get old fast, I thought, and Pluck made a threatening woof, flicking an ear to coat Benedict's hand in a haze of black.

Breath catching, Benedict jerked his hand away, wringing his fingers as if stung. "That's . . . interesting," he said, and the dog utterly dissolved into a hazy puddle and oozed under the couch. "He's still cold."

"He likes you," I said, then stifled a shiver when a faint *I do not* iced through me.

"That's great. I, ah, like him, too." Unnerved, Benedict eased back into the cushions.

"When shadows kill someone, it's by accident." I hesitated, lips pursing when Pluck hazed into a fog and drifted into the kitchen and away from Benedict. "Usually. Once they are bound to a weaver, they are not as dangerous. Anyone can touch them unless the shadow feels threatened."

Or annoyed, Pluck grumbled, twining about my feet like a cat making a go for the life insurance. *What does Lev want?*

"Good question." I opened a cupboard and found a plate for the Danish. "Lev, Pluck wants to know what you want that Benedict had to be here for."

"He does, huh?" Lev looked up from pouring out a coffee. Setting a Danish on top of the mug, the small man returned to the living room and sat down. A faint haze followed him, settling between his feet. Clearing his throat, Lev shifted to a nearby chair instead. "It's time for you to start earning your MREs, Grady." Lev's gaze flicked to Benedict. "If your gunshot wound checks out, you and your, ah, partner are on your way to Detroit."

Finally. A thrill dropped to the pit of my gut as, with an ear-slapping shake, Pluck solidified.

"You didn't say anything about a trip," Benedict said, clearly affronted. "I thought this was about getting the rezes out of the auditorium. The workers can't get in to even assess the damage."

"No?" Lev smirked at him. "Maybe I didn't tell you because you're not cleared to hear any of this." Lev took a bite of his Danish, one leg going over a knee. "Grady, we have identified three possible separatists who are using their magic in an adverse, illegal manner. They stunned the team that we sent to talk to them and fled. Nodal wants to see what you and your shadow can do."

"Petra got shot," Benedict protested. "You can't be serious."

I was so ready to get out of here it wasn't funny. Two weeks of forced immobility was starting to get on my nerves. It wasn't as if the sweepers' guild would have anything to do with me. "Really?" The coffee was done, but I was willing to ignore my "no business over coffee" rule and I filled two more mugs to their brims. "I did what I told Nodal I'd do. How are misbehaving mages in Detroit my problem?"

"Because you're a weaver," Lev said as he devoured his pastry. "It might help if you could . . . you know, show us your stuff." He licked his fingers. "Otherwise, someone is going to kill them."

"Separatists? What a shame," I said insincerely.

"You want to send Petra to arrest the same people who want her dead?" Benedict said, his face creased in anger. "No way in hell."

"How much does it pay?" I asked, and Benedict made a huff and pushed back into the cushions. But all I really wanted was the chance to talk to people who didn't know who I was and weren't scared to death of me. That, and maybe eat something that I hadn't cooked myself.

Grinning, Lev took an envelope from a back pocket and set it on the table. "I didn't invite you on this magic carpet ride," he said when Benedict took it and opened it.

"These are travel papers . . ." Benedict's brow furrowed.

Lev yanked the envelope out of his hand and set it on the table once more. "You get the rest of the information on the way," he said, putting his feet on the table in warning when Benedict reached for it again. "That is, if you accept it."

"Just like the movies, eh?" I mused aloud.

"Militia transport. Bring earplugs," Lev said, and I smiled.

"That sounds great." Plate balanced on a mug, I grabbed the second and sashayed into the living room. "Where's the rest?" The question had been for Lev, but my eyes were on Benedict. He was agitated, worried about me, and that was endearing after all that we'd been through.

"Rest of what?" Lev asked, while I handed Benedict one of the mugs. "I assumed that the dog—"

"Not for Pluck," I said, one hand gentling him as he flopped onto my feet as if he were begging for a treat. "For Benny and Herm."

"Ha!" Benedict almost barked.

"We lost track of Herm three days ago. It might take some time to find him." Lev winced. "You, ah, think you can text him? He won't answer us."

That Herm would talk to me and not the militia was kind of nice, but my stomach had knotted. "He didn't leave, did he?"

"No one leaves St. Unoc without us knowing," Lev said, and Pluck huffed, little streamers of shadow drifting from him like dust.

"He didn't leave, did he?" I asked again. "You checked his junkyard lair, right?"

Benedict reached across the space and took my hand. "I'm sure he's sulking, but I think he'd clean himself up and come if you asked."

"Good." Eyes wide, I took a bite of my Danish. I hadn't had anything but cereal and toast for breakfast for two weeks, and the sweet dough was like heaven. That is, until a jet roared overhead and the dishes rattled. With a soft *pudunk*, my phone vibrated off the table and hit the floor, and the music cut out.

"This is supposed to be a small, covert task," Lev complained when he could be heard again. "Just you, me, and—"

My eyebrows rose. "If you didn't want Benny to come, why did you ask me in front of him? There is no way I'm stepping out of St. Unoc without Benedict and Herm." Coffee in hand, I stood to go shut the big slider. If the jets were doing maneuvers, they might be at it for hours. "Benny, I'll leave it up to you to hammer out the details."

Smug, Benedict eased into the cushions with his coffee. "I'm not good on a plane. What do you have that is fast? I like stick shift."

"To Detroit? I don't think so," Lev said. "You can forget about that right now."

Smiling, I peered out the glass door as I shut it. Pluck dissolved into an excited haze, only the barest hint of a dog shape to him as he stood in my shade. *We are going to find more weavers?*

"Yup. We are going to find more weavers." My hand dropped to him, fingers playing in his chill haze as the cactus wren sang. Excited, I gazed out over St. Unoc, little shimmers of dross lighting the desert-hot air like mirages. For all the problems and hard-to-explain incidents, the world didn't know about us yet. And as I looked out over the scaffold-laced auditorium, I vowed that they never would.